HISTORY OF LIES

T.S. MAYNARD

W.J. MCNALLY

PROLOGUE

September 15, 2017

This day changed the world. No one knows why, except for a select, perhaps unlucky few. Most defining moments in history center on a death or deaths—assassinations, coups, wars, revolutions, executions. This day was no different. While morbid that humans so often use death as a historical marker, it makes logical sense. Death is the end of something or someone. It is the culmination of events that leads to an inevitable conclusion— an ending that begets a new beginning.

For most historical events, no one focuses on the moments leading up to them. The reason is simple enough. They're innocuous and seemingly unrelated, but after enough time, history reveals that everything is connected, and everything is important. Most people think "enough time" means a few years, maybe a decade, or at most a lifetime. That's because people focus on things from their perspective, but what if enough time hasn't passed?

It is widely accepted that history was written by the victors. If that's true, it means history has one-half of the story at best, and at worst, it is full of lies. But which is it? The key to unlocking that answer—September 15, 2017.

CHAPTER 1

It was a crisp fall morning and patrons enjoyed fresh coffee, handmade pastries, and other breakfast delights in an upscale café in Arlington, Virginia. In a faded red booth, two sisters in their mid-30's, Dr. Riya Patel and Dr. Anjali Patel, finished their fruit plates and espressos. Of the two, Riya was more beautiful, but Anjali placed more effort into her appearance. A crimped hairdo, designer clothes, and meticulously applied makeup belied a deep-seated insecurity. In contrast, Riya, the older sister by three years, preferred a natural clean face and simple ponytail.

"You have to give me a hint," Riya asked, as she popped a piece of melon into her mouth.

Anjali smirked, then sipped her coffee.

"You can't tell me you're working on a big scientific discovery and then not say anything."

Anjali remained firm. "It's top secret. Dr. Guthrie would have me fired."

"Fine. I guess I'll have to wait."

Anjali enjoyed being the center of attention and couldn't let go of the moment. She blurted out, "It has something to do with the hippocampus, but that's all I can say."

Riya mulled over the new information. "The hippocampus?"

"At least we think so," Anjali corrected.

"Hmm. Hippocampus. Is it related to memory?" Riya asked.

Anjali smiled. Riya was warm.

"Something with savant syndrome?"

Anjali turned up her nose. "I said this was going to be really big."

Riya rolled her eyes, feigning insult. "That could be really big."

"It's much bigger, but I can't tell you until after our trials finish next month. This is going to change the world," Anjali declared.

Riya sipped her espresso, now concerned. "Anjali, I hope this isn't some fringe science thing."

The conversation shifted from playful to tense—that simmering insecurity triggered by one small comment loaded with subtext.

Riya had been looking out for her sister for years. Their mother died from cancer, and their father just months later. Most people might bemoan the cruelty and unfairness of life after losing both parents so young, but Riya threw herself into her schoolwork and caring for Anjali. By any standard, except her own, Riya was an unmitigated success. Her intellect and work ethic got her a full ride to Harvard Medical School, where she graduated in the top 1% of her class. She went on to become a preeminent neurologist and pioneered breakthrough methods to improve outcomes for stroke victims. She'd helped hundreds of people, but her achievements came at a steep price. Her work first lifestyle left little room for personal relationships. The only person Riya loved was her sister, but her accomplishments made Anjali feel like she was never good enough. In recent years, the relationship had improved, but all it took was one unintended insult to set things back.

Anjali glowered at Riya. "You're not the only one who can work on something important."

"I didn't mean it like that. It's just… you're not positive it's related to the hippocampus, and you're announcing next month? Guthrie's reputation isn't the best."

"Because he's a trailblazer," Anjali fired back.

"Once you get a certain reputation, it's hard to be taken seriously," Riya said.

Anjali bit her lip to stop it from quivering. "You don't think I'm a reputable doctor?"

Riya reached out to grab her sister's hand. "I didn't say that."

Anjali recoiled and sat back against the booth. "Maybe I didn't graduate from Harvard like you." Her resolve hardened as she spoke. "And maybe I'm not some superhero neurologist, but *this* is going to change the world." She snatched her Strathberry black leather brief and stood to leave.

Riya's head dropped. She didn't want their breakfast to end like this. "Anjali."

Anjali stopped.

Riya searched for something to say, but she was a terrible liar, and everything Anjali feared her sister believed about her, she did.

"I'm going to change the world, not you." Anjali stormed out.

Riya stared at her coffee. This was a setback. She'd work through this and fix it like she always did. After one last sip, she signed the check and left.

She'd make it up to Anjali next time.

——————

WITH HER LEATHER brief by her feet, Anjali stewed on her morning subway commute. Why did Riya always find a way to put her down? A passenger in a ratty sweatshirt stood over her, holding a bottle of booze in a crumpled brown paper bag and belched like a foghorn. Anjali recoiled with disgust. *Can the day get any worse?* The subway slowed for its next stop. The drunk passenger lost his balance and fell on to Anjali's lap. There was her answer.

A bystander in a gray suit with the exact same leather brief rushed to Anjali's aid. He heaved the drunkard off Anjali. "It's too early to be drunk, pal."

3

"You know what they say? It's five o'clock somewhere," the bum slurred as he mixed back into the crowd.

Anjali thanked the good Samaritan. He nodded, grabbed Anjali's leather brief, left his in its place, and exited.

Three stops later, Anjali hurried out of the subway station toward a bland commercial real estate complex subdivided into multiple units. Companies renting these spaces were either scraping to get by or hoping to hit it big one day. Anjali's employer, Guthrie Research, was both.

As she entered the building, two beefy security guards, Daryl and Bobby, greeted her. Anjali flashed her ID badge and strutted by. The security was unusual for a corporation in this type of complex. She opened a door that led to the office bullpen, an unimpressive area filled with cubbies separated by cheap sterile walls. This room was not the reason for the guards.

Anjali reached a nondescript desk. Her space contained a computer screen on one side of the desk, stacked manilla folders on the other, and a white coat hung on the wall partition. She tossed the briefcase under her desk as a man in a similar coat, Dr. Cushing, passed by.

"You're late," he said and continued on his way.

Anjali grabbed the hanging coat, slipped it on, and darted down the hall. She approached the door marked "Image Lab."

The Image Lab contained three monitors. Cushing sat in front of the first, which displayed a computer rendering of a human brain. Anjali plopped herself in front of the second, which tracked a patient's heart rate and blood pressure, even though there was no patient in sight. Wayne, a nerdy bearded middle-aged man with a potbelly and sweater vest, stood beside the third monitor, a black screen. The technology in this area still didn't justify the security detail out front. The only other feature in the Image Lab was a window into the next room.

"Any bets on what we're going to see today, Wayne?" Anjali asked with a sly grin.

Wayne rubbed his hands as he considered the question. "I'm feeling something BC."

4

Anjali raised an eyebrow. A bold prediction. "We've only had two of those. Ten bucks says AD."

A stern, male voice interrupted through the intercom and ended the office fun. "Did Dr. Patel finally arrive?"

Anjali blushed as Cushing responded affirmatively into the intercom.

The voice declared, "We're administering the stim."

The heart rate displayed on Anjali's monitor increased. Erratic scarlet lines pulsated into the brain rendering on Cushing's screen, and a tiny area in the center turned a bright crimson.

Wayne's monitor flashed, and an image faded into view—a Nordic boat with a dragonhead on the bow.

Wayne stared, slack-jawed. "Would ya' look at that?" He ran his fingers over the screen. "This never gets old."

Even Cushing and Anjali couldn't help but stare at Wayne's screen.

"You don't have to be a historian to know that's a Viking ship," Cushing said.

"Is that AD or BC?" Anjali asked.

Eyes still glued to the monitor, Wayne held out a ten-dollar bill.

Cushing pressed the intercom, "We got one."

The voice responded, "Okay, we're stopping the stim. Have Dr. Patel meet me in my office."

Cushing eyed Anjali. Trouble. She stood up and gazed through the window into the adjacent lab. Two doctors attended to a sedated man in his forties. He reclined in what looked like a futuristic dental chair and had three metallic probes attached to his head. *This* was the reason for the security.

As Anjali exited the Image Lab, she bumped into Dr. Guthrie—the voice from the intercom. In his early sixties, Guthrie had salt and pepper hair and acne scars from when he was a teen. It gave him a weathered look that matched his gruff personality. "Dr. Patel, come with me."

Guthrie led her down the hallway to his office. He maintained the appearance of chivalrousness as he opened the door for Anjali, but once

5

inside, all façade of politeness vanished. He motioned for her to sit in the chair. It was not a request.

Once seated, Anjali glanced around the messy room. Despite her years of service, she'd not been in here before and was surprised to find such disorganization from a man she both feared and respected. Dr. Guthrie remained standing to make Anjali feel as uncomfortable as possible. It worked.

Anjali jumped in to explain, "Dr. Guthrie, I'm sorry I was late. I was…"

Guthrie held up his finger to silence her. He had no interest in excuses. "Do you understand the significance of our discovery?"

Anjali nodded.

"No. Do you truly understand it?" Guthrie asked again.

Anjali stammered for a response. She had already acknowledged she did. What more did he want?

"We have scientific proof that we have past lives." He let that sink in before proceeding. "That will fundamentally change everything about our society."

"I know, and I'm honored to be a part of this groundbreaking research. I'm sorry for being late. It won't happen again."

Guthrie stared at Anjali. Something more significant than Anjali's tardiness had upset him. "If anything leaks before we're ready, it could compromise the entire study."

"I understand," Anjali replied.

"I have reason to believe otherwise."

A knock at the door jolted Anjali.

"Come in," Guthrie commanded.

The door opened and Daryl, one of the security guards, entered carrying Anjali's leather brief. He placed it on Guthrie's desk.

"IT monitors all computers," Guthrie explained. "Yesterday, classified files were downloaded to a Zip drive from your computer."

"That's not true," Anjali protested.

Guthrie continued to stare at the brief. "Open it, and let's find out what's inside."

"Dr. Guthrie, I'd never do anything to jeopardize this study," she pleaded.

"Open it, Dr. Patel," Guthrie ordered. He was not going to ask a third time.

On the verge of tears, Anjali's fingers trembled as they unhooked the clasp on her brief. She lifted the flap and peered inside. "Oh, God."

Guthrie's head slumped. She was guilty. Or was she? She was scared, but not of being caught. She was scared to death.

Guthrie motioned Daryl to take her into custody. As he grabbed her arm, Daryl glanced inside the brief. His eyes widened in horror, but he didn't even have time to scream.

Boom!

A bomb exploded.

CHAPTER 2

MACEDON, 343 B.C.

To UNDERSTAND the history of lies, it is essential to know how it all began. One person who knows the truth would say 343 B.C. was the beginning. It occurred during the Macedonian Empire, the forerunner to the more widely known Greek Empire.

SUN PEEKED out from behind the mountains, illuminating the slumbering capital of Pella, the capital of ancient Macedon. Dominated by white-pillared buildings, one stood out in dramatic fashion, a magnificent 70,000 square foot palace that doubled as a protective fort if the city was ever attacked. Dutiful soldiers, decked out in cuirasses, photo-Telamon shields, helmets, and armed with short swords, guarded the estate. This complex was the home of Philip II, King of Macedon, and father of a son who would one day become a legend.

The thirteen-year-old boy, Alexander, slept on a soft bed made from sheepskins and an ivory frame. His face grimaced as he tossed and turned until he bolted upright and startled himself awake. Dripping with sweat, his tired eyes begged for the torment to end. His dreams had been an ongoing problem. They haunted Alexander nightly and chilled him to the bone. He slid out of bed, eager to begin his day and take on the actual world rather than whatever lurked in his mind.

GUARDS STOOD alert at each entrance to a grand dining hall. The vaulted ceiling, marble floor, and crafted cedar table reeked of ostentatious decor, but fitting for a king's house. Philip II, King of Macedon, slouched forward with his elbows on the table. A bearded warrior, his scarred face was a testament to a man who lived by the sword.

Servants tip toed in with platters filled with fresh fruits, loaves of bread, and meats. They placed them before the king with shaky hands and then darted back out. Philip was like a volcano that could erupt at any moment. It kept everyone on their toes, which was how he liked it.

Alexander entered, now dressed in a chiton. In between bites of lamb, Philip motioned him to come hither. Alexander obliged and sat beside Philip, but his distant gaze showed he had little interest in his father's words.

In a gruff voice, Philip asked, "How are your studies?"

Alexander ignored the question. His attention turned to his mother, Olympias, who slipped into the back of the room to keep tabs on things. There was little affection toward her, as she hadn't come to protect him. She'd come to defend her position as the king's favorite wife.

"Boy! I'm speaking to you," Philip said.

"He had another dream." Olympias spoke for Alexander to assuage the king's growing anger.

Philip dropped his lamb. "Always with these ridiculous nightmares." He eyed Olympias. "Is he still a baby sucking off your teat?"

"Alexander said his dream was a battle. A very bloody one," Olympias said. Brilliant and beyond ambitious, Olympias would have been the one wearing the crown if she were a man. Philip raised an eyebrow, intrigued—her desired effect.

"Are you ready to start the military academy?" Philip leaned back in his seat and stared at his son.

Alexander shrugged.

"He's doing well with his studies," Olympias said. "He should continue, at least for another year. It will prepare him to be a wise king."

Philip grunted in agreement. How could such a fragile boy handle the horrors of war? He stabbed at a hunk of lamb. "Is that what you want, Alexander?"

"Either is fine," Alexander said as his thoughts drifted back to his nightmare.

Philip bit into the tender meat. "Either is fine," he muttered as he chewed. "You've got a big wrestling match coming up. I understand Hephaestion is undefeated like you. Do you want to win or lose, or is either fine?"

Alexander didn't respond. Philip slammed his fist down, startling everyone except Alexander.

"Your king is talking to you!"

Alexander raised his gaze and looked Philip square in the eye. He showed no fear, which was unsettling. How could a boy be afraid of his dreams but hold no fear of the king, a terrifying warrior who had cut down hundreds of men?

"Winning the tournament shows everyone you're not just the king's son," Philip said.

Olympias rubbed her hands. The conversation had drifted into dangerous territory. "Win or lose, Alexander is still a good boy," she said, hoping to calm matters.

Philip ignored Olympias. He could not stand for insolence from anyone, much less his teenage son. Philip leaned down, just inches from Alexander's nose. "Do you want to be a good boy or a great man, Alexander?"

By his father's standards, "great" meant conquering and expanding the kingdom, activities that didn't interest Alexander. Since no answer would appease Philip, Alexander didn't offer one.

Philip slammed both fists against the table. "It is not a given that you will be heir to my throne."

The guards stood frozen like statues, afraid to draw attention to themselves.

"Let's calm down. Alexander will be king and a great one," Olympias said in as soothing a voice as possible.

"You think I will trust my legacy to a weak boy spooked by his own shadow?" Philip asked.

"This is just a phase," Olympias said. "He will grow out of these dreams."

"No. I will get a new wife and make a new heir."

A silence befell the room. Olympias clutched her hands against her chest as if Philip had sentenced her to death. She stammered for a response. "He will win the match. He will be a great ruler. Your legacy will live on forever," she said in an unveiled attempt to play to his ego.

Philip took a deep breath before dispensing his wisdom. "In battle, a loss means you're dead, and the kingdom destroyed." Philip stared at his son with dead eyes. "Lose the match, and you only lose the crown."

He stood up and left in a huff, his decision final. Olympias chased after him, hoping in vain to change his mind.

All the guards followed.

"I just want to get rid of my nightmares," Alexander whispered as he surveyed the giant room. It was empty. He was alone in the world.

———————

THE WEALTHY AND ordinary citizens of Pella packed the gymnasium for the wrestling match between the two teens once word spread about the contest's significance. The building itself was not remarkable. A large dirt floor served as the "mat," and the people watching formed the "ring."

Alexander stood on one side, wearing nothing more than a loincloth.

11

Even though puberty had given him the beginning of a warrior's physique, he felt naked and exposed. He kept his eyes glued to the floor, which helped him from becoming overwhelmed by the bustling energy. Whispers and wagers were placed, and people openly gossiped about who would be heir if he lost. He also didn't want to make eye contact with his father, who watched from a small balcony on the second floor.

Hephaestion, also thirteen, paced back and forth like a lion on the other side of the ring. Based only on appearance, Hephaestion would win easily.

The referee, a fit man in his forties, motioned the boys to the center. Hephaestion and Alexander obeyed and stepped toward each other. Hephaestion's steely gaze bore down on Alexander.

Despite Alexander's indifference to his father's wishes, he did want to win, but it was not about keeping his claim to the throne. He simply had a will to win, or perhaps a fear of losing.

The referee swung his arm between the boys and signaled the start of the match. The teens sized each other up, probing for weaknesses. Hephaestion shot at Alexander's legs, corralled them, lifted him in the air, and brought him down hard.

The crowd both gasped and cheered.

Alexander escaped Hephaestion's grip and sprung back to his feet, even though the body slam bruised his entire left shoulder. The two squared off, then locked arms. Hephaestion grappled behind Alexander and again slammed him to the ground, this time on his right side.

Alexander refused to give up. He broke free from Hephaestion's vice grip and struggled to his feet. Breathing heavy and primed for defeat, he staggered across the ring. Hephaestion pursued and shot high.

In the blink of an eye, Alexander's mind *flashed*.

Two bloodied soldiers squared off in hand-to-hand combat. One lunged to attack, but the other shifted his weight, flipped the attacker, put him in a chokehold, and then broke his neck.

Alexander snapped back to reality. No time to think as Hephaestion barreled towards him. He turned, knocked Hephaestion off-balance, performed the reverse flip from his mind, and put Hephaestion in a choke-hold. Left with no option, Hephaestion submitted and tapped out.

The crowd roared in delight at the fantastic finish. A cheer started that built in intensity.

"Future king. Future king. Future king!"

Alexander took it all in. He glanced up and even caught the smallest hint of a smile from his father.

Gracious in defeat, Hephaestion approached Alexander. "Congratulations, that was an incredible move."

"Thank you. I was fortunate to win," Alexander said.

Hephaestion locked eyes with Alexander and bore down with the same intense gaze as before the match. Something else was on his mind.

"What is it?" Alexander asked.

"I was hoping I could talk to you," Hephaestion said. "We have something in common."

Alexander's curiosity was piqued.

Hephaestion leaned in and whispered, "The visions."

CHAPTER 3

THIS IS THE PRESENT-DAY, even though "present" is a fleeting concept. Everything, save for a microsecond, is the past or the future. However, "present" can also mean focused and aware. For perhaps the first time in his life, a history professor was "present." His awakening began after a fateful lecture early in the semester.

History may lie, but we're the authors of it.

THE UNIVERSITY OF MARYLAND comprised a 1,250-acre picturesque campus filled with red-brick Georgian buildings, and included Francis Scott Key Hall, a pillared edifice that could double for a government building in Washington, D.C. It housed the history department, and inside one room, Ben Preston delivered a gripping lecture to a full class. Dressed in a professorial sport coat and jeans, Ben was handsome in a nerdy kind of way. A favorite among students because he somehow made history engaging, Ben struggled to connect with most people on a personal level. Driven in some ways and yet drifting in others, Ben searched, like we all do, for a meaning to his life. Currently an adjunct professor, he aspired to be a full-fledged, tenured one. He wasn't sure if that would fulfill him, but it at least gave him something to strive for and take his mind off feeling lost.

"As they ran through the streets, they were not met with cheers and high fives." Ben paused for dramatic effect. "The Roman people were horrified. Stupefied. Demoralized."

Ben commanded the room, and his students hung on every word. It was as if they had been living this story. Ben rubbed his chin in pensive reflection. History wasn't a collection of facts or a description of events. For him, it was life—a record of our existence and the highs and lows of humanity. It was about individual people and their nuanced complexity.

"Julius Caesar was a tyrant," Ben preached. "By killing him, the senators thought they were saving a republic and an ideal. The ideal that no one man should control Rome."

A female student raised her hand. Ben pointed at her to speak.

"Why do so many people think of Julius Caesar as a great leader?" she asked. "You made him sound... awful."

Ben rubbed his head as a headache set in. He hated it when his students missed the point of his lectures. "I didn't intend to present him that way. People are often more complicated than their historical summation." Ben glanced at the clock. "That's it for this week, and I guess that's it for 'awful' Julius Caesar."

Ben smiled as he gave a curt wave to his students to signal their dismissal. As they gathered their things, Ben added, "Next week, we're going further back in time to explore the life of another ancient world leader—Alexander the Great."

An arrogant student in a Sigma Chi sweatshirt chimed in, "Do you hate him too?"

"I'd better not since I've spent the last year working on an article about him. That said, after you learn how his life ended, I think you'll find that his real moniker should be Alexander 'The Failure.'"

The arrogant student rolled his eyes. "C'mon. It wasn't his fault he got sick. He may have died young, but he became ruler of one of the largest empires. Professor, are you going to rewrite everyone's history?"

Ben froze. One harmless off-handed comment from a *thinks-he-knows-it-all* teenager caused his body to go numb. "Um, make sure to do the reading. And, uh, enjoy the rest of your week." He waved with a smile, but as soon as he turned to collect his things, concern filled his face.

Minutes later, Ben sat on the edge of his chair at his antique Stow-Davis desk. Books, journals, and boxes of documents packed his cramped office like a miniature library, albeit a disorganized one. He skimmed a paper, flipping back from one page, then to the last. He stopped only long enough to pop an Advil as the headache from class intensified.

A middle-aged man, dressed like Ben, knocked on the open door. Lost in the mysterious riddle of the paper, Ben didn't respond.

"Hey," the man said.

Ben paused reading and glanced up. "Hey, Frank."

Frank was Ben's closest friend at the school, and if Ben was honest with himself, which he wasn't, Frank was his only real friend.

"Heading down to the pub for a beer. Want to join?"

A couple of beers didn't sound like a bad idea, but the paper beckoned Ben. He rubbed his head in frustration.

"You okay?" Frank asked.

"I can't find my sources for a couple of key items in my article." Ben put his paper aside.

Frank shrugged. "So, it doesn't get published."

"If I don't get published, I'm off the tenure track. I won't get promoted to associate professor." Ben grabbed his coat, and the two headed out.

Frank remained unconvinced. "So, you won't be stuck in this little prison cell for the rest of your life."

Ben closed the door of his "cell" behind him.

McGINTY'S WAS a classic Irish pub with circular maple wood tables and a dartboard in back, but as with most pubs, the dominant feature was the mahogany archetypal wrap-around bar. Frank and Ben sat on two of the stools drinking, although Frank did most of the drinking while Ben tore at the label on his Guinness.

In the upper corner behind the bar, a college basketball game played on a Sony flat screen. Frank stared slack-jawed and pumped his fist when his team scored.

"Did you know the publisher for the *Journal of Global History* is the world's oldest publishing house?" Ben asked, even though he knew Frank wasn't listening or interested. A small part of him hoped Frank would understand his dilemma. Ben continued to prod for a reaction. "Definitely the most prestigious history journal."

Frank kept his eyes glued to the television. "Yeah, if you don't get published by them, your career is definitely over."

Ben jabbed Frank in the ribs with his elbow.

"I'm kidding. Lighten up." Frank sipped his beer.

The career path in historical academia was not a secret. A person usually began as an adjunct professor. After enough time schmoozing with tenured professors and having at least one article published, one could expect a promotion to associate professor, then to tenured professor, and maybe one day becoming a dean of a department.

"It isn't just my career," Ben said. "Beth wants to get married. I told her we need to wait until I get promoted, so we have enough money, so we can buy a home together—actually start a life."

"Come on. Beth doesn't care if you're an *adjunct* or an *associate* professor." Frank's bluntness was one of his faults and also one of his endearing qualities. He didn't mind calling out someone's BS.

Ben continued to find excuses to avoid addressing the riddle stuck in his head. "I'm turning thirty on Friday."

Frank side-eyed Ben. "What's this really about, Ben? Don't tell me this is about a paper or turning thirty."

Ben tore at the label on his beer until there was nothing left. "Do you ever feel like this isn't your life?"

"No. I always dreamed of being a history professor," Frank joked.

"I'm serious," Ben said, and he was. Dead serious. "I always feel... afraid."

"Afraid of what?"

"Like I'm doing it all wrong," Ben said. "I teach history. I talk about people that have done all these amazing things. What if I haven't done anything? What if I'm nothing?"

Frank mulled on the weight of Ben's admission and then slapped him on the back. "Congratulations! You're having your mid-life crisis ten years early. That's something, right? Know what will help?" Frank took a chug of beer and raised an eyebrow for Ben to follow suit.

On the television screen, a headline scrolled at the bottom. *Virginia Congressman Tom Vance is taking an indefinite medical leave. Reports have surfaced that Vance may be suffering from brain cancer.*

"Oh, man. That guy can't catch a break." Frank pointed to the TV. "Tommy Vance was one of the best college players I've ever seen. No one shot the ball better. Blew out his knee sophomore year. NBA dreams, gone. Guy picks himself up, goes on to become a congressman. Some thought he might become president. Now, he's got brain cancer." Frank let that sink in. "Kind of makes your problems seem small, right?"

Ben shrugged. Maybe.

"I'm sure you're overreacting about this article," Frank said. "It will get published. You'll get promoted, and then married. Life will be grand. Until then, drink your beer."

Ben took one small sip. "I describe Alexander the Great as a failure."

Frank chewed on that doozy for a moment. "Have a few beers."

"I know it's a crazy conclusion," Ben said. "But I did the research. I traveled to Pella, Macedon, and India. I talked to other professors. I found new sources—obscure texts." Ben took one more defeated sip. "But I reread my paper, and I couldn't find citations for some of the key moments

—like how he died. But I know someone gave me that information. I just don't remember who. I have to find my sheet."

"Your what?"

"My sheet—my list of sources," Ben said. "It shows all the people I talked to and the key info I got. I have to find it."

Frank polished off the last of his beer, then motioned to the bartender for another. He then swiveled on his stool to face Ben. "You realize you're telling me that the importance of your life depends on finding a bibliography?" Frank let the words hang for a moment.

But this wasn't about a bibliography. Ben had been chasing this promotion like it was a destination. It meant forward progress. Movement. But what happens when the goal isn't reached? What happens if everything stops moving? Ben found that the voices in his head got a little louder, and he didn't like what he heard. He needed to know that his article was right. He needed *something* in his life to be right. History was the one thing he excelled at, and getting the promotion gave him a purpose. Without that, he didn't have one. Without a goal, he couldn't stop the worst voice in his head from taunting him.

The world would be better off if Ben Preston didn't exist.

CHAPTER 4

The Virginia Hospital Center looked like any other hospital—a rectangular box with alternating horizontal bands of windows and concrete. The paved semi-circle entryway provided for easy pick-ups and drop-offs.

Dr. Riya Patel, Anjali's sister, sat in her office on the third-floor, scanning papers strewn about her rosewood desk. Dozens more filled a thick file in front of her. A framed picture of herself and Anjali from her sister's medical school graduation rested on the corner. Both smiled and looked happy. Amidst the mess was an old newspaper article that described the explosion at Anjali's lab and a highlighted police report. Another document listed the names of the deceased scientists, their schools, majors, and previous jobs. It included Wayne Glassman, a history professor.

There was a knock at the door, but it opened almost immediately. Greg Yates, the CEO of the hospital and, thus, Riya's boss, entered in a dark blue Armani suit. He was the picture of superficial health from Botox, skin tanners, and teeth whitening, which made guessing his age a useless exercise, but most assumed he was in his late fifties.

"Greg, what can I do for you?" She scooped up the papers and stuffed them in the file.

Greg walked over and sat on the edge of her desk. He reached down and opened the file. Caught red-handed, Riya avoided eye contact. Instead, she stared at the framed photo.

"Want to take some more time off?" Greg asked.

"No. Being alone is worse," Riya said. And it was. The last year had been brutal. Anjali didn't have any immediate family, at least not nearby. Her mother and father emigrated from India to the U.S. just before she was born. After they died, she lost touch with her remaining relatives. When Anjali died, she had no one. Left to her own thoughts, unresolved wounds surfaced and joined forces with new ones. Why did her parents die? Why now her sister? There must be a reason for their deaths.

Greg picked up the photo of Riya and her sister. "It's a nice picture of you two."

"I found it when we cleared out her apartment," Riya said. "There isn't much else to remember her by." After Anjali's funeral, Riya never visited her sister's grave because she wasn't there. The explosion obliterated everything and everyone. The funeral director suggested that Riya place personal mementos into her sister's coffin, which she did, even though it felt like a hollow gesture.

Greg respectfully placed the photo back on the desk. "Listen, Riya. You are one of the best neurologists in the world... when you're doing your job." Known to many as "the velvet hammer," Greg understood these were the tough conversations a CEO had to make, and he was always up to the task. "I care about you," he started in his velvety way, but finished with a hint of the hammer. "But I have a hospital to run and patients who need their doctors focused on them."

"I'll do better," Riya promised.

"Anjali's death was a tragic accident. A gas line ruptured. A freak occurrence. You have to let it go."

A tear streamed down Riya's face. "The last time I saw her, we got into a fight. She said her research was going to change the world. I didn't believe her. I didn't believe *in* her. And she knew it. I know she's gone, but I need at least a part of her not to be."

Greg stood back up. "All the research is gone."

"Something must have survived. I need to find it. I need to know what she died for," Riya's voice trailed off into a whisper.

Greg offered one last attempt to be the velvet. "If you want to honor her memory, you can do it with *your* research and your practice."

"I don't know if I can." Riya looked down, ashamed.

Greg took a deep breath. "If you can't, then I have to let you go. Take a couple of days, okay? Let me know by the end of the week."

Riya nodded, and Greg left.

And there it was, Riya's choice—keep her job and forget her sister, or lose the one thing she'd worked for her entire life.

CHAPTER 5

Macedon, 343 B.C.

Alexander and Hephaestion shared a meal of figs and lamb atop a crumbling wall at the city's edge. They were now cleaned up after their match and dressed in chitons. Hephaestion also wore a necklace with a stone medallion crafted with ornate symbols.

"What do you see in your dreams?" Hephaestion asked.

Alexander opened his mouth to speak, but fear stopped him.

"If you don't want to talk about it…"

Alexander blurted out, "Battles. War. Fighting…" Once started, he couldn't stop, perhaps realizing that Hephaestion might be the only person who could understand. "Pain. Death. Sometimes, there are other things, but mostly I see… suffering." Alexander stared at Hephaestion but then looked away, embarrassed that he'd opened himself up.

"Me too," Hephaestion said.

"Really?"

Hephaestion nodded. "Given your father's connections, I was hoping maybe he knew what causes them."

Alexander shook his head. "He's had doctors, medicine men, wise men, and philosophers all treat me. No one can fix it."

The boys picked at their food in shared mystery.

"The visions are why I don't know if I want to be king." Alexander gazed at the city below, ashamed to make such an admission.

"Why's that?"

"They feel real to me," Alexander said. "I'm afraid they could happen if I become king."

Hephaestion mulled his response as he finished a bite of lamb. "Then why would I have similar visions? I can't be king."

A valid point that comforted Alexander.

"And if you didn't want to be king, maybe you should've lost." Hephaestion shoved Alexander playfully.

The two smiled.

"It's a relief to know I'm not alone anymore and can talk to someone who doesn't think I'm crazy," Hephaestion said. "I hope we can be friends."

"I'd like that." As the words left Alexander's lips, something amazing happened inside him. He no longer felt isolated or alone. He had a genuine friend.

"These visions are the only reason I have an interest in fighting," Hephaestion said.

"What do you mean?"

"What if the people who are suffering are haunting us because we need to save them? What if these dreams are our destiny?"

"You mean we're seeing our future?" Alexander asked.

Hephaestion nodded. "What if we're supposed to save the world?"

The message resonated with Alexander.

INDIA, 323 B.C.

· · ·

TWENTY YEARS LATER, a Greek army stood ready for battle, with the infantry positioned in phalanx formation. The soldiers wore blood-stained armor and tired faces. Bandages covered gory wounds. They looked like they'd been to hell and back and were being asked to do it again.

Hephaestion, now in his early thirties, attempted to rally the men from atop a white stallion. As a boy, his physique was impressive, but as a man, his rippling muscles inspired awe as if he'd been born from the Greek gods. But some things hadn't changed. Hephaestion still wore the same medallion necklace. "Men, I know we just fought an epic battle, one that will be remembered for all eternity. You're tired. You're hurt. But we must fight again."

The hearts of the men sank. After so many years of fighting, there wasn't a man who hadn't lost at least one friend in battle, and they barely emerged victorious in their most recent clash against a fearless enemy. For some, the thought of dying was less cruel than this never-ending campaign of war.

Alexander, a modern-day Achilles, sat atop his black stallion named Bucephalus. Covered with dried blood, not a drop of it his own, Alexander stared in the opposite direction of his men. They adored him and would do whatever he asked, something that weighed on his conscience. After campaigning for over a decade, they'd sacrificed so much, but the evil of the world seemed never-ending. A leader by example, Alexander always fought in the front lines, something the men respected and admired. He also treated them as equals rather than subordinates.

Hephaestion tried again to lift their spirits. "We embarked on a journey many years ago—a journey to free the world from tyranny and injustice—a journey that the gods have blessed. We must honor that. Today, we face a new enemy. One that doesn't qualify as human. These barbarians steal, enslave, rape, and pillage. Imagine they did this to your daughters. Would you stand for it?"

The men shouted in an obligatory show of support. They believed in the cause, but the fervor of their youth had left after so many years of fighting.

25

Many felt they'd done their fair share in the pursuit of justice, and all wanted to go home and be with their families.

Alexander looked back at his men. Fear and frustration filled their eyes. As Hephaestion rode up beside him, Alexander whispered, "You sure the men are up for this?"

Hephaestion had assumed the role of the dogged drill sergeant and pushed the men hard. Many resented him for it, but the army didn't have room for error if it was to achieve its goals. He leaned over and whispered, "If we wait, it will be worse. The enemy will have time to organize." Hephaestion signaled the army forward with his sword.

The men slogged forward in unison. The cavalry, led by Alexander, came together and trotted in formation.

General Craterus, a beast of a man, commanded the infantry. His orders were simple but not easy—engage the enemy head-on and hold. The cavalry would find a weakness in the enemy's line and break it. Once broken, the Greeks would surround the enemy and slaughter them.

As the cavalry thundered forward, Hephaestion yelled out, "Stay together!" This command, above all else, would see them through the assault. In ancient battles, the biggest army didn't always win. Discipline decided victory, something the Greeks had mastered.

A camp came into view—huts and corrals, and only a small force of defenders, maybe a few dozen. They formed a thin defensive line. It would be an easy victory, but Alexander never underestimated his opponent. He glanced back once more at his haggard men. He hated what he'd put them through, even if it was for a greater good. Without warning, he spurred Bucephalus to charge.

Hephaestion watched with frustration. He motioned the rest of the cavalry to try to keep up. It was an effort in futility.

Confused, the defenders prepared for battle as this lone horseman stormed closer. Alexander rode with a fury and maybe even a death wish. He spotted a small gap in the line, steered Bucephalus toward it, and smashed through the weak enemy position. The rest of the cavalry followed and overwhelmed the barbarians.

Alexander scanned the camp and discovered confused elderly women bound by rope in a corral. Cries for help diverted his attention. He spied a cage-like structure built into the hill. Alexander dismounted, hurried up the embankment, and found a group of terrified women and girls locked in a wooden prison made of bamboo rods secured by a crude lock. As he struggled to open the cage, battle cries echoed from the trees on the hills above him. In seconds, a swarm of fighters emerged in an ambush. The Greeks had been tricked, but Alexander's premature attack forced them to engage sooner than planned, and the barbarian army faced the Greek infantry from the front rather than the flanks, its intended target.

Hephaestion turned the cavalry around to meet the new enemy. Seeing their brethren in need, the Greek infantry charged the barbarian hordes.

As Alexander assessed the battlefront, a barbarian sprang down from above and smashed Alexander in the stomach with a club. He fell back, his sword knocked to the ground. One of the imprisoned women attempted to reach the sword but couldn't.

The barbarian raised his massive club to lay a death blow on Alexander.

CHAPTER 6

MARYLAND, 2018

THE EARLY MORNING skyline of College Park, Maryland, lay behind a faded eight-story apartment building, which was home for Ben and his girlfriend, Beth. They rented a one-bedroom unit on the fourth floor. One side of the building overlooked a manicured courtyard and faced a sea of loblolly pines. Their side faced another apartment complex. Views were a luxury that cost extra money, something they didn't have.

In their lone bedroom, both slept, but only one peacefully. Beth rested on her side, a soft smile on her face and her long blonde locks facing Ben, who laid on his back. About every twenty minutes, his eyes flashed open and then drooped down. It was like sleep apnea, except breathing wasn't the issue. When his eyes popped again, they remained open until his gaze fell on the digital clock on the nightstand—4:12. His body craved sleep, but his mind refused to cooperate, in part because of the raging headache that had not stopped since class the day before. Ben convinced himself the stress of his missing list of sources caused it, and there was only one remedy—he needed to find it. Before crawling out of bed to begin the hunt,

Ben opened a secret compartment in the back of the nightstand. Inside, a 9mm pistol rested on its side, along with wads of cash. He grabbed his wallet beside the clock, pulled out a couple of twenties, and added to the stash. When he closed the nightstand, he was too tired to notice the corner of a bill sticking out. He slid out from under the sheets and disappeared into the living room.

Ben opened the coat closet, revealing stacks of giant cardboard boxes. He lifted one down, which had "Research" scrawled in heavy marker on the side. He tossed the top off and began rifling through papers, skimming sheet after sheet. Within minutes, a colossal mess surrounded him.

"What are you doing?"

Ben jolted in shock and turned to find Beth, half-awake, looming over his shoulder. He stumbled for a response. "Nothing. Just looking for some old notes... for a lecture."

"Any news about your article?" Beth asked in a sweet voice. She was one of those blessed few who looked beautiful rolling out of bed.

"Not yet."

Beth gave Ben a comforting hug from behind. "You know it's okay if you don't get published, right?"

Ben nodded, but it wasn't okay with him. He rubbed his head.

"You sure you're okay?" Beth asked.

"Just tired. And my head hurts."

"You've been having a lot of headaches lately. Maybe you should go to a doctor." Beth said, concerned.

"It's fine. I've been dealing with these since I was a teen."

Beth raised an eyebrow. This was news to her. Ben had suffered through at least three dozen headaches in the last four months, but he experienced one in the two years prior. When they first began, he'd suffer through one every few days, and it would subside after an hour. The frequency and intensity had increased where he now had one, at least every other day.

"Stress brings them on," Ben said.

"All this over your article?"

29

Ben nodded.

"Well, don't let an article about someone who is dead kill you, okay?" Beth half-joked as she kissed the top of Ben's head. He smiled, but it faded as soon as she returned to the bedroom. Any guy would be lucky to have a girl like Beth, which was why he carried a guilty conscience 24/7.

LATER THAT MORNING, Ben commuted via a public bus through a part of town losing the battle with urban blight. The ride reminded Ben that there were many in this world far worse off than he. The brakes of the metro bus belched and squealed at the next stop. The driver pulled the lever and opened the door. Three gang bangers swaggered on. Sporting red bandanas, baggy jeans, and arms covered with tattoos and muscles, they scoped out the bus, hoping to find trouble. The leader of the trio, T-Roy, eyed a pretty young Asian girl sitting by herself reading a book. He parked himself beside her as his cronies found seats nearby and snickered. They enjoyed watching their pal cause mayhem.

"Hey, sweet baby girl," he said.

The girl pretended not to hear and kept her head in the book.

He raised his voice. "You don't speak English?"

No reaction.

"You deaf?"

Still nothing. T-Roy nudged the now frightened girl. The cronies cackled like hyenas. The other passengers eyed one another and hoped someone else would help.

Ben's heart raced. *Thump, thump. Thump, thump.* Something was going to go down. *Thump, thump. Thump, thump.* Or was it? The brakes of the bus squealed. It was Ben's stop. The middle door opened, and he scurried off to escape the potential confrontation.

Hours later, Ben delivered another engaging lecture to his students, but he wasn't nearly as composed as yesterday. He struggled with his balance and perspiration pooled in the armpits of his shirt and beaded on his forehead. *Was it the stress of the article? The incident on the bus? Or something else?* He didn't know, but he felt like he should, which only added to his anxiety.

"Alexander the Great had all the advantages one could ask for." He wiped sweat off his brow. "Born into nobility. Well educated. It is undeniable that he did a lot in his short lifetime. He conquered one of the largest empires ever known. But is that success?" He pensively rubbed his chin as he addressed the students, then wiped away more moisture. "What was his purpose? What did he want to accomplish? Was it to conquer the world? If so, then he failed."

Ben held his head as searing pain shot through his brain. "We may never know his true purpose." He staggered forward.

Several students stood up in shock. One yelled, "Call 9-1-1."

Ben snapped out of it and caught himself from falling. "I'm fine. Just a little dizzy." In a half-daze, something dawned on him. He knew where to find his sheet of sources. A surge of adrenaline filled his body as he gathered his things. "We'll let out a little early today. See you next class," Ben said to his bewildered students as he raced out of the room.

Ben dashed through the hallways until he reached his office. He threw the door open, rushed in, and slammed it shut. In one corner, there was a stack of historical trinkets on top of three boxes. He shoved the bobbles aside and slid the second box out. He flung the top off and rifled through stacks of paper until he pulled out two sheets.

"Found you," Ben said with a huge smile. He scanned the list of names, and his grin slowly disappeared. He finished and reviewed the pages again. Then, a third time. The harsh reality set in. He didn't source his paper, an elementary school blunder. Ben's blood boiled, but he had only himself to blame. His fury turned to despair as he slumped down on the ground, now on the verge of tears. He grabbed his head as a raging headache hammered away.

"What's wrong with me?"

CHAPTER 7

RIYA SIGNED in at the front desk of a live-in rehabilitation center. A nurse in a white shirt and slacks escorted her down the hall to the communal room. Several residents sat on couches watching a Disney movie. Two others played ping pong. Behind them, a man in a wheelchair faced the window with his head slumped. Bobby was the security guard and lone survivor from Anjali's lab.

"Bobby? I'm Riya Patel." She offered her hand. Bobby looked at her with forlorn eyes and shook her hand. Riya glanced down at his legs, which appeared mangled even with clothes on.

"Do I know you?" He asked in a whisper of a voice.

"I'm Anjali Patel's sister. She was a doctor who worked at the lab."

Bobby studied her again. "You kinda look like her."

Riya cut to the point of her visit. "I was wondering if you knew anything about the research at the lab."

Bobby looked away. "I was just a security guard. They kept everything secret."

"Please. Anything at all would be helpful," Riya said.

"Why do you want to know so bad?"

Riya suddenly became defensive. "Whatever she was working on was very important."

"How do you know it was important if you don't know what it was?"

A fair question and one Riya asked herself every day for the last year. "Because I believe in her. And I believe she's still with me. And she wants me to know." Riya choked up, unable to utter another word. Her speech didn't even work on herself anymore. She glanced down at her feet, vulnerable. "I need her death to matter. To know that it wasn't some random accident."

Bobby nodded, appreciative of her honesty. Now it was time for his own. "On the day of the explosion, my partner and I got a call for one of us to help with something. We were lazy. Neither wanted to go, so we flipped a coin. He's dead, and I'm here. Not sure who lost that flip. But if that isn't random, I don't know what is."

Maybe Bobby didn't realize how cruel his words were, but they enraged Riya. She leaned in, grabbed his shirt, and pulled his face to hers. "Listen, Bobby, it's the end of the week. That may mean nothing to you, but it means a lot to me. I need to decide if I'm going to live the rest of my life believing that my sister died for nothing, or if I'm going to end my career. The next thing out of your mouth is going to weigh heavily on my choice. Do you understand that?"

Taken aback by Riya's physical aggressiveness, Bobby sat in shock, unable to respond to the massive responsibility she just threw in his lap.

"Do you know anything at all about what they were researching?" Riya asked.

Bobby still sat speechless. Riya let go of Bobby's shirt, realizing her physical outburst was a mistake, and so was this visit. He was a victim, too. "I'm sorry for your injury." She turned to leave.

"I remember one thing," Bobby said.

33

CHAPTER 8

India, 323 B.C.

Time seemed to slow down as the massive barbarian held his club to the sky to smash Alexander's skull in, who appeared calm and ready to accept his fate. The women and girls fled from the prison, which interrupted the execution and caused the barbarian to pause. *How did they get out?*

The woman who had tried to reach Alexander's sword was now free and could. She slid the weapon between the barbarian's legs to Alexander, and their eyes met. Her eyes—her beautiful brown eyes—there was something about them. They served as a magical elixir for his fighting spirit. He snatched the sword just as the barbarian struck with all his might. Alexander deflected the strike, then sprung to his feet. The barbarian possessed the size advantage, but Alexander's skill was otherworldly. He slashed and thrust his sword until the barbarian dropped in a bloody heap. He spotted the shell-shocked woman who saved him, offered a quick, curious nod of gratitude, then left.

Hephaestion re-organized the cavalry and plowed through the attackers. From behind, Alexander became a one-man army, cutting down any adversary who stepped toward him. Through the chaos, Bucephalus emerged. Alexander mounted him and then sped towards the infantry battle. As he drew near, Alexander let out a primal scream. The barbarians turned to see the grim reaper in the form of a Greek madman barreling down.

The rout was on.

BODIES LITTERED the field of battle, and there was barely a Greek among them. The victorious soldiers pillaged anything of value from the enemy corpses—the proverbial spoils of war—but most looked disappointed by the lack of treasure they uncovered.

Hephaestion approached Alexander, who surveyed the carnage. His rage had been replaced with melancholy, and his gaze fell upon the blank expression of a dead "barbarian," no older than sixteen.

"Scouts report only a couple dozen escaped," Hephaestion said, pleased with the result. "How did you know they had an ambush planned?"

"I didn't," Alexander said.

"Then why did you—"

"My nightmares have not gone away, Hephaestion," Alexander interrupted as he continued to stare at the dead boy. "They're worse."

"We rid the world of a bunch of lawless thugs. You saw the condition of their slaves," Hephaestion said.

These bouts of depression both frustrated and worried Alexander, who nodded and wanted to take comfort in his friend's words.

"We didn't have a choice. We acted. We saved. Good triumphed," Hephaestion said. "War against evil will never be pretty."

"I just need the visions to go away."

Hephaestion handed Alexander an animal skin filled with wine. He snatched it and took a huge gulp.

That night, the soldiers celebrated their victory under the star-filled sky. The barbarian camp was now the Greeks', and they had converted it from a place of depravity to one of joy. The men sang and danced with the people they freed or at least got drunk enough to forget the violence they just endured and inflicted. One soldier played music with a kithara, a stringed instrument that was a cross between a harp and a guitar, and another blew into an aulos which resembled a double flute. A third soldier belted out lyrics that the dancing soldiers often repeated.

A tipsy Alexander meandered through the revelers to congratulate them on their victory. Out of nowhere, an elderly woman grabbed him and planted a big, wet kiss on his lips before scurrying off. Two of Alexander's men, Diodorus and Varus, erupted with laughter from the prank. Alexander smiled as he wiped his mouth. When he turned, he came face-to-face with the woman who saved him. No longer in the heat of battle, Alexander now got a good look at her. She was stunning, with jet black hair and olive skin. Alexander did his best to conceal his drunk condition as the woman kneeled.

"There is no need for that," he said in perfect Sanskrit, the native language. Alexander made a point of learning as many languages as possible, which he also encouraged his top lieutenants to do. It allowed direct communication with the enemy during negotiations as he hated relying on an interpreter. It also garnered goodwill from liberated people. Alexander had become proficient in Sanskrit, Persian, and Illyrian through the years, along with his native Macedonian and Greek languages.

Alisa stood, revealing a bruise to her left eye.

"What is your name?" Alexander asked.

"Alisa."

"Thank you for your help today," Alexander said. The mention of their first encounter reminded him of a nagging question. "May I ask how you opened the cage?"

"The key," she said.

"The key?" Alexander struggled to come up with an explanation as to how that made sense. "How—"

"It's a story I'd rather not repeat."

Alexander looked closer at her bruise. "Did that happen in battle today?"

"Yesterday," she said, offering no further details.

Alexander could empathize. Except for Hephaestion, he didn't believe anyone could understand how he felt, so he stopped trying to explain. "I'm sorry for your suffering," he said without prodding further.

They gazed at each other for a moment. Alisa was striking, but it was more than that. Something about this woman intrigued and captivated Alexander. He wanted to kiss her, but he was afraid she didn't feel the same. He reminded himself that fortune favors the bold as he tried to work up his nerve.

It was now or never.

CHAPTER 9

LIKE A DEAD MAN WALKING, Ben shuffled down the longest hallway of Francis Scott Key Hall. Of all the days to get the call to come to the dean's office, today was Ben's 30th birthday, and the dean didn't summon him to wish him a happy day. Ben would be told the fate of his article, and thus, the fate of his job.

Ben reached the dean's door and knocked.

"Come in," a voice answered.

Ben took a deep breath. Time to get it over with. He turned the knob and entered to find John Hammersmith, the dean of the history department, an elderly gentleman with a receding hairline, donning a charcoal colored Brioni double-breasted suit with black wingtip shoes. His wood-paneled office was large and meticulously organized—the opposite of Ben's. The dominant feature was the elegant, hand-crafted mahogany desk. Despite his intimidating name, Hammersmith cared for people.

"Mr. Preston. Please, have a seat," he greeted. "I want to talk to you about your article."

Ben swallowed hard.

"As you know, Cambridge Press is a prestigious publishing house. Their reputation is stellar," Hammersmith said.

Ben nodded, already knowing what's coming next.

"So, when one of their editors wants to meet with an author, it's a pretty big deal."

Ben looked at Hammersmith, confused. "It's going to be published?"

Hammersmith grinned. "Yes, and one editor wants to discuss your research."

Ben sat, mouth agape.

"They had one request," Hammersmith noted. "There were a couple of items that weren't sourced, which they assume was just an oversight."

Ben's spirit dropped. "I can't do that."

"Why not?"

"I don't know the sources," Ben said.

"I'm afraid they won't publish without it."

Hammersmith didn't need to say more. Ben would not be published or promoted.

HOURS LATER, Ben sat alone in his office, re-thinking his stupidity. He couldn't even offer the world a simple recitation of historical facts. Morose thoughts filled his brain, including the emptiness of his life. It didn't matter that they were irrational. It was how he felt, and depression isn't rational, anyway.

Frank popped his head in. "Happy birthday, bud."

Ben's face spoke for him. It was not a happy day.

"What's wrong?" Frank asked.

"Got the news about my article," Ben said, and then shook his head.

"Sorry, pal. At least you know and don't need to stress about it anymore, right?"

"Yeah. Sure." Ben resumed brooding.

Frank bit his lip. "Listen, for the sake of your relationship, you might want to cheer up a little, or at least pretend to. Beth might be planning something for your birthday."

"I know she planned a surprise party," Ben said without any improvement in his mood.

Frank lingered. "I don't want to pry, but do you think there's a little more going on here?"

"What's going on here, Frank?" Ben asked, irritated. He had no interest in putting on a fake smile for his birthday, and he had less interest in being psychoanalyzed.

"It's just... this feels like self-sabotage. Creating historical events in your thesis article. Then, using your article as a reason you can't ask Beth to marry you. Have you considered that maybe you don't want to be a history professor, or maybe you don't want to marry Beth?"

"Wow. Amazing insight. You should teach psychology, Frank, because you sure as shit don't know history." Ben grabbed his coat and left.

Ben rode the bus home in silence. He was tired, angry, and his head throbbed. It was one of those days, and it wasn't over yet. The brakes belched as the bus stopped for a pickup. The doors swung open, and the thugs from yesterday hopped on. Ben eyed them as they passed.

T-Roy scowled back, "What'cho looking at, Professor Dick Cheese?"

The cronies snickered. Ben boiled but looked away, not interested in a fight.

T-Roy continued on until he found another unlucky lady sitting alone. He plopped himself beside her. "What's up, beautiful?"

The lady squirmed in her seat. "I just want to go home."

"That's good cause I want to go to your home too." T-Roy licked his lips suggestively.

The lady looked out the window.

"Don't turn away from me, bitch," T-Roy said.

The lady didn't respond. T-Roy shoved her in the back.

"Hey!" The physical contact triggered Ben, and the outburst startled everyone, even himself.

T-Roy glared at Ben. "You got a problem, Professor Dick Cheese?"

Ben's courage melted. He looked at the floor like a child being scolded.

"Yeah, I didn't think so, boy. You got nothing." T-Roy turned his attention back to the lady.

Thump, thump. Thump, thump. Ben's heart raced. T-Roy's words swirled in his head, but it wasn't T-Roy's voice. It was strange and a thousand times more ominous. *You got nothing. You got nothing.* The words echoed louder and louder, and Ben's heart raced faster and faster.

The brakes squelched, and the bus came to a stop to pick up more passengers.

You got nothing.

Ben's anger erupted. He jumped to his feet, grabbed T-Roy's head, and smashed it into the metal seat in front.

There was no turning back now.

CHAPTER 10

Virginia, 2018

Riya gazed at Bobby with hope-filled eyes. Finally, she'd learn the truth about her sister's research. She imagined herself finishing it, writing a paper on it, and delivering a powerful speech, giving all the credit to her amazing, brilliant sister. "What do you remember?" she asked.

"They were giving people some sort of history test."

Riya eyed him, confused. "A history test?"

"Yeah, they were seeing what they knew about history."

Riya shrugged. "That's it?"

Bobby nodded.

Riya struggled to put the pieces together. "That wouldn't change the world."

"I never said it would."

Riya sat alone in the breakfast café; the last place she saw her sister alive. She sipped a cup of coffee, deep in thought. It was possible Anjali exaggerated the significance of the research. But that would mean she died randomly and for no reason. Did that mean all the time they spent together was for no reason, too? Riya placed a couple of dollars on the table, got up, and left.

She returned to her office, but the same nihilistic thoughts attacked as soon as she reached her desk and found her sister smiling at her from the graduation photo. The thick file about Anjali's death rested beside the picture. She'd wasted a year searching for something that wasn't there, and she'd spent even more time helping and supporting her sister. All of it was for no reason. All of it was a waste. Riya shook her head as if that would get rid of the melancholy. She stuck the file as far back in the desk drawer as it could go. Tears welled up as she refused to look at the photo any further, but it remained on the corner of her desk, staring at her. She abruptly grabbed it, tossed it in the drawer, and shut it. Her sister was dead, and there was nothing she could do about it.

Riya left her desk, marched down the hallway to Greg's office, and tapped on his glass door. He glanced up from his work and motioned her in.

She charged in, eager to get the words out before she could change her mind. "I'm here to stay, Greg."

Greg folded his hands and studied Riya. The internal struggle radiated across her face. "Are you sure?"

Riya wasn't sure of anything. Anjali's death created new wounds and opened up old ones. Why did her parents and Anjali have to die? What's the point of loving someone if they die randomly? And if everything is random, what's the point of anything? She wasn't prepared to deal with such existential questions. She didn't know if she wanted her job back, but she craved the routine that came from it. The job was a beautiful distraction that allowed her to avoid dealing with life's tragedies. She did it before, and she intended to do it again. She wanted the blue pill.

"Yeah, I'm sure."

"I need to know that you'll be focused 100% on your job. I can't have you doing this side investigation thing. And really, I think it's best for you. Can you commit to that?"

Riya swallowed and fought her emotions from bubbling up. "I've let her go, Greg."

Greg exhaled and smiled. He leaned forward in his chair. "I'm happy for you, Riya. You have a gift, and you should use it."

Riya nodded, appreciative of the pep talk even if she didn't fully embrace it.

"We just got a VIP case, and I want our best neurosurgeon on it." Greg pointed to Riya. "Our guest would like to keep a low profile, so he's going to enter and exit through back doors, and he'll be coming during off-hours. He was diagnosed with a malignant tumor, but he wants a second opinion."

Riya's curiosity piqued. This was precisely what she needed to take her mind off things. *Who was this mysterious VIP?*

"It's Congressman Tom Vance," Greg said.

THAT EVENING, Riya found herself in her office, sitting opposite the congressman. Distinguished and handsome, Tom was an African American in his early forties. He held a manila envelope and wore a black shearling jacket and baseball cap—his incognito look. For a man diagnosed with a death sentence, Tom appeared healthy and confident. "It's leaked out to the press, which can severely impact my line of work, but I feel great," he said.

Riya motioned to the envelope. "Are those your test results?"

He nodded and handed it over. Riya opened it and pulled out CT scans —the equivalent of 3D X-rays that show soft tissue. She held one up to the light, revealing black and white ghost-like images of Tom's brain. Unusual masses in the middle of the brain grabbed her attention. "Your hippocampus is abnormally large, and it has a couple of unusual masses, so I understand why the cancer diagnosis was made. Do you have nausea?"

Tom shook his head.

"Flashes of, or sensitivity to, light?" Riya asked.

"Just weird images that flash in my mind from time to time."

"Tumors can sometimes cause hallucinations."

"It's not cancer." Tom shook his head, frustrated. "I feel too good. My brain isn't dying. It's never felt so alive."

Riya found it rude when her patients tried to tell her what they did or didn't have. Why visit a doctor if they felt confident in their Googled-diagnosis? She cut Tom some slack and assumed he was in denial. "What do you mean?" she asked and played along.

"Cancer is debilitating, right?"

Riya nodded.

"My mind is getting sharper," Tom said. "Let me give you an example. I was flipping through the television and came across a Bollywood channel. I started watching it and realized I liked it."

"My parents watched a lot of those. Some are pretty good." Riya smiled to connect with Tom.

"Here's the thing, they weren't in English, and all of a sudden, I realized I understood what they were saying. I picked up the language in a matter of hours."

Riya exhaled. Time to burst Tom's delusion with actual medical knowledge. "Tom, sometimes tumors can trick you into thinking you're experiencing something, but you're not. You might have thought you understood what they were saying, but your brain created the narrative."

Tom stared back at Riya and replied in perfect Sanskrit, "Adara vartase aparaddhi, Doctor Patel."

Stunned into silence, Riya understood the words because her parents had taught her the language. But how did Tom Vance know it?

CHAPTER 11

INDIA, 323 B.C.

ALEXANDER STARED at Alisa's soft lips, then her eyes. He wanted to kiss her more than anything, but he hesitated. Something stopped him. The moment passed, which left him standing awkwardly and avoiding eye contact. He bowed his head and moved on.

As he pushed through the throngs of drunken soldiers, Hephaestion pulled him aside and out of earshot of the other men. "We have a problem," he said. "The barbarians barely had a pot to piss in."

Alexander shrugged, failing to see the dilemma.

"This party will keep the men happy for tonight, but tomorrow they'll demand payment. They fight for freedom, but they also need to support their families back home."

Alexander stroked his chin and considered the issue. "What do you suggest?"

"Malli is a day's march. The ruler has taxed his people to death and hoards the gold in his palace," Hephaestion said.

Alexander's shoulders slumped. Another battle.

"He won't dare challenge us."

Alexander wasn't convinced.

"I know it's hard, but if we don't fight for those who can't, who will?" Hephaestion asked.

"The enemy is never-ending."

"You're tired from battle today. Get some sleep," Hephaestion said. "You'll feel like yourself in the morning."

Alexander scoffed. Sleep? That was the last thing he wanted. Alexander downed a drink and was about to rejoin the revelers, but paused. "We're friends, right?"

"Best friends," Hephaestion said.

Alexander looked down at the ground. "What if this isn't my destiny?"

"Then what is your destiny?"

With downtrodden eyes, Alexander murmured, "I don't know if I have one." Afraid to hear Hephaestion's response, Alexander rejoined the party.

THE NEXT MORNING, the Greek army slogged through the rugged countryside. Slumped atop Bucephalus, Alexander rode half awake and half sick.

Hephaestion motioned his horse up alongside him. "Too much ale?"

Alexander remained hunched over. "I can't even drink my nightmares away anymore."

Hephaestion shook his head. "The men worship you. You rule an empire larger than anything known in history. And you've saved thousands, maybe millions, from evil rulers. Does nothing help at all?"

Alexander considered the question. "It felt good when that woman thanked me."

"Which woman? The old lady that kissed you?"

Alexander shot him a look.

Hephaestion smiled. "Ah, the gorgeous slave girl. If she's your elixir, we can send a rider to bring her back."

"No," Alexander said.

"You don't think she'd want to lie with Alexander the Great?" Hephaestion joked.

"She'd feel like she couldn't say 'no.' Like I'm the next tyrant, imposing his will on her." Alexander kicked his heels into the sides of Bucephalus. His mind was made up, and he was done talking about it.

THE GREEK ARMY NEARED MALLI, a mid-sized city for the time. The citadel, the primary feature, peeked over foreboding walls. Crude buildings and shanties surrounded the flatland outside the city, but they appeared deserted. Inhabitants of towns often retreated behind the safety of the walls when enemy armies approached, but no guards patrolled the walls and the main gate was open. *Had the Mallians abandoned the city entirely?*

A Greek scout rode back from the town to deliver an update to Alexander and Hephaestion. "The city is deserted."

From atop Bucephalus, Alexander turned to Hephaestion. "Doesn't look like we'll be finding any gold today."

A small, ominous tent was pitched on the outskirts of the shanties. A second scout rode back from that direction. "An old man says he knows of the treasure you seek."

Alexander squinted at the small tent. *Were they being set up for another ambush? How did this old man know what they sought?* He rubbed his chin and considered the possibilities.

"Why are you worried?" Hephaestion mimicked Alexander's chin rubbing. "You always rub your chin when you're deep in thought or worried. It's a tent with one old man. I can send in the heavy cavalry if you'd like," he joked.

Not amused, Alexander stopped rubbing and pushed Bucephalus forward as Hephaestion followed with a playful smirk.

They reached the tent and dismounted. Alexander kept his hand on his sword, took a breath, and entered, with Hephaestion following.

A bearded old man dressed in a modest tan robe sat on a sheepskin rug with three cups made from gourds. A campfire crackled beside him. Alexander exhaled and let his guard down.

"A pleasure to meet you both. My name is Gabriel," he said but remained seated, something not done in the presence of high royalty.

"Where is the Malli gold?" Hephaestion asked.

"I know nothing of gold," Gabriel said.

"There are repercussions for lying." Hephaestion withdrew his sword to intimidate, but Gabriel didn't flinch.

"Why aren't you afraid?" Alexander asked.

"Afraid of what? Leaving this old body?" Gabriel said in a soothing voice. "And I did not lie. The treasure you really seek is the truth about your dreams."

CHAPTER 12

BEN SMASHED T-Roy against the back of the metal bus seat in front. T-Roy held his hands up to blunt the impact, but it didn't matter. The rage-fueled beating continued until a crony sprang to his feet to protect his friend. Ben spun around and kicked him in the stomach, knocking him back into the other crony. The move was seamless, powerful, and impressive, but it interrupted Ben's fit of rage. *What did he just do?* Fear grabbed hold, and he dashed out the middle door of the bus as T-Roy and the cronies regrouped and chased after him.

Fast and full of adrenaline, Ben whipped around a street corner, then over a planter. T-Roy and the cronies pursued with blood in their eyes. Ben kicked up dirt as he crossed a softball diamond and onto a soccer field. He pulled away, leaving T-Roy and the cronies sucking wind.

Still infuriated, T-Roy shouted, "You better hope I don't find you!"

Ben didn't stop running until he turned a corner and found himself outside his apartment complex. Exhausted, he scanned the area to make sure the cronies were gone. Ben entered the key code to the main door of the complex, raced to the elevator, and punched the call button. As he waited, his anger flared back up, thinking about what had happened. "Idiots. I don't have nothing. I got everything. I'm Ben Preston. History professor." He paused and corrected himself. "Adjunct history professor. I have a nice place to live." He hesitated again and assessed the building. "Nice enough place to live." He continued to fume as he stepped into the elevator. "And a beautiful, amazing girlfriend who wants to marry me." No qualification was necessary on that one. As that sank in, his tantrum melted. Beth loved him. Why couldn't he love her back?

The elevator stopped at his floor. The doors opened, and he ambled down the long hallway to his unit. He unlocked the door and entered the pitch black apartment. Ben tossed his keys on an IKEA end table, then locked the door behind him. The room lit up, and friends burst out from behind furniture and shouted, "Surprise!"

Ben almost jumped out of his shoes, much to the delight of the guests, including Frank. Beth emerged from the kitchen, hurried over, and hugged him as everyone clapped. "Happy birthday, hon." She noted his disheveled appearance. "You okay?"

"Fine. I just, uh… I'm fine." As Ben looked into Beth's eyes, an impulsive idea popped into his mind. He turned and addressed the crowd. "I got some bad news today. I didn't get published."

The guests reacted in unison. "Aww."

"I'm so sorry, hon," Beth said.

"It's okay. I'll get it next time. It made me realize something. I don't want to waste any more time worrying… or waiting." Ben dropped to a knee.

A collective gasp from the room. Beth touched her heart.

"Beth Marie Murphy, will you marry me?"

Overwhelmed, Beth stammered. "Are you sure?"

Ben nodded, then a moment of awkward silence. Would she accept?

"Yes," Beth said, smiling ear-to-ear.

Cheers erupted, and Frank played the part of the peanut gallery. "Kiss her! Kiss her!"

Ben rolled his eyes and gave Beth a cute peck on the lips. People stepped forward and took pictures.

Frank goosed Ben again. "C'mon. Give her a real kiss."

A little embarrassed, Ben obliged the audience and dipped Beth into a romantic pose. As he leaned in to kiss her, camera flashes from iPhones burst in rapid succession. Time slowed down as the burst of light blinded Ben. His mind *flashed.*

Ben floated somewhere else in his thoughts, a mysterious location—a tent lit only by the warm glow of a small fire. He was present, but in spirit only. Two people were enmeshed with one another, making passionate love. The face of neither could be seen, but long tresses of black hair flowed down the back of the woman. This was not Beth. The moment was ethereal. Total bliss.

Eyes closed, Ben kissed Beth passionately. As he opened them, he startled when he found Beth staring at him, breathless. That was the most intense kiss Ben had ever given Beth.

"Wow," she said.

Frank shouted from the crowd, "That doesn't mean you're getting out of buying her a ring."

Everyone laughed, and the party began. Ben smiled but looked away, guilty.

What just happened?

CHAPTER 13

Riya reviewed her medical notes in front of the MRI suite, a small office containing three monitors and a built-in desk. A large window provided a view of the actual MRI room. She overheard Macy, the MRI technologist, leading Tom down the hall while asking the standard safety questions.

"Just want to confirm that you have no metal on you, or in you, including no pacemaker or joint replacements."

"That's the fifth time I've been asked," Tom said.

"Just our normal safety checks."

Tom raised an eyebrow. "Doesn't sound safe if you have to check that many times."

"An MRI is essentially a giant magnet. You'll be fine." Macy led Tom into the control room.

"We've got a nervous patient, doc," Macy said to Riya.

Tom fidgeted with his hands and kept reaching back to check on the open flap of the less than flattering blue hospital gown he now wore.

"Don't worry," Riya said. "The test is painless, and these images will

53

help us determine whether you've got cancer or something else." She resumed her review of the medical notes.

"I already told you it isn't cancer."

Macy led Tom into the MRI room. As soon as he'd left, Riya felt guilty for not paying closer attention to her patient. Tom was nervous and maybe even a little scared. She peered through the window to make sure he was okay.

The MRI itself took up about a third of the area, with the bore in the middle of the machine taking center stage. It looked like a giant eye, which was fitting since it could see through people. An MRI-safe gurney rested just outside the bore and Macy motioned Tom on to it. He sat down, and as soon as he was flat on his back, Macy slid him into a head coil, a device resembling a clunky helmet from a bad sci-fi movie. Tom's eyes widened as he glanced from side to side.

Macy put her hand on his shoulder to comfort him. "You won't feel anything physically, but if you're claustrophobic, you may feel a little uneasy. There are some odd sounds. Booms and rattling. That's normal."

Riya listened through the intercom system, which allowed them to communicate and monitor the patient during the test.

"Is Dr. Patel a good doctor?" Tom asked, very matter-of-factly. "She seems... distracted."

Riya's guilt intensified. Tom was right. He received a death sentence, and she was trying to use it as a distraction to avoid thinking of her sister.

"She's just focused on the test. She's the best doctor on the East coast," Macy said. "No one works harder than her." She handed Tom a call button. "Press the button if you need to stop the test. There's an intercom inside. You're in good hands. Try to relax."

"Yeah, this all looks very relaxing," Tom said.

Macy patted his leg, slid him into the bore, and retreated into the control room. She sat in front of the last monitor and entered all the data to begin the test.

"Guess he doesn't know we can hear what he says, does he?" Riya asked. "And thanks for the kind words."

Macy smiled. "I'm glad you decided to stay."

Riya nodded. Macy pushed the intercom. "We're starting, Tom."

The MRI machine kicked into gear, and metallic banging and whirring filled the room. The first image emerged on the monitor in front of Riya. Macy pressed the intercom. "You're doing fine. Continue to stay still."

Tom responded, almost inaudibly, "Magni aestimo."

Riya glanced at Macy. "What did he say?"

Tom mumbled, "Inveniet eam. Thesauros. Hernando Cortes."

"Is that Latin?" Macy asked.

"How can he speak multiple languages like this?" Riya wondered, fascinated by whatever was going on in Tom's brain.

Tom continued to babble, but it became quieter until he fell silent.

Riya jumped to her feet and looked through the window. Her face dropped. "Get me a crash cart, now!"

CHAPTER 14

India, 323 B.C.

Flies buzzed inside the tent, but neither Alexander nor Hephaestion noticed. Sweat beaded on their foreheads as they assessed this strange, old man named Gabriel. How did he know about their visions? It was both intriguing and worrisome.

"Please, sit down. Have a drink," Gabriel said.

Hephaestion scoffed. "Trust a drink from a stranger?"

Alexander rubbed his chin as he contemplated the proposition. Hephaestion eyed him. Alexander quickly put his hands down.

"Now you should be worried," Hephaestion said. "Don't touch whatever he's offering."

Alexander considered, then motioned for Gabriel to pour. Hephaestion grabbed Alexander's arm, pulled him close, and whispered, "Don't let a wrinkled nobody defeat the world's most important man."

Amused by the exchange, Gabriel poured himself a drink from an amphora, then raised his glass to Hephaestion and downed it. Alexander sat, took a sip, and assessed the flavor. "It's just wine."

"Flavored with myrrh," Gabriel added. "Which will help open your mind. Keep drinking, and you shall see the truth."

Alexander chugged the rest and motioned for a re-fill. He needed answers. Over the next hour, Gabriel sipped while Alexander gulped. After tossing back his sixth cup, wine dribbled down Alexander's chin. Gabriel shook the empty amphora. No more. Alexander glanced up at Hephaestion, a blurred mess through his drunk eyes. "You don't look so good, Hephaestion."

Hephaestion bristled.

Gabriel noted Alexander's "calm" state and nodded. "You are ready. Relax your mind and let go of your thoughts." He waved his hand over the small fire. "Look at the brightest flame. Watch how it dances."

Alexander did as instructed. On edge, Hephaestion kept his hand on his sword. At first, nothing happened, then Alexander's drunk stupor transformed into intense focus. Then, it was like he wasn't there anymore—at least not mentally. Suddenly, his body shook and convulsed.

Hephaestion sprang into action and unsheathed his blade. "What did you give him?"

Alexander grimaced, and his eyes filled with horror. Hephaestion raised his sword to end Gabriel. Just as he was about to strike, Alexander snapped out of the trance. "Stop! I'm okay. I saw. I saw it."

"What did you see?" Hephaestion asked.

"These visions aren't of our future. They're of our past."

CHAPTER 15

GUESTS LAUGHED and sipped bargain-priced wine and beer at Ben's birthday party, which had unexpectedly turned into an engagement celebration. Except for Ben, everyone reveled in the joy of friends and free-flowing alcohol. He found a quiet moment alone on his balcony. He leaned on the railing, nursing his beer, lost in thought. The vision from his mind perplexed him. *Who was that woman?*

Frank opened the sliding glass door and disturbed Ben's solitude. He carried a bottle of wine and two glasses. "Hey. I'm sorry about what I said in your office. It was none of my business."

Ben shook his head. "No, I'm sorry. I shouldn't have snapped like that."

Frank handed Ben a glass and poured. "Happy birthday. You'll appreciate this too. Special import. Handmade. The way they did it hundreds of years ago."

Ben took a sip and nodded in approval. He chugged the wine, then motioned for a refill. Frank obliged, and then both men leaned on the railing, enjoying the breeze in awkward silence.

"Sorry about the article," Frank said. "At least the headaches will be gone with that out of the way, right?"

Ben looked down at his feet and kicked at the railing. "I don't think that's what's causing them."

Frank eyed him.

"This isn't supposed to be my life… I do things… I can't explain." Ben paused before revealing the bombshell. "I'm not in love with Beth."

Frank chugged his own wine and glanced back inside, hoping no one had heard Ben's confession. He leaned over and whispered, "Then why did you just propose to her?"

Ben chuckled to himself. He'd been asking himself that same question. He should love her. He *wanted* to love her. His mind swirled with random thoughts. "I have a gun in my bedroom."

Frank stepped back, fearful. This was more than a mid-life crisis. "Why do you have a gun, Ben?"

"I'm always afraid… or something."

"You need to talk to someone," Frank said, realizing Ben's issues were way out of his league.

"Maybe. I have to use the bathroom." Ben stumbled back inside.

As Ben floundered through the living room, his heartbeat accelerated. *Thump, thump. Thump, thump. Thump, thump.*

He passed by Beth, who gave him a sensual grin. Ben forced a return smile, but as soon as he turned, it disappeared. *Thump, thump. Thump, thump. Thump, thump.* What was happening to him? Was this a heart attack? He ambled down the hall and into the bathroom. He locked the door. *Thump, thump. Thump, thump. Thump, thump.*

He glanced at his reflection in the mirror. He didn't like the man staring back. A decorative scented candle in the corner caught his eye. The dancing flame mesmerized him. His body was present, but his mind was not. His eyes remained fixed on the little flame until, finally, he blinked. *Thump, thump. Thump, thump. Thump, thump.*

He glanced up at the mirror, and Alexander stared back.

"They're hunting you. Stop trying to remember her," his reflection commanded.

Stunned, Ben punched the mirror, shattering it.

CHAPTER 16

India, 323 B.C.

THE SUN BEAT down on a desolate landscape dominated by dirt and rock. The only vegetation was scrub brush and a few lonely trees. A vagabond covered in a robe and head wrap rode a donkey along a winding trail through the uninhabited region. He continued along the route, which ascended through a craggy pass. As he crested the bluff, he scanned a narrow valley below. Trees and a rock outcropping provided lots of hiding places.

The vagabond removed the wrap from his face. It was Gabriel. He pulled out an animal skin filled with water and took a sip. He hopped off the donkey and led the animal into the gorge. Half-way down, the rocks shielded the sunlight, making it darker and more ominous.

Gabriel paused before entering the narrowest part of the trail. His eyes darted from side to side. Danger lurked. He slipped his hands inside his robe. "Is this the road to Malli?"

Silence.

He beckoned again, "Kind men, hiding in the rocks and trees, would you share your wisdom of this area with an old man?"

A moment later, a brigand emerged from behind a rock. Covered with a dirty cloak and thick black beard, he threatened with a rusty sword. A second bandit, armed with a club, appeared from a thicket of bushes. Two more, holding spears, revealed themselves further up the trail. All three fell in line behind the first brigand.

"My name is Gabriel. To whom do I have the pleasure of speaking with?" Gabriel asked.

"Give us your possessions, and you may die a quick and painless death. Fight and you shall suffer." The brigand pointed his blade at Gabriel.

"I'm old. I don't wish to fight," Gabriel said.

A crooked smile spread across the brigand's face. Gabriel would be an easy target. The brigand took a step towards Gabriel with his sword at his side.

"But my treasure is not for the taking," Gabriel said.

The fearlessness from Gabriel paused the brigand. He motioned for his men to come with him. They fanned out, creating a semi-circle of death, but the narrow pathway prevented them from surrounding Gabriel.

"Is this the road to Malli?" Gabriel asked.

The brigand didn't appreciate Gabriel's plucky disposition. "Why are you worried about a place you'll never see?"

"So, it is the right road." Gabriel smiled and nodded in gratitude. "Many thanks. I am meeting Alexander of Macedon."

The brigand scoffed. "The warrior king? What do you want with him?"

"Why are you worried about someone you'll never see?" Gabriel asked, and his eyes narrowed.

All pretense of playfulness ceased. The brigand raised his sword and prepared to attack.

"Alexander must give up his crown," Gabriel said, giving the brigand a final chance to avoid a lethal confrontation.

The brigand howled with mocking laughter. His men mimicked their leader until he halted and sneered. "Last chance for a quick death."

"It will most certainly be quick," Gabriel said.

The brigand took a step forward. From under Gabriel's robe, he unsheathed a scimitar. For the time period, this curved blade was advanced weaponry. Even in the shadows, it appeared to glisten, especially compared to the brigand's rusty sword. In one swift strike, Gabriel slashed the brigand's throat. The two men armed with spears attacked, but Gabriel side-stepped the first, cracked him with the butt of his sword, and swung the scimitar back at the second, slicing his throat. The club-wielding bandit let out a ferocious battle cry and attacked Gabriel with wild swings. Without fear or hesitation, Gabriel avoided the assault, waited for his opening, spun and struck. Another body lay at his feet. The lone survivor, who was lucky enough to only get bashed on the head, fled in horror, but as he glanced over his shoulder, he ran right into a tree and knocked himself out.

The entire sequence happened in seconds, and "old man" Gabriel didn't even break a sweat. He wiped the blade on one of the brigand's cloaks, sheathed the weapon, and continued on his way.

CHAPTER 17

Riya and Macy analyzed Tom's limited MRI results in the cramped control room. Both puzzled over the images. Macy traced white masses with her fingertips. "Looks like scar tissue," she said.

"That doesn't explain his language abilities." Riya racked her brain for answers. "Have you ever had anything like that happen before?"

Macy shook her head. "No, and I haven't had anyone crash like that either. That could've been bad. If a congressman died getting an MRI…" She exhaled in relief.

Riya glanced at the clock. "It's late. Go home."

Macy took one last look at the MRI results, then left.

Riya opened the digital file that contained the recording of the MRI test. She leaned down and focused on Tom's whisper. "Magni aestemo. Invenient eam. Thesauros. Hernando Cortes."

Riya scribbled on a paper beside her: *hippocampal mass, foreign language savant, Hernando Cortes.* She stood up and wandered the halls of the hospital, staring at her notes.

She reached her office, plopped down in front of her computer and Googled, "Hernando Cortes." The search results revealed "Spanish explorer" and "Conqueror of the Aztecs."

She opened her desk and pulled out the framed picture of her sister, along with the file about her death. Her thoughts raced as she removed the page with her handwritten notes from her interview with the security guard and ran her finger across the words *"finding out what people know about history."* The impossible crept into her mind.

She rifled through the papers until she found the list of individuals killed in the explosion. It showed their names, ages, and professions. She scanned the sheet and paused on one name—Wayne Glassman, History Professor, University of Virginia.

The pieces came together, and she turned to the photo of her sister. "You were right. This will change the world."

Riya typed "Past Lives" into the search bar of the internet browser. She hit enter, and the results included several topics, including "27% of the world's population believe we've been here before," "Indications you have had a past life," and "Past lives: Why can't we remember them?"

TOM LAY IN A COMA. Machines monitored his vitals, including his heart rate. *Beep, beep. Beep, beep. Beep, beep.* Except for the slight movement of his chest rising and falling, Tom didn't move a muscle.

Beep, beep. Beep, beep. Beep, beep. Tom's heart sped up to 120 beats per minute, and his eyes flickered. The monitor jumped to 150 beats per minute. His closed eyes darted back and forth as if he was experiencing a vivid dream. The heart rate spiked to 200 beats per minute, a rate achieved during intense physical activity. His eyes twitched like crazy and his heart rate hit 220 beats, a dangerous level.

As quickly as it escalated, his heartbeat and breathing dropped to a resting state. Tom's eyes snapped open. They were calm, composed, and certain.

CHAPTER 18

MARYLAND, 2018

IN A COMFY SUEDE CHAIR, Ben sat straight up and scanned the psychiatrist's office. Emerald green plants, vibrant flowers, and paintings of scenic beaches, waterfalls, and sunsets adorned the room. Everything about the space inspired a relaxed atmosphere. The only thing not relaxed was Ben.

He eyed Dr. Brown, a psychiatrist in his mid-40's, in the adjacent love seat scribbling notes on a pad of paper. The good doctor wore hip glasses and an argyle sweater. He attempted and succeeded in portraying the confident intellectual.

"So, you just got engaged," Dr. Brown said in a soothing voice. "Congratulations."

Ben dug his fingers into the suede cushions.

"I understand you're having second thoughts. That's normal when you make a big life decision."

Ben nodded in agreement, but remained on edge. He couldn't believe he was in a shrink's office.

"Is your fiancé here?"

"No. I haven't told Beth about my issues," Ben said. "A little hard to tell your new fiancé you're crazy."

"Psychiatrists don't like that word," Dr. Brown said, "and it will be helpful if you include her in your therapy."

"We'll see," Ben said, with absolutely no intention of considering the request. How helpful could it be if Beth knew he'd been dreaming about a woman he'd never met?

Ben was a classic new patient, closed off and distrustful. Dr. Brown switched topics to spur more conversation. "Tell me about the gun. When did you get it?"

"A little over a year ago," Ben said.

"Does Beth know you have it?"

Ben shook his head.

"Why did you get it?"

Ben hesitated before answering. "I felt like I was in danger."

Dr. Brown jotted down notes. "Why do you feel you're in danger?"

Ben paused even longer. "People are out to get me."

"Out to get you?" Dr. Brown repeated and wrote more on his pad, which made Ben nervous and curious. "Why would they want to 'get' you?"

"Because of what I know," Ben said.

"And what do you know?"

Ben opened his mouth, but nothing came out. He should know the answer; otherwise, how, or why, would someone want him? He rubbed his head and tugged at his hair in frustration.

"Who is out to get you?"

"They're… uh…," Ben stumbled for an answer. "They're very dangerous."

"But you don't know who they are?" Dr. Brown asked to emphasize the fact that Ben didn't have an answer.

Ben tugged again at his hair and shook his head, embarrassed.

"It's okay," Dr. Brown assured. "You can't remember for a reason, and the reason is that it's not real. I know it feels very real, but Ben, you have a disorder called paranoid schizophrenia. That means you have trouble differentiating between what is real and what is imagined."

Ben sunk into his chair. "So, I'm crazy."

"No, and I still don't like that word."

"You said I'm imagining things."

"Aren't you?" Dr. Brown leaned forward to connect with Ben. "You've added your spin to historical events. You wake up with nightmares that make you feel like mysterious people are out to get you."

Ben shrugged. "How is that not crazy?"

"It's simply a problem, and a treatable one," Dr. Brown said. "At the moment, you have a mild case, but it has the potential to get worse."

"What should I do?"

"I want you to get an MRI to verify there's nothing physically wrong with the brain. Let's make sure there are no cysts or tumors. If that checks out, we'll put you on some medication. In the meantime, I want you to integrate some cognitive behavioral therapy into your daily routine."

Ben crooked his neck. He'd never heard of such a thing.

"It starts very simple," Dr. Brown said. "The next time you're afraid or anxious, I want you to stop. Don't react. Instead, ask yourself, why? And when you answer that, I want you to decide if it's a rational fear or anxiety."

Ben puzzled over the doctor's advice. "That's it?"

"To start," Dr. Brown said.

Ben stood up to leave, but he had one last question. "Has anyone's visions ever been real?"

Dr. Brown smiled and patted Ben's shoulder. "No, Ben. No one's visions have been real."

CHAPTER 19

INDIA 323 B.C.

A QUARTER-MILE outside the walls of Malli, the Greek army waited in the scorching sun in attack formation. Some glanced at each other out of the sides of their helmets. Others stared at the tent where their two leaders had disappeared hours ago.

General Craterus stood in front of the phalanxes. He did his best to project confidence and that everything was under control, but that could only last so long in the blistering heat.

Varus, one of Alexander's top soldiers, cracked and shouted, "Are we going to fight or melt?"

Craterus grunted in irritation, then marched down to Gabriel's tent.

Inside, Gabriel counseled Alexander and Hephaestion around a campfire. Alexander leaned forward, enthralled by the shared wisdom.

"How many lives have you lived?"

Gabriel tallied it up on his fingers. "I'm in my twelfth... that I remember."

"Twelfth!" Hephaestion said. "Were you anyone of note?"

"I was a ruler several times, but... that was a long time ago."

"Why don't you rule now?" Alexander questioned, hoping for insight into his situation.

"We'll get to that later." Gabriel eyed Alexander with a gaze that pierced into his soul.

Craterus opened the flap of the tent and interrupted. "Apologies for the intrusion. The men grow restless."

Gabriel nodded and collected his things. "I have more to share, but if you're too busy with a war, I'll be on my way."

Alexander considered his options before turning to Craterus. "The city is deserted?"

"Yes," Craterus said while keeping a watchful eye on Gabriel.

Alexander turned to Hephaestion. "I'd like a moment alone with Gabriel. Go with Craterus and order the men to set up camp."

Suspicious of his dismissal, Hephaestion nevertheless obeyed.

As soon as Craterus and Hephaestion left, Gabriel sat back down. "I'm pleased you'd like to learn more."

Alexander stared at Gabriel, believing and hoping this man had the answers to the questions that had vexed him for so long. "Why did you stop leading your people?"

Gabriel cocked an eyebrow, surprised by the question.

"You said you'd get to that later. I'd like to get to it now," Alexander said.

Gabriel took a deep breath and poked at the fire with a stick. "In my early lives, I succumbed to the temptation of power and wealth. I conquered. Pillaged. Killed."

Gabriel let those words hang in the room.

"That's not what I'm doing. I'm liberating people," Alexander said.

"That town you were ready to sack," Gabriel waved his hand toward Malli outside, "you seemed more interested in gold."

"We need to fund our army," Alexander said, then admitted, "but you're right. Our purpose has become clouded in politics and finances."

"This gift comes at a heavy price. Not even death spares us from remembering our sins and failures."

"Is that why I have nightmares?"

Gabriel glanced at Alexander, and his eyes answered for him.

Alexander's shoulder's slumped. "Is there a way to stop them?"

"I believe there is. This ability gives us a memory that spans lifetimes. But why do we have this gift?"

Alexander shook his head. No idea.

Gabriel waxed philosophic. "I believe the purpose is to record history without bias or involvement. I've seen history re-written, altered, and fabricated. The victors and those in power are the worst offenders. And yet, they are immortalized as heroes."

Alexander listened, confused. "So, you use this gift to be a historian?"

"Yes. I travel the world telling people the truth about what has happened and what is happening in other lands. I also leave written accounts to contradict the false histories."

Alexander struggled to believe this was any sort of solution. "But you're not really helping."

"In a world filled with lies, I find the truth is always helpful. And are you helping the world now?"

Alexander stumbled for a defense. "I'm trying to."

"How many people have you killed in your efforts to help humanity?"

The coldness of the statement silenced Alexander.

"I understand the desire to take part in and create history, but the temptation to indulge in power is too great," Gabriel said.

"Are you suggesting I give up my crown to be a historian?" Alexander asked in disbelief.

"Do you want to be free from the nightmares?"

Incredulous, Alexander paced about the room. "Walk away from my army? My empire?"

Gabriel nodded. Alexander could not believe what he was hearing, but even more shocking, he was not dismissing it outright.

71

CHAPTER 20

Riya sat in her darkened office with the only light coming from her computer monitor. Documents from the file about her sister's death lay strewn across her desk in an organizational system that only she understood, but her focus was on the screen. An article about past lives regression captivated her. Half the information seemed like pseudo-science, but the other half kept her brain in overdrive as she considered the implications of this discovery.

The door flew open, and Greg rushed in, distraught. With her sister's file exposed, Riya's jaw dropped. She was busted. Or was she?

"I need you. It's Tom Vance," he said.

Riya followed Greg out. The two raced down the long hallway, then turned a corner and continued until they came to Tom's room. Dressed in the clothes in arrived in, Tom calmly tied his shoelaces. He did not look like someone who just emerged from a coma.

"Congressman Vance. Um, can I help you with anything?" Greg asked.

"I feel much better. I'm ready to leave." Tom laced up his second shoe and then stood.

Greg held out his hand to stop him from walking out. "Glad you're feeling better, but we need to continue to monitor you."

Tom smiled as only a politician can. "I'm ready to leave, but thank you for your help."

"We didn't do anything except run one test which wasn't completed," Riya said.

"And which put me in a coma. MRIs are harmless, huh?" Tom eyed Riya.

Riya stumbled for a response as a man in a suit rushed in with a document and pen. She recognized the man—he was one of the hospital's many attorneys. Greg snatched the paper, then waved him away.

Tom motioned for Greg to step aside. "If you'll excuse me, I have some important state matters I need to attend to."

Riya shook her head. She couldn't let Tom leave. There were too many questions. "Congressman Vance—"

Tom interrupted, "Please call me, Tom."

"Tom, something serious is going on in your brain. Do you remember speaking in Latin?"

Tom paused. "I don't, but I feel fine now. Great, actually." He stepped around Greg to leave.

Greg softly grabbed Tom's arm to stop him. "It is not in your best interest, medically, to leave."

Tom pointed to the document in Greg's other hand. "I'll sign whatever waiver you need."

That satisfied Greg. He handed the paper and pen to Tom, who quickly scribbled a signature and gave it back.

Tom was seconds from leaving. Riya panicked. The one person who might hold the answer to her sister's research would be gone. She blurted out, "I have a theory about your language abilities."

This caught Tom's attention. "What is it?"

Tom and Greg stared at Riya. She remained silent, now afraid to reveal her thoughts about Tom's condition.

"Dr. Patel, what's your diagnosis?" Greg asked.

Saying anything about past lives would kill her credibility and, likely, her career. Everything Riya warned her sister about—the loss of reputation, never being taken seriously again—would all happen to her. She vamped, "There's scar tissue in the hippocampus that's causing anomalous brain waves. If we can just run a couple more tests—"

"I'm not interested in more tests. Good day." Tom walked out.

OVER THE NEXT couple of days, Riya attempted and failed to slip into a routine at work. She kept thinking about Tom, his test results, and her theory. *Why did she let him leave?*

As she reviewed a patient file at her desk, the picture of her sister distracted and unnerved her; it was like she was being judged from the grave. The guilt became unbearable. "Quit looking at me. I know it wasn't random that this guy came into my hospital."

Riya resumed her work, but every so often her eyes locked onto her sister's. "What do you expect me to do if he won't take my calls?"

Her sister still smiled and stared.

Angry, Riya snapped the patient file shut and pulled out Tom's file. She thumbed through the pages until she found his address and considered her next move. "Fine," she barked at the picture, then grabbed her car keys and left.

An hour later, Riya drove her Prius through a wooded neighborhood filled with large estates. She turned onto a street and discovered a bustle of reporters, cameramen, and several news vans in front of a gated compound.

Riya parked a couple of hundred feet short of the melee and walked over to a cameraman stationing his equipment outside the wrought iron gate of the Tudor mansion. A fence ran the perimeter of the property, which was unusual for the area. Most of the plots were open, interconnected yards.

"What's going on?" she asked.

"The Congressman is stepping down. Rumor is he has brain cancer," the cameraman said.

"I don't understand. He said he felt fine."

"Are you a neighbor?" the cameraman asked. "They might want to interview you if you know him."

Riya shook her head, flummoxed. "Uh, no, thanks." She returned to her car to figure out her next step. Her phone rang, and when she answered, Greg's booming voice greeted her.

"Where are you?"

"I'm outside Tom's house," she said.

"What the hell are you doing there?"

"I'm checking on my patient, but I can't get in to see him. He's resigning, Greg."

"I know. That's why I called. It's all over the news."

"Why would he resign if he felt fine?"

"The official statement is to spend more time with his family, but Riya, you need to get back here immediately," Greg said. "His attorney called and sent a threatening legal letter to have all of his medical records turned over and any copies destroyed."

"He can't do that."

"It's not worth the legal risk. The negative PR alone could cost us millions."

"Greg, there's something miraculous about Tom's case," Riya said.

"What are you talking about?"

"My sister said her research was going to change the world—"

"You said you were done with that," Greg snapped. "You gave me your word."

"And then Tom Vance came into my office, and his symptoms fit what my sister was researching," Riya fired back. "I need to run more tests so I can prove it."

"Riya, this has the potential to bankrupt the hospital. You need to get back here, turn over everything related to Tom Vance, and drop this case, or you're fired. Do you understand?"

Riya stuttered, taken aback by Greg's bluntness. "Yes, I understand." She hung up, deflated. The velvet hammer had struck. Riya started her car and pulled a U-turn, but as she drove away, a side street caught her eye and gave her an idea, albeit a risky one. She veered onto it, and the road wound through another part of the neighborhood to an open estate that backed up to Tom's property. She parked and stared at the back of his mansion—a moment of truth, or a moment to remain innocent. Disobeying a direct order from her boss would get her fired, but trespassing on a patient's property might get her thrown in jail and end her career. There had to be another way. She tapped her fingers against the dashboard as the wheels turned in her head.

"Screw it." She opened the car door.

CHAPTER 21

Ben graded papers in his cramped office. Most professors hated this part of the job, but not Ben. He didn't care if his students' understanding of history was sorely lacking. Even when the papers were drastically wrong, he could still lose himself in the stories of the past. It made the grading easy as he scribbled notes about the right takeaways from whatever subject he was covering.

A knock at the door interrupted the solitude. Ben glanced up to find an old man in an expensive black suit and thick coke-bottle glasses.

"Ben Preston?" the man asked in a raspy voice.

"Can I help you?" Ben asked.

"My name is Professor Thomas," the man said while remaining in the doorway. "I specialize in Ancient Greek history. I reviewed your article about Alexander the Great. An intriguing read. The details about his childhood, his motivations, the relationship with Hephaestion were inspired. Truly enlightening."

Ben appreciated the praise. "Thank you."

"I was curious about your description of his death," Professor Thomas said. "It is widely accepted that he fell ill in Babylon. Other theories are pure speculation, and your paper presented the circumstances of his demise with such certainty."

Ben dropped his gaze to the floor, embarrassed. "I know I failed to source that."

"That's why I'm here. I'm curious as to how you arrived at such a conclusion." Professor Thomas stared at Ben through his thick glasses. His gray piercing eyes caused Ben to shift uneasily in his chair.

"I know it seems off. Maybe I made it up by accident. I don't know." Ben held his head and grimaced in frustration.

"Are you okay, Professor Preston?" Thomas asked.

Ben continued to hold his head. "Just a headache. Bad migraines. I'm sorry for the error."

"No worries, Mr. Preston. Good day."

Ben looked up, and Professor Thomas was gone. He jumped out of his seat, dashed to his door, and peered down the hallway. There was no sign of Professor Thomas. Ben stroked his chin. *Was that real or imagined?*

I<small>T WAS</small> a typical Thursday night at McGinty's bar. College basketball played on the television, a few people chatted, and Ben and Frank sat on their same stools drinking the same beer as last time. Ben stared at the screen, but his mind was elsewhere. The strange visit from Professor Thomas perplexed him, but more than anything, his thoughts focused on the vision of the woman when he kissed Beth. Who was she, and why was he so drawn to her? Since that kiss, the mysterious woman haunted him. Almost anything reminded him of her. On his way to work that morning, he scraped his arm on a thorn bush. When he inspected the minor cut, he slipped into something of a trance, imagining the woman's captivating eyes. He was so mesmerized that he almost missed his bus.

"So, what did your shrink say?" Frank asked.

Ben snapped out of his daze. "I'm crazy, but he doesn't like using that word."

"Seriously, what did he say?" Frank pressed, still worried about his friend.

A strange man wearing a black overcoat squeezed between Ben's stool and the table behind him. As he passed, he bumped into Ben.

"Pardon me," the man said.

Ben didn't give it a second thought as he leaned in and whispered to Frank, "Remember when I told you I'm not in love with Beth?" Even saying those words out loud made Ben cringe with guilt. "I think I'm in love with another woman."

"Who?" Frank asked.

"I don't know. She keeps popping into my brain. She's this mysterious, beautiful woman." Ben smiled as the literal girl of his dreams danced in his mind.

Frank looked at Ben side-eyed, more worried than ever. "But you don't know her?"

Ben shook his head. Nope.

"Did you get any medicine from the psychiatrist?" Frank asked.

Ben glanced up at the mirror behind the bar. The man who bumped into him sat in a booth in the back and stared in Ben's direction. "Frank." Ben subtly elbowed his friend. "Is that guy in the booth staring at me?"

Frank turned around to look, but Ben grabbed his arm.

"No, no, no. Don't turn around. Look in the mirror."

Frank indulged Ben and looked. "Tough to tell from this far away." Frank motioned to the television in the corner. "He's probably watching the game."

Ben slumped his head. Time to heed Dr. Brown's advice—*ask if it's real.* After a moment of internal deliberation, he turned to Frank. "You're right. He's watching the TV." Ben took a deep breath. "The doctor said I have paranoid schizophrenia, which means my imagination creates weird things I think are real. It's why I don't feel like myself all the time." The admission was hard and embarrassing. Ben continued, "I have an MRI this week to make sure it isn't brain cancer. So, I guess I'm hoping I'm only crazy."

"You're like that guy from that movie, 'A Beautiful Mind' with Russell Crowe," Frank said. "He was a little crazy, but he was also a genius who won the Nobel Prize. Maybe you're gonna win the Nobel Prize."

Ben smiled. That would be nice. He took one more look at the mystery man in the back. To Ben's horror, the man stood up and walked straight for him. When the man was just a step away, he reached down near Ben's feet, causing Ben to jump in his seat.

"You dropped your phone." The man offered Ben his phone off the floor.

Ben stared for a long, uncomfortable moment, then grabbed the device.

"Have a good night," the man said.

Ben continued to stare.

Frank attempted to help with the awkward situation. "Thank you, sir."

The man returned to his booth, and Ben relaxed.

"Have you talked to Beth about all this?" Frank asked.

Ben chuckled. "Psychiatrist suggested I do that, too." He took a big, defiant chug of beer. "And no, I will not let my imagination ruin the best thing in my life. I'm going to figure this out. I'm going to get better." Ben tipped the bottle back and polished it off. Then, he shouted to the bartender, "Another round. And get one for the kind gentleman in back."

The bartender popped the top off another Guinness and slid it in front of Ben, who snatched it and continued to self-medicate. "I just need to keep telling myself this woman isn't real, and no one is out to get me."

HOURS LATER, a half-drunk Ben fumbled with his keys outside his apartment. With unsteady hands, he unlocked and opened the door. He attempted to toss his keys on the IKEA table in the corner, but missed.

"Beth? Hon? Where's my beautiful, wonderful, amazing fiancé?" He stumbled further inside.

Beth sat at the kitchen table with his 9mm and the stack of cash in front of her. She wore a grim look as she stared at the gun. "I was cleaning the bedroom and noticed something sticking out of the back of the nightstand. You can imagine my surprise when I found out it was a twenty-dollar bill. And then you can imagine my utter shock when I found a stack of money and a *gun*."

"It's not what you think."

"What is it then?" Beth's eyes locked onto Ben. "Is it drug money?"

"Of course not."

Unconvinced, she motioned to the pistol. "Then why do you have a hidden gun?"

Ben sat down at the table and reached out for Beth's hands, but she leaned back and crossed her arms, not interested in anything but answers. For a split second, Ben considered telling the truth, but instead offered, "I got the gun because of the burglaries in the neighborhood. I didn't want to freak you out, but I wanted to protect you."

Beth softened. It was plausible. There had been some car thefts and a burglary at the complex. "And the money?"

"I was saving up for the engagement ring. You like balancing the checkbook, so I couldn't keep the money in the account. But I guess I couldn't wait to propose." Ben couldn't believe how easily the lies flowed. He wasn't proud of it, and he almost convinced himself.

Beth craved for Ben's words to be true. "Really?" Her hands moved to the table.

Ben grabbed hold of them and nodded.

"I don't like secrets," she said.

"I know, and I'm sorry." Still on thin ice, Ben squeezed her hands to emphasize his sincerity.

"And you know how I feel about guns," she said.

"I just want us to be safe." Ben hoped his excuse would enable him to keep the gun. After all this, he still felt a strong need for the weapon.

"I want it out of here," Beth said.

Ben paused. He did not want to lose the gun.

Beth pulled her hands away. "It's the gun or me."

Ben couldn't talk his way past this one. "I'll get rid of it tomorrow."

He reached for the pistol, but Beth snatched it. "I'll take care of the gun." She shoved the stack of money towards him. "You take care of the ring."

Beth stood up and retreated to the bedroom. Once alone, Ben breathed a sigh of relief. He opened the fridge, took out a beer, and popped the top. Between sips, Ben wandered to the glass door that led to the balcony. He stared out and replayed the argument with Beth. It troubled him how he could lie so easily. He remembered his diagnosis—paranoid schizophrenia. If he boiled it down, wasn't that just a bunch of lies that he told himself? What if he believed his own lies? How would he ever know the truth?

As he looked into the night sky, something caught his eye on the building across the way. *Was that a person on the roof?* He leaned in and squinted. It looked like someone with a camera. *Was he being watched?*

As the paranoia set in, Beth called from the bedroom. "Dean Hammer-smith left a message. Professor Jadali, from Cambridge Press, is going to meet you in your office to talk about your article on Friday."

Ben glanced towards Beth in the bedroom. "You mean Professor Thomas? He already came."

"No. It was Jadali. Friday."

Then who was Professor Thomas? He stared out at the rooftop again. The person, if there was one, was gone.

CHAPTER 22

India, 323 B.C.

Greek soldiers rested under trees and played games with one another. Some look bored, many appeared restless. Alexander and Hephaestion walked together through the now established camp outside the walls of Malli.

Hephaestion assessed the troops as they passed. "The men grow impatient, Alexander."

Alexander waved off the comment. "We've been campaigning for so long. They can use the rest."

Hephaestion gritted his teeth. "We're in a land with people that want to kill us. We don't have the luxury of resting."

"Perhaps it is time we left this land and went home," Alexander said as if he were suggesting which type of wine they should drink.

Hephaestion stopped and grabbed Alexander's arm. "If we leave, the warlords and barbarians will enslave the people as soon as we're gone. How difficult will it be to sleep then?"

Alexander swallowed. The mention of his visions was always a sore topic of conversation. He eyed his friend. "What if this isn't our purpose? There are so many other things to do and learn. Gabriel has traveled the world learning about so many subjects."

"Yes, Gabriel is fascinating indeed." Hephaestion's words dripped with sarcasm.

"I can't believe you're not more intrigued by him. I feel like we're finally getting answers to the questions we've searched for all these years."

Hephaestion pulled Alexander close. "Something scares me about Gabriel. There's something he's not telling us. Knowing about this gift for centuries provides a huge advantage. What if he's playing us?"

Alexander scoffed. "How can he play us? He's but one man among the world's most powerful army."

"One man who has stopped the advance of that army with nothing but his words. What does he even want?" Hephaestion asked.

Alexander paused, afraid to tell Hephaestion about Gabriel's proposal. "To share his wisdom with us."

Boisterous yells interrupted the argument. They hurried to the raucous to investigate. Five soldiers and Gabriel engaged in some sort of contest that had drawn the interest of a dozen others. A wooden board leaned against a wagon about thirty feet away. In the middle, a melon dangled on a rope.

Alexander grabbed the arm of Balakros, a young soldier watching. He recoiled upon seeing the king in his presence.

"At ease," Alexander said. "What's going on?"

"Diodorus and the old man got into an argument," Balakros said. "Diodorus threatened him, and the old man said if Diodorus took one more step, he would not live to see the sun set. Before it got out of hand, the old man offered an alternative. He told Diodorus that if he or any man could beat him with the knife, he'd give that man a day's wage."

"And if Gabriel wins?" Alexander asked.

Balakros raised an eyebrow. "Sir, I don't think anyone considered that a real possibility."

They turned their attention to the contest. The board already had three knives embedded in the wood, all about a foot from the melon. A soldier hurled another knife that hit two inches from the fruit. The group cheered the shot.

Diodorus, a muscular twenty-year-old with an arrogant smirk, stepped up for his turn. He flung the knife, and it grazed the very top of the melon.

The soldiers roared with delight. Diodorus reveled in his apparent victory.

Without hesitation, Gabriel launched not one, not two, but three small daggers. *Thwack. Thwack, Thwack.* They tagged the melon in rapid succession, leaving nothing but a pulpy wet mess dripping down the board.

The performance silence the crowd and humiliated Diodorus. Before he had time to react, Alexander stepped in. The soldiers snapped to attention.

"Pay Gabriel whatever is owed," Alexander commanded.

Embarrassed, Diodorus stared at the ground. "I don't owe anything."

"You lost."

"I didn't have to put anything up," Diodorus said.

Gabriel interjected, "Losing was never a possibility, so it didn't seem fair."

Alexander stepped to Diodorus just inches from his face. "No one bothers Gabriel again."

Diodorus trembled, afraid to meet Alexander's eyes. Even without the order, it is unlikely the men would challenge Gabriel after that unexpected performance. They scampered away to resume their duties, with Diodorus leading the flight. Gabriel bowed to Alexander, then retreated towards his tent.

Hephaestion leaned into Alexander. "We have no idea who we're dealing with."

Alexander rubbed his chin, unsure what to believe himself.

———

THE NEXT DAY, Alexander and Hephaestion visited Gabriel for another counseling session. They sat, legs crossed, in front of the crackling fire in the center of Gabriel's tent. Gabriel sat next to them and guided them to relax.

"Deep breath. Deep breath," Gabriel coached like a master yogi. "Calm your thoughts. Listen to the voices of the past trying to come through."

Hephaestion remained rigid, unwilling to yield his mind. Alexander wanted to submit and remember more of his past, but Hephaestion's palpable frustration prevented any such progress. The elephant in the room had to be addressed. Alexander uncrossed his legs and turned to Gabriel. "How did you learn to be so good with the daggers?"

Gabriel paused, then remembered the contest with the soldiers. He pondered his response, then glanced at Hephaestion. "That necklace you're wearing. Why did you choose it?"

Hephaestion stared at the necklace, taken aback by the unrelated question.

"Bought it at a market when I was a kid. Looked interesting, I guess."

"Maybe it looked 'interesting' because something inside you recognized the inscription on it," Gabriel said. "That's Sumerian, a text few people know how to read. Do you know what it says?"

Hephaestion held up the medallion and, perhaps for the first time, really looked at the etched shapes and symbols. His eyes widened.

Alexander put the pieces together. "Our skills are transferable from one life to the next?"

"For the most part, yes. How many times do you throw something in one lifetime? Imagine that skill after twelve. With each new body I inherit, it takes a little time getting used to the physical characteristics, but the mind remembers how to do it."

"What skills do you know from past lifetimes?" Hephaestion asked.

Gabriel leaned back and considered his answer. "It would take some time to list them all. There are things like throwing, but then within that, there are specific skills like throwing a spear. Styles of fighting and languages are transferable. Through my lifetimes, I've come across others with the gift, and they've become experts in things like math and science."

Hephaestion shot a concerned look at Alexander. "There are others like us?"

"Yes," Gabriel said.

Alexander's mind raced. For every answer he received, three new questions emerged. "Why can't we access our past lives the way you can?"

"That's what we're trying to figure out," Gabriel said.

Hephaestion remained on alert. "These others. Who are they?"

"Almost all have abused the gift. As I discussed with Alexander, the temptation to indulge in power is great. It will cloud your judgment." Gabriel turned to Alexander. "Have you considered my proposal?"

"What proposal?" Hephaestion glared at Alexander, who avoided eye contact.

"I'm still evaluating it," Alexander said.

Hephaestion stood up, flicked the dirt off his chiton, grunted, and left. Alexander clenched his teeth, angry with himself. He bowed to Gabriel, rushed out of the tent, and spotted Hephaestion storming off.

"Hephaestion," he called out.

Hephaestion kept walking. Alexander hurried and grabbed his arm. "Hephaestion."

His friend turned and faced him. "Yes, your highness."

"I should have told you."

"I have followed you unconditionally since we were kids," Hephaestion said. "You were my best friend."

"I still am."

Hephaestion stepped back. "Really? A few days with this old man, and you've already got secrets with him."

"I was ashamed."

"Of what?"

"I'm considering his proposal."

"What did he say?" Hephaestion demanded.

"He thinks I should end the campaign." Alexander looked away as he spoke. "And give up my crown."

Hephaestion's eyes bulged.

"Gabriel said the nightmares are memories of my sins and failures from past lives. The temptation to abuse power is too great. The nightmares will keep getting worse."

"That is the most ridiculous thing I've ever heard." Hephaestion stepped into Alexander's face and whispered. "Think about your men. Imagine how they'll feel if you tell them that after a few conversations with a man you just met, you've concluded that all of these years of fighting were a mistake? They'll revolt, Alexander."

Alexander hadn't thought about his men's reaction. They'd risked everything for him. "What if it was a mistake?"

Hephaestion paced back and forth to release his growing anger. "Do you honestly believe the gods would bestow these tremendous skills upon us and not intend for us to use them?"

"What are we supposed to do? Continue to fight battles forever? And what are we fighting for? To free people from one ruler to be my subjects?"

"There will always be someone to rule… to lead. Have the courage to lead," Hephaestion pleaded.

Alexander craned his neck to the sky for divine guidance. "What if I'm not fit to do so?"

"You're the world's most revered ruler. You fight to free people."

"How many have we killed in that pursuit?" Alexander asked.

"We've killed the enemy," Hephaestion shot back.

"Who are we to decide who that is?"

Hephaestion looked at Alexander in utter disbelief. "I don't even know who I'm talking to right now." He resumed pacing in frustration. "If the lion isn't the king of the jungle, the hyenas will be. Is that the world you want to live in?"

Both men fell silent, their relationship on the brink.

Alexander looked to the ground and, in a hushed tone, asked, "Do you remember when you told me that your visions are why you fight the way you do?"

Hephaestion nodded.

"You wanted to save people. I wish my reason was as noble as yours.

The dreams are why I wanted to fight too, but it's because I wasn't afraid of death. I welcomed it and the relief it would bring. When Gabriel revealed the truth, my heart sank. Every night since then, I've prayed to the gods, begging for their mercy." Alexander faltered as the words got caught in his throat. "I don't want this gift."

Hephaestion glared. "You've already made your decision, haven't you?"

Alexander couldn't look his friend in the eye, which was a good thing; otherwise, he'd see the crushing disappointment.

"The men are going to mutiny over this." Hephaestion walked away.

CHAPTER 23

Virginia, 2018

Riya hopped down from the fence onto Tom's property. As soon as her feet touched the ground, she'd passed the point of no return. She was now trespassing, and if things went as planned, she'd transition from a misdemeanor to a felony within minutes, as the goal was to break into Tom's home.

Riya scampered behind a large tree. Peering around the trunk, she spied another tree closer to the back door. She dashed and hid behind it. Filled with adrenaline and panting, she took a moment to collect herself. Another hundred feet and she'd be at the back door, but there were no more trees to hide behind. She crouched low and maneuvered around the tree where a large foot greeted her. When she glanced up, she stared down the barrel of a 9mm Glock. The owner of the foot, Ron, a giant black man, towered over her in a black suit.

Poised to end Riya's life, Ron said, "Don't move an inch."

Riya froze as Ron touched his earpiece. "Backyard. Intruder. Doesn't seem to be press."

"I'm Dr. Patel. I'm Tom's doctor."

"Shut up. I said, don't move." Ron gripped the gun with both hands.

"I need to speak with Tom. Please."

Ron touched his earpiece again. "She claims to be Tom's doctor."

A tense moment of silence followed as both waited for the response. Finally, Ron ordered, "Get up with your hands behind your head and move to the back of the house."

Riya followed the instructions as Ron walked behind her with the gun aimed and ready. As she neared the house, Tom waited just inside the French doors. He opened one. "She's okay, Ron."

Ron relaxed as Tom waved Riya over. Once inside, Riya soaked in the lavish living room with a wraparound couch, rustic fireplace, and huge flat-screen television. She zeroed in on the massive bookshelves lined with hundreds of books. Most were about historical subjects—the world wars, Ancient Rome, the Dark Ages, early explorers, and the Knights Templar.

Tom waved Ron away for privacy. Once the two were alone, Tom skipped any pleasantries. "Dr. Patel, what are you doing trespassing on my property?"

Riya opened her mouth to speak, but like at the hospital, she couldn't find the right words. "I wanted to make sure you were okay. How are you feeling?"

"Brain feels fine. As you can see, I've got a lot going on, so I need to get back to work. Let me show you out the front door."

Riya stood still. She didn't come all this way to be shown the door. "Why did you have your attorney demand your test results?"

Tom eyed Riya. "Speculation about my health is something I can't afford in my line of work."

"But you resigned. Why?"

Tom crossed his arms. "The reasons for my resignation are personal, and I value my privacy."

Riya attempted a softer approach. "Tom, I realize you're scared about the cancer diagnosis. And you're confused about how you know these languages."

"Dr. Patel, you have no idea what I'm going through, and I'm going to have to ask you to leave." He pointed to the front door.

"My sister died about a year ago," Riya said, still not moving from the living room.

"I'm very sorry to hear that, but I don't know what that has to do with anything," Tom said, now irritated.

"She was researching something when she died. It was a big discovery that was going to change the world."

"Please leave, Dr. Patel." It was no longer a request. Tom grabbed her by the arm and guided her to the front door.

Even as Riya was yanked, she continued to press her case. "I think your symptoms are related to what she was studying. You have an abnormal hippocampus. You can speak random languages. You're fascinated with history." She pointed back at the bookcases.

They reached the front door. Tom turned the knob and was about to shove her out.

"Tom, you've had past lives!"

Tom stopped.

Riya turned and came face-to-face with him. His expression was not one of shock or disbelief, and the unsettling realization washed over Riya. "But you already knew that. You remember your past lives."

CHAPTER 24

Dressed in a hospital gown, Ben lay on his back on the patient bed outside the MRI machine. Just like with Tom, a technologist slid Ben's head into the coil. He then handed Ben a call button. "If you need to stop the test, press the button; otherwise, just relax."

Ben chuckled. "You're scanning for tumors."

The technologist slid the bed mid-way into the MRI tube. Ben's breath quickened as soon as he was inside.

Through the intercom, the technologist asked, "You doing okay in there?"

"Yeah. Fine," Ben called out.

Silence filled the room before the machine began its sequence. Obnoxious whirring and banging pierced the calm, and Ben's head exploded with pain. He squeezed his eyes shut, and voices swirled in his mind. His eyes fluttered, and he fell into a dream-like state.

"No. I can't remember." Ben grimaced and shook his head.

"Try to lie still," the technologist's voice interrupted.

The voice stirred Ben back to consciousness. He forced his eyes open and attempted to wiggle out of the tube. "Stop. Stop. Stop!" He shouted while pressing the call button.

The technologist dashed into the room and slid the patient table from the machine. Ben didn't wait for further help and yanked himself free from the contraption.

"Are you okay?" the technologist asked.

"I can't. I can't," Ben said, out of breath.

"It's okay," the technologist said. "Many people are claustrophobic. We can give you a sedative."

Ben elbowed the technologist aside and disappeared into the changing area, where he swapped clothes in under a minute. He rushed to the elevator, pressed the call button, and glared at the doors as if that would make it arrive faster. When the doors opened, he jumped in and pushed the button for the ground floor. As the elevator car traveled, strange voices assaulted Ben from all sides. Disoriented, he turned around and searched for their source.

The elevator stopped a couple of floors short of Ben's destination, and a Hispanic mother and her teenage daughter hopped on, engaged in a heated argument.

"Usted pan no trae a aquel idiota alrededor de la casa otra vez," the mother said.

"El no es un idiota. El es mi novio," the teenager protested.

As Ben listened, something miraculous happened. The words melded into English.

"He's not going to school," the mother raged on. "He doesn't have a job. He's an idiot, and he's no good for you."

The daughter crossed her arms. "You can't stop me from seeing him."

Ben watched, mouth agape. *Are they speaking in Spanish or English?* As Ben stared, the mother scowled at him.

The elevator settled on the ground floor and the doors opened. The mother grabbed her daughter's hand and hurried away, eager to escape the creepy gawker.

Ben stumbled out and caught the first bus he could. After a nauseating ride home, he entered his apartment, holding his stomach. Queasy and tired, Ben dragged himself into the bedroom and collapsed on the bed. His eyes closed, and he drifted into a fugue-like state. Every so often, he flinched or muttered things.

The toilet flushed. "Ben? Honey, is that you?" Beth called out from inside the bathroom.

Ben didn't answer.

Beth emerged and found Ben sleeping on the bed. She leaned down and rubbed his back. "Are you okay, hon?"

Ben mumbled, "Alisa. I've missed you."

CHAPTER 25

INDIA, 323 B.C.

THE SUN DRIFTED toward the horizon of the Indian countryside. It would have been a serene setting were it not for the Greek military commanders, including General Craterus, arguing atop a bluff that provided a 360-degree view of the surrounding area. Alexander rode up on Bucephalus and assessed the situation. Given the intensity of the shouting, something serious was wrong. As he dismounted, he scanned the group. "Where's Hephaestion?"

"I assume he's on his way," Craterus said.

Alexander considered waiting, but the urgency of the atmosphere didn't permit it.

Craterus pointed to the east, where small billows of smoke rose into the sky. "Sir, our scouts have located the Malli army. They are east of the Akesines river." He then pointed to the west, where dust kicked up from a large army on the march. "And a scout has reported troops moving west from the Hydroatis."

Alexander surveyed both locations and gritted his teeth. "They're trying to flank us."

"Yes," Craterus said. "We believe the Malli army split up their forces when we stopped our advance."

"How many?" Alexander asked, fearing the worst.

"At least ten thousand on each side."

"At least we'll have the numerical advantage for this battle. Don't let them converge. Let's force the fight with whoever is closer," Alexander said.

A mounted messenger galloped up the hill. When he reached the top, he jumped off his horse and hurried to Alexander. Eyes filled with fear, the messenger did not want to speak. "Sir," he stuttered. "May we speak in private?"

Alexander stepped aside. The messenger leaned in. As the words left his lips, Alexander's face turned white. He bolted to Bucephalus, hopped on, and raced away at breakneck speed. He maneuvered the horse down the hill, giving no regard for the animal's safety or his own. When Alexander reached the bottom of the slope, he spurred Bucephalus as fast as he'd ever driven him. When he arrived at camp, he dismounted and sprinted into Hephaestion's tent.

Hephaestion lay on his small cot with one leg dangling off the edge and beads of sweat all over his body. His ghastly white skin and massive black pupils revealed the obvious—he was gravely ill. A servant applied a damp towel to his forehead. When Alexander entered, the servant stepped away and left them alone.

Alexander knelt beside his friend. "Hephaestion."

Hephaestion coughed and sputtered. "The Malli army is advancing."

"I know. What happened?" Alexander looked at his sick friend, wanting desperately to help.

"Poison. In my tea." Hephaestion coughed.

"Who?"

Hephaestion shot him a look.

Alexander drew his sword. "Where is he?"

97

"He's not been here. He disappeared," Hephaestion said.

Alexander looked at Hephaestion, confused.

Hephaestion wheezed, and his breath became more shallow. "He's been manipulating us from the moment we met him." He used what little strength he had left and pulled Alexander close. "There are others with the gift. They are here. *Among our people!*"

A chill went down Alexander's spine. "Who?"

"I don't know. Trust no one," Hephaestion counseled in his final breaths. "Look at my hands." Hephaestion placed both hands in front of his chest and clasped them together in a distinctive grip. One was upside down, the other right side up. "We both must remember this signal."

Alexander imitated the grip.

"Rome. Meet me in Rome."

Alexander nodded.

"And promise me you'll continue to lead."

Alexander nodded.

With one final gasp of energy, he bellowed, "Don't let Gabriel win. Promise."

Tears streamed down Alexander's face. "I promise."

As the last bit of life faded from Hephaestion's body, his breath rattled, and his eyes fell blank. Then, silence. He was dead. Alexander respectfully closed Hepahestion's eyes and removed his medallion necklace. He gripped it tightly and buried his head in Hepahestion's chest. His best friend, his only friend, was gone. Once again, Alexander was alone in this world, but the isolation hurt less than the guilt. Alexander let this happen. He befriended Gabriel. He chose a stranger over Hephaestion.

Alexander's despair and guilt turned into a burning rage. He roared, "Find Gabriel!"

CHAPTER 26

VIRGINIA, 2018

IN THE MIDDLE of Tom's Italian marble foyer, time and Riya stood still. She stared at Tom, slack-jawed. *He could remember his past lives.* A million thoughts and questions raced through her mind, and she peppered Tom with them all at once. "How is this possible? Did it happen in the MRI? My sister was right. This is going to change the world."

As Riya reveled in the monumental nature of the discovery, Tom held up his hand and interrupted. "Dr. Patel, you need to stop pursuing this now, or you're going to end up dead like your sister."

Riya stiffened. "My sister died in an accident."

Tom shook his head. "She was murdered."

The words hit Riya like a punch to the face. Her legs became wobbly, and she put her hand against the wall for support. "What did you say?"

Tom didn't respond, but his eyes told Riya he knew *a lot* more. "Who?" she asked, but it wasn't a question.

Tom remained silent.

Riya stepped at Tom and pointed her finger in his face. "Tom, if you know, you have to tell me."

Tom pushed her finger aside, then pointed his finger in *her* face. "You need to stop. These people are ruthless."

"Who are they?"

"If you don't stop, they will kill you," Tom said. "If you're lucky, you won't see it coming. It will just be over." He snapped his finger inches from her face. "Like that."

"Why would they do that? Why would they kill innocent people?" The words stuck in her throat. One of those innocents had been her little sister. "Why?"

Tom stared at Riya. She wasn't ready for the truth. "To protect their secrets."

"What if I go to the press and tell them you remember your past lives?"

"I'll deny it," Tom said, not the least bit worried.

"I'll show the video of you speaking strange languages," Riya said.

This wasn't Tom's first rodeo with intimidation tactics. "My lawyer is requiring that you hand over all my files and test results immediately."

"I have a copy," Riya said.

Tom didn't flinch. "It will be dismissed as some fluke, a fake tape, or that I'm some type of savant. If anyone asked me, I'd claim it's bogus."

Riya wanted to scream at the top of her lungs. "My sister died trying to make this discovery. Why won't you help?"

Tom leaned into Riya and grabbed her arm. "You clearly have not been listening. I am helping." He pulled her to the front door. "Turn over that tape, forget all about me and what you think you know. If you don't, I'll file a massive lawsuit against your hospital and you personally. You will lose your medical license, and your career will be over. But none of that will matter because you'll be dead."

Tom shoved Riya out the door and slammed it shut.

CHAPTER 27

Maryland, 2018

After a deep sleep, Ben stirred, and his eyes popped open. He rubbed his head and sat up, confused. Strange dream. He turned and found Beth sitting in the corner chair with red and puffy eyes.

"What's wrong?" he asked.

"Who is she?" Beth choked on the words.

"Who?"

"I was surprised you came home," Beth said. "Thought maybe you weren't feeling well. Then you started talking in your sleep. You kept talking about some woman—Alisa."

Panic set in. What did Ben say? What did Beth know? Did he talk about his feelings for this strange woman? "I don't know her." Ben shook his head to emphasize his ignorance.

Beth stared at Ben with daggers in her eyes. "Then how do you know her name?"

Ben couldn't fast-talk his way out of this one—time to come clean.

"There's something I need to tell you. I've started going to a psychiatrist. I've been having these strange visions. I keep thinking people are following me, and I keep seeing this strange woman in my head, but I haven't met her. I swear."

"Stop lying to me!" Beth shouted and rose to her feet.

"I'm telling you the truth. That's why I got the gun. It was because of these feelings. And the money was in case the people came, and I needed… in case *we* needed to leave in a hurry." Ben hoped Beth didn't realize the slip of the tongue. He failed to recognize the bigger error.

Beth stood frozen, aghast. "That's what the money was for?" She stammered as she forced herself to admit the truth. "You don't want to marry me, do you?" Tears rolled down Beth's cheek as her heart broke in front of Ben. He slid off the bed and stupidly attempted to put a comforting arm around her.

"Don't." Beth recoiled in disgust. "Just go away. Go. Go to Frank's for a while or somewhere else. Just don't stay here."

Ben hated himself. He never meant to hurt Beth. He knew it was a mistake to ask Beth to marry him, but he wanted to make her happy, and Ben wanted to want to marry her. He failed. Big time. "I'm sorry."

BEN EXITED his apartment complex and dialed Frank on his cell. "Hey. Can I crash at your place?" He paused as Frank reacted. "I'll explain later." He listened again as Frank offered to pick him up. "No, I'll just walk. I could use the fresh air."

Ben hung up. As he roamed, all the ways he screwed up tugged at his conscience until something odd distracted him—footsteps ever so subtle echoed behind him. Ben stopped, and so did the sound. He walked, and the footsteps resumed. *Were those his footsteps?* Ben paused again and turned around, afraid of what he might find. The shadows appeared especially ominous on this night. He squinted into the darkness. *Was that someone hiding in the shadows, or was it just in his head?* The more he stared, the more his eyes acclimated, and the more a figure emerged.

Ben swallowed as fear filled the pit of his stomach. A city bus passed. Ben glanced down the street and spotted a bus stop. "Hey. Hey. Stop!"

The bus pulled over. Relieved, Ben raced over, hopped on, and sat in one of the front seats. He peered through the window into the darkness, trying to find his pursuer. As the bus pulled away, Ben settled into his seat and let down his guard until a familiar voice from the back of the bus raised the hairs on his neck. "I'm gonna get lit tonight. Gonna find me a nice, tasty 'ho.'"

Ben stole a glance to confirm his suspicion. Yep, it was T-Roy and his dumb ass buddies. Ben stared ahead, hoping they wouldn't recognize him from behind.

The brakes of the bus belched and squealed for its next stop. Ben escaped down the front steps of the bus, but not before T-Roy caught a glimpse of him. Time for payback.

Hurrying down the road, Ben hung a right down a side street as soon as he could, but the two cronies emerged on the far end. Ben turned to flee, but T-Roy now blocked that path.

"Well, well, well. If it isn't Speedy Gonzalez," T-Roy said. "Nowhere to run here, is there?"

Ben looked around for a way to escape. There was none.

One crony snickered. "I think he's gonna cry."

T-Roy cracked his knuckles. "No, homes. He's not gonna cry. He's gonna bleed."

Behind T-Roy, something more ominous emerged in the distance, a man in a black overcoat. Ben recognized the man—it was the guy that bumped into him at the bar, and the stern look on his face revealed this was not a coincidence and he was not here to help. Ben was in danger, and it wasn't from T-Roy and his lowlife friends.

The man in black closed in.

T-Roy turned and glowered at the man. "Get lost, fool."

The man didn't speak as he drifted closer. T-Roy stepped at the man and took a swing. The man blocked the punch, wrenched T-Roy's wrist back, and kicked him into the wall.

The cronies raced past Ben to help their friend. Ben watched dumbfounded as this mystery man performed a flawless sequence of something akin to Jiu Jitsu. In seconds, all three thugs were bleeding on the ground.

The man turned his focus to Ben.

CHAPTER 28

INDIA, 323 B.C.

A BLUEBIRD FLUTTERED and chirped through the picturesque landscape. Like an ethereal Disney movie, it popped from one tree branch to the other. It glided over to inspect a radiant hibiscus bloom. The adorable bird took to the skies, revealing rolling hills decorated with trees and grasses in every shade of green and yellow imaginable—*nature at its finest.*

The bluebird descended and landed on what looked like thin brown grass. It pecked, but the sod wouldn't come out, so it moved onto something beside the "grass"—something olive-colored and malleable. It was an ear that belonged to a dead Greek soldier. The brown grass was his crusted hair.

Sensing danger, the bird darted away to escape the smoke billowing into the sky. Just to the west, fire transformed the hills into a black, charred wasteland. Most harrowing were the thousands of dead bodies strewn about —*humanity at its worst.*

In the aftermath of the battle with the Mallian army, anxious Greek soldiers, including General Craterus, carried a wounded Alexander into a tent. An arrow protruded out of his left shoulder—a grotesque sight. It was the type of injury that proved fatal more often than not, and his men knew it. With his good arm, Alexander wrestled free from their grip and then clutched Hephaestion's medallion necklace that now hung around his neck.

"Let me go. Get your hands off me," Alexander shouted.

His men placed him on a small cot. General Craterus pointed to one of his soldiers. "Get the doctor."

The soldier rushed out of the tent.

"No! No one comes near me."

Craterus waved the rest of the soldiers away to give Alexander space, hoping it would calm him. "Alexander, if we don't treat the wound—"

"I don't care," Alexander interrupted with wild, scared eyes. "Where is Gabriel? Have you found him yet?"

"Our men are still searching," Craterus said.

"Have them search faster."

"Alexander, we just fought a battle."

"Are you making excuses, Craterus?"

"We'll find him. We'll double the number of men searching."

"You're lying! All of you," Alexander screamed. "You're with them, aren't you?"

"With who?" Craterus asked.

The doctor, Philip of Arcania, an older bearded man in a simple robe, raced in. He approached Alexander and reached towards the wound. Alexander punched Philip with his good arm, sending him reeling to the ground.

"No one touches me. Do you understand?" Like a cornered lion, Alexander prepared to defend himself to the death.

Holding his jaw in pain, Philip pulled himself off the floor. "I am here to help."

The baffled soldiers watched Alexander's bizarre behavior—this was not the leader they'd been following.

Alexander scanned the faces of his men. He trusted no one. "I will avenge Hephaestion. If you want to help, bring me Gabriel."

Craterus motioned to the sky. "As the gods are my witness, we will find him."

"Alexander!" Philip said.

The sternness in Philip's voice broke through Alexander's paranoia.

"You *will* die if we don't treat that wound." Philip let that sink in. "You can't avenge anyone if you're dead."

Alexander considered his options. "Only one person will treat me."

CHAPTER 29

Maryland, 2018

Ben's heart raced a hundred miles an hour as the mystery man closed in. *Fight or flight?* Filled with adrenaline and a primal fear, his body chose for him. Ben turned tail and fled. With blazing speed, Ben leaped and jumped over obstacles and fences. He glanced back over his shoulder. No one was in sight, but he refused to stop. Something drove him forward. Whatever danger pursued, he was determined not to let it catch him.

Every chance he got to make a turn, he did. He kept up the pace until his legs gave out. Frantic and breathing heavy, he searched for a place to hide. A pile of bushes behind a concrete bench at a bus stop would have to do. He dove in and concealed himself. No one could find him there.

Seconds later, the man emerged at the far end of the street. *How was this possible?* The man studied his phone as he got closer to Ben.

A sickening sensation enveloped Ben as he reached into his pocket and pulled out his phone. He remembered the man bumping into him at the bar. Later, the man gave Ben his phone back after it "fell" on the floor. This man had stolen it and put some sort of tracking software onto it. Left with one risky option, Ben snuck out from the bushes and slipped the phone onto the bench near the bus stop. He retreated to his hiding spot and watched through the leaves as the man closed in.

With every step, Ben's heart thumped harder and he couldn't have been more afraid if the devil himself approached. The man surveyed the area and stood just a few feet from the bushes where Ben hid. Chiseled cheek bones, dark eyes, and a scar across his chin all made him even more intimidating. A scowl infected his face when he spotted Ben's phone on the bench. Using his own phone, he dialed a number. "It's me. He knows we're following him."

The man listened for a response as Ben peered through the bushes, petrified. "I don't know what he knows yet. I've got all his info. We'll monitor his friends, family, and keep tabs on the police. I'll get him. It's just a matter of time."

The man retrieved Ben's phone and walked away.

Ben remained frozen, too terrified to move. The night sky was black, with clouds covering any hint of the moon or stars. The wind blew just enough to rustle the leaves and add an extra chill to the bone. Still, Ben waited. Terror filled the pit of his stomach, and the thought of moving made it worse, but after three hours, he couldn't take the cold any longer. He shivered out from his hiding spot and scanned the road. *It looked safe, but was it?*

Arms crossed for warmth, Ben wandered the streets, unsure where to go. The only thing he had to keep himself company were his thoughts, and they did little to comfort him. *What are you gonna do now? They're tracking you. Can't go to the police. They wouldn't believe you, anyway. Can't go home. Can't go to work. Can't use credit cards.*

Ben searched the streets for anything familiar, but everything felt different and foreign at night. He was lost in more ways than one. "No one's visions have ever been real, eh, Dr. Brown?" he said out loud. "I better get a refund."

Ben labored on—destination unknown. Just one night in the elements, and he already looked beaten. Up ahead, the glow of a small fire beckoned.

As Ben neared, he discovered a homeless camp—tents and cardboard boxes served as dwellings for people, most of whom were passed out from any combination of fatigue, despair, drugs, and alcohol. Two older men were awake, sitting in broken lawn chairs beside the fire that burned in a barrel of refuse.

"May I?" Ben asked as he put his hands up towards the flames.

In a thick Appalachian accent, the smaller of the two men said, "Fi' dollas."

"Excuse me?"

"This ain't no free hotel," the man said.

Ben wasn't sure how to respond and turned back to the street.

"I'm just playin' wit' ya'." The man chuckled. "You can get warm. I'm Jim. This is Harvey." Jim motioned to the second homeless man, who said nothing and stared at the fire.

Ben stood closer to the fire. "Nice to meet you. I'm Ben."

Jim looked Ben up and down and noted his fresh clothes. "I ain't seen you before out here. You new?"

"You could say that." Ben rubbed his frigid hands together.

"So, what's the story?" Jim asked, eager for some entertainment.

Ben considered his audience, then figured, why not? "I'm either crazy, or I'm being followed by some strange guy."

"I know that guy!" Jim leaned forward.

"You do?" Ben cocked an eyebrow.

"Yeah, yeah. Scary, dude. Dark, mysterious." Jim's eyes bulged as he spoke. "He used to follow me. Every day, sun come up, there he be. I'd run, but he'd still be there. Always right behind me."

Ben shook his head in disbelief that Jim knew the mystery man. "What'd you do?"

"Nothing." A big grin spread across Jim's face. "It was my shadow. I was afraid of my own shadow, get it?" Jim burst out laughing at his own terrible joke. He smacked Harvey on the back, who continued staring straight ahead. Jim then offered up some actual advice. "If you're afraid of the fella' and need to disappear, you should go into the hills. Ain't no one come lookin' in the Appalachians. You can disappear *forever*."

Harvey glanced up and showed a small sign of life. "Why would he want to hide forever?"

"Better than being dead forever," Jim said.

"We all end up six feet deep."

Jim gave Harvey a stern look. "Go back to watching the fire."

Harvey ignored Jim and turned to Ben. "What does the man want? Why is he following you?"

Ben shrugged. "I have no idea."

"Then why are you afraid of him?" Harvey asked with genuine curiosity.

Ben stopped and considered the question. "I don't know."

"Maybe you should find out," Harvey said.

"And how's he gonna do that?" Jim smirked. "Just go up to the fella' and ask?" He shoved Harvey and giggled. "That's a stupid idea, and my pal Ben ain't stupid."

The wheels turned in Ben's head. "Harvey, that's a great idea." He nodded in gratitude, then left.

Harvey resumed staring at the fire, leaving Jim to listen to himself talk. "That's what I thought too. You find out what the man wants."

CHAPTER 30

Virginia, 2018

Riya sat in a chair with cracked black vinyl padding in the Arlington police station. She tapped her foot on the grey and white checkerboard floor as she glanced at the five other people waiting. An older, rotund man in his early 50s, Officer Mike Fisher, opened a door holding a file. Mike looked like he'd struggle to apprehend a spunky toddler, which probably explained why he was a desk jockey. "Ms. Riya Patel," he called out and surveyed the room for a response.

Riya raised her hand. "That's me."

Immediately smitten by her natural beauty, Mike sucked in his gut, smiled, and shook her hand. "I'm Officer Fisher, but you can call me Mike. Come with me, Ma'am," he said while motioning her to the back of the station. "Can I call you, Riya?"

"Uh, sure."

"Riya. That's a beautiful name." Mike led her down a hall to a bullpen of small cubes separated by cheap walls that only went half-way up to the ceiling. When they reached his organized cube, he gestured for Riya to sit in the only chair for guests. He sat behind his desk, which had a computer off to the side. "So, Riya, how can I help you?"

"I'd like to report a murder... well, seven, actually."

"Murder." Mike leaned forward, intrigued. "That's a very serious crime."

"One of them was my sister," Riya added.

"I'm very sorry to hear that. Why didn't you call 9-1-1?"

"This happened a year ago," Riya said.

Mike scratched his head and leaned back in his chair. "And you're reporting it now?"

"They died in an explosion at the lab where they worked. It was determined it was an accident, but I just received information that it was done intentionally."

"We will certainly investigate this, Riya." Mike shifted his attention to the computer and began inputting data into an electronic file. "So, who gave you this information?"

Riya opened her mouth to answer, but stopped after remembering Tom's warning. "I can't say."

"We need to know who told you so we can follow up with them." Mike motioned to his report.

"It's complicated. I don't know if my source knows for sure this was a murder."

Mike leaned back in his chair, now suspicious of Riya's claim. "Hmm. Listen, Riya. I want to help you, but I need more information to re-open an investigation."

Flummoxed, Riya struggled to come up with a reason for Mike to believe her. "This person is confident there's a group of people responsible. They're very dangerous."

"Who is this group?"

"I'm not sure. It could be a gang or the mob or maybe a terrorist organization." Riya lost hope as she listened to herself. Her words sounded crazy. She could only imagine Mike's reaction if she told him that people remember past lives.

"Riya, we can't start an investigation without more information," Mike said with an apologetic frown.

Riya reached out and grabbed Mike's hands. If she had to flirt to get this done, then so be it. "Please, Mike. Can you look into it?"

"I can't. All I can do is file a report, and then a detective will review it."

"Will you at least file the report?" Riya begged.

"Yes, but I know how this all works. An overworked officer is going to see there's nothing new to follow up on unless you give me the name of the person."

This investigation needed to happen, but if Tom was right, other lives were at stake. "I need to think about it. But please file the report."

Mike nodded. He'd do it even though it was a waste of time.

Riya stood to leave.

Mike sprang to his feet and shook her hand goodbye. He also handed her a card. "Here's my number if you change your mind. Or call if you just need someone to talk to."

Riya forced a polite smile and left. As she exited the police station and walked to her car, she didn't see the skinny, middle-aged black man with cold dark eyes watching her in a black SUV. His name was Carlos, and he studied her as she slipped into her car. As she pulled away, Carlos placed a call on his cell.

"She's leaving the police station," he said.

CHAPTER 31

INDIA, 323 B.C.

THE GREEK MILITARY caravan trudged back to the village of the people they freed. The survivors watched in shock as their liberators returned. These once joyous soldiers lumbered with their heads to the ground. Alexander rode slumped over on his horse, the arrow still protruding from his shoulder.

Craterus pointed to several men. "Set up Alexander's tent." He then scanned the faces of the stunned villagers until he spotted Alisa in the crowd. "You." He pointed at her.

Alisa's eyes widened in surprise. A young girl, Maya, grabbed her arm, not wanting her to leave. Alisa whispered something in Maya's ear, pulled away, and approached the general.

Craterus leaned down as Philip of Arcania listened nearby. "Do you have any medical knowledge?"

Alisa glanced at Alexander, then at Craterus. "Very little."

Philip turned to Alexander. "This is madness."

Alexander barked from his horse. "She's the only one." The pain from his wound was excruciating, but Alexander lifted his shoulders and gaze to show he was still the king and still in charge. His decision was final.

Now with a black eye, Philip approached Alisa, pulled her aside, and whispered something as he handed her a cloth case filled with medical instruments.

Alexander glanced around at his men. Many had confused stares. He knew what they were thinking—that he'd gone mad from his wound. His shoulders slumped down again. Maybe they were right. He didn't trust his doctor or anyone in his army. The only person he trusted with his life was a woman he barely knew.

AN HOUR LATER, the Greeks had re-built much of their camp. Through the years, they'd had plenty of practice setting up their traveling home. Alexander's tent was just like the other soldiers, except a little bigger, and he didn't share it with anyone else. Two soldiers stood guard outside.

Inside, Alexander lay on a small cot, and a fire crackled beside him. A bowl full of warm water and clean towels sat atop a wooden table at the far end of the tent. Craterus escorted Alisa inside. Her fingers trembled as she placed the cloth case on the table and then soaked a towel in the water.

Alexander waved Craterus over. "You find him. Use any means necessary. Now go."

Craterus bowed, then exited, leaving Alexander alone with Alisa. Just the sight of her lifted his spirits, but barely. He tried to remain strong and intimidating in front of his men, but he was dying and getting weaker by the second.

"Hello," Alisa said, hoping to break the awkward silence. She inspected the wound and found the arrowhead buried deep in Alexander's shoulder with the shaft partially broken. The swollen flesh oozed a mix of dried and fresh blood. Alisa dabbed the injured area with the towel. As she wiped away dried blood, fresh fluids seeped out.

"You must remove the arrow," Alexander said.

Alisa took a deep breath, then naively reached for the shaft.

With his good arm, Alexander blocked her hands. "No. If you pull, and it breaks, the arrowhead will be much harder to get out."

"Then how do I get it out?"

Alisa's question revealed just how little medical knowledge she possessed. Alexander swallowed. Maybe this was a mistake. He fell back into his cot and rubbed Hephaestion's medallion with his good arm. His resolve hardened, and he clenched his jaw. If he was going to die, it was going to be on his terms. "You must cut the wound open."

Alisa's jaw dropped. "Alexander, I can't. You need a doctor."

Alexander grabbed Alisa with one arm, pulled her close, and whispered. "No. People are trying to kill me. I don't know who. They already murdered my best friend."

"Why me?"

Alexander shook his head, not sure. "You already saved me once. I need you to do it again."

Alisa retreated to the small table and unrolled the cloth case, revealing an array of intimidating metal instruments capable of causing tremendous pain. Alisa returned to Alexander's side with a knife in her quivering hand. The sight of the blade caused Alexander to recoil. Sure, he had been through horrifying battles, but this was different. He prepared himself for the worst. "If I pass out, do not let anyone in. Understand?"

Alisa nodded, then brought the scalpel down and cut. Alexander clenched his jaw and did everything he could to stop from screaming in agony as the blade pierced his already mangled flesh. After several excruciating seconds, Alisa returned to the table with bloody, shaking hands.

A voice whispered. Alexander was used to voices swirling in his mind, so at first, he didn't give it much thought, but then he realized it was coming from a crease in the tent. As he listened closer, he recognized the voice. "Open the wound with your fingers and use the pincers to grab the arrowhead." It was Philip.

Alexander shouted, "Out! Or I'll have your head."

The whispers stopped. Alisa returned to Alexander with the pincers and a towel. Her eyes were red and filled with tears. This was horrifying for her as well.

Alexander offered words of encouragement, which he needed himself. "Don't listen to him. I trust you, okay?"

Alisa's hands froze as she stared at the gruesome wound. "You need a doctor, Alexander," she said as tears streamed down her cheek.

Alexander shook his head. He needed Alisa to remain strong. "Don't let anyone else near me. There's a traitor among my men. Please. You must do this."

Alisa nodded and took a breath to compose herself. She then began the next step, splaying the wound with her fingers.

Through gritted teeth and tears of his own, Alexander whimpered, "Don't let anyone else near me. There's a traitor..." The pain became too much, and he passed out.

Complete darkness and silence. Then, a pinprick of white light. A swirl of indistinguishable voices came from the light, which became bigger and bigger. Alisa's voice broke through the clutter of random voices in strange tongues. "The gods brought us together for a reason."

Alexander cracked his eyes and found Alisa standing over him. With the light radiating behind, she looked angelic, and his pain was gone. Had he died and arrived at a better place? He didn't care. He smiled at the comforting sight of her and drifted back unconscious.

CHAPTER 32

Maryland, 2018

Frank carried his briefcase and strolled down the hallway of Francis Scott Key building until he reached his office. He twisted the doorknob and entered. As soon as he shut the door behind him, Ben revealed himself, startling Frank to death. "Holy sh—."

Ben held up his hands. "It's just me."

Frank tossed the briefcase on his desk and collected himself. "What the hell are you doing? What happened last night? I thought you were coming over."

"I was jumped by some gang members," Ben said, eager to talk to his friend. "And do you remember the creepy guy from the bar?" His eyes bulged as he spoke. "He's been following me. He bugged my phone."

Frank sat down in the chair for guests. "Are you sure you're okay?"

"No, I'm not okay. Did you hear what I said? I'm being followed."

"Don't you think maybe this is what your psychiatrist told you to be wary of?" Frank asked, hoping Ben would make the connection.

Ben clenched his teeth. This hadn't been some manifestation in his mind. This happened. "Give me your phone." He didn't wait for a response and reached towards Frank's pockets. To spare the awkward pat-down, Frank handed it over.

Ben pressed the home button, then looked to Frank for the passcode.

Frank considered objecting, but at this point, he'd given up. "2. 4. 6. 8. 1. 0."

Ben glanced at Frank. *Really?*

Frank shrugged. "It's easy to remember."

Ben entered the code, then pulled up the "Find My Phone" app. He inputted his phone number and waited. A moment later, a map revealed the location of Ben's phone.

"See." Ben held up the screen. "He's got my phone."

Frank studied the display. "I'm not sure what that proves other than your phone is…" He inspected the map closer. "Near your apartment."

"What?" Ben searched the map.

"Maybe it fell out of your pocket."

Ben's mind raced. Why was the man near his home? "I need to borrow your car. I need to find out what he's up to."

"I can't give you my car, Ben. I think you should talk to your psychiatrist."

"This is real, Frank. I need your car. Beth might be in danger."

Frank stood and put his hand on Ben's shoulder. "Listen, I care about you, man. I really do, but you need help."

Ben slumped against the wall and covered his face with his hands. Frank patted him on the back. "It's okay, buddy."

Ben dropped his hands. "I know I sound crazy. I do. But let me show you something." He grabbed Frank's wrist and squeezed.

"What are you doing?"

Before Frank could pull away, Ben cracked Frank above the carotid artery on his neck. The move stopped the blood flow to Frank's brain for a brief second. He dropped like a rock, but Ben caught him and eased his fall. Frank was out cold.

"Crazy, right?" Ben said to a sleeping Frank. "No idea how I know how to do that."

Ben searched Frank's pockets and collected his keys and phone. "You'll get these back by tonight. Sound good?" Ben tapped Frank on the back and left.

BEN DROVE FAST, bordering on reckless, in Frank's Ford Escort. He glanced at the map on Frank's phone that showed *his* phone's location. He turned down the street he lived on and parked on the side of the road. The map display revealed that his phone, and likely the mystery man, were only a few parked cars ahead.

Ben climbed over the center console into the passenger seat and cracked the door open. He slipped out, crouched low, and crept forward, staying close to the sides of the cars. He passed one. Empty. He moved on past a truck. Also empty.

Someone sat in the third car, a BMW. Through the side mirror's reflection, Ben could see the chiseled cheeks and scarred chin of the mystery man, which sent a chill down his spine.

Ben ducked behind the truck to hide. He took three deep breaths to compose himself and then peered around the back bumper for another look. The mystery man appeared to be on a stakeout, waiting for Ben to return home. Ben considered his options. He could call the cops, but the mystery man said they were monitoring the police. Maybe he could get the license plate and find out the man's identity. With nothing better coming to mind, Ben pulled up the camera app on Frank's phone, but before he had time to implement his plan, a pedestrian turned the corner ahead. It was Beth.

Ben stayed hidden behind the truck as Beth disappeared into the apartment complex. The mystery man exited his vehicle and followed her.

Ben slipped out of his hiding place and observed from a safe distance. He peeked around the doorway as the man entered the elevator. As soon as the doors closed, Ben hurried into the lobby and sprinted to the stairwell.

He leaped up the stairs, taking them three at a time. One floor. Two floors. He kept going as fast as his legs would carry him until he reached his floor.

Gassed and breathing heavy, Ben cracked the door and spied the mystery man breezing down the hallway towards his apartment. When the man arrived at Ben's door, he pulled out a pistol and chambered a round, then re-holstered the gun. Not a good sign. The mystery man knocked on the door.

Ben panicked and whispered to himself, "No, no, no. Don't answer, Beth."

CHAPTER 33

Virginia, 2018

Riya reviewed documents from her sister's file on her rustic kitchen table from Pottery Barn. Her entire home looked like an advertisement for the company. Everything was new and decorative knick-knacks provided the perfect accent to each space. A mahogany bookcase contained classics like *War and Peace*, *Pride and Prejudice*, *The Great Gatsby*, and *Wuthering Heights*. Her kitchen contained eclectic devices and utensils, like an espresso machine and a Belgian waffle maker. All the extra touches suggested that Riya was something of a Renaissance woman, but while she had indeed read the books, it wasn't because she enjoyed them. She'd done it years ago as a requirement in her college classes. For Dr. Patel, "leisure reading" meant medical journals. As for her kitchen accoutrements, she'd used everything at least once and at most twice as the life of a top neurosurgeon left little time for things like baking.

Her only other pastime had been helping Anjali, which had since morphed into discovering the truth behind her death. She poured over the material from the file, something she'd already done a hundred times, but this was the first time it had been a murder investigation.

Her phone rang and interrupted her work. She answered and heard a familiar voice. "Riya, it's Mike. Um, I mean, Officer Fisher."

Riya arched her eyebrow, intrigued by the call. "Oh, hey. I didn't expect to hear from you."

"I wanted to check up on you. Make sure you were okay," Mike said.

"That's kind of you. I'm fine."

"I also have some good news. The detective from your sister's case, Harper Peterson, is going to contact you. Guess I was wrong that nothing would happen."

Riya exhaled with joy, relieved she'd get some help. "That's fantastic, Mike. I can't thank you enough."

"My pleasure. If there's anything else I can do, please let me know."

There was a knock at Riya's front door. "Riya. It's Greg. I need to talk to you." Greg knocked louder.

Riya walked to the door with the phone in hand. "Will do, Mike. I need to run, but thank you again." Riya hung up and opened the door, revealing a stern-looking Greg.

"You know why I'm here, right?"

Riya shook her head.

"I got a call from Tom Vance's lawyers a short while ago." Greg invited himself in. "You went to his house! After what I told you? Do you realize how many jobs you put at risk? This is people's livelihood, Riya."

"I'm sorry, Greg."

"They said you have a copy of Tom's test results. I need those now." Greg held out his hand.

"Come on, Greg."

"Now."

Riya grabbed her brief off the table, pulled out a Zip drive, and handed it over.

Greg held up the drive. "This is it, right?"

"That's it," Riya promised.

Greg pointed to the papers on the table. "What about those?"

"That's *my* file about *my* sister." She placed herself between Greg and the papers. He wasn't taking those.

Greg eyed Riya, doubtful. "I'll have the hospital's attorney contact you to make sure nothing has slipped your mind. I also need your ID badge."

"What do you mean?" Riya handed the badge to him.

"You're fired." Greg turned and showed himself out the door.

Riya stood there, stunned, even though she should have seen it coming. Anger simmered as she thought about Tom and his unwillingness to help. Now he'd gotten her fired, too. She snatched her cell and dialed his number.

"Hello, Riya." Tom said in a calm voice, like he'd been expecting the call.

"What the hell are you doing?" she demanded.

"What are *you* doing?" he asked, flipping it back on Riya. "I told you to forget about me and what you think you know."

"I did," she said, lying through her teeth. There was a lot of chatter in the background on Tom's end. Riya wondered if he was home or somewhere else.

"Why were you at the police station?" Tom asked.

"How did you know that?"

Tom kept his voice low and measured. "I had you followed."

"You did what?" Riya snarled at the phone, as if that would do any good. "Is that why you got me fired?"

"I didn't ask for that. Whatever happened between you and your boss is on you. I told you yesterday I need my medical records, and now I need to know what you told the police."

Riya couldn't believe Tom's nerve. "I don't have to tell you anything."

"You're right," Tom said. "Even though you may have put my life in danger. But I also don't have to tell you the name of the group responsible for murdering your sister."

"You know?"

"Yes, but you have to tell me what you told the police."

"I just asked them to re-open my sister's death as a homicide." Riya paced about the kitchen.

Tom chuckled, the first hint of any emotion. "You have no idea how stupid that was. What else did you tell them? Did you give them my name?"

"No."

Tom spoke slowly for emphasis. "I need to know exactly what you told them."

"I didn't use your name. I told them a group murdered the people at the lab, and they needed to investigate it. And they do. Who are these people, Tom?"

"I told you before; they're ruthless. And they're beyond connected. Do not go to the police again. Or the FBI. They have people there. You never know who you can trust. They monitor the major crime databases and all the intelligence agencies. *Your* report about *their* crime has probably already been seen by them."

"Who are they?" Riya pleaded.

"First, do not call my number again."

"We had a deal, Tom."

"You want to put yourself in danger? That's fine. But as soon as we hang up, this line is disconnected. You don't know me, and you don't mention me, ever. Is that understood?"

"Understood. Who are they?" Riya continued to pace around her kitchen. She had to bring her sister's murderers to justice.

"They're called the Pantheon. They are probably already on their way. If I were you, I'd disappear." Tom hung up.

Riya now stood frozen with the phone in her hand. She had the information she needed, but was she a dead woman walking? Riya ventured to the front window and peered out at the vehicles parked along the road. *Was someone already out there, watching?* She snapped the blinds shut.

CHAPTER 34

India, 323 B.C.

His arm healed, Alexander strolled with Alisa along a dirt trail lined with vibrant flowers. Birds chirped, and the soft morning light gave everything a magical glow.

"Where are we going?" Alisa asked with a giant smile.

"You'll see," Alexander said with a wry grin.

The two continued their hike until they came upon a bubbling brook. Shaded by trees and surrounded by reeds and lotuses, the setting appeared too picturesque to be real.

"It's beautiful," Alisa marveled. She turned to Alexander. Their eyes met, and emotions rose.

Alexander leaned in and kissed her. The two fell into the grass in paradise. As the romantic energy built, Alexander and Alisa rolled onto something hard and lumpy. It was the decayed corpse of Hephaestion. Alexander pulled Alisa away, terrified. The eyes snapped open. "Avenge me," it bellowed.

Alexander bolted upright in his cot with his injured arm wrapped in a sling and sweat covering his body. Disoriented, he took slow, deep breaths to calm himself. It was just a dream. Still unsettled, Alexander rubbed Hephaestion's necklace for comfort. His gaze fell on a second bed and Alisa's cloak resting on top.

Philip opened the front flap of the tent. "You're awake. May I come in?"

Alexander nodded. Philip stepped inside but kept his distance, remembering the last time he got too close to the king.

"Where's Alisa?" Alexander asked.

"Filling the water bowls," Philip answered. He pointed to Alexander's shoulder. "May I have a look?"

Alexander hesitated.

Philip held his hands to his heart. "I've been your physician for many years, Alexander. I've served you faithfully, and I will continue to."

Alexander nodded, then undressed the wound himself. Once exposed, he marveled at how well it appeared. "Have you ever seen an injury heal like this?"

Philip pursed his lips, not impressed. "Truly, the gods are with you. There's no other explanation for how a peasant woman could do this." His words were loaded with subtext and innuendo.

"Perhaps you have some things to learn from the peasant woman."

Philip bit his tongue. "Of course. You know she's quite fond of you. She's certainly fond of your authority."

"What do you mean?"

Philip leaned down and studied the wound closer. "Rumor is she's taken to our stores and has generously donated to her people."

Alexander pulled his shoulder away. "Do you feel threatened by her?"

Philip huffed. "Of course not."

"Then why would you imply she stole from my army based on a rumor?"

Philip had wandered into dangerous territory and attempted to backtrack. "I didn't say she stole. I—"

Alexander cut him off. "And why would you suggest that she alone didn't heal me? Did you help her against my direct orders?"

Philip bowed his head in deference. "My sincerest apologies for implying anything."

Alexander studied Philip for a long, uncomfortable moment. *Was he the traitor?* "You're dismissed."

Philip bowed again and left.

Alexander stewed on Philip's words.

Alisa entered, carrying two jugs of fresh water. "Thirsty?" she asked.

"Not right now," Alexander rubbed his chin, distracted. "What do you think of Philip, my doctor?"

Alisa poured the water from the jugs into pitchers. "I don't think he likes me very much."

Alexander smiled. "I love your honesty. And I don't care what he thinks. I don't trust him. He may be a traitor."

"Why do you think that?"

Alexander continued fiddling with his chin as he thought. "I don't know. But I need to find out if he is, and I need to find out if anyone else is."

Alisa finished with the water, then tended to Alexander's exposed wound. She grabbed a towel and bowl filled with a translucent amber gel. "How will you do that?"

Alexander sat up to provide easier access to his shoulder. "Have you overheard anything from the men in camp?"

Alisa dabbed the wound with the towel. "Just that many are tired of fighting. Is it true you've been campaigning for eleven years?"

Alexander nodded.

"Will you ever be done fighting?"

Alexander exhaled, a question he asked himself daily. "One day. Hopefully."

Alisa took a clean strip of cloth and dipped it in the amber gel. "Maybe it would be good to settle down. For a bit, at least. Let the men regroup. It will give you time to find the traitors."

"Maybe. It's complicated. There are things about me... things I've done. Things I must do. I spoke of these things only with Hephaestion."

"Your friend that was killed?" Alisa applied the gel to the injured shoulder.

Alexander nodded as he closed his eyes for a moment and enjoyed the soothing relief of the medicine. "If he were here, he'd know what to do."

"My people believe that when someone dies, their spirit lives on. Maybe he will tell you what to do," Alisa said.

Alexander remembered his dream and the horror of Hephaestion's corpse. "Maybe."

Alisa finished applying the dressing to the wound and leaned back. "If you're feeling better, I'd like to visit some of my friends in my village."

Alexander looked at his shoulder, disappointed she'd finished. "Of course."

Alexander watched her leave with longing eyes, and melancholy set in as soon as she'd left. He had no one else in the world that he trusted. He rubbed Hephaestion's medallion between his fingers, the only physical token from his friend. "I miss you," he said, slipping into conversation as if Hephaestion was present through the medallion. "What do you think about her? Pretty amazing, right?" He smiled until the guilt from his dream wiped it away. "I haven't forgotten. I will avenge you. I'll find Gabriel." Alexander gripped the necklace tight in his hand.

THE ARMY STOOD in formation with a palpable curiosity as they were unsure why they'd been called. Alexander emerged in regal attire with his arm still bandaged. He strode through the men, who gazed upon him like a god in the flesh.

When Alexander reached the front of the group, he turned and shouted so all could hear. "Many of you have been wondering about my condition. As you can see, I'm fine." He emphasized the last point for both his friends and the unknown traitors within the ranks. "For over a decade, we've defeated all our foes. It's time to get back to work."

The spirit of the men dampened—more barbarians, more battles, and more death.

Alexander expected the reaction. "But it's time for a new work."

A sparkle of hope filled the men's eyes.

On a small hilltop behind the army, Alisa raced to the top with her friend Maya. Both listened intently.

"It's time to tend to our fields. Re-build our cities. And lead our people." Alexander paused before declaring. "It's time to go home."

The men fell silent. Were they really going home?

Alexander grinned. "We leave tomorrow."

A deafening cheer erupted as the soldiers hugged and kissed one another. Tears rolled down the cheeks of many.

Alisa's face dropped. She turned and disappeared down the hill.

THE EVENING TURNED TO NIGHT, and the party was in full swing. Liquored up, the soldiers danced and sang. Alexander made the rounds, stopping to thank each man for his service. Satisfied with his efforts, he retreated to his tent to let his men enjoy the moment. Upon entering, he found Alisa gathering her things.

"What are you doing?" he asked.

Alisa didn't look up to greet Alexander. "You're leaving tomorrow."

"No, we're not," Alexander said, dropping the pretense of the jovial commander. He had other plans.

Alisa stopped packing, confused. "But you said—"

Alexander stepped towards Alisa and interrupted. "I'm glad I caught you before you left." His words were warm and inviting.

"Why?"

He moved closer. "Because I don't want you to leave."

Both stared into the other's eyes as the music from the party played in the background. They longed for one another and not just physically. "It feels like we were almost at this same moment a few weeks ago," Alexander said.

Alisa gazed up at Alexander, the attraction mutual and deep.

"It's not often you get a second chance," he said.

"A second chance at what?"

Alexander looked at her beautiful, full lips and her flowing, dark hair. He settled on her big, auburn eyes. "That first night, I wanted to kiss you."

"I didn't."

Alexander deflated.

"But I do now," she said. Alisa leaned in and kissed Alexander.

It was a wonderful, passionate first kiss. One they'd never forget.

***

HOURS LATER, the party concluded. It was well past midnight, and several soldiers lay passed out, drunk. Most had retreated to their tents.

In the king's tent, Alisa laid on Alexander's chest, reveling in postcoital bliss. The night had been everything either could have imagined and more, but Alexander was troubled.

"What's wrong?" Alisa asked.

"I must tend to something." Alexander slid out from under Alisa, dressed, and was gone in seconds.

Except for the random soldier snoring, the camp was silent. Alexander snuck from tent-to-tent searching the beds. He stopped first at Philip's tent. To Alexander's surprise, Philip was there, snoring. He checked more tents, finding nothing but sleeping soldiers. He entered one more and discovered three empty bedrolls.

He'd found the traitors.

CHAPTER 35

MARYLAND, 2018

HIDDEN IN THE STAIRWELL, Ben watched through the cracked door as the mystery man knocked on Beth's door. His heart raced. *She couldn't let the man inside.* Thinking fast, Ben pulled out Frank's phone and texted her. *Don't answer.*

The mystery man knocked again. "Beth Murphy?"

Ben's fingers pounded on the phone screen. *Don't answer it!!!*

"Who is it?" Beth asked from inside.

"I'm with the FBI. My name is Agent David Drake."

Ben typed. *He's not with the FBI.*

A moment later, Ben received a return text from Beth. *Who is this?*

Ben shot back a response. *This is Ben. The man at the door chased me last night. He's dangerous.*

"Can I see a badge or some ID?" Beth asked, still safe inside.

David Drake, if that was his name, pulled out his wallet and held up an authentic FBI badge to the peephole.

"What do you want?" Beth asked.

Drake slipped his wallet back into his pocket. "I need to speak to you about your boyfriend, Ben Preston."

Ben typed. *Don't open it. Please trust me.*

Silence, then Beth called out, "I kicked Ben out last night. I don't know where he is."

Drake stuck his hands in his pockets, annoyed this was taking so long. "Ma'am, I really need to speak to you. We can do this the easy way or the hard way. If you obstruct justice, that's a felony. You need to open the door."

Ben texted. *Ask him what crime I committed.*

"What did Ben do?" Beth asked.

"He has important information that will help us," Drake said.

"Then why is he a fugitive?"

Drake paused. "He's been helping a terrorist named Alisa."

Ben froze. Alisa was real.

"Have you ever heard him talk about her, Ms. Murphy?" Drake pressed.

A long moment of silence. Drake put his ear to the door and heard the muffled sound of Beth crying. "Ms. Murphy? Are you okay? Let me in, and we can talk about it."

Ben texted one more time. *I have no idea what's going on. Don't open the door. I don't want you to get hurt.*

From inside the apartment, Beth screamed, "It's too late!"

Drake backed off, confused. "What's that, Ms. Murphy? What's too late?"

"I told you, he's gone," Beth said in a forced, calm voice. "I'll meet you in your office with my attorney."

Drake huffed with irritation and pulled out a tool from his pocket to pick the lock. Just as he inserted the thin metal rod into the keyhole, his phone buzzed. He answered and listened. "Understood," he said before hanging up and turning his attention to the door. "Ms. Murphy, I'll have my office reach out to you."

Drake hurried to the elevator. Ben closed the stairwell door to avoid detection. He then slumped down on the steps, rubbing his head. He couldn't believe what he'd heard. Alisa was real. Then it hit him.

They wanted her, not him.

CHAPTER 36

VIRGINIA, 2018

RIYA SEARCHED the *Pantheon* on her laptop at the kitchen table. She had been at it for hours, working non-stop until night, not even resting to eat. Instead, she consumed search results. With her latest batch, she scrolled through images of the famous pillared Pantheon temple in Rome. Several captions read, *Pantheon: The house of the gods.*

A car rumbled down the street. Still edgy and nervous from Tom's warning, she paused and listened for any signs of danger. After a few seconds of silence, she resumed her work.

A knock at the door startled her out of her chair. *Who would be here at this hour?* Was Tom right? Had they already found her?

She stepped to the door with apprehension. "Who is it?"

A voice answered, "Detective Harper Peterson."

Riya exhaled and chuckled at herself for being so paranoid. She slid the chain off and opened the front door, revealing David Drake, a/k/a Harper Peterson now holding an official *detective* badge.

"Detective Peterson. I wasn't expecting you. Mike mentioned you might call. Thank you for coming."

"It's no trouble." Drake reached out and shook Riya's hand. "I understand you have some questions about your sister. And first, let me offer my condolences." He put his other hand on top of Riya's and patted it.

"Thank you. Come in." Riya waved Drake in.

Drake took one step inside and surveyed the house. "You have a lovely home, Dr. Patel."

Riya led him to the kitchen. "Thank you. Would you like some coffee or something?"

"Coffee would be just fine."

Riya opened a cabinet and pulled out a box of Keurig pods.

The large stack of papers on the table caught Drake's attention. "You've got quite an investigation going here."

"Feel free to look through those." Riya filled the water bin on the Keurig.

Drake casually rifled through the documents. "I understand someone told you that your sister was murdered."

"That's right."

"Who told you that?"

"Um…" Riya stammered as she fiddled with the machine. "I don't know who exactly… but I know the group who committed this crime. Have you ever heard of the Pantheon?"

Drake stopped. Riya had his attention. "The Pantheon? Hmm. Don't think so, but walk me through your investigation and show me what I missed. I'll get the coffee. I know how to work a Keurig. Would you like one?"

"Sure."

As Drake worked the Keurig, Riya pulled out some dog-eared papers. "The key was the medical research. For a year, I had been trying to figure out what they were up to. No one knew, and there was nothing public about it."

She sorted the notes and pulled out the list of people killed with their occupations. A dog barked on the side of the house. Riya froze. Still worried about Tom's warning, she was oblivious that she had let the danger in her front door. "Excuse me for a moment." Riya disappeared into the side bedroom to investigate.

The moment alone gave Drake an opportunity to slip a pill into Riya's coffee. She returned seconds later. "Everything okay?" Drake asked.

"Yes. Just the neighbor's dog."

"Cream or sugar?" Drake offered a polite grin.

"Just a little sugar, thanks."

Drake took the sugar off the counter, poured a touch, and stirred until the pill dissolved. "So, you were telling me about the research."

"Oh, yes." Riya sat down. "It was so important the Pantheon killed to keep it secret."

Drake sat down next to Riya and placed the tainted coffee in front of her.

CHAPTER 37

INDIA, 323 B.C.

BIRDS SQUAWKED from the banyan trees, signaling the start of a new day. After spending the last couple of hours alone thinking, Alexander ambled into his tent and found Alisa asleep in his cot. He sat on the edge of the bed and rubbed his head, still shocked he'd been wrong about the traitors' identities. He'd been wrong about so many things. Alisa awoke behind him and draped her arms around him. He shrugged her away.

"We found the traitors."

"That's good, right?" Alisa asked.

"It's not who I thought it would be." Alexander stood and faced Alisa. "Philip told me some things that surprised me. He said you didn't heal me..."

"Alexander, that's not—"

Alexander interrupted, "And he said you were taking supplies."

Alisa pulled the blanket over her chest, now feeling vulnerable. "People were starving. They were going to die."

"So, it's true?" Alexander shook his head and scoffed at his wishful imagination. "We were brought together for a reason."

This struck a nerve. Alisa threw her clothes on and rushed out on the verge of tears.

Alexander kicked at the ground, angry at her but furious at himself. He turned to chase after her, but Craterus entered. "We have the men you requested."

Alexander nodded. He'd make amends later. "Bring them in."

"How did you figure out it was them?" Craterus asked.

"If I announced we were leaving, the traitors would need to communicate to Gabriel where we are heading, and they'd need to do it last night."

"Very clever, sir."

Craterus left and returned a moment later with three men, who shuffled into the tent, hands and feet bound. Varus, one of Alexander's best infantry soldiers, was among them. Craterus shoved them to their knees in front of Alexander.

"Leave them with me," Alexander said.

Craterus assessed Alexander's injured arm. "Are you sure?"

Alexander picked up his sword with his good arm. Craterus nodded, then left.

"You remember your past lives?" he barked.

The men remained silent with their heads tilted to the ground.

"Where is he?" Alexander ran the tip of the blade along the dirt in front of them.

More silence.

"Varus," Alexander said, still in disbelief at the betrayal. "You were one of my best men. We fought together. Why?"

Varus didn't respond or even acknowledge Alexander.

"Look at me!"

Varus raised his gaze, revealing eyes, not of a loyal soldier but of a cold, arrogant, and manipulative enemy. "Why would we ever tell you anything?"

Alexander placed the tip of his sword under Varus's chin. "Because I will end you."

Varus stared at Alexander. "That's not a real threat when you come back, now is it?" He taunted Alexander with a wry smile.

The other two chuckled under their breath, and the lack of fear rattled Alexander's confidence. "What is it you want?"

"You've already given what we want, but you can't take it away. What you want, you can no longer have." Varus said cryptically.

"And what do I want?"

"The answer to why you have this gift. But you blew it. You don't deserve this gift." Varus snarled and glared at Alexander with contempt.

Alexander's blood boiled. "Craterus."

Craterus rushed in.

"Separate the prisoners. Torture them until they tell you where Gabriel is hiding."

Alexander kept his eyes on Varus as he spoke. "If the answers don't match perfectly, continue to torture them until they do. Do it far away from the men so they don't hear the screams for mercy.

Craterus kicked the captives until they got to their feet. Alexander still eyed Varus as he shuffled out. "Gabriel can't stay hidden forever. He's finished, and so are you."

Varus snickered under his breath. Something about his laugh worried Alexander.

"Until we meet again," Varus said, as he bowed with false reverence.

CHAPTER 38

Ben tailed Drake's car, careful not to get too close. Drake turned down a residential street—Riya's street. This was the moment just before Drake entered Riya's house.

Ben glanced at the map on the iPhone. The road was a cul-de-sac. He drove past it, parked, and jogged back down the road. Ducking behind a large bush, he spied Drake approaching Riya's house. Riya answered the door, then invited Drake inside.

Ben snuck up to the side of Riya's house and found a gate, which he unlatched, careful not to make a sound. He silently slipped into the back-yard when the neighbor's pit bull charged and barked viciously. Ben held his arms up and braced for the worst. The dog's leash stopped the animal's attack a few feet from Ben. The dog continued to bark and snarl until Ben turned the corner.

A moment later, Riya looked out the side window to investigate. Finding nothing, she returned to the kitchen.

Ben ducked low and maneuvered his way to the kitchen window, where he could hear Riya talking to Drake inside.

"And did you ever figure out what your sister was researching?" Drake asked, intrigued.

"Yes," Riya answered, holding her spiked coffee in her hands. She took a sip.

"And?"

Riya looked down, embarrassed. "It will sound crazy."

"As a detective, I've found that some of the craziest things turn out to be true." He offered a reassuring smile and nodded for her to continue.

Riya avoided judgmental eye contact as she said, "They were researching past lives."

"Hmm," Drake said, with no emotion.

Riya took another sip of tainted coffee. "I know how it sounds, but look." She pointed to a paper. "One researcher was a historian. Why would you need a historian for a scientific study?"

Drake put his coffee down, folded his hands, and leaned forward. "I can tell you're very intelligent, Dr. Patel." Drake now spoke in a haughty tone. "You must have more evidence to make a claim like past lives."

Riya blinked hard as her eyes grew heavy. "Well, uh, I may have some evidence."

"I need that, and I need to know who told you about the Pantheon," Drake said.

Outside, Ben listened on edge. He worried that even his breathing might give him away. *Pantheon?* He repeated the name in his head. Something seemed familiar. If nothing else, it filled him with dread, the same almost instinctual terror he felt when he fled from Drake.

Thump, thump. Thump, thump. His heart pounded the more the Pantheon bounced around his mind.

Inside, the conversation between Drake and Riya continued, even though it sounded more like an interrogation at this point.

"I told you, I don't know who told me," Riya said.

"I don't believe you."

Drake's accusation caught Riya off guard. Her eyelids grew heavier. She glanced down at her coffee and realized, "What did you give me?"

Drake sipped his coffee and winked.

Riya whipped out her phone and dialed Officer Mike. "Pick up, Mike. Pick up," she begged as the phone rang and rang.

She got out of her chair to get away from Drake, but stumbled backward. She leaned against the wall for support. Terrified and fading fast, there was nothing she could do to stop it.

"Please pick up. Pi…" Riya slid down to the floor.

Ben peered through the window in horror. As Riya passed out, he ducked out of sight. His heart raced out of control. *Pantheon.* The word continued rattling through his brain, stirring up emotions—agony, fury, helplessness, but mostly terror. He wanted to flee, but fear gripped hold. When he calmed himself enough to move, he snuck another glance in the kitchen. Drake and Riya were gone. He stood up a little further. Drake slung a massive garbage bag over his shoulder and walked to the front door. There was a slight moan from the bag.

"Shhh. We'll talk more later. It will all be over soon," Drake said.

Ben mustered enough courage to slink to the side of the house that didn't have the pit bull. With his back against the wall, he sidled towards the corner so he could peer around without being seen.

Drake walked to his BMW and pressed the electronic key to open the trunk.

Ben held his head in pain as voices swirled. *You can't stop them,* one taunted.

Drake dumped Riya into the trunk.

Other voices mocked Ben. *Go back into hiding. Don't remember her. Don't remember.*

Ben clenched his teeth. He had to do something. He had to act. One more voice played in his mind, one he recognized, but he didn't know why. It was Gabriel's. *How many times do you throw something in one lifetime? Imagine that skill after twelve.*

Without thinking, Ben grabbed a rock from the bushes and threw. It sailed through the air and tagged Drake on the back of the head, knocking him out instantly. A one in a million throw.

CHAPTER 39

INDIA, 323 B.C.

ALEXANDER WALKED with purpose through the Greek camp, past his men. Confused, they watched as he left the safety of their ranks and entered the remains of the village. As he marched, he got a good look at the dwellings. Compared to his tent, the homes of these people were destitute. Several had torn roofs and collapsed walls—courtesy of the barbarian invaders. The villagers stared. What was the king doing in their midst, and alone, no less?

Alexander searched the grounds until he found Alisa beside her old home grinding millet with a mortar and pestle. Consumed by her task, she didn't hear Alexander approach.

Just the sight of her made Alexander feel better, but he was at a loss for words and could only muster a single word. "Hello."

Alisa continued grinding away.

"Hephaestion was one of the few people I trusted," Alexander said, before clarifying. "He was *the* only person I trusted. When he died, I didn't know who to turn to. But there was something about you." He sat down on

146

his knees, hoping she'd turn around. "Something I was drawn to. I can't explain it."

Alisa kept working.

"I don't care about the supplies," Alexander said.

Any reconciliation was interrupted as Craterus rode over with two members of the royal guard and Bucephalus. "We broke the traitors," he said.

Alexander held up a finger. He needed more time with Alisa. "I don't care that Philip saved me."

Alisa dropped the pestle and faced Alexander. "You know what hurts the most? I thought someone believed in me—believed I was capable of more. Philip didn't save you."

"But you said…"

"I took some food." She waved her hand at the obvious poverty of the village. "People were starving."

Craterus held out the reigns of Bucephalus. "The information led our scouts five miles west. They spotted an old man escaping on a donkey. We've found him."

Alexander was torn. He needed to leave, but he wanted to stay. He leaned into Alisa and whispered, "How did you know how to save me?"

"I had a vision. A dream."

Alexander was stunned. *Did she remember past lives, too?*

"If he gets to the Hydroatis River, we may lose him forever. We must go now." Craterus turned the horses around, dropped Bucephalus's reigns, and led the other soldiers to pursue.

Alexander stood and walked backward. "I have one more battle to fight. But we will continue this talk when I return."

"Killing this man will not bring your friend back."

"I gave him my word." Alexander turned and dashed towards his horse, but stopped before mounting. "I'll return soon. And when my army leaves, you and your people will all come with us."

"I don't believe you," Alisa said.

Torn between vengeance and blossoming love, Alexander wanted to

147

stay, but he needed to fulfill his promise to Hephaestion. "Now, you have my word." Alexander mounted Bucephalus. He groaned from the pain in his arm as he settled in. He kicked his heels into the sides of Bucephalus and charged off, quickly catching up with the others.

Craterus glanced at Alexander's arm. "Are you sure you're ready for this?"

Alexander eyed him, then spurred Bucephalus in front.

The sun beat down as the quartet kicked up dust along the dirt trail. It was exhausting as they attempted to make up ground. Alexander rode full tilt and pushed the others to keep pace. As he crested a hilltop, fatigue set in. He stopped to survey the valley below, and the delay gave Craterus time to catch up. The other soldiers were too far behind.

"We should pause for water and wait for the others," Craterus said.

Alexander glared at Craterus. Water? He didn't need water. He *needed* to find Gabriel.

Craterus rolled his eyes. This pace couldn't last. "Fine, *I* need water." He pulled his flask from his side and chugged.

Alexander relented, grabbed the canteen from the side of Bucephalus, and drank. He slumped forward and held his injured arm.

Craterus noted his deteriorating condition. "Are you sure you're able to continue, Alexander?"

Far in the distance, Alexander spotted something. Eyes straining, he could barely make out a lone man riding a donkey. Alexander kicked Bucephalus's sides, and the animal charged off like a rocket. He was about a half-mile away and closing fast. Alexander grimaced in pain, but he gave no concern for his health. Even Bucephalus labored, but they were too close to stop now. The two drove forward, leaving the support of Craterus behind.

Alexander closed in, now just fifty feet away. He pulled the reins on Bucephalus and stopped the animal. Pallid and sick, he dismounted, then stumbled forward as he withdrew his sword. "Gabriel!" he shouted.

The donkey stopped.

The man hopped off the animal and faced Alexander. It was not

Gabriel. It was Varus. "Looks like we meet again. Sooner than you thought, I'm sure," he said with a sinister grin.

Alexander staggered backward in shock. He raised his weapon and prepared to defend himself against Varus, who did nothing to suggest he would attack.

Craterus rode up. Alexander didn't notice as his world spun. The injured arm and the ride had taken its toll. Or maybe it was something else.

"You don't look so well. Have more water." Varus eyed the canteen. "You can trust me. And Craterus." He laughed.

Alexander glanced back at Craterus and realized he'd been poisoned. As the toxins overtook him, he stumbled and fell on his back.

Varus cackled as his words played in a loop in Alexander's head. *You can trust me.*

Craterus and Varus stepped closer. The two men towered above as Alexander looked up from the ground. He'd been outsmarted and beaten. As his life faded, they drifted further away, as if Alexander traveled in reverse into a dark tunnel.

"It's too bad. He could've been a great asset to us," Varus said.

"He was a great asset," Craterus noted as Alexander struggled to breathe. "We gained more wealth in this lifetime than in the prior five combined, and we know where this wealth is located."

Varus shot Craterus a sideways glance. An odd statement. He turned his attention back to Alexander. "Listen up. Remember these words. You have one more chance to make the right choice. If you go against us again, you never get another. *Ever.*"

From Alexander's perspective, Varus and Craterus were now far in the distance until they were but a speck of light that went black.

Alexander the Great was dead.

CHAPTER 40

Drake rested unconscious, propped up in a chair in Riya's kitchen, with his hands duct-taped behind his back. His head, with a large welt, drooped against his chest. Ben laid a sleeping Riya on the white wraparound couch in the living room. He returned to the kitchen, patted Drake down, and discovered a 9mm pistol and wallet. He sat across from him and searched the wallet. Ben uncovered several types of IDs with a different name on each. *Who the hell was this guy?*

Drake stirred, and his eyes opened. He collected himself, then found Ben staring at him.

"Who are you?" Ben asked. "And don't bother with one of these fake names." He flicked the IDs across the table.

Drake surveyed his surroundings like a predator.

"Why are you following me?" Ben moved his head in Drake's line of sight to get his attention.

Drake ignored Ben and continued to assess the situation.

Ben cocked the gun and pointed it at Drake. "I will end you."

Drake chuckled under his breath. "Forgive me. Déjà vu."

Ben arched his eyebrow. *What did he mean?*

Drake stared at the barrel of Ben's gun, unafraid. "Go on then. Make it a quick one and be done with it."

Ben put the pistol against Drake's forehead. "Where's Alisa?"

Drake leaned into the gun.

"Why do you think she's a terrorist?"

Drake raised an eyebrow, perplexed that Ben knew that.

Ben smirked and regained his confidence. "I was outside the apartment listening."

Drake nodded, somewhat impressed. "I see. Well, I bugged your place and had been listening, too. I told Beth what I thought would get me inside."

Ben clenched his teeth. What other personal information did Drake know about him? He lowered the gun and sat back down. "Why do you want Alisa?"

Drake leaned forward. "First, let me ask you a question. Why don't you remember your past lives?"

Ben shook his head. He didn't know.

"I do." Drake sounded like a salesman who had the cure for whatever ailed someone.

The offer tempted Ben.

"I can help you with your memories. I can help you find Alisa too." Drake tilted back in his chair.

"How?"

"You asked why I want Alisa. I'd be remiss not to clarify that it isn't what I want." Drake leaned in again towards Ben as if he was about to share something topic secret. "It is the way it will be. Right now, you have a choice. Join us, or you'll be killed—by me or someone else. If you join, you'll have a life you've only dreamed about. Power, wealth, luxury. Pretty simple decision, I think."

Ben held the gun, but Drake possessed the leverage.

"And let me add one more sweetener to the offer. We won't harm

Alisa."

This resonated with Ben, even if he couldn't fully remember her.

"We just need information from her, that's it," Drake said.

Ben inched closer to Drake, suspicious, but he wanted to believe.

Drake watched with a twinkle in his eye. "That's it. You can trust me."

The words triggered something inside Ben, replaying in his mind but in a different voice. *You can trust me.* Ben knew this man. It was Varus.

A sinister grin crept across Varus's face. Unknown to Ben, he'd been using this time to free himself from his restraints. Without warning or hesitation, Varus cracked Ben with a right hook. He followed with a left. Ben blocked it, but the strike knocked the gun from his hands, sending it sliding into the living room.

The torn duct tape dangled from Varus's hands. He tossed the last bits off as Ben squared off against him. Varus parried a series of punches from Ben, then kneed him in the stomach.

Ben doubled over in pain.

Varus seized his advantage and put Ben in a rear-naked chokehold. Ben flailed as he struggled to breathe.

Varus whispered in his ear. "Go to sleep, Alexander."

Ben's struggles became weaker, but he fought on. Varus whispered again, "We'll take away your pain. We'll end you. It's what you've always wanted. And don't worry about Alisa. After we find her and get what we need, we'll end her, too."

Ben's resistance subsided, both from Varus's bleak message and lack of oxygen.

"You killed my sister."

Ben glanced up, stunned to see Riya awake in the living room with the gun pointed in his direction. Varus jerked him in front as a human shield.

"You killed her, didn't you?" Riya asked with venom in her voice.

"Careful, now. You wouldn't want to shoot an innocent man," Varus said from behind Ben.

Riya had zero interest in negotiating. *Bang!* She fired a shot that fortunately missed Ben, but it also missed her intended target and only winged Varus's shoulder.

Varus shoved Ben at Riya, ducked down, and raced to the side of the kitchen.

Bang! Bang! Bang! Riya fired as Varus launched himself through the window. Shards of glass crashed to the floor. Riya hurried over and glimpsed Varus disappearing into the night. She returned to Ben with the gun trained on him.

Ben collected himself. "Do you remember your past lives?"

"No. Do you?"

Ben rubbed his neck, still catching his breath. "I think so."

"Who are you?" Riya kept the weapon aimed at Ben.

"Ben Preston. I'm a history professor."

"Who is Alisa?"

"I don't know. I just know I need to find her before they do." Ben looked up at Riya, hoping she'd lower the gun.

She eyed him for a moment, then slipped the pistol into her pocket. "We need to get out of here. These people will be back."

Ben struggled to his feet while Riya collected the papers on the table and crammed them into the folder. The picture of Anjali stopped her. Riya grabbed that too and hustled to the front door.

Ben stammered behind her. "We should take my friend's car. They track everything. Credit cards, cell phones, your car. You can't use any of it."

Ben opened the door and surveyed the neighborhood. It was quiet and appeared safe. Together, they hurried down the street to Frank's car. As they reached the door, Ben stumbled and held onto the hood for support.

Riya put the file and picture of her sister in the back seat, then assessed Ben. "You're in no condition to drive."

"I'm fine," Ben said.

"You might have a concussion."

Ben shook off the suggestion. "Are you a doctor or something?"

"A neurosurgeon, actually."

Humbled, Ben handed the keys over and climbed into the passenger seat.

Riya hopped into the driver's seat, turned the ignition, and then hesitated before shifting the car into gear. "Where are we going?"

Ben buckled his seat belt. "We can't go to the police."

"I know. That's how they found me." Riya gripped the steering wheel.

"A motel or something?" Ben asked.

"Yeah, because taking a stranger to a divey motel always ends well." Riya shook her head. "Does this Alisa remember her past lives?"

"I think so."

Riya shifted the car into drive. "I know where to go."

CHAPTER 41

Port Royal, Jamaica, 1665

Sloops and schooners bobbed in the waves, anchored in the port. A rickety boat about half the size of a sloop sailed into the bay and docked. Torches illuminated a shanty town built just beyond the sand. Boisterous laughing and drunken yelling bellowed from several of the establishments. The loudest was a beat-up tavern advertised by a painted sign with three scrawled words, "The Three Tunns."

A bearded man dressed in ratty clothing ambled into The Three Tunns with a noticeable limp. Two flintlock pistols hung on each side of his belt, along with a sheathed dagger. He surveyed the scene and found a raucous, motley crew of privateers, adventure seekers, prostitutes, and barmaids reveling in drunken debauchery. No one gave a second look as he shuffled to the barkeep.

"Ale," the bearded man said.

The barkeep filled a wooden tankard and slid it over. The bearded man left a copper and studied the patrons. He zeroed in on a group of privateers playing a card game with a small pot of money in the middle. He limped over and stood right behind one man. "What 'er ye' playin'?" He said with no worry about manners.

Beeman, a privateer with a perpetual sour-puss face, kept his eyes on his cards. "Who's asking?"

"Name's Edmund."

"Well, Edmund, why don't you piss off?"

The table erupted with laughs and mockery.

Edmund remained where he stood. "Looks like a game for money. Small money, to be sure, but I guess that's something."

Another privateer, Fitzy, took mild umbrage from the dig. "You don't look like Sir Money Bags from where I'm sitting, Edmund."

The group snickered.

"Looks can deceive," Edmund said.

A third privateer, Robert, the most intelligent and refined of the bunch, found Edmund intriguing. "What can we do for ya, Money Bags Edmund?"

"I need a crew."

"What job?" Robert asked.

"Gold. Silver. Jewels," Edmund enticed.

The drunkest man, O'Leary, belched. "Do you have whiskey on this here voyage of treasure?"

"Aye."

"I'm in!" O'Leary giggled at himself.

Everyone else ignored the drunk. Robert pushed for details. "Sounds like the type of cargo that will be guarded."

"Not if we move fast. This treasure is hidden but unguarded," Edmund said.

Beeman scoffed. He didn't like Edmund. "Bugger off, mate. Not interested."

Edmund shrugged with disappointment. "It was worth a shot. Pardon thy intrusion as I did not know ye were a lily."

The revelry at the table stopped.

Beeman stood and eyed Edmund. "What did you say?"

Edmund cleared his throat and stared back at Beeman. "I. Did. Not. Know. Ye. Were. A. Lily."

Beeman withdrew a dagger from his shirt. A hush fell upon the room as other patrons watched, knowing that a fight to the death was about to break out. Beeman wanted to attack, but Edmund's stare unsettled him. He walked with a limp, his clothes were rags, and yet his eyes were like those of a lion ready to pounce.

"You'd be well to know yer place. You don't bring a poking stick to a gunfight, mate." Edmund tapped the handle of one of his pistols.

Beeman's bravado melted.

Edmund had no desire to waste his bullets. That wasn't what he came for. "You can challenge me aim... or you can get rich?"

"How rich?" Beeman asked, not interested in dying this moment.

"More than you'll earn in six lifetimes," Edmund said. "And speaking of six, I need six men. No more. No less. Six. I'll be at me boat."

Edmund limped back out of the tavern. The revelry at The Three Tunns resumed except at the table. The men stared at one another. They had a big decision to make.

Edmund stood on the dock and looked out to sea, smoking a pipe. For all he'd experienced, a moment like this was something he cherished. It was peaceful and honest.

Fitzy, Robert, Beeman, O'Leary, and two other men, Big Henry and Little Henry, named for obvious reasons, walked on the dock.

"You said there's enough treasure for six lifetimes," Robert said.

Edmund savored the taste of the tobacco from the pipe. "Aye."

"And that's for each of us, right?" Beeman asked.

"Aye, mate. You won't have to work for six lifetimes. Not that you'll need that much."

O'Leary belched. "You haven't seen how much I can drink." He guffawed at his own joke. No one else made a peep.

"How do we know we can trust you?" Beeman asked, still suspicious of Edmund, but this offer of treasure tantalized his imagination.

"How do I know I can trust *you*?" Edmund turned to face the men.

Beeman didn't have an answer.

Edmund puffed away. "You can trust me, mate, because there's nothing I value more than loyalty. And if I'm marching you into danger, I'm marching myself in with ya's. If I meant you harm, there's six of you against one of me."

Beeman pointed to Edmund's weapons. "You've got two pistols."

Without hesitation, Edmund tossed one to a stunned Beeman. "If the treasure ain't there, shoot me dead. If the treasure is one penny less than my word, you can have my share. And if you break your word, well, I can at least take one of ya's out." Edmund tapped his finger on his remaining pistol. "Fair enough?"

Fitzy stepped forward. "So, whose treasure are we taking?"

"Does it matter so long as you get rich?"

Robert held up his hand, now worried. "Aye, it matters. We're not stealing from the Crown. We ain't hanging fer this."

Edmund smiled. He had his crew. He enjoyed the last of his pipe as he looked back out to sea. "You don't need to worry about hanging. We're not taking from the Crown."

"So, who are we taking from?" Robert asked.

Edmund exhaled a large puff of smoke. "The Pantheon."

CHAPTER 42

SOUTH CENTRAL LOS ANGELES, 1992

THE SWELTERING SUN beat down on the local park in the ghetto. "Park" was a generous term as it included a broken swing, faded jungle gym, and grass so torched by the heat it was nothing but brown kindling waiting for a spark. The cracked basketball courts had rusted rims with metal nets. Three words summed up the park and its surrounding neighborhood—hard, drab, and depressing. The one ray of hope in this otherwise bleak environment was a lone African American teen working on his jump shop. This was a young, fresh-faced Tom Vance. He had big aspirations, even if he didn't know what he wanted in life, but two things were certain. First, this gloomy existence wasn't for him, and second, he couldn't go through life alone. The world was too big and mean. He needed people he could depend on, people who would have his back no matter what. No one in his circle of supposed friends and family had ever been like that, which left him isolated and dreaming of a way out.

As he continued to work out, two wannabe gang bangers in baggy pants, wife beaters, and black bandanas swaggered on to the court. One was skinny and angry. The other was muscular with a doughy midsection.

Skinny boy called out to Tom. "Yo. You want some kush?"

Doughboy stepped up and gesticulated with his hands like he'd seen in the rap videos. "It's da' bomb, dawg."

Tom didn't respond, too locked into his practice. He shot. Count it.

"Yo," Skinny boy said louder. "I'm talking to you."

"No, thanks. I'm good." Tom continued with his training.

Skinny boy, ever the hustler, pushed for a sale. "You need Mad Dog or a forty?"

Tom shot from further out. Swish. "Nah."

Skinny boy gritted his teeth, frustrated by Tom's lack of interest. Tom dribbled further out, stepped back, and shot. Basket.

Doughboy broke his tough-guy character and marveled at Tom's shooting. "Do you ever miss?"

Tom retrieved the ball and dribbled it between his legs. "Once in a while." Tom shot again and scored.

"You practice all the time?"

Skinny boy smacked Doughboy on the shoulder. "We playing twenty questions or working?"

"I'm building customer relations," Doughboy said.

Tom sized up his next shot. "I read an article about Michael Jordan's net worth. If I earn a fraction of that when I'm in the NBA, I'll be set forever."

Skinny boy rolled his eyes. "You think you're going to the NBA?"

Tom shot from near mid-court. It dropped. "For starters. I'm not sure what I really want."

Tom's arrogance irked Skinny boy. "So, you're just gonna breeze in and out of the NBA?"

"Maybe. Why not? Seems easy enough."

Skinny boy pulled out a Smith & Wesson 357 and pointed it sideways at Tom. "Because of this."

Tom glanced at the gun, not phased in the slightest.

"Look, dawg, I was trying to do you a solid and give you something for your money, but if you ain't buyin', then I'm takin'." Skinny boy cocked the hammer.

"I don't have any money. Not in the NBA yet." Tom heaved up a hook shot. Bucket. Now he was just showing off.

"Then give me your shoes," Skinny boy said.

"What are you going to do with my smelly old shoes?" Tom retrieved the ball and dribbled.

Skinny boy stepped at Tom with menace. "Doesn't matter."

Tom stopped dribbling. "It matters. You want money, right? My shoes ain't gonna get you no money. No one gonna pay for these. Look at the holes." He lifted a foot, revealing cracks along the toe-box.

"I want them because I want them. Now do it!"

Tom's demeanor flipped. He wasn't about to be pushed around by some punk. He moved towards Skinny boy. "Or else what? You gonna shoot me. You want to go to jail for the rest of your life over shoes?"

"You want to be dead over shoes?" Skinny boy put the gun against Tom's forehead.

"Do it." Tom leaned against the barrel of the gun and met Skinny boy's stare.

Skinny boy gritted his teeth. He was being put to the test.

In a flash, Tom cracked Skinny boy's forearm and snatched the revolver. The situation had reversed in a microsecond. In another second, Tom opened the chamber, revealing no bullets. "This piece of junk couldn't fire even if you had bullets." He chucked the garbage gun across the park.

His bluff called, Skinny boy asked, "How'd you know?"

"No one selling forties and stealing smelly shoes has a working gun. Guns are for cowards anyway."

Skinny boy stepped forward like he wanted a fistfight. "What'd you say, dawg?"

Tom tapped his forehead. "This is a real weapon. Why don't you try using it?"

"You want to go?" Skinny boy raised his hands, ready to box.

161

Tom had other ideas. "How much you making slinging that bullshit weed?"

"Two bills, bitch." Skinny boy said.

"A week?"

Doughboy chimed in, "A month."

Skinny boy punched Doughboy in the shoulder.

Tom rolled his eyes. Pitiful. "I got a way to make a lot more if you want to work together."

Skinny boy dropped his fighting façade, not at all the response he expected. "Doing what?"

"First, I need to know I can trust you. Can I trust you?" Tom asked.

"We just threatened to kill you," Doughboy said.

Skinny boy shoved Doughboy.

Tom smiled. He liked Doughboy's honesty and Skinny boy's fearlessness. "We'll work on the trust. What are your names?"

Skinny boy pointed to himself, then to his friend. "I'm Carlos, and this is Ron."

"So, Ron and Carlos, what do you say? Want to work together?"

CHAPTER 43

V<small>IRGINIA</small>, 2018

I<small>N THE DEAD OF NIGHT</small>, Riya and Ben drove. Except for the hum of the engine, it was quiet. Ben reclined his seat and rubbed his neck.

"Are you alright?" Riya asked.

"Fine. My neck and head are a little sore," Ben said as he kept thinking about Varus and his cryptic message. He tried to trick Ben into joining "them," and they wanted to kill Alisa. Why? And why did they think Ben could find her? Questions filled his brain, and as Riya turned on to Tom Vance's bricked driveway, another came to mind. "Are you sure we can trust this guy?"

"He's a congressman."

Ben arched an eyebrow. "We're trusting a politician?"

"He *was* a congressman," Riya said.

Riya pulled up to the gate and rolled down the window. "Look, he remembers past lives like you. He warned me about the people that would try to kill me—the Pantheon. Have you heard of them?"

Ben racked his brain. It sounded familiar, but he couldn't come up with anything concrete, no tangible memories. Just emotions. "Maybe. I don't know."

"Well, he knows," Riya said. "If there's any chance of figure out what's going on, it's with him. He may know about Alisa too." Riya pressed the call button. As she waited, a video camera mounted above one of the brick pedestals turned and pointed right at her.

The gruff voice of Carlos crackled through the speaker. "This is a private residence."

"I'm Dr. Riya Patel, Tom's doctor. I need to speak with him."

"Go away," Carlos said.

"This is important." Riya stared up at the camera. "Let Tom know there's someone he needs to meet."

"Why is that?"

Riya hesitated. "He has the same medical condition that Tom does."

"What condition?"

"I'm sorry, that's something I can only discuss with the patient." Riya threw up her hands to the camera. Nothing she could do. A long silence followed. "Please. This is a matter of life and death."

More silence.

Ben tapped Riya's arm. "Let's go. We'll figure something else out."

Riya dug her nails into the steering wheel and waited until it became awkward. They weren't going to be let in. She shook her head and shifted the car into reverse when the gate opened. Riya smiled at Ben and drove into the compound.

Carlos stood at the doorway and motioned for Riya to pull to the side and park. She followed his directions. As soon as she turned the car off, Ron emerged from the shadows with his gun aimed at them. "Hands raised where I can see them."

Ben held hands to the sky in shock and fear as Ron approached.

"What's going on?" Riya asked with her arms raised.

"Standard security check." Ron pulled Ben out of the car and frisked him. He ripped out Ben's phone, wallet, and then he discovered Varus's gun. "What's this about?"

Ben fumbled for an answer. "Personal safety."

Ron eyed Ben, then patted down Riya. Satisfied, he motioned them to the door.

"Where's Tom?" Riya lowered her arms.

"He's not here, but he said you're welcome to stay until he gets back," Carlos said in a less than inviting tone.

Ben walked up the steps to the door and studied Carlos. He seemed just as scared as Ben.

"Is this how you welcome guests?" Riya asked.

"Or you can leave right now?" Carlos pointed to the gate, unappreciative of the sarcasm.

"When will Tom be back?" Riya asked as she entered the foyer.

"Morning. There's a guest room on the left." Carlos directed them down the hallway.

Ben walked with trepidation. He turned into the guest bedroom, fearful this was all some sort of trap. Upon entering, he found a cozy space with a queen-size bed and a small sofa in one corner. He looked at Riya and exhaled in relief, but then the door slammed shut. A lock clicked into place.

Riya tried the door. It was locked, with no way to unlock it from the inside. She pounded on the door. "Hey! What are you doing?"

Silence.

"Still feel like we can trust the politician?" Ben asked.

Riya banged her fist against the door again.

Ben darted to the window and felt around the frame. He assumed it would be locked like the door. To his surprise, the lock twisted, and it slid open. The cold nighttime air whipped into the room. This wasn't some sort of prison.

Ron and Carlos were afraid of them.

165

CHAPTER 44

THE CARIBBEAN SEA, 1665

EDMUND SURVEYED a tropical coastline through a spyglass as the ocean breeze powered the sloop forward. The crew manned the sails and wheel, guiding the ship through the whitecaps.

"What are you looking for?" Robert asked as he pulled the boom to better angle the sail.

"The sleeping man," Edmund said.

"The what?" Robert eyed Edmund, confused.

Edmund continued searching through the spyglass and then smiled. He limped over to Robert and offered the device. Robert lifted it to his eye and found a rolling hill covered with densely packed trees. The contours of the mounds did indeed resemble a man sleeping on his back.

"The sleeping man." Robert grinned and handed the glass back. They were getting close. "Who are the Pantheon, Edmund?"

"It would take a long time explaining the history of the Pantheon." Edmund walked away. He had no interest in discussing them.

Robert pressed for more information. "Where did they get their treasure?"

"Everywhere," Edmund said. "Take us ashore, lads."

HOURS LATER, the men had traded sailing with the refreshing ocean breeze in their face to hiking in ninety-degree heat and stifling humidity. They trudged through the thick, tropical jungle, swatting mosquitoes with every step. Big Henry lugged an enormous pack with lanterns dangling off the side. The rest carried empty packs and canteens. Despite his handicap, Edmund ambled along without a peep. He led the motley crew to a massive rock wall covered with moss and vines. A second rock about fifteen feet high with rounded corners rested in the middle of the wall.

Edmund ran his fingers around the smooth edges of the stone. "This is it." He said with a twinkle in his eye.

"It's a rock." Beeman threw up his hands, frustrated and exhausted.

Edmund dismissed Beeman's pessimism. "Think of it like a very heavy door." He brushed away the vines and creepers that had grown over the edges. "On the other side of this rock is more than enough treasure for everyone. Each of ya's has a pack. Whatever you put in it is yours and yours alone. Is that understood?" He raised his voice to emphasize the point.

Big Henry nodded. "Sounds fair."

"I'm sure it does." Little Henry shoved Big Henry's huge pack, then appealed to Edmund. "He can carry twice as much."

Edmund had no interest in petty squabbles. He inspected the crack separating the gigantic rock from the apparent stone door. "That's the deal. You don't go into anyone else's bag. Greed will get you killed. Are we clear?"

Everyone in the crew looked at one another and answered in unison, "Aye."

Edmund waved them to the rock. Big Henry put his pack down and went to one side of it. The others, minus Edmund, followed his lead, and

167

together they pushed. As they strained, Edmund removed flint from Big Henry's bag and built a small fire with twigs, other kindling, and a touch of gunpowder.

The men struggled with their footing. The rock didn't budge.

Edmund glanced up, displeased with the effort. "Come on. Come on. Did I bring men or a bunch of wee lasses?"

While glaring at Edmund, the men dug in and pushed harder. The massive rock yielded and rolled, revealing an ominous cave. The men cheered and patted each other on the back.

O'Leary leaned into the darkness. "The treasure!" Fleet-footed, he dashed inside.

"Wait," Edmund called out in a dry tone, making it tough to tell if he intended to stop O'Leary. Regardless, it was too late. The ground swallowed the drunkard. A blood-curdling scream followed, and then a muted thud.

Edmund muttered, "Greed will get ya' killed." He struck the flint, which ignited the gunpowder, and a small fire blossomed.

Fitzy inched towards the cave and discovered a pit that had been covered with sheepskin, twigs, and dirt. "O'Leary?"

"He's dead." Edmund fed more fuel to the growing fire.

Robert looked at the cave, then at Edmund. "Traps?"

"Aye. You best listen to me, mates. There is treasure to be sure, but be careful what you take." Edmund sat back to admire his crackling fire. He used a burning twig to light three lanterns, handed two out, and kept the third for himself. Then he grabbed a small log, lit it on fire, and approached the cave.

As the lanterns and crude torch illuminated the darkness, it revealed an open treasure chest in the middle of the cavern with gold coins spilling out —a sight more alluring than a siren's song.

"Look at that!" Fitzy marveled, his mouth agape.

As the men ogled the booty, Edmund tossed the burning log down into the pit.

"Look at that." Edmund pointed down.

Fifty feet below, spears stuck up from the ground, impaling O'Leary's body and two other skeletons. Others had made this mistake before. Reality set in. The treasure was close, but they didn't have it yet.

Beeman curled his lip with displeasure. "That chest doesn't look like six lifetimes worth of treasure for each of us, Edmund."

"Let's have a closer look-see before you cast judgment." Edmund leaned against the wall and began sidling around the pit. "Step where I step. Touch what I touch."

The others followed single file. After twenty feet, Edmund stopped and pressed down with his foot. The ground bowed down from the weight—another sheepskin covered pit. Edmund inched forward towards the middle of the cave. Solid ground. It became clear from Edmund's zig-zagging that there was a narrow pathway that led to the middle of the cave—a maze of sorts. Edmund continued to sidle around, twisting and turning along the path. He kept his arms out for balance—a slight slip on either side meant death. Almost to the treasure, Edmund stepped down with one foot and broke the false ground, revealing a four-foot gap between the path and the chest. He backed up and ran as best he could with his limp. Edmund launched himself over the chasm and cleared it by inches. He took a moment to collect himself as the others made the jump. With two healthy legs, they hurdled it with ease.

Big Henry smiled with delight and hurried to the chest. "We did it!" He dug his hands into the gold coins.

"No," Edmund said.

Too late, Big Henry triggered another trap. A spring-loaded dagger shot out of the coins and struck him in the chest. He staggered back towards the pit.

Little Henry raced over to help. Big Henry reached out his hand. Little Henry grabbed hold, but physics won as the weight of Big Henry pulled Little Henry down with him into the abyss. A moment later, a double thud.

"If you would all listen to me, maybe ya wouldn't die. I said walk where I walk and touch what I touch! That gold…" Edmund emphatically pointed to the chest. "Do not touch!"

Robert, Beeman, and Fitzy glanced at one another, perhaps regretting the decision to embark on this journey. Edmund searched the back of the pedestal with his foot until he found another pathway. He sidled forward until he reached the back wall.

Beeman threw up his hands. "It's a stupid wall, Edmund. Now what?"

"Always so negative, mate." Edmund traveled along the wall and then disappeared into it.

"Where the hell did he go?" Beeman asked.

Robert followed Edmund's footsteps, stepping where he had. Fitzy went second, and Beeman last. They discovered a crevice illuminated from Edmund's lantern from inside a secret chamber. Squeezed against the rock, they emerged in a massive archaic vault organized with rows of chests. One possessed gold coins from ancient Egypt, another from ancient Rome, a third contained gold bars, and a fourth held silver bars. The final row overflowed with jeweled rings, bracelets, and necklaces. The designs of the jewelry varied from Chin Dynasty dragons to Egyptian scarabs.

Fitzy, Robert, and Beeman stared slack-jawed. This was every pirate's dream and then some. Even Edmund appeared in awe of the wealth displayed before him.

"What say ya' now, Beeman? Is this enough fer ya'?"

"There's more," Beeman said, perhaps the first positive words he'd spoken in his life.

Ready to loot, Robert asked, "Is it safe?"

Edmund nodded. "Aye. Take what ye' can carry. But remember, what you take is yours and yours alone."

The men pulled out their packs and approached the chests with giddy smiles. Fitzy targeted the coins, Beeman the bars, and Robert zeroed in on the jewels.

While they filled their pouches, Edmund searched the back of the vault and found a hidden chest about two feet long, but not very wide or high. Edmund slipped it into his bag.

Beeman eyed Edmund suspiciously but pretended not to notice.

What was in that chest?

CHAPTER 45

SOUTH CENTRAL LOS ANGELES, 1993

STUDENTS AND PARENTS filled the stands of a beat-up gymnasium. The scoreboard displayed tonight's matchup: Compton Raiders versus Bellevue Academy. Poor versus Rich. As the players warmed up, it was easy to tell them apart. Bellevue wore designer blue warmups, while Tom and his teammates sported faded gold jerseys.

Tom held a ball in his hands, stepped back, and took a shot. Clank. Off the front of the rim. A teammate fed him another ball. He let it fly. Airball. Tom grimaced and shook his head. He looked nothing like the kid from the park who made every shot. He seemed either nervous or just bad, which was exactly how he wanted it to appear.

Ron and Carlos lined up bets with visiting fans and even intimidated several prepsters into placing a wager. Ron and Carlos might be wannabe gangsters in Compton, but they were the real deal to Bellevue kids. It also seemed like a no brainer. At worst, the students would owe nothing, and maybe they'd get paid a sucker's bet. Of course, the Bellevue kids were the suckers, even though Compton had zero chance of winning. Bellevue was

171

one of the top high school teams in the country, with an All-American being recruited by all the college blue bloods, but Tom made wagers on things he could control. In this case, it was based on what the Bellevue kids didn't know. The bet was simple enough. Pick a player: Tom or Mr. All-American. Whoever scores more wins.

Was it fair? No, but was it fair the prepsters were born with a silver spoon dangling out of their mouths? Why should they get the best of everything? Tom hated the rich fans. He imagined them looking down on him and thinking they were superior. It served as motivation, even though it probably was all in his head.

Carlos walked down the bleachers to the floor and waved Tom over. With a big grin, he whispered, "We got eight bettors and a little under three grand on the line. We got more than we've made in the entire season."

Tom looked up at the Bellevue supporters. Three grand was nothing. Most wore name brand clothes, and many of the female students carried designer handbags that cost that much. An Asian parent sat with his arms crossed, wearing a polo shirt and khaki pants. Tom focused on this guy and imagined the type of expensive car he drove and the mansion he'd be sleeping in later tonight while Tom went home to his small one-bedroom apartment with less than a grand in his pocket.

"Three grand? Small-time," Tom said.

"It will be a big-time loss, so you better outscore King Kong." Carlos motioned to Reggie Gibbs, the All-American built like a Mac truck.

Tom peeked over. "I ain't worried about him. Line up more bets. We need more money."

"How much is enough?"

Tom went back to his warmups. He didn't ignore the question, but he also didn't have an answer. An unquenchable hunger drove him, and whatever Ron and Carlos lined up would never be enough. As the Bellevue cheerleaders smiled and giggled on the sideline, Tom's anger simmered. It wasn't just money that he craved. He wanted to be on top.

Each team's starters took the court. The two tallest players from each squad prepared for the tip-off. The ref tossed the ball up to start the game, which was knocked to Gibbs. He immediately drove the lane for an easy lay-up. A Compton player in-bounded the ball to Tom. He dribbled down and heaved it up from outside the arc. Nothing but net.

The match continued, and the superiority of Bellevue became apparent. By the fourth quarter, the contest had turned into a rout, but the hidden game between Tom and Gibbs was close. Gibbs had the edge 27 to 22. Coaches usually pulled their starters at this point to avoid injury, something Tom counted on, but Gibbs remained on the court. His teammates on the sideline cheered him on as he closed in on the league's all-time scoring title.

With less than a minute remaining, Gibbs drove the line and skied for a thunderous dunk. The Bellevue supporters and teammates went wild. Tom's world spun, and a pounding headache racked his skull. His entire body felt like it was being tortured. Maybe that's why they called it the agony of defeat.

Tom received the inbound pass and raced down the court. He jumped up from way behind the arc. Swish. A Bellevue player lazily in bounded the ball. Tom saw his moment. He darted towards the ball, intercepted the pass, and laid it up. He was now down two, with fifteen seconds left.

This time, the Bellevue player delivered a firm pass to his teammate. With Compton down fourteen, the rest of Tom's teammates had given up, and several fans filed out. Tom chased the ball, but Bellevue kept passing. Finally, Tom got close enough to lock onto the player's arm. The ref blew the whistle. Foul. Three seconds left. Everyone in the gymnasium, except those in on the bet, seemed perplexed and annoyed. Then Tom saw who he had fouled. It was Gibbs.

Tom's fate was out of his hands as Gibbs stepped to the free-throw line. The first shot dropped along with Tom's head. He was down three, and Gibbs still had his second free throw. Gibbs bounced the ball twice, then shot. The ball arced high in the air, clanked off the side of the rim, and bounced out.

Hope.

The ball fell in the hands of a Compton player, but Tom yanked it away.

He dribbled frantically as the clock counted down. 3-2-1. From mid-court, Tom launched a prayer as the buzzer sounded. The ball sailed through the air and swished. He did it! Elation filled Tom's face, and he dropped to his knees until reality set in. He didn't win. He just didn't lose. And he was lucky.

He thought he had controlled everything, but he was wrong. He underestimated the situation and his opponent.

After the game, Ron and Carlos waited by the bench with scowls on their faces. They needed that money, but they were still there, waiting for Tom. They were loyal. Tom sat on the edge of the bench and took off his sneakers and sweaty socks, revealing large painful blisters. The sight caused something to stir in Tom's mind—a shriek and a cry. A strange voice rang in his head. *Stop. Please. Stop.* Tom doubled over in pain.

"Tom? You okay? Tom?"

Tom glanced up and found a balding white man with a massive beer gut, Mick Majors, towering over him.

"Don't take losing so hard. You played great. Loved how you played until the final whistle." Mick reached out and shook Tom's hand.

Tom wondered what this man wanted. "Thanks. Just got a headache and a couple of blisters. I'm fine."

"I'm Mick Majors. I coach over at MCU. Quite a game. Thirty points, twelve of fifteen shooting. I've been following you this season. I'm very impressed. You going to college?"

"NBA, but I'll make a stop at college." Tom put on a new pair of socks.

Mick smiled. He liked Tom's confidence. "I'd like to offer you a full scholarship if you're interested in playing for me."

Tom glanced over at Ron and Carlos and considered life at college. He'd be alone again with no one he could trust. "I'll consider it, along with the five other offers." Tom stuffed his old socks in his gym bag and stood to walk away, but then paused. "Your offer would be more appealing if you gave my two associates a full ride, too." Tom motioned to Carlos and Ron, who now watched.

Disarmed, but also impressed by Tom's moxie, Mick said, "That's admirable you want to take care of your friends, but I don't think the rules would permit that."

"That's fine. I'll take my talents to Tech. I'm sure they won't mind winning another championship." Tom turned to leave.

"You know what?" Mick said, his tone now more accommodating. "Let me see what I can do. Good to meet you, Tom." Mick passed Ron and Carlos on his way out. "Boys."

As soon as he was gone, Ron and Carlos hurried over to Tom.

"What the hell just happened?" Ron grinned from ear-to-ear and shoved Tom.

"We're going to college. For free," Tom said.

Carlos put his hands over his head and his mouth hit the floor. "My mom is never gonna believe her boy is going to college. Dawg, I'll never doubt you again. That was huge."

Tom shook his head and walked away. "Still small-time."

Carlos and Ron looked at each other. Was Tom serious? Carlos called out, "What's big-time?

Tom wished he knew the answer.

CHAPTER 46

Virginia, 2018

Riya's eyes popped open. Fear grabbed hold as nothing looked familiar. The country quilt wasn't her beige Pottery Barn comforter. The twin-sized bed wasn't her queen. And she definitely didn't have a strange man sleeping on a cramped sofa with his feet spilling off the edges. As she gathered her senses, she remembered. They were at the home of Tom Vance, the patient who could remember his past lives and who was at least partially responsible for getting her fired. This stranger sleeping near her feet had saved her from the mysterious group who murdered her sister. Or, maybe, she had saved him. She covered her face with her hands. Everything was a mess, and nothing felt right.

"You okay?"

Riya glanced up. Ben rubbed the sleep from his eyes, pulled his feet off the couch, and swiveled them around to the floor.

Riya shrugged and offered a forced smile. "Yeah. I'm fine." But she wasn't. Riya didn't know what she should do or who she could trust.

"Should we see if your friend is back yet?" Ben asked.

"He's not my friend, but he should be able to help us."

Ben ambled to the door and pounded. Footsteps clopped on the wood floor outside, then the metallic clanging of the key turning in the lock. Ron opened the door and greeted them with his hand resting on his holstered gun. "What do you want?"

Ben backed away as Riya rose to her feet. "Where's Tom?"

"Not back yet."

"You can't keep us locked in here," Ben said.

"These are Tom's instructions. Safety concerns."

"Safety concerns? How does that make sense?" Riya asked.

Ron didn't have an answer, but that changed nothing.

"Where's Carlos?" Riya looked past Ron into the hallway. Maybe they'd have better luck with him.

"He had some work to do."

Ron's vague answers raised concern. He was concealing something, or he knew nothing. Neither option offered any benefit, and Riya couldn't take the chance that it was the former. "You know what, since Tom doesn't seem to be in a hurry to return, we'll be on our way. If he wants to get a hold of me, have him call me."

"You can't leave," Ron said, with his hand still on his holstered gun.

"The hell we can't." Ben stepped towards the doorway.

Ron moved aside and was careful to keep enough distance between himself and Ben. Riya followed Ben out of the bedroom and hurried down the hallway. She opened the front door. The driveway was empty.

"Where's our car?" Riya asked.

"Tom needed it removed for security reasons."

Riya lost it. That car contained the only photo of Anjali that Riya had access to, and it had the files of all her research about her sister's death. She charged Ron and pointed at him like a mother scolding a child. "I want that car back here now! I had important documents... personal items..."

"Calm down. It's just a precaution. Tom's instructions. You gotta trust him."

Riya stepped closer still. "Trust him? He's not here. We don't know what he's doing, when he's coming back, or if he's coming back."

Ron walked backward down the hallway. "He'll be back. He always keeps his word."

Riya continued to pursue Ron. "Get him on the phone now."

Ron backed up into the wall. With nowhere else to go, he unholstered his pistol and aimed.

Riya positioned herself in front of the barrel, unafraid. "This is the third time you've stuck a gun in my face, and I'm tired of it. Get Tom on the phone."

Ron placed his finger on the trigger.

Ben waved his hand in the line of fire to diffuse the situation. "Just get our car back, Ron. No one needs to get hurt."

Riya didn't back down. Maybe it was because she had just stared death in the face last night, or maybe it was that she didn't believe a congressman would want to explain why his guard killed someone he invited inside. Regardless, Ron had a choice. Pull the trigger or call Tom.

Ron swallowed hard, then pulled out his phone and dialed. "They want to talk to you. They want their car back, too." He listened for a moment and then tossed the phone to Riya.

"Tom?" Riya asked.

"Hello, Riya."

"What the hell is going on, Tom?"

"Be quiet. I warned that you were in danger, didn't I?"

"Yes." Riya drifted around the hallway as she listened.

"I said the Pantheon would come for you, didn't I?" Tom said.

"Yes."

"I told you never to contact me again, and you showed up at my house with a strange guy you just met, correct?"

"Yes."

"So just recapping here. Everything I said has been right, and you went back on your word. Do you want to bring down the Pantheon, or do you want to bring them to my front door?"

"Maybe if I had a little help from you," Riya snapped back.

"Who is this guy?"

"His name is Ben Preston. He needs to find someone named Alisa. Do you know her?"

A long pause. "No. How do you know the Pantheon didn't trick you?"

"He saved me, Tom. I'd be dead if it weren't for him."

"I told you how dangerous they are. You never know who you can trust. You need to keep an eye on this guy."

Riya glanced over at Ben, now a little worried. Who was he? She knew what Ben had told her, but when she woke up from the tainted coffee, it seemed like Ben was about to make some sort of deal with the man that tried to kill her. Then all hell broke loose. Maybe Tom was right.

"I'll be back in two days," Tom said.

Riya's mouth fell on the floor. "You won't be back for two days!"

"Do you want my help or not?"

"You're going to help?"

"Yeah. Two days. Watch him." Click. Tom hung up.

Riya stared at the dead phone, then at Ben.

"He won't be back for two days?" Ben said, incredulous.

Ron lowered the gun. "You gotta trust him. He's a man of his word."

The phone beeped in Riya's hand. It was a text notification from Tom. *Let them out of the room, Ron.*

Riya held up the message as she handed the phone back to Ron. "Guess we gotta trust him."

As Ron read the message, Riya walked past him towards the kitchen.

AN HOUR LATER, Riya sat at the kitchen table, nibbling on a bagel, and sipping coffee she made herself. She'd never trust a drink from anyone else again. With each slurp, she replayed each moment with Tom and Ben. Making matters worse, Ben plopped himself right next to her.

"Do you think Ron and Carlos know? About past lives?" Ben whispered as he subtly pointed to Ron, who watched the television in the living room.

Riya studied Ron. Every so often, he'd glance over at them. He was still "on guard," but oblivious otherwise. She shook her head.

"Why wouldn't he tell them?" Ben asked.

"Maybe he doesn't trust them."

"They sure trust him. They do whatever he says." Ben took his plate to the sink.

Riya considered whether that meant she could trust them, but the idea of relying on the guy who stuck a gun in her face filled her stomach with knots. Everyone around her seemed to be lying or hiding something. Riya wasn't religious, but she prayed for a sign to let her know who she should believe.

The door leading to the garage opened, and Carlos entered.

"Did you get Tom's text?" Ron asked.

Carlos held up his answer—a full garbage bag. He placed it on the kitchen table in front of Riya. "Tom told me to bring this stuff back to you."

Riya looked inside. "The files!" She dug around in the bag until she found the graduation picture with her sister. Unfortunately, the glass was smashed.

"Sorry about the picture," Carlos said.

Riya ran her finger over her sister's image, and she choked up.

Ben glanced at the photo over her shoulder. "She's beautiful."

Riya nodded as she walked into the kitchen, never taking her eyes off the photo. "Anjali was also smart, funny, and... a great doctor." She dumped the broken glass into the trash can. "She didn't deserve—" Something caught her attention as the shards fell into the can. Riya removed the photo and found a zip drive hidden in the frame.

Her prayer had been answered. She could trust her sister.

CHAPTER 47

THE CARIBBEAN SEA, 1665

EDMUND MANNED the wheel of the sloop and enjoyed the soft breeze on his face as the boat cruised along the calm waters. Fitzy, Robert, and Beeman drank ale and sang tunes on the deck below. Every so often, they'd toast their tankards and yell with a drunk cheer followed by a laugh.

Fitzy raised his cup and motioned for everyone's attention. "To our good captain. Thought he was full of shit, but he was full of treasure."

"Here, here." Robert raised his mug.

Even Beeman obliged. Edmund tipped his hat.

"Hey, Captain," Fitzy slurred. "How did you know about all of them traps?"

An interesting question. Edmund steered the wheel as he considered his answer. "If you're going to rob someone, ye' best do yer' research."

Fitzy raised his tankard. "Here, here. To... research!"

The three drunks clanked mugs and toasted to research.

Beeman glanced at Edmund. He then eyed the ladder leading into the hull. "Anyone need a refill?" Beeman didn't wait for a response and climbed down. Below deck, he passed by the galley and headed to the bow, where he found the bags filled with everyone's treasure. Beeman placed his tankard on a barrel, grabbed Edmund's bag, and began rummaging. He discovered coins, jewels, and a couple of gold bars, but not the chest. Where could it be?

"Looking for this?"

Beeman whipped around and found Edmund behind him, holding the small chest.

"All that treasure ain't enough fer ya?" Edmund scowled at Beeman like he did in the tavern—like he could and would kill him. "Remember what I said about greed?"

Beeman swallowed hard. He eyed Edmund's pistol, then considered reaching for his own. "I wasn't gonna take it. Promise. I just wanted to know what's inside."

The air hung heavy and tense, like someone was going to die. Suddenly, Edmund relented and placed the chest down on a crate. "Fair enough. Have yerself a look-see." He waved Beeman over to open it.

With shaky legs, Beeman inched over.

Edmund stepped aside. "Go ahead. It's fine."

Beeman moved towards the mysterious wooden box. It looked old—ancient perhaps and had ornate bronze clasps. He flipped them up, then lifted the top. Beeman's eyes widened as he marveled at the contents. "What is it?"

"Power." In a flash, Edmund kicked Beeman's knee, causing it to buckle, then twisted his neck around, snapping it. Beeman fell dead instantly. Edmund spilled Beeman's drink on the ground beside him and grabbed the chest. He gave one dismissive glance at Beeman, then reached down and reclaimed his flintlock pistol. As he brushed the dust off the weapon, he called out, "Robert, come quick. Something's happened to Beeman."

Edmund waited as Robert climbed down from the top deck. He rushed over and recoiled upon seeing Beeman's lifeless blue eyes gazing up.

Edmund stood in the galley and watched Robert check Beeman's body to confirm what he already knew—Beeman was dead.

"What happened?" Robert surveyed the area. Beeman's mug rolled back and forth on the floor with the rhythm of the waves.

"Not sure. Found him like this. Must've slipped on his drink." Edmund sipped his own stein.

Robert studied Edmund. Both pistols now hung on his belt and his eyes, those cold brown eyes, pierced back, daring Robert to say what he thought. He refused to take the bait. "Beeman wasn't one to be trusted, anyway. Caught him sniffing around my bag earlier."

Edmund held up his stein for a cold-hearted toast. "Then I'd say he got what he deserved. Without trust, there's nothing. Ain't that right?" He took a sip.

Robert nodded in agreement. Fitzy peeked his head down from the top deck. "There's a ship in the distance!"

Edmund and Robert scampered up the ladder. Edmund pulled out his spyglass and scanned the ocean where Fitzy pointed. A massive galleon headed towards them.

"You think it's following us?" Fitzy asked.

Edmund lowered the spyglass. "Aye."

"The Pantheon?" Robert asked.

Edmund looked at Robert, and for the first time, his eyes showed fear. "Aye."

Fitzy paced the deck in fright. "They've got at least sixteen cannons on a ship like that."

"He won't sink his treasure," Edmund said as he rubbed his head, trying to think of a solution.

"Who's 'he'?" Robert asked.

Edmund ignored the question. His mind focused on survival. "We can't outrun a galleon with only three of us manning the sails." Edmund pointed at the shoreline. "We need to go where he can't."

Fitzy and Robert pulled the boom as Edmund jumped to the helm and spun the wheel. The ship swung ninety degrees and now headed towards shore. Edmund glanced back at the galleon—it was closing fast. Edmund searched the coast and pointed. "There. The river."

Fitzy and Robert looked on with fear as the galleon continued to close the gap with its enormous sails engulfed by wind. Someone stood on the deck, but they were too far to make out any detail.

Fitzy scanned the water along the side of their boat. Panicked, he shouted, "We're passing over a reef! We're gonna run aground!"

With masterful skill, Edmund guided the ship. "Pop the jib, thirty degrees starboard!" Robert and Fitzy followed the order. Edmund spun the wheel, and the boat split an opening in the reef.

"Fifteen degrees port!"

Robert and Fitzy executed the command. Edmund steered the ship into the mouth of the river. They survived—for the moment, at least.

Robert exhaled. "Nice work, Captain. They can't follow us upriver."

"Not with that ship. Load the treasure in the dinghy," Edmund said.

Robert and Fitzy looked at Edmund, confused.

Edmund hopped down from the helm. Danger still lurked. "There's not gonna be enough wind. Hurry!"

Robert and Fitzy disappeared below deck. The sails fluttered and fell as the trees along the river blocked the wind. The boat slowed to a meander.

Robert and Fitzy emerged with their packs. Edmund hurried into the hull, reached behind a barrel, and withdrew the hidden chest. He tossed it in his pack and left.

Robert and Fitzy waited in the dinghy. Edmund climbed down, tossed his pack in the middle, and grabbed an oar. He motioned Robert and Fitzy to do the same. "Row as if your life depends on it because it does."

All three dipped their oars into the water and got to work.

"Where are we going?" Fitzy asked, his arms straining.

"Just row," Edmund said, not wanting to waste a breath or energy talking.

For the next two hours, the men rowed in silence, each man lost in his thoughts. They traveled up the river, destination unknown. As the men fatigued, each paddle became weaker and less frequent. The blazing sun didn't help either.

Fitzy cracked first. "I need a break." He pulled his oar up and slumped over for a much-needed rest.

Edmund was as tired as Fitzy, but the penalty of capture drowned out his body's cry for mercy. "We have to keep rowing."

Robert raised his oar and took a deep breath. "We've been rowing for hours."

Edmund didn't have time to argue. He scanned the shoreline and spotted a beachhead covered by tree branches. "Take her ashore."

The trio paddled and maneuvered the boat into the trees and onto the sand. Edmund grabbed his pack, hopped out, and limped into the forest at a fast march.

Fitzy watched Edmund's unrelenting energy with despair. "We need a rest, Edmund."

"No. He doesn't rest."

"Who?" Robert asked.

Without turning back, Edmund charged on. "We must keep going."

Hearing the urgency in Edmund's voice, Robert and Fitzy heeded the warning. They pulled their bags over their shoulders and set out into the woods.

After miles of trudging through trees, vines, and creepers, Robert and Fitzy were on the verge of giving up. Mercifully, Edmund spotted an unusual group of rocks and pointed. "There!"

With the end in sight, Robert and Fitzy mustered the strength to complete the hike. When they reached the rocks, Robert looked around. "You think we're finally safe?"

Edmund nodded. Fitzy sprawled out on the ground, breathing heavy but thankful. Robert took a knee, grateful to be off his feet. Edmund leaned against a rock.

"Edmund, who are we running from?" Robert asked.

Fitzy rolled over and faced Edmund. "I thought we were running from the Pantheon."

"We are. We're running from the creator of The Pantheon. And that was his personal vault."

"One man had all that?"

Edmund nodded.

Robert scratched his head. "How is it I've never heard of someone that wealthy?"

"You've heard of him, mate. You just didn't know it was him."

Robert and Fitzy eyed each other, puzzled. Edmund had a habit of answering most questions with responses that raised more questions. He pulled out the chest from his pack and then handed the bag to Robert and Fitzy. "This is for the both of ya's."

Fitzy opened the bag and found jewels and gold coins. "This is your share."

"I told you, loyalty is something I value. Trust me when I tell you that loyalty is rarer than the treasure in that bag, so take it." Edmund motioned to the chest in his hands. "This is what I came for."

"What is it?" Fitzy sat up, intrigued.

Edmund looked Fitzy and Robert square in the eye. "This is very important. He can't have this. Ever."

Robert stood up. "What is it?"

"This is how he keeps his power. I need your help burying this here chest." Edmund tapped the ground with his foot. "And I need your word that you won't ever come looking for it. Do I have your word?"

Robert and Fitzy looked at one another, then nodded.

CHAPTER 48

Mid Central University, 1997

Manicured jacaranda trees, Bermuda grass, and stone pathways created a relaxed atmosphere on MCU campus, even though it was located in the heart of a bustling city. Students ambled to and from classes, while some hung out in front of the dormitories.

Inside Vanholm dormitory, a five-story modern building, Tom lay in his room with the shades drawn. A pillow covered his face, but it couldn't stop his mind from tormenting him. It was as if Tom had a severe case of tinnitus, but instead of a constant high-pitched ringing, horrific screams echoed in his ears. Strange images accompanied the shrieks, and since he started college last year, they'd gotten worse. Things flared up as the relationship with his coach soured. During the recruitment process, it was all sunshine and rainbows with Mick Majors, but since Tom's arrival on campus, the coach had turned into a taskmaster who demanded more each day. If they lost, Coach Majors belittled Tom and put the defeat on his shoulders, even though he was the best player and leading scorer. Winning was the only acceptable outcome. If Tom realized his dream and became like Michael

Jordan, he now recognized he'd still have a coach and team owners controlling him. He was their puppet, and if he made millions, they'd make ten times that.

Ron and Carlos opened the door without knocking and flicked on the lights.

Tom winced and shielded his eyes with his hand. "What the hell? Turn it off."

Carlos sat in the only chair in the room. "Yo, Tom, Coach is asking about you."

"I got a headache, man."

Carlos fiddled with the mouse next to the computer on Tom's desk. "He's getting pissed. You've been missing practices."

Tom rolled over. "How does he expect me to play like this? I can't even get a good night's sleep."

Ron stood with his hands in his pockets. "He said he's gonna pull our scholarships if you don't play."

Tom rolled back over. "Would that matter? You dumb asses don't even go to class."

Carlos continued to tinker with Tom's computer. "Why do we need to go to class if we're going to the NBA?"

Tom rubbed his head. "We're not doing that anymore."

Carlos dropped the mouse. "What?"

"The NBA is small-time, man."

Carlos stood up. He'd had it. "This is bullshit. Everything is small time. You told us we'd be rich. We followed you here."

Tom snapped back, "That's right. You follow me. If you didn't, you'd still be slinging dope for chump change."

"You gave us your word, Tom," Ron said.

This struck a chord with Tom. "You still smoking the kush, Carlos?"

Carlos looked down at his feet. Guilty.

Tom reached out his hand. "Give me some of it."

A HALF DOZEN conference championships hung from the rafters of Felski indoor stadium. On the court, the basketball team warmed up for practice. Ron and Carlos slipped in the back and sat in the bleachers. Coach Mick watched from the sideline as Tom trotted by with a stupid grin on his face.

"Nice of you to show up today, Tom."

"Feeling a lot better today, Coach. Thanks for asking."

"You better be feeling good. We got Tech in two days."

Even high on marijuana, Tom seethed as Mick ordered him around. He doubted his tubby coach could run one lap with his massive beer gut, let alone play an actual game. Tom giggled at the thought of his coach wheezing, trying to keep up with him.

Mick blew his whistle, and the team huddled up. "A-Team on offense. B-Team on defense. Remember ball movement. We gotta be faster with our passes." Mick blew the whistle again. The team split and lined up in their positions. Naturally, Tom prepared to go on offense.

The point guard dribbled, and a defender engaged. Tom cut and received a pass. He stepped back and pulled up for a jumper. Basket.

"Easy." Tom kept his hand raised in a shooting pose.

His defender eyed him. Mick pointed to Tom's spot on the court. "That's a low percentage shot. If you miss, we're not in position for a rebound. Look for the extra pass. Go again."

The players reset, and this time the offense passed the ball around, but as soon as it got in Tom's hands, he launched a wild-looking shot. Swish.

"Easy peasy," Tom said as he pretended to brush a little something off his shoulder.

His defender bristled.

"What the hell was that?" Mick asked.

"Two points," Tom said.

"Come on, Tom. You're not going to take that in a game. Do it again."

They reset the play. Tom received a pass, turned, and from a deep three, swished it.

"I'm on fire." He blew on his fingertips and mocked his defender. "You like that one?"

His defender gritted his teeth.

"Again!" Mick blew the whistle for a restart.

The A-Team reset. They passed the ball around, and when it reached Tom, he elevated for a high jump shot. His defender launched himself to challenge the attempt, but his momentum propelled him through Tom's legs.

Tom landed awkwardly, and his knee buckled. He grabbed it in agony. "Oh shit. My knee! My knee!"

Mick hurried over as Tom writhed on the floor in pain. From the bleachers, Ron and Carlos looked sick—like they'd just witnessed someone die.

TOM RESTED in a hospital bed with his knee bandaged after surgery. Ron and Carlos walked in, nervous to see their friend, who was also their meal ticket.

Carlos kept his worry in check and radiated confidence as he fist-bumped Tom. "What's up, dawg? How you feel?"

"Great. Pain meds are working. Been sleeping like a baby."

Ron strolled to the edge of the bed. "Doc said the surgery went well."

Tom nodded. A moment of silence followed as Ron and Carlos stared at Tom's bandaged knee—the elephant in the room. "Ron and I have been doing some reading," Carlos blurted out.

"That's new." Tom snickered.

Ron stepped to the other side of the bed. "For real. We've been reading the NCAA rules. You can take a medical red-shirt, and by next season, you should be all good. NBA is just delayed one year."

Tom remained quiet. Frustration swirled inside. He was tired of having people boss him around, and he hated that a coach could dictate his future. Even with the right coach, a random injury could ruin everything.

"What is it, dawg?" Carlos asked.

"Something is telling me this isn't the path for us."

Ron and Carlos glanced at one another. Not this again.

"I know I told you we'd go to the NBA, but that was so you could get money, right?"

Ron and Carlos nodded.

An idea had been percolating in Tom's head. It was crazy, but it was an idea. It was time to take control of his destiny.

"There are other ways. And I can get you even more money—and power."

"What are we gonna do about money today?" Carlos rubbed his head in frustration. Their immediate financial situation was dire.

"You gotta trust me, Carlos."

Carlos sat in the chair for guests and dropped his head down. "We're gonna lose our scholarships. We'll be back on the streets."

Tom tapped his brain. "We've got insurance."

"Yeah, yeah, I know, having an education is insurance against something like this."

"Yes. And I have actual insurance."

Ron smacked Tom's shoulder. "What the hell are you talking about?"

"I insured myself. Against injury."

"You can do that?" Ron asked.

Carlos leaned forward. "How much?"

"A million."

Carlos's and Ron's eyes widened.

"You trust me now?"

Carlos smiled. "Hell yeah, dawg."

"Good, because for what I have in mind, I need you both to educate yourself. You're going to become refined. Well-spoken. Genteel."

"What the hell? Where are we going instead of the NBA?" Ron asked.

Tom replied with three simple words, "The White House."

CHAPTER 49

Virginia, 2018

After a grueling adventure, Tom arrived home with bug bites and scraped hands, but he didn't care. Things were looking up. After so many years, he finally had a chance at the power he'd sought, but he needed to remain calm. Tom couldn't make the same mistakes as before. He had to see all the angles this time. Who was Ben? Was it possible he stumbled upon someone with the gift?

He entered through the front door carrying two duffel bags and a pistol in his pocket. After dropping the bags in his study, he went into the living room. Ron and Carlos jumped to their feet, swaggered over, bumped fists, and gave Tom a bro-hug. "Yo. Glad you're back," Carlos said.

"I told you I'd be back." Tom stared in the kitchen at Ben and Riya, who stood up from the table.

"Never had a doubt," Carlos said.

Tom motioned to Ron and Carlos. "Guys, meet me in my office."

Ron and Carlos disappeared into Vance's study. Tom walked over to Ben and looked him up and down. His assessment: Ben didn't seem like much, but he knew better than anyone that underestimating people had dire consequences. Still, Ben wasn't at all what he expected. Most people with the gift remember their past lives when they're a teen. Ben was middle-aged. Tom knew how he'd blocked his past for so many years, and he also knew the reason. Maybe the same thing happened to Ben. Or maybe Ben was hiding something.

"Ben, I presume."

Ben nodded.

"So, what do you remember—about your past?"

Ben took a deep breath. "I think I was Alexander of Macedon."

The words hung in the air. They sounded odd and impossible, but they were the truth. With each second that passed, it became more uncomfortable as Tom studied Ben, his face showing zero emotion.

"Did you know—" Riya corrected herself. "Do you know him, Tom?"

"No."

But that was a lie. Tom did know Alexander, and he hated him.

CHAPTER 50

THE CARIBBEAN, 1665

THE CANOPY of lush trees concealed anything and anyone below it. Edmund studied the treetops and listened for any human sounds. A slight breeze rustled through the leaves, and cuckoos squawked to one another. Nothing else. He turned to Fitzy and Robert, who shoveled dirt out of a giant hole about six feet deep.

"That's enough," Edmund said.

"Finally." Fitzy leaned on his shovel and exhaled.

Edmund handed the chest down to Robert, who held it gingerly. What mysterious item was in it?

"I have your word, aye?" Edmund asked.

Robert and Fitzy eyed one another—a moment of doubt, perhaps. "You do indeed." Robert placed the box in the deepest part of the hole.

As soon as he turned to climb out, he found Edmund's two flintlock pistols pointed his way. He opened his mouth to plead. Too late. *Boom! Boom!* Fitzy took a bullet to the head and dropped dead. Robert was shot in the chest and fell on his back. He clutched the injury and struggled to breathe.

Edmund heaved the bags of treasure into the hole and then started shoving the pile of loose dirt on top. Terror spread across Robert's face as more rained down. Covered up to his neck, he stared up at Edmund with his last bit of energy, praying for mercy.

"Sorry, mate. I've been burned before. I don't trust ya'." Edmund sent more dirt down and covered up Robert's face.

CHAPTER 51

Washington D.C., 2017

Senator Hugh Howley, late 60s, Caucasian, intimidating, and dressed in a sharp, custom black suit, tapped his finger on the armrest of an Italian leather chair. Two aides sat on his right. Congressman Tom Vance sat across from him on the other side of the teak coffee table. U.S. flags and photographs of Howley posing with various world officials adorned the walls of his office. Given the rigid posture of the aides, this meeting carried serious significance. In a display of position and confidence, Hugh leaned back and stared at Tom as if he was evaluating him. Tom leaned back in his chair as well and attempted to exude greater confidence. It was like a weird stand-off where one had to appear more relaxed and comfortable to gain the upper hand. Tom might have won were it not for the dark bags under his eyes.

Hugh gazed across his office and out the window to maintain an aura of indifference. "If that damn health care bill isn't passed, there will be hell to pay. I've heard Gaines is waffling in his support."

Tom remained calm. "It won't happen. I have his ear. He knows the consequences if he doesn't support it."

"Good." Hugh crossed his legs. "Let's talk about the future."

Tom mirrored Hugh and crossed his legs. "Let's."

With steely grey eyes, Hugh glared at Tom. "I know what you want. You know I can help you get it. But here's the thing, I don't endorse losers, so if I'm backing you for president, I need to know you're gonna win."

"I have the support of the minorities," Tom said.

"Obviously."

"I've raised the minimum wage, so I've got the working class—"

Hugh interrupted, "You don't need to sell me on your political record. Are you still using? Because Americans don't vote for druggies, Tom."

The words stung, but Tom refused to let it show. "No. Nothing."

Hugh glowered at Tom. "At present, you don't look like the picture of a president."

Tom exhaled, the only sign of genuine emotion. His fatigue came from a variety of reasons, including having to suck up to people like Hugh. Once he was president, he could stop the charade. He would be on top. Hugh would answer to him. "I'm just tired from pushing this health care bill through."

Hugh grunted.

"Check my test results from the last six months if you don't believe me."

Disinterested, Hugh shrugged. Tests could be cheated.

Tom leaned forward to argue his case. "I only used marijuana, which will be legal soon. And no one knows about it, anyway."

Hugh shook his head and smirked. Not a positive sign for Tom. "They always find out. You know that."

"Good. The only reason I used was because of the pain from my knee. By the time the election rolls around, I'll be three years sober. People will rally behind someone who overcame adversity."

A valid point Hugh hadn't considered. "What other skeletons are in your closet?"

"There's nothing, Hugh."

"There's always something, Tom." Hugh leaned in, his tone now cold and calculated. "Here's the deal. Tell me now, and we figure out if we can work with it, but if I find out later, you will not be the Democratic nominee for President of the United States. You can guaran-damn-tee that."

"Hugh. There's no—"

Hugh raised a finger and cut him off. "Go home. Think hard about who is coming for you. Who will want to take you down if you run for the most powerful position in the world? And most importantly, how are they going to do it? We clear?"

There was only one answer Hugh would accept. Tom bit his tongue and nodded.

TOM RODE IN HIS SUV, chauffeured by Ron. He leaned against the side of the car as it pulled into the driveway of his estate. He exited the vehicle, slogged into the house, tossed his briefcase by the door, and entered the living room, where he collapsed onto the couch. Something other than fatigue bothered him. He was so close to achieving his goal, and maybe that's why he was so worried, afraid something could take it away. What was he missing? How could he lose the presidency?

Carlos emerged from the kitchen munching on a granola bar.

Tom perked up. "You get it?"

Carlos handed him a bag with a strange plant inside.

Tom studied the light green, bulbous shrub. "You sure this won't show up on any of the drug tests?"

Carlos took a bite of his bar. "Peyote is used so rarely they don't screen for it. And it should definitely help those headaches."

Tom handed the bag back and stood. "Okay. Cook it, prepare it, or do whatever I got to do to take it. I'm going to get ready for bed." He ambled like a zombie into his bedroom. He needed sleep. Since kicking his marijuana habit, his nightmares resumed with a menace. At first, they were irregular and woke him up maybe once a night, but they'd increased in intensity and frequency.

After throwing on a pair of sweatpants and T-shirt, he drifted to the edge of his bed, slumped into it, and held his head. The voices already swirled, almost taunting him. Soon, he'd be asleep, and they'd have him.

Carlos entered with a cup of "tea." He handed it to Tom, who eyed the brown liquid with unease. "You drink it?" Tom took a sip and grimaced. "That's nasty."

"You're not drinking it for the taste."

"Yeah, if I focus on the taste, it will definitely make my headache seem less terrible." Tom held the cup as far from his nose as possible.

"You're welcome, by the way." Carlos exited.

Once alone, Tom took one more look at the disgusting liquid, then chugged it. He leaned back in the bed, held his head, and rocked back and forth to comfort himself. Hugh's voice played in his mind. *Who will want to take you down?* Tom closed his eyes. *Who's coming for you?* He let go of his head and found calm. The tea was working! A smile crept across his face until an ominous voice shattered the moment of Zen.

I'm coming for you.

Tom scanned the room. Who was that?

I will find you just like before.

Tom looked all around for the source of the voice.

Here I am.

Tom turned left. Nothing.

Here.

Tom turned right.

The voice laughed. *I've already got you.*

Tom grimaced in anguish as his feet blistered and melted. His fingers fell off one by one and tumbled to the floor. Blood poured out of his eyes. The voice cackled louder.

Tom staggered to his feet. "Help me!"

He put his weight down on his injured feet, and they buckled. He fell forward and cracked his head on the base of the bed.

Carlos and Ron rushed into the room. Tom was semi-conscious, and his feet, hands, and eyes were all uninjured. It had all been in his head.

Ron patted Tom's face. "Tom. Tom!"

A semi-conscious Tom whimpered in despair. "I know what I need."

"What? What do you need?" Ron asked.

Tom passed out.

CHAPTER 52

Tom sat behind his desk with his hands clasped together and placed under his chin. With glazed eyes staring down, he could've been praying, but he wasn't. Memories raced through his mind, and strategies percolated. Ron and Carlos sat in the chairs on the other side of the desk and looked at Tom, confused.

"Yo. Tom? You alright?" Ron asked.

"Yeah, I'm fine."

"What's going on, Tom? Who are these people, and why are you helping them?" Carlos asked.

"The doctor said this guy has the same condition as you, but I thought they cleared you of cancer," Ron said.

"You know that trust is something I value more than anything. You both have stood by me, even when things haven't gone as planned."

"We always got your back, dawg," Carlos said.

"I need you to continue to trust me, but I can't tell you more until I get more information from them. Are you okay with that?"

Ron and Carlos looked at each other. In all the years, Tom had said some cryptic things, but this was the most bizarre.

Tom expected they might require a little convincing. He placed one of the duffel bags on the desk and motioned for the two of them to open it. Carlos unzipped the bag, revealing stacks of hundred-dollar bills. Both Ron and Carlos stared in awe.

"Where'd this come from?" Ron asked.

Tom smirked and leaned back in his chair. "An old relative. An inheritance of sorts. I needed time to sort the paperwork and sell some of the assets. There's more where that came from, too."

Carlos flipped through a stack of cash. "Yo! This is huge."

"What's in that one?" Ron pointed to the other duffel bag under the desk.

Tom grew serious. "That one is for me." He studied Ron and Carlos for any sign or glimmer of betrayal. Anything less than total obedience was unacceptable. "Are we good?"

"Yeah. We got you," Carlos said.

WHILE TOM HAD his private meeting with Ron and Carlos, Riya sipped coffee in the kitchen and Ben paced back and forth in the living room. Like Tom, Riya thought about her memories, most of which were about Anjali. She also assessed Ben, trying to find any hint of deception and manipulation.

"What do you think he's doing?" Ben asked.

"I don't know," Riya said.

"He's gone for days and then meets with his guards behind closed doors. What do you think they're saying about us?"

"I don't know." Riya took another sip of coffee and wondered the same thing.

Ron and Carlos walked out of the study and into the living room. "Tom's ready to see you both."

Riya stood up and held up her hand to stop Ben. "Let me have a moment with Tom, okay?"

Ben opened his mouth to object, but Riya started down the hallway and disappeared into the study. She closed the door behind her.

Tom startled as he stuffed something back into the remaining duffel bag. "Where's Ben?"

"I wanted to talk to you first."

"Okay. I'm all ears."

"What are you looking to do here?" Riya asked.

"I offered to help, remember?"

"Yeah, I remember. A few days ago, you wanted to get rid of me as quickly as you could, but now you want to help."

"If you don't want my help—"

Riya interrupted, "I want to know what changed."

Tom leaned back in his chair, and his eyes bore down on Riya. "I don't trust easily."

"What?" Riya asked, confused by the bizarre statement.

Tom remained like a statue, still staring, still studying. "I don't trust people. Not anymore."

"You can trust me," Riya said, thinking that's what Tom needed to hear.

Tom leaned forward. "Here's the problem with trust. You never know who you can really trust, but you definitely know who you can't."

Tom's statement felt like a test and implied so many things, including that he didn't trust Riya. She weighed her response. "Can I trust you?" It was a loaded question, and one she hoped would reveal something of an honest answer. Based on Tom's description of trust, she knew she couldn't. If he said "yes," she'd know the truth.

"Of course not. We just met. The only thing you can trust is whether we have the same interests," Tom said.

"And?" Riya asked.

"Like you, I want to take down the Pantheon," Tom said.

Riya considered the leap of faith she'd been debating for the last two days. "I think I know how we can."

Tom leaned forward further and furrowed his brow. "How can we bring them down?"

"We expose them and show people who they are, so they can't hide in the shadows anymore. We make them answer for their actions."

Tom chuckled. "The Pantheon has remained hidden for thousands of years. What are you going to do? Call up a newspaper and say there's this group that remembers past lives, and they've been manipulating the world for centuries? Who's going to believe that?"

"The Pantheon killed my sister because she proved past lives exist, so clearly, there is a way to prove it."

"If only you knew how they did it."

Riya pulled the zip drive from her pocket. "I found this hidden in the frame of my sister's picture. I think it's her research."

Tom held out his hand. For a moment, Riya debated whether to give it to him. He couldn't be trusted, but he wanted to take down the Pantheon. She placed the drive in his hand. He inserted it into his computer and clicked the mouse to pull up its files. The first document showed a schematic of a device. Riya hovered over Tom's shoulder and studied it, hoping it was the proof she needed. Tom pulled up another drawing that depicted a brain with marks showing electrode placement. He opened a patient dossier that included JPEGs. The first photo revealed an image of El Castillo, the famous Mayan temple. Priests stood atop the structure with arms outstretched to the sky. The brilliant white stones weren't weathered or faded from time. It wasn't a painting, and it wasn't photoshopped. It was a real image from the time of the Maya.

Riya marveled at the work and put the pieces together. "They figured out how to convert brain waves into images. Tom, we *can* prove past lives exist."

Tom processed the revelation, but there was no joy or elation.

"Did you hear what I said? We can stop the Pantheon."

"What are you doing to do with this?" Tom asked.

"What do you mean? We're going to use it to bring them down," Riya said.

"You know what they did to keep this secret. You don't think they'll do that again?"

Tom's aggressive response perplexed Riya. How could Tom not see the power of this information? "We can send it to the press. We can post it on the internet. YouTube. Everywhere. They can't kill everyone."

Tom shook his head. "They'd find a way to dismiss it."

"How could they do that?"

"Every time you post that..." Tom pointed to the screen. "You do it from a computer—something they can trace. They will find us, kill us, and then take down the posts. Most people won't believe it, and anyone who does, they'll eliminate. They don't view murder the way we do. They don't care who they kill. You, of all people, should know that."

A lump formed in Riya's throat. She couldn't believe Tom would use the death of her sister to scold her. His reluctance also raised a red flag. Maybe he didn't want to bring down the Pantheon. She reached down and snatched the zip drive from the computer.

"How will you ever stop them if you don't try?"

Tom clasped his fingers together and placed them against his chin. "Even if this discovery got out into the world, you'd still need to use it on them to show what they did, right?"

"I suppose."

"How can you do that if you don't know who they are? If you want to bring justice to your sister, we need to find them first. I suspect Ben can help with that, but we need to find out who he really was. We're going to find them, Riya, but you have to trust that we're at least on the same side."

She didn't. She trusted nothing about Tom. It seemed these people with past lives all had secrets, and they had all learned how to manipulate and lie brilliantly. In that instant, Riya knew she'd better learn how to do the same.

"I do, Tom."

CHAPTER 53

India, 328 B.C.

A PEACEFUL VILLAGE of mud huts sat tucked along the bend of a winding, sleepy river. Inside one home, a bearded man in a turban, Anga, eyed a fifteen-year-old girl dressed in a simple tan sari. He circled and assessed her, then groped her breasts non-sexually. The girl looked to her mother and father for help, but they stood by and watched. Anga pawed her hips like he was evaluating an animal, then shrugged, unimpressed. One final judgmental stare at the girl, then he turned to the father and nodded. They had struck a deal.

The girl's eyes dropped, crestfallen.

Weeks later, the villagers gathered for a wedding—the union of Anga's son, Mahendra, and the scared girl. Both were now dressed in attire extravagant only relative to their daily clothing. The girl wore a sari, dyed bright red from madder berries. Together, they performed the sacred Saptapadi ceremony, circling a holy fire seven times while stating their vows.

After the service, the village celebrated—one of the few moments in these people's lives where everyone laughed and smiled. Happiness was all around, except for the young bride. Her distant eyes traveled to some place in her mind, far away. Anga led her and Mahendra to their new mud hut. He waved the newlyweds into the home to consecrate the union. The girl eyed her new father-in-law with contempt but proceeded inside. Anga gave his son a sly grin, then closed the flap on the hut and shouted for the party to resume.

When night fell and the deed had been done, the girl laid awake with her back to a sleeping Mahendra. Filled with resentment, the girl hated her existence. None of this was her choice, but choice was not the way of the world she had been born into. Her subsistence village survived by placing needs and obligations over wants and desires, which meant defined roles. The men farmed and hunted. The women cooked, brought water from the river, built mud huts, and made babies. They were supposed to be thankful to the gods that they'd existed for five generations in relative peace because marauders and barbarians had attacked most villages in the area. When that happened, the men were killed, and the women were abused and sold into slavery. Given those options, the fifteen-year-old girl understood why she should be grateful, but she wasn't.

Now married to a boy she didn't care for, her reality would be the same thing every day until the day she died or became too decrepit to carry water pots. Nausea filled her stomach as this sank in, but she willed herself to sleep and to an enchanting dream she'd had since she was thirteen. An effective coping mechanism, it filled her with hope, even if it was just a dream. Every once in a while, she'd experience a nightmare of times and places similar to this reality. Those nights were the worst. Over time, she trained her mind to have this one special dream. She made it feel so real, and with each dream, she'd add extra details and experiences.

Over the next several years, the girl grew into a beautiful young woman. Her name was Alisa, the woman who would one day save Alexander the Great from the barbarians.

ALISA SLEPT, lost in her wonderful dream, when something tugged on her hand. Her eyes popped open, and she found her mother-in-law, Bahula, hovering over her. Missing most of her front teeth, Bahula wasn't winning any beauty prizes, but she possessed a kindness that Alisa appreciated.

"We start breakfast," Bahula said with a toothless grin.

Alisa forced a smile, then trudged out of the hut. The ancient rat race had begun, and it was the same race she'd run for the last four years. Alisa took two clay pots and began the march down to the river. She passed a neighbor's hut. A thirteen-year-old girl, Maya, peeked out, snatched her own pots, and joined Alisa on the journey. Born with a deformity in her right leg, Maya walked with a severe limp.

"What happened in your dream this time?" Maya asked excitedly. Hearing about Alisa's dreams had become entertainment for Maya.

Alisa smiled. Maya reminded Alisa of herself at that age—still energetic and naïve, not jaded by the cynicism of the future that awaited her. Alisa didn't dare reveal her true feelings about her actual world. "I always talk about my dreams. Tell me about yours."

Maya looked down at her feet. "I dream of getting married, but my parents can't find me a husband." She glanced at her deformed leg, ashamed. Marriage was a union to ensure survival, so parents didn't want a daughter-in-law who might bear children with the same ailment.

Alisa pursed her lips. She hated that Maya carried such thoughts. "Why do you need to get married? I'm married and look." She held up her pots. "We're both carrying these."

"Yes, but you have someone to care for you. And one day, you'll have kids," Maya said, then realized her blunder.

Most women Alisa's age had multiple children. That she had none had become the talk of the village. In such instances, the woman was always to blame. Alisa couldn't tell folks she was grateful she didn't have kids, especially girls. She also couldn't tell them that her husband had little interest in her, which suited her just fine. She suspected he had a closer relationship with his childhood friend.

"I suppose. But don't you think you have more to offer than this?" Alisa motioned again to the pots.

"Maybe, but right now, I just want to hear about your dream."

Alisa smirked and launched into the latest story. The two ventured further into the forest and reached the river as Alisa finished her tale.

"Why do you think you have your dream?" Maya asked.

Alisa paused. It was something she'd asked herself many times. "I think it is from the gods. They're letting me know I'm meant for something more. We both are."

"What is it you want to do?"

"I don't know, but I know I can do more." Unsatisfied with her own answer, Alisa thought longer about Maya's question. "I want people to look at me like I matter. *I* want to feel like I matter."

The sorrow in Alisa's voice caught Maya by surprise. Alisa realized that her words implied that she and Maya didn't matter, which was the exact opposite of what she wanted Maya to believe. "But I know we do, Maya. And somehow, I'm going to prove it to you."

Alisa forced a smile and put her arm around Maya's shoulder. She squeezed to provide comfort and make her believe the words, even though Alisa needed it even more. She let go, tiptoed into the river, and bent down to fill her pots. The cool water danced across her fingertips. These simple moments provided a serenity and kindness to a world she despised.

"What do we have here?" A gravelly voice shattered the calm.

Alisa and Maya startled. They looked up and found a grotesque heathen with mangy hair towering over them. His name was Tirdad.

"It's going to be a good day." He growled with a mischievous grin.

He raised a fist to the sky. Hundreds of men, armed with clubs and swords, emerged on the other side of the river. Before Alisa had time to react, Tirdad cracked the back of her skull with the butt of his sword.

She was out cold.

CHAPTER 54

PONTIC STEPPE, 287 B.C.

BLACKNESS AND SILENCE. Then, a muffled noise. Over time, the obscured sounds became more frequent and clear. Streaks of color broke through the darkness. Then, a small circular white light appeared far off in the distance. It grew larger until the black had been swallowed by this now blinding white light.

A newborn cried. Through fuzzy vision, he surveyed the strange new world and found himself in the arms of his mother, Coba. She beamed at her creation.

Another woman, Numi, left the modest tent where the baby had been born.

Warrior men, dressed in animal skins, huddled by a fire. These were Scythians, horsemen from the Southern Eurasian steppes. It was 287 B.C., but the year was irrelevant to them. They followed the seasons and the animals they could hunt.

The largest man and leader of the tribe, Sasan, stood up from the fire as Numi approached and bowed her head. "It's a boy."

An ear-to-ear smile filled Sasan's face, and his men let out a huge cheer. Magnificent news. Sasan was a well-liked leader, and the tribe prospered under his rule. A son meant the good times were likely to continue. And this new baby boy who would be named Azes was special.

Azes walked at six months. Less than a week later, he could run. His father often held him to the sky with pride, confident he'd lead the tribe to new heights.

On his tenth birthday, Azes hunted for the first time with the men. Typically, boys waited until they were thirteen or fourteen. Early in the day, the expedition yielded nothing—a bad omen for a first hunt, especially for the future leader of the tribe. After hours of fruitless searching, the men stopped near an alcove with a small stream on the other side. Azes drifted away from the group to explore. He peered around a rock. A black grouse landed and perched on a small tree. Sasan took note as Azes slipped into a hunter's crouch. The other men crept behind.

Azes maneuvered around the rock with his bow and arrow at the ready, but the tree branches blocked a clean shot. He worked his way around to the other side.

The men watched with awe as Azes, a first-time hunter, snuck around as if he'd done it for years. The hunter in the back couldn't see above the other men. He crawled up a small hill to get a better view but slipped, causing a rock to roll down.

The bird sensed danger and flew off. Azes didn't lose focus, aimed and let the arrow fly. The bird fell from the sky, struck through the neck.

Sasan cheered, then smacked the clumsy hunter.

FOR THE REST of his adolescence, Azes hunted with tremendous results and even killed a brown bear once. His reputation and stature in the tribe rose as a provider and a protector. Azes reveled in the peace that hunting brought from being outside in the elements. He also used it to escape his mind. The activity required an almost spiritual focus on the sights, sounds, and smells of the world, which left little time to think about anything else.

In contrast, at night in the family tent, the mental isolation tormented him despite the fact that his mother, father, two sisters, aunt, and uncle all slept around him. Voices and images assaulted him as soon as his eyes shut. One vision stood out. A man warned him of danger, and even though he wore strange clothes and had a dark complexion unlike anyone in his clan, something about him was familiar. This man urged Azes to come to him.

Azes never spoke of his dreams until he could contain his emotions no longer. Riding with the other warriors of the tribe, they reached a bluff that overlooked their small village. A now graying Sasan paused, proud of the community he'd built and the legacy he'd leave. He turned to his son, now a young man. "Azes, this will be yours soon. You shall multiply our kingdom tenfold. It is your destiny."

Azes looked down at his horse, troubled.

"What is it?"

"I keep having dreams, Father. Of a place called Rome. I must meet someone named Hephaestion. We must defeat a demon among men. Gabriel."

Sasan listened to his son, confused and concerned. "I have heard stories of this city—Rome. It is too far and too dangerous of a journey."

With his head still bowed, he lowered his voice to almost a whisper. "I must try. I must leave."

Sasan's face hardened. "You are the future of the Scythians. You cannot leave."

The warriors followed Sasan down the trail, leaving Azes alone and conflicted.

That night, Azes slept in the family tent beside a crackling fire. His mind *flashed.*

Alexander shared a meal with Hephaestion when they first met as teenagers after the wrestling match.

A comforting thought. Azes smiled in his sleep. His dream skipped forward.

Gabriel shared his words of "wisdom" to Hephaestion and Alexander.

The smile disappeared from Azes's face. The image *flashed* one more time.

Hephaestion coughed and sputtered on his deathbed. He showed Alexander the secret hand signal.

Azes turned and grimaced in his sleep. Then the moment that had plagued Azes for years.

Hephaestion died, and the image of Alexander blended into Azes as he yelled, "Find Gabriel!"

Azes startled awake in a sweat. He glanced around. His parents and other relatives, who now seemed foreign to him, slept in silence. This person named Hephaestion felt more like family than any of these people. There was a bond—a friendship that was unlike anything he'd experienced. And he no longer felt like Azes. The name Alexander rattled in his head.

The pit of his stomach ached. Hephaestion needed him. The world needed him. He could no longer stay in the mountains hunting fox and antelope. He got up, grabbed his bow, then slipped out.

Azes walked to the stable and found his horse, a black stallion very similar to Bucephalus—a conscious or unconscious desire on his part. He mounted the horse and rode out. As he reached the edge of the village, he turned back one last time. He cared for these people, and he would miss them. Tears welled in his eyes because he'd never see them or the village again. He loved the peace of being Azes, but he was Alexander, and he must find his friend. The demon Gabriel must be destroyed. He kicked the side of his horse and left.

The Eurasian mountains were home to many tribes. Alexander had heard stories about them from his father. A few were peaceful, but most were not. Instructed never to venture into another tribe's territory, Alexander must violate that warning to find Rome.

After a day of riding, Alexander maneuvered his horse through a craggy trail. No flies buzzed. No birds chirped. Everything remained still, which caused the hairs on Azes's neck to stand up. With his eagle eyes, he scanned the area. Someone hid behind a bush. Further up, a figure peeked around a rock. Another ducked behind a tree.

Alexander snatched his bow from his back as men revealed themselves and attacked. He released an arrow that tagged one assailant. He searched for an escape route, but an attacker armed with a bow took aim and fired. An arrow sliced through the air and impaled in Alexander's thigh. He bellowed in pain, then kicked his heels into his stallion and charged the attacker. The horse stampeded through and sped away. Alexander distanced himself from the ambush as the horse found open space. The attackers attempted to follow, but Alexander's stallion was too fast.

After riding for another hour, Alexander paused long enough to inspect his injury. The arrow was lodged deep within his thigh. Blood oozed out and dripped onto the ground. He cut a strip of animal skin from his clothing and wrapped the leg, hoping to stop the bleeding. He'd need to find help soon if he wanted to live.

Days passed, and he and his horse slogged ahead. Both needed rest and Alexander still required medical attention. The skin around the swollen wound was a sickly purple with green streaks. He was dying. Half conscious, he rode slumped forward.

He muttered to himself, "Rome. Hephaestion. I'm coming."

CHAPTER 55

Virginia, 2018

A love seat had been placed in front of a cozy fire in Tom's living room. Classical music played in the background. In the kitchen, Tom uncorked a bottle of a red blend. An empty bottle rested beside it. He poured two glasses, then brought them into the living room, where Ben and Riya sat on the couch. Tom offered one glass to Riya. To an outsider, the moment might've looked like some sort of yuppie dinner party, but this was no party, and it was eleven in the morning.

Riya held up her hand. "Still a no for me." Anything that would cause her to relax and let her guard down around Tom was of zero interest.

Tom placed the glass on the coffee table and shoved the other glass in Ben's hand. He did not have the option of declining.

Ben swirled the wine. "This isn't what I had in mind when you said I'm going to find Alisa."

"We're simulating the transition from one life to the next." Tom tapped the empty love seat. "Sit down and get comfortable."

"Transitioning? You mean dying?" Riya asked.

Ben settled in and got comfortable in the love seat. "Funny. I always thought of death as an unpleasant experience."

"Death, yes, but passing, no," Tom said. "We're simulating the passing. You've heard of people with near-death experiences describing a white light and seeing their life flash before them?"

Ben and Riya nodded.

"There you go. We're getting you into that state." Tom pointed to the fire. "Focus on the brightest flame and relax."

Ben stared at the fire.

Riya leaned forward and watched this ritual with intense curiosity.

Tom stood behind Ben, and in a soothing voice, whispered, "Travel to the white of the flame."

Ben followed Tom's instruction. The flame flickered and danced, and his gaze transfixed. Suddenly, he zoomed towards it, and his mind *flashed*.

He emerged on a peaceful hilltop with a spectacular view—like something from *The Sound of Music*—rolling hills covered with grass, flowers, and charming trees. Ben soaked it in. Was this a dream or a memory?

At the bottom of the next hill, he spotted someone waving. He squinted, then shouted, "Alisa!"

Ben sprinted down the bluff as fast as his legs would carry him. All of his questions would be answered, and he'd be reunited with this mystery woman he burned with desire to be with. Then a strange thought crossed his mind. He reached the bottom, tripped on the tip of a rock, and fell down hard. Ben bounced back up and crashed into a massive stone wall, bigger than the Great Wall of China, that appeared out of nowhere. He dropped on his back in pain and held his throbbing head. The wall stretched as far as the eye could see.

On the other side of the barrier, answers waited. On his side, ignorant bliss remained, except it wasn't blissful at all. For years, he'd felt empty, even cowardly. He'd tried to create a life that wasn't meant for him, afraid to face the one that was. Tears rolled down his cheek. He couldn't hide from whatever was on the other side anymore. He needed to confront his fear, no matter how painful. As he lay on his back, the sky morphed from a beautiful azure blue to a glimmering orange, which then transformed into a firestorm.

His mind *flashed* again.

Ben found himself on the floor, dangerously close to the fire. The flames flickered like a snake's tongue towards his face.

Riya pulled him away. "Ben! Are you okay?"

Ben blinked and snapped out of his daze. "What happened?"

"You passed out."

Tom remained standing and studied Ben. "What did you see?"

Ben replayed the last moments of his vision. "I hit a wall."

"Like a mental block?" Riya asked.

"No, I literally ran into a wall. I saw Alisa, and then this wall just... emerged out of thin air." Ben stood up.

"It didn't come out of thin air. It came from your brain. That's not a memory," Tom said.

"What is it then?" Riya asked.

"The wall is a physical representation of an event that's stopping you from remembering." Tom continued to study Ben like a poker player, searching for his opponent's tell. "Why don't you want to remember her?"

"I do. And I will."

Tom sipped his wine, eyes glued on Ben, not convinced.

Riya focused on the science of this phenomenon. "How are these mental blocks created?"

"There's a connection between the manner in which you die and how easy or difficult it is to remember your past lives," Tom said.

"What do you mean the manner in which you die?" Riya asked.

"If your last memory is painful, it's like your brain locks up." Tom squeezed his fist to illustrate his point.

Ben rubbed his chin, processing this information against his visions. "Isn't dying always going to leave you with a painful memory?"

"I'm not talking about just dying," Tom said in a pointed tone. "I'm talking about something horrific. Imagine your worst fear coming true. When that happens, your brain—no—your psyche is scarred." Tom's eyes widened for the briefest of moments. A memory of his own, perhaps.

Riya noticed. "Is that why you couldn't remember?"

"Yeah."

"What happened to you?" she asked.

Tom's flash of vulnerability passed as quickly as it came. "Let's focus on Ben right now." He snatched the wine glasses and marched them to the kitchen.

"How do I get past this 'mental scar'?"

Tom opened the trash can and dumped the empty glasses, breaking several. He slammed the trash shut. "With something stronger than wine."

CHAPTER 56

INDIA, 323 B.C.

CAMPFIRES REVEALED the outline of Alisa's village. Howls and wicked laughter emanated from the creatures around the flames. Alisa stirred awake and found herself in a bamboo cage built into the small hill near the village with the other young women and girls from her tribe. She searched the faces and discovered Maya huddled in the corner.

Petrified, Maya scooted over to Alisa. "I thought you were dead."

Alisa hugged Maya, and the two held one another, trying to comprehend this horrific situation.

"Why did this happen to us?" Maya wept.

Alisa squeezed her tight. "I don't know. We'll be okay."

Another young woman from the tribe, Nisha, chimed in, "No, they're going to use us for their pleasure. And then kill us."

Alisa glared at Nisha. "The gods wouldn't do that to us. We have a purpose."

Nisha, ever the pessimist, pointed outside the cage. "What was their purpose?"

Corpses of friends and family littered the ground around the village. Among the dead, Alisa's husband. A heathen grabbed one leg of the body, then tossed it down a ravine. Alisa never loved Mahendra, but she fumed at the callous disrespect. She switched her focus to her captors—not a sober one among them—as they feasted after a day of pillage and murder.

The men showed deference to a herculean man, Marduk. He hunkered near the fire with a large chunk of meat that took both hands to hold. Tirdad, the vile man who knocked out Alisa, attempted to sit next to Marduk, but the other barbarians squeezed him out. Even his own people didn't like him. Insulted, he marched to the cage. He opened the lock, and the captives squirmed into the back. Tirdad eyed the women and girls, then pointed to Maya.

Maya clutched Alisa in horror. "Please. No."

Tirdad smiled with lust in his eyes. Sick and perverted, this was going to happen.

Alisa stepped in between them. "You don't want her. She's unclean now."

Tirdad sneered. Who was this slave speaking to him? Alisa bowed deferentially. When she glanced up, he decked her across the face. Another heathen watched the exchange and stepped in to stop the abuse, but for a less than noble purpose.

"These are for Marduk! Don't make them ugly. He doesn't like that." The heathen waved Tirdad away from the cage.

Tirdad slammed the door of the cage shut and stepped to the heathen. "I fight in the front lines! For what? Like a dog, I get scraps—the last cup of wine, the ugliest slave girl."

The heathen nodded without paying attention to the rant. He was used to this from Tirdad. In a band of disgusting miscreants, Tirdad stood head and shoulders above the rest.

Tirdad scowled in frustration, then stormed off.

Alisa exhaled as Tirdad walked to the other side of the camp. Something caught her eye hidden in the bushes. A strange man spied on the barbarians. The man slinked back into the trees and disappeared. Was he part of the heathens or a random person in the forest? She dismissed the stranger and focused on the danger at hand.

She needed a plan to save everyone, or they'd all end up like her husband.

THAT NIGHT, the women and girls slept uneasily in the cage, except for Alisa. She searched for a way to escape. She dug at the bamboo pieces, but they were too deep and secure. The lock was a strange device she'd never encountered before. The back of the cave was no luck. She could tunnel for months and still not reach the other side.

The keys clanked against the lock, causing a few to stir and Alisa to freeze. It was Tirdad. The door swung open. Tirdad motioned everyone quiet and gestured with a dagger across his throat. Disobeying meant death.

He pointed to Maya. She crawled forward, petrified.

Alisa jumped in front again. "Take me instead."

Tirdad looked Alisa up and down with predatory eyes, then smiled. "I'll have you both. And if either of you makes a peep, I'll slit your throat and rip out your tongue." He flickered his tongue obnoxiously.

Alisa and Maya left the cage. Tirdad relocked it, then led the two to the ravine by the river. Alisa's heart raced. Helpless to stop what was about to transpire, she looked around at the surroundings. She couldn't believe that of all places, the river was where this heinous act was about to happen. The river had been the one peaceful place she had escaped to for sanctuary. It had always held a special spot in her heart, but now it was just flowing water—worthless in this dire moment. The cattails on the bank grew six feet in the air. Alisa loved picking those and feeling the pillowy ends with her fingers. Why couldn't they be hard with sharp points—something she could use as a weapon? A log rested in the middle of the ravine. She'd sat there on many warm evenings thinking about her favorite dream—but it was far too heavy to be of use now. All these things that had comforted her were useless, and all of it was about to be desecrated.

Tirdad pushed Maya over the log, so her butt stuck in the air. He motioned Alisa to put her face down on the ground until it was her turn. Alisa's mind swirled, and her heart beat faster. *Thump, thump. Thump, thump. Thump, thump.*

Tirdad pulled the cloak off Maya.

Thump, thump. Thump, thump. Thump, thump.

Alisa closed her eyes. She needed to escape this nightmare and flee to her dream. No, she couldn't run from the moment. That would be cowardly. She forced her eyes open to face the fear. In the bustle of leaves and mud, a small log lay half-buried. Something inside of Alisa exploded—a pent up rage. She snatched the log, sprang to her feet, and smashed Tirdad in the head. He crumpled like a sack of potatoes, but she did not stop. *Crack. Crack. Crack.* She pummeled him again and again until a bloody corpse lay in the mud.

Alisa stood in shock and out of breath. Lip quivering from fear, Maya rushed over and fell in her arms. Alisa embraced Maya and comforted her even though she needed the hug just as much. Voices from the camp reminded Alisa they weren't safe yet. She grabbed Maya with both hands. "We must hide the body."

The two sprang into action from the surge of new adrenaline. Maya clutched the feet of Tirdad, and Alisa pulled on his arms. Together, they dragged him down into the thicket of cattails. Heathens rustled about on the other side of the river. Others joked from the camp behind Alisa and Maya. Nowhere to run. No way to escape. Only one choice remained.

Alisa patted the body of Tirdad down until she found the keys to the cage. She grabbed Maya's hand and led her back. Alisa opened the lock, they slipped inside, and she relocked it.

One heathen called out to another. "Where's Tirdad?"

Alisa and Maya stared at each other in fear, wondering if they had only delayed their doom.

Another heathen shouted, "I found Tirdad. He's dead."

Marduk, the leader, boomed with authority, "I told you I saw someone in the forest."

Alisa and Maya clung to each other.

Another heathen screamed, "Cavalry is on its way! Now!"

Heathens darted throughout the camp. Marduk ordered several men together. "Prepare for battle! Lead the men into the woods and flank them when they reach the village."

The men fanned out in a surge of commotion, fear, and tension. Despite the chaos, the heathens organized themselves rapidly. Some disappeared into the hills above the cage. Most ran into the trees near the trail leading into the camp. A few dozen remained and set up a defensive line. The entire process took less than a couple of minutes, and then everything fell silent.

A slight pitter-patter echoed through the forest. What was it? The sound intensified, growing louder until it became a thundering pounding that shook the ground. In all their lives, Alisa and Maya had never heard such a noise. Was it an earthquake? The gods? Terror filled their eyes.

The heathens in the defensive line pointed at the horseman riding toward them at a breakneck speed. Behind him, cavalry rumbled and kicked up dust. Alisa watched, transfixed, as the lone horseman broke through the enemy position. Majestic, fearless, and in total control, he gave her hope. One man took on these heathens. She had no idea this was the famed Greek army. She'd never heard of them nor of Alexander the Great. These strangers wore helmets with plumes on top, and glistening metal contoured to their chests offered almost mystical protection. Even their horses wore metal around their faces. It all mesmerized Alisa, but her fellow captives shrieked as the two armies collided.

The screams caught the attention of the lone horseman. Alexander walked towards them, his arms and legs rippling with thick, powerful muscles. The men in Alisa's village all had thin, wiry frames. Who was this stranger and what did he want? He had to be better than the alternative. Maybe the gods sent him?

Battle cries rang out. A heathen jumped down from the hill and smashed Alexander in the stomach with a club, knocking his sword to the ground. Alisa reached through the bamboo cage to grab the blade, but her fingertips could only graze the tip. About to give up, she remembered she had the key. As soon as she opened the lock, the other girls and women fled past the heathen, who raised his massive club to lay a death blow on Alexander. Alisa leaped to the side, seized the sword, and slid it to Alexander just in time. He snatched it, blocked the club, and sprang to his feet. Within seconds, barbarian corpses surrounded Alisa. Alexander offered a curious nod of gratitude to Alisa, then left. Shell shocked, Alisa sat alone, trying to process the multiple near-death moments in just the last hour. A part of her felt like crying, another like vomiting, and still another felt hopeful.

ALISA'S VILLAGE, BRIEFLY THE HEATHENS', now belonged to the Greeks. Inebriated soldiers danced and sang in the early night. For the survivors of Alisa's village, there was an eerie similarity to the night before with the heathens when they drunkenly celebrated death and destruction. At least these men didn't put people in cages. Unsure of their liberators' intent, the villagers offered forced smiles, hoping they weren't spoils of war that would be sold into slavery, or worse.

Alisa stood in the shadows with the group of girls from the cage. She comforted and kept their spirits up, but even she had concerns after watching Alexander for the last few hours. He was just a man, like all the others who drank and shouted too much.

Bahula, her mother-in-law, wandered on the other side of the dancing men, hoping to find her son. She passed Varus and Diodorus.

"Old lady. How would you like to kiss the king of the known world?" Varus held out a coin and pointed to Alexander.

Bahula eyed the weapons that hung off their hips. She didn't dare refuse the 'request.' With trembling legs, she walked into the sea of dancing men, grabbed Alexander, kissed him, and then scurried off.

Diodorus and Varus erupted with laughter from the prank.

Alisa sprang to her feet and hurried to help Bahula. As the soldiers danced, they bumped Alisa off course, and she came face-to-face with

Alexander. Love at second sight? No. Alisa maintained a cautious hope for survival, but there was something different about Alexander. She kneeled before the king.

"There is no need for that," Alexander said.

She stood and found Alexander staring at her. Was he just another Marduk or Tirdad?

"What is your name?" Alexander asked.

"Alisa."

"Thank you for your help today. May I ask how you opened the cage?"

"The key."

"The key? How..."

Alisa remembered Tirdad and the horror of the heathens. "It's a story I'd rather not repeat."

Alexander motioned to her eye. "Did that happen in battle today?"

"Yesterday."

Alexander paused. "I'm sorry for your suffering." His words were soft and genuine.

Alisa believed him, or at least she wanted to. She couldn't resist looking up into his eyes. They stood there, gazing at each other for an awkward moment. Alexander was handsome, but Alisa found him attractive for different reasons. He seemed to care about her and how she felt. He wanted to protect her and make sure she was okay. Or was it all in her head and just another wishful dream? Alexander licked his lips ever so slightly. Alisa's heart raced in fear. He was going to kiss her, and then he'd want more. He *was* too good to be true. To her surprise, Alexander nodded goodbye and moved on. Hope filled her heart.

The next morning, the village survivors began their chores and attempted the impossible task of getting back to normal. Alisa searched for unbroken clay pots to fill with water. She overheard Maya and Nisha talking as they explored the rubble for food.

"We can't trust them." Nisha picked nuts from a small basket. "I heard them talking about needing to get paid."

Bahula stood in shock above the corpse of Mahendra, her son. Tears streamed down her face. Alisa rushed over, hugged her, and brought her away from the body.

"What do you think, Alisa? Can we trust them?" Maya asked.

Alisa continued to hold on to Bahula, who cried into her shoulder. "They are led by someone good. The gods brought them to us. To help."

"Then why are they leaving?" Nisha pointed to the Greek caravan gearing up to leave.

Alisa watched with concern. Alexander mounted his horse, slumped over, and left the camp. That small glimmer of hope she let herself feel the night before vanished.

CHAPTER 57

STILL HAGGARD AND GRAVELY WOUNDED, Alexander, in his lifetime as a Scythian, crested a small hilltop atop his horse. A city bustled below. He prayed for it to be Rome—his destination. Hephaestion might only be a brief ride away.

Alexander rode down the rolling hill and reached the town gates. Inside the walls, homes and shops made of mud bricks and thatched roofs lined the streets. A few pedestrians glared as Alexander passed by. Having grown up in the steppes of the mountains, Alexander had not seen anything like this before, at least not in this lifetime. The concept of a town felt familiar, even if this one did not.

He motioned to an old man and pointed to the ground. "Rome?"

The man shook his head. Alexander's spirit and shoulders slumped. He then pointed to his injured thigh with a pained face. The man gestured down the dirt path towards a mysterious triangular shaped structure surrounded by peculiar sculptures. Alexander nudged his horse down the street until he reached the odd dwelling and its unusual half-man, half-horse statues. He entered the building and discovered a dark and ethereal temple of sorts. Frankincense burned, which filled the air with a musty pine aroma. More statues of half-horse animals decorated the interior.

Kastor, a man in his early 40s, swept into the room and sized up Alexander. Part doctor, part shaman, and a sprinkle of a charlatan thrown in for good measure, Kastor wore a striking white tunic, colorful necklaces, and rings. "What do you seek, young man?" He spoke in a strange dialect.

Alexander pointed to his wound, then said something in Scythian.

Kastor sighed, annoyed by the foreigner. "How are you going to pay?" His words were slow and deliberate, as if that would help Alexander understand his language. The Hippocratic Oath hadn't made its way to this town, and even if it had, Kastor was not the type who would have honored it.

Alexander looked blankly at him and kept pointing to his wound. Kastor held up a finger, then disappeared into a back room, and returned holding a handful of coins.

"Pay. How?" He pointed to the money.

Alexander glanced at the circular discs of metal and realized Kastor sought a trade. He nodded and offered his bow, along with a hunting knife.

Kastor turned up his nose, then flicked his wrist for Alexander to leave.

Alexander pleaded in Scythian, which only irritated Kastor more. He had no time for a poor, backwater refugee. He seized Alexander by the scruff and showed him out. When he opened the door, Alexander's stallion chortled and neighed in surprise. Kastor immediately marveled at the magnificent beast. He held his hands out to the animal, then to the sky, as if to thank the gods.

"You give me your horse. I save your life." Kastor pointed to the stallion, then to the wound. Alexander's heart sank. In Scythian culture, the horse meant life. Used for travel, hunting, and war, a man's horse became a close friend. Alexander ambled to the animal and nuzzled his nose. They'd been through a lot, but their journey together must end. If he did not agree to the trade, he would die. Alexander turned to Kastor and nodded.

Kastor led Alexander back into the temple and laid him down on a small mat on the floor. He tore Alexander's leather pants, exposing the injured leg and the arrow's shaft. With every step, Kastor swung his arms in a melodramatic dance. He added more frankincense into the burners, then gestured to several of the statues—apparently gods—for their favor. He poured a strange liquid into a wooden cup and handed it to Alexander.

"Drink. You're probably going to die, but it will help with the pain."

The words still didn't register with Alexander, something Kastor realized and had fun with. Alexander smelled the liquid and grimaced at the biting odor. Kastor touched the bottom of the cup to encourage Alexander to drink. He obliged.

Kastor inspected the swollen, black, and blue flesh around the arrow. "They say when you die, you find out what's really important in your life. What's it for a simpleton like you? Your family?"

Alexander stared at him.

Kastor stuck his face close to the wound and smelled. The pungent stench hinted at an infection. "A wife?"

No reaction from Alexander.

"Your horse." Kastor gestured with his hands in a perverse, sexual pumping motion.

Alexander mumbled, "Hephaestion."

Kastor eyed him. Did he understand? He shrugged it off and pulled out a jar of honey. "Legend has it that this stuff once saved Alexander the Great, so I think it can work on a nobody like you."

Alexander winced as the viscous liquid traveled from the jar into the wound in a long, thin, sticky line. Kastor marveled. "Incredible, really. The honey cleans the injury of evil, and it also helps seal the wound when I pull the arrow out."

Alexander writhed in pain.

Kastor poured another drink and handed it to him. "This is only going to get worse."

Alexander snatched the cup this time. Anything to help with the pain. Kastor placed a tourniquet around Alexander's upper thigh and prepared for the moment of truth. He bowed towards one statue. "May the gods find favor."

Kastor seized the arrow shaft and yanked it out. Sensory overload. Alexander's eyes widened in shock, then he fell back on the mat and passed out.

Unconscious from the world outside, his mind remained conscious within itself. Random voices in various languages swirled in a chaotic medley. Time stood still or raced forward; he couldn't tell. Then, silence.

Alexander's eyes opened, and he lurched up. What happened? How long had he been out? The blanket fell down to his waist, and Alexander realized he was naked except for a cloth wrap on his injured leg.

Kastor emerged from the backroom in a casual blue robe, chomping on a handful of grapes. He popped one in his mouth. "Wow. Didn't think you were going to make it. Almost was ready to bury you."

"Where am I?" Alexander now spoke in perfect Greek, Kastor's language.

Kastor dropped the grapes and stumbled backward until he hit the wall. "What did you say?"

"Where am I? How long have I been out?" Alexander rubbed his head and looked at his leg. "Do you know how to get to Rome?"

Trembling with fear but trying to remain brave, Kastor stayed as far away from Alexander as possible. "You're not speaking in tongues. You must've come back from the dead." Kastor sidled his way to the front door, then dashed out, screaming, "Demon. Demon!"

If Alexander had any chance of going to Rome, he needed to leave fast. He struggled to his feet and gingerly maneuvered his clothes on. As Alexander left the temple, bright sunlight blinded him. Shielding his eyes with his hand, he surveyed the foreign town. The street was quiet, his horse gone. Disoriented, he limped towards the city gate. Four soldiers with swords drawn rushed over and surrounded him.

Alexander was not going to Rome.

CHAPTER 58

Virginia, 2018

BEN SAT on the edge of the bed in the guest room and swirled a cup of brown liquid. He leaned down and smelled it. Not much of an odor. He raised it to his lips but paused, uncomfortable with the prospect of drinking.

Tom paced the room in thought while Riya stood at the bedside. "So, how is this process supposed to work?"

"What do you mean?" Tom asked.

"How do people like you normally remember past lives?" Riya asked.

Tom eyed her with suspicion.

"I'm a brain doctor, Tom. This is fascinating stuff."

"It starts around puberty. We get flashes of memories. Things we can't explain. At first, you feel like a weirdo, an outcast... that is, until you realize all that you know and all that you can do. But learning to remember is a process."

Ben swirled the tea again. He'd had his share of feeling like an outcast. "Why is this going to work any better than wine?"

"Peyote is a hallucinogen. It will help your brain see the mental block differently," Tom said.

Ben looked to Riya for confirmation. "Doctor?"

Riya shrugged. "This is unchartered territory, but the drug itself should be relatively safe."

"Relatively safe. Nice."

Riya asked, "Why are you so confident he'll know how to find Alisa if he gets his memories back? They would've known each other years ago."

"Having this gift is lonely. Few people can relate. The gifted will often have meeting places to reconnect. We commit it to memory." Tom locked eyes with Ben. "Hopefully, you have a place with Alisa."

"Hopefully? So, you don't know this is going to work?" Ben asked, now even less sure.

"I know it's the best chance we have to find her," Tom said.

Ben flicked the liquid with his finger.

Tom continued to pace the room. "You need to understand. We don't have time. The Pantheon came for you before. They will keep searching. They don't stop. They *never* stop. We need to hurry this up, so drink the tea and relax."

Ben glanced up to find Tom and Riya leering down at him. "Two people staring at you waiting for you to relax... isn't relaxing."

Tom stopped pacing. He glanced at Riya and nodded. The two exited the room, which left Ben with no more excuses. He psyched himself up with three quick breaths, and, like a cup of bad medicine, he tossed the peyote tea back with one big chug. The foul, bitter liquid hit his tongue and caused his face to pucker.

Several minutes passed. Ben rested on the edge of the bed and assessed how he felt. The tension and worry had left him, replaced with a calm, or maybe it was fatigue. He couldn't tell which, nor did he care. His eyelids grew heavier. He laid down and closed his eyes. All the muscles in his body seemed to exhale at the same time. Total relaxation. Then his eyes twitched, and his breathing sped up.

Ben's mind *flashed*, colors erupted, and he re-emerged on the peaceful hilltop. He spotted Alisa at the bottom of the next hill, waving to him just as before. Instead of breaking out into a run, he took a deep breath. "Okay. You're not real. Just my imagination, so stay calm."

Ben jogged down his hill and tripped on the exact same rock as before. When he regained his footing, the massive wall confronted him. "And you're not real either."

Psychedelic clouds streaked the sky. "Wow." Ben giggled. The hallucinogen was working. Ben touched the cold stone wall and, without hesitation or effort, he scaled it like Spider-Man. Up, up, he climbed until he reached the top.

Now only a couple hundred feet away, Alisa turned and ran up the hill. Confused, Ben shouted, "Wait! Where are you going?"

He crawled down the other side. As soon as his toes touched the bottom, he broke out into a sprint but ran into Alexander's chest. Where did he come from? With his hands on his hips, Alexander blocked Ben's path as if he was guarding it. Ben studied Alexander, who was both foreign and familiar. Ben smirked. Alexander smirked back.

Alisa dashed further up the hill. Ben stepped to the side of Alexander.

"Whoa." Alexander put his hand to Ben's chest, letting him know he couldn't pass.

Ben swatted Alexander's hand away. "Move out of the way."

"Or what?" Alexander asked in a confrontational tone.

Showdown. A fight was going to break out. Or was it?

Alexander tried to make eye contact with Ben, who averted his eyes. "I'm doing this to protect you. And her," Alexander said.

"I need to know the truth."

Alexander shook his head. "Here's a glimpse of the truth."

Alexander stepped back, closed his eyes, and held out his hand towards Ben. A strange moment of silence and then Ben clutched his stomach and knelt on the ground. What did Alexander do to him? As he wallowed in pain, he glimpsed Alisa cresting the top of the hill and disappearing.

Ben's mind *flashed* again. He startled awake, pale-faced. He rolled out of the guest bed and struggled into the bathroom. A moment later, awful sounds filled the room—first retching and then vomit splashing into the toilet.

Tom and Riya rushed into the bedroom.

"Ben, are you okay?" Riya asked from the doorway of the bathroom.

Ben shook his head, still buried in the toilet bowl.

"It's a side effect of the peyote. You'll be okay," Riya said.

Ben rinsed his mouth in the sink and came out, still unsettled. "It wasn't the peyote."

"What was it? What did you see?" Tom asked.

Ben stared at the floor, angry at himself. "I keep stopping myself from getting past it."

Tom pointed his finger deep in Ben's chest. "You need to get past it."

Ben swatted Tom's finger aside. "I don't know how."

Tom's frustration boiled over. He grabbed Ben and shoved him against the wall. "Figure it out!"

Riya stepped in between the two and pushed them apart. "Let's calm down for a moment." She glanced at Tom, suspicious. "Why is it so important to you that he remembers this girl?"

Tom paced the room and ran his fingers through his hair. His outburst had exposed too much. "I told you, the Pantheon always finds you. You never see them coming. They've mastered the art of manipulation and infiltration."

"What does that have to do with Alisa?" Ben asked.

"Alisa is special. Even among people like you and me."

"How is she special?" Riya asked.

"She knows who they are. We don't know how she knows, but she knows."

Ben didn't need his memories back to recognize what this meant. "You know her, don't you?"

Tom rubbed his head, irritated. "I know of her."

"I thought you wanted to avoid the Pantheon," Riya said.

"I do, and it's a lot easier if I know who they are. And if you want to bring them down, find justice for your sister, then we need Alisa."

In one sentence, Tom flipped the attention back to Ben. Riya needed closure, and there was only one way to get it—find the people that killed her sister. She looked at Ben.

He slumped back in the guest chair. "A part of me won't let me remember."

Tom racked his brain for a solution. "I've encountered mental blocks before, but nothing like this. By this point, you should have worked through the painful memories and should recall things from multiple lives."

"All I remember are pieces from the one life. Maybe two. And Alisa. What else can I take? Is there a stronger drug?"

Tom thought for a moment. "We'll get you an MRI."

"That put you in a coma," Riya reminded Tom.

"I was fine in a few hours."

Ben waved off the idea. "I had an MRI already. I pulled myself out of it. Couldn't take it."

Tom asked Riya, "Can you get us an MRI and sedate him?"

"I was fired, remember?" Riya sneered at Tom. "But I might be able to call in a favor." She turned to Ben. "When you're sedated, you won't be able to stop it, so whatever you're afraid of, you'll have to face it. Are you prepared for that?"

Ben wasn't, but that didn't change his mind. "I have to do this."

CHAPTER 59

INDIA, 323 B.C.

ALISA AND MAYA tossed handfuls of nuts onto a blanket in the middle of the camp. Nisha watched from inside a hut where several elderly rested. Pale, sick, and feeble, they were all knocking on death's door.

Nisha assessed the pathetic food haul. "Is that it?"

Alisa put her hands on her hips, refusing to give in to Nisha's pessimism. "We'll find more. The gods will deliver us."

"Stop talking about the gods. Look around you." Nisha waved around at their bleak existence.

Maya drifted away from the argument. Something caught her attention down the long trail leading to their village. She pointed. "The Greeks return!"

As the Greek caravan neared the village, the other survivors stood up in shock. Nisha and Alisa made eye contact. The work of the gods?

As the military procession entered the village, Alisa spotted Alexander riding slumped over on his horse, the arrow protruding from his shoulder. Maya scurried behind Alisa.

General Craterus guided his stallion toward the villagers. He scanned their faces until he zeroed in on Alisa and pointed. "You!"

Alisa's eyes widened. Maya clutched her arm, not wanting her to leave. Alisa leaned down and whispered, "I'm sure it will be fine."

AN HOUR LATER, everything was not fine as Alisa stood beside the table inside Alexander's tent. She unrolled the cloth case, which revealed an array of intimidating medical instruments. She had no idea what each was for or how she should proceed. Despite her desire to appear strong, tears welled up. She couldn't do this. A simple village girl couldn't perform a surgical procedure on a king.

"Psst," a voice whispered.

Alisa glanced around for the source. Philip peaked through a crease in the tent. "Use the knife in the middle. Two cuts. Top. Bottom. This big." He held up his fingers, half an inch apart.

Nervous but relieved by his guidance, Alisa nodded.

"And this deep." Philip expanded his fingers another inch.

Alisa's jaw dropped. Trembling, she returned to Alexander's side with the scalpel.

"If I pass out, do not let anyone in. Understand?"

Alisa nodded, then brought the knife down. She struggled to maintain her composure as the blade sliced into Alexander's already mangled flesh. After several excruciating seconds, Alisa returned to the table with bloody hands. Sick to her stomach, she looked at Philip, who watched through the crease.

"Open the wound with your fingers and use the pincers to grab the arrowhead."

Semi-conscious, Alexander overheard the mumblings. "Out! Or I'll have your head."

The crease shut, and Philip disappeared. Alisa was alone again and terrified. Alexander's death would be on her hands. Armed with the pincers, she returned to his side.

Alexander croaked, "Don't listen to him. I trust you, okay?"

Alisa bobbed her head, even though she didn't trust herself. Tears streamed down her cheeks as she stared at the mess of flesh, blood, and other fluids. "You need a doctor, Alexander."

Alexander clutched her with his uninjured arm. "Don't let anyone else near me. There's a traitor among my men."

Alisa had no choice but to proceed. She splayed the wound with her fingers. Alexander writhed in agony, which only made it worse and prevented Alisa from maneuvering the pincers inside to retrieve the arrowhead. Mercifully, Alexander passed out.

"Psst. Psst. Did he pass out?" From a crease in the tent, Philip waved her over.

Alisa exhaled, relieved. Someone who knows what they're doing can take over. Alisa took one step toward Philip but then stopped. The king of this army believed *she* could save his life. Yes, it was crazy, but still. Alexander trusted her.

The cozy fire in the middle of the tent popped and distracted her. Her gaze transfixed on the dancing flames. Her mind *flashed,* and she disappeared into her favorite dream.

A Vedic healer looked down at his new baby daughter with awe and wonder. The girl met her father's stare, and a bond formed.

The healer tended to a patient's injured head. His daughter, now eight-years-old, played in the corner with a doll she made of twigs and grasses. She mirrored his actions and pretended to help her doll.

Later, the healer showed his daughter various powders, gestured to different parts of his body, and explained what each did. The little girl marveled at the medicines and absorbed the information.

As a teenage girl, she watched her father, now graying, treat a patient. He squinted at the vials of medicine. The girl stopped him when he reached for one. He inspected the vial closer and nodded, grateful for her help.

Older still, the girl observed her father treat a man with a horrific gash on his forearm—a life-threatening injury. He cleaned the wound with a towel, then poured honey into it, and bound it with a clean strip of cloth.

Alisa's mind *flashed,* and she snapped back to reality. The strange vision confused and comforted her. She'd had many dreams about this wonderful man before, but none had dealt with such a bloody injury. It gave her more confidence and composure to resume the surgery. A moment later, she retracted the pincers with the arrowhead.

Philip pushed the main flap of the tent open. "It's quiet. Did he pass out?"

Alisa rushed over and escorted Philip out so as not to let him see Alexander's condition. "Do you want to lose your head? He's adamant no one enters."

Philip tried to hold his ground, but Alisa guided him back out of the tent. "I am here to help. It doesn't make sense that he'd trust you with his life over an esteemed doctor."

Alisa handed the arrowhead to a stunned Philip. "If you want to help, get some honey."

"Honey?" Philip asked.

"And clean strips of cloth. Hurry." Alisa gave him one last shove out of the tent and then closed the flap.

Confused by the request and from a peasant woman of all people, Philip left to carry out Alisa's instructions.

OVER THE NEXT SEVERAL DAYS, Alisa remained by Alexander's side as both protector and doctor. He drifted in and out of consciousness and had shaking fits, either from a nightmare, an infection, or both. Alisa kept her word and didn't allow anyone into the tent. She convinced General Craterus and the other commanders that Alexander demanded the isolation, and to disobey would result in a severe penalty.

At the one week mark, Alexander's health turned the corner. When Alisa cleaned the wound, she could see that it had almost closed. Any sign of infection had disappeared. After she finished applying more honey, she washed her hands in the bowl of water, shook them dry, then sat down and enjoyed a moment of peace with a small plate of fruit.

Craterus pulled the flap of the tent open but did not enter. "You have some people to see you."

Before Alisa had time to respond, Craterus waved her outside, then disappeared. With a piece of melon in hand, Alisa walked outside the tent and found Maya and Nisha. Maya rushed over and hugged Alisa. Nisha stood behind.

Maya peeked back inside the tent at Alexander, sleeping. "Did you save this king?"

Alisa gave her a curt nod and attempted to conceal the pride of her accomplishment.

Nisha soured the moment. "You saved him, but we're dying. Your friends. Your family. We have no food. Nothing."

Alisa had been so overwhelmed taking care of Alexander, she had forgotten about the suffering in her village. "I will ask him for help when he wakes. The gods sent them to save us. I know it."

Nisha stared at the melon in Alisa's hand. "Maybe the gods aren't interested in all of us. Bahula died," she said without emotion. "Maybe she starved. Maybe it was a broken heart. Others aren't far behind."

Alisa held the melon with guilty hands. Bahula had always been so kind to her. They had a strange, unspoken bond over their lives of obligation and obedience. Alisa felt Bahula loved her as much as she did her own son. "I'll get food. Now go, so I can ask him." She wanted to be alone.

Maya gave Alisa one more hug and then left with Nisha. Alisa disappeared inside the tent and tossed the melon back on the plate. Her moment of peace was already a distant memory. She paced back and forth, overwhelmed by the responsibility of protecting the king and now having to save the village. Someone might be starving to death that very second. She had to get food. But how?

If Alexander were conscious, she could simply ask him. Alisa nudged him with her finger. No response. She poked him again. Still nothing. He was on the mend, but not out of the woods yet.

Alisa's head slumped. She began speaking as if Alexander were awake. "You trusted me to help you. It makes no sense... unless the gods brought us together for a reason."

An idea percolated, but it was risky, and she was unsure. As if by a divine miracle, Alexander's eyes cracked open. He smiled, then drifted back unconscious. Alisa needed no more of a sign. She marched out of the tent and searched the camp until she reached the supply wagons. She approached Diodorus, the soldier responsible for managing the rations. Most of his day had little action, so he spent his free time throwing daggers into the wagon's side. Alisa interrupted the activity.

"I need food for my people."

Diodorus stopped and sized up Alisa, a simple villager. "These supplies are for the army. Not people like you." He threw a knife and tagged the center of the wagon.

Alisa ignored the callous dismissal.

"Alexander sent me. I'm the one who saved his life. The only one he would trust."

Diodorus's arrogance vanished. "You?"

"You can ask him, but I don't think he'll be pleased, as he's still recovering."

Given Alexander's recent erratic behavior, the last thing Diodorus wanted was to upset him. "How much do you need?"

"A couple of bags of grain, some fruit, and some salted meat."

Diodorus smirked. Crumbs. He could do that no problem.

Alisa pursed her lips. She aimed too low with her ask. "Each day," she added. "And bring it to the huts over there."

Her bravado stunned Diodorus into submission, and he did what a soldier does. He obeyed. He told Alisa he'd have men deliver the rations every day at sundown. Alisa feigned that evening was an inconvenience, but accepted. She turned and walked back to the tent, shocked that her ruse had worked, with one exception.

Throughout the entire exchange, she failed to notice Philip lurking and listening nearby.

CHAPTER 60

SIRMIUM, 268 B.C.

TWO SOLDIERS SHOVED Alexander onto the stone floor of a dark, dank dungeon. A wretched, naked cell mate covered in grime and feces lay curled in the corner. Alexander pulled himself to his feet as the door of the chamber boomed closed behind him. He shouted through the barred window. "I'm not a demon. Listen to me. I have to get to Rome."

One soldier muttered, "Tell it to Pyrros."

The soldiers exited the jail to continue their patrol of the town. They passed a father and son selling fruit.

The father called out, "What did that man do? He looked injured."

The soldier in command kept walking and said, "He's a demon! Back from the dead. Speaks in strange tongues."

The father tossed a fig to the soldier. "Thanks for keeping us safe."

As soon as the men turned the corner, the father whispered to his son. The boy darted away. He traversed the city streets, taking short cuts between buildings until he reached a primitive tavern. Inside, several people drank wine and ate fruit, some of which he and his father had harvested. One patron stood out because of his clean blue linen tunic. The rest of the people wore tan or brown clothing made from animal skins that hadn't been washed in weeks. The patron sipped a glass of wine and read a scroll. Precursors to books, scrolls were possessions of the wealthy, and this individual had many.

The boy headed straight to the patron, leaned in, and whispered in his ear. The patron handed the boy several coins, collected his scrolls, and left.

ALEXANDER INSPECTED the dungeon for a way to escape. He ran his fingers across the damp back wall, hoping to find a weakness. After everything he'd been through, he couldn't believe he was stuck in this hellhole. And why? For speaking Greek? Then it dawned on him. He could speak in Greek, and his memories were no longer hazy or jumbled. Alexander remembered campaigning to save the world, meeting Gabriel, and looking into the eyes of Hephaestion as he died. He had failed in his previous life. He couldn't fail in this one.

His cellmate, Smeme, stirred in the back. "Did you say you're a demon?"

"I said I'm not a demon."

Smeme ignored the response. "Wow. This is my lucky day. Pyrros won't bother with a petty thief like me if he's got a demon."

"I'm *not* a demon." Alexander turned to his cellmate. Maybe he had some useful information. "Who is Pyrros?"

"He's worse than a demon." Smeme held out his bloody, mangled fingers with the nails torn off. "What's in Rome?"

"My friend. I have to get there."

A thundering voice erupted from the front room of the prison. "Why was my dinner interrupted?"

Alexander listened as a trepid voice responded. "Sir, Kastor was treating the wound of a foreigner. The foreigner died, but a demon took possession of his body. Nearly killed Kastor."

The booming voice commanded, "Then we shall kill this demon."

A moment later, a small, diminutive man, Pyrros, accompanied by two muscled soldiers, entered the narrow hallway just outside the dungeon. Pyrros stared at Alexander through the window of the door and turned up his nose. "You don't look like a demon."

Alexander breathed a sigh of relief. Finally, someone with a brain. "I'm not a demon."

Pyrros held up his hand for silence. "We will follow the legal process to determine the veracity of your claim. You will be tortured for three days, but if you confess to being a demon, we will kill you quickly."

Alexander thought about enduring three days of torture. "And if I don't, you'll let me go?"

"Probably not," Pyrros said.

Alexander's mouth dropped. "Then what difference does it make what I say?"

"It matters how much pain you'll endure. Ask Smeme about the pain. I'll give you the night to sleep on it—if the rats let you sleep." Pyrros smiled and then strolled out.

Smeme laid back in his corner. "That's Pyrros."

Alexander reached his hand through the window of the dungeon door and down to the lock. He touched the keyhole, but it was too small to get a finger in there, not that a finger would do any good.

Smeme watched with amusement. "There's no way to open that. Believe me, I've tried."

Alexander scoured the cell for anything of use, but there were no windows, no furniture, and no toilet. There was nothing inside this dungeon except human excrement and Smeme. When reality set in, Alexander slumped down on the cold, hard rock floor and took a deep, frustrated breath, but he refused to quit. He'd made a promise to Hephaestion that he intended to keep. He whispered to himself. "As the gods are my witness, I will find a way out of this. I will meet you in Rome, my friend."

Smeme overheard the wishful vow. "Friend, you're not getting out of here alive."

Alexander turned to his cellmate. "Do the rats really come at night?"

Smeme held up his hands about two feet apart. "Big ones."

CHAPTER 61

Virginia, 2018

A black Escalade drove up and parked near the rear entrance of the hospital where Riya formerly worked. Carlos sat in the driver's seat, Tom rode shotgun, and Ben and Riya were in the back. Riya stared at a door about fifty yards away and anxiously clutched a bag. If security caught them, they'd be arrested, and the Pantheon would find them. She didn't want to imagine what would happen after that. Instead, she focused on her sister. If she could figure out how this past life phenomenon worked, maybe she could bring the Pantheon to justice. She glanced at Tom and Ben. At the moment, she'd settle for knowing who she could trust. In the pit of her stomach, she knew that neither told her the truth—at least not the entire truth.

"You sure she'll do it?" Tom asked.

"Already spoke to her. She'll leave the back door open when she goes on her lunch break," Riya said.

After ten minutes, the door opened, and Macy, the MRI technologist, emerged. She cracked the door, then walked towards the Escalade. Riya rolled the window down as Macy approached, unnerved.

"All set up. No one is there," Macy said.

"Thanks, Macy. I wouldn't have asked if it wasn't important."

"Keep an eye out for security," Macy said, and then hurried away.

Guilt set in. It was one thing to get herself fired; Riya couldn't get Macy fired, too. The MRI needed to be done in a half-hour. Most of the doctors and nurses in this hospital wing were on lunch break, but some always came back a little early. Riya had to make sure they were well gone before that happened.

Carlos drove the Escalade up to the door. Ben and Riya hopped out, but Tom paused and turned to Carlos. "Be ready to get us."

Carlos shook his head, confused. "Why are we doing this, Tom?"

As was so often the case, Tom said four words. "You gotta trust me."

Tom, Riya, and Ben slipped through the back door into an empty hallway. They moved with stealth across the laminate floors until they reached the MRI Center. Riya opened the door, and they scampered into the vacant reception area.

Riya led Ben through reception and pointed to Tom. "Stay here and watch for security." She didn't wait for a response and continued with Ben. They passed a small changing area. Riya tossed a gown at Ben. "Put it on, and make sure you don't have any metal on you." Riya left Ben and moved into the control room. She threw her bag on the desk, sat down, and glanced at the computer. As promised, Macy had already set up the imaging sequence.

Meanwhile, Tom stood guard in the reception area. He peeked through the door's small glass window to see if anyone was coming down the hallway. So far, so good.

Now dressed in a baby blue hospital gown, Ben hustled into the MRI control room. Riya pointed to a gurney. "Get on, but make sure you remove your belt buckle and anything else that's metal."

"You already said that."

"Because it's important," Riya snapped. She wasn't in the mood to have her orders questioned.

Ben laid down on the gurney. "All good. No metal."

Riya found the IV, specially designed for MRIs. She swabbed the back of Ben's hand and inserted the needle. "This should make you feel sleepy in a couple of minutes." As the words left her mouth, she realized something. Patients under anesthesia often let down their guard and speak their mind with no filter. This was her chance to get some answers. She wheeled him into the MRI room and brought the coil down around Ben's head. "Ben, did you have headaches when you were a teen?"

Ben blinked as the drugs kicked in. "Yeah, why?"

"Why did they go away?" Riya pushed the gurney onto the slide that led into the MRI bore.

Ben stared at the ceiling with glassy eyes, the drugs already kicking in.

In the reception area, Tom ducked down out of sight as a security guard passed by the doorway and continued on his way.

"Ben?" Riya shook his arm. "When did you remember you were Alexander?"

Ben looked at Riya with glassy eyes. "When I was researching my thesis in Pella, Greece. That's when my headaches came back."

Riya nodded, making some connections. "What made you pick Alexander for your research?"

Ben considered the question for a long moment.

Tom peeked his head in and interrupted. "We gotta hurry it up, Riya."

"You need to stay out of here, Tom. It's not safe." Riya motioned him out. She wanted him gone, not only for safety reasons; she also didn't want him overhearing the conversation. Tom returned to the reception area.

Riya looked into Ben's eyes. "Ben, are you telling me the truth?"

"Yeah. It hurts, though."

Riya tapped Ben on the shoulder. "It's okay. We'll talk more later."

"Okey dokey," Ben said, now in la-la land.

Riya slid Ben into the MRI. "Just sit still. We need some good pictures."

A goofy grin spread across Ben's face. "Cheese."

Riya rushed into the control room, sat down, and clicked the mouse on the computer to start the sequence. The MRI kicked on, and the banging and whirring began. Tom stepped in to check on the progress. Riya pulled out a file containing MRI images from her bag.

"What are those?" Tom asked.

"Your MRI results."

"You were supposed to give those back, Riya."

"Yep." Riya ignored Tom and studied the image, even though she'd already studied it for hours.

"What are you using it for?"

"I need something to compare against." She pointed to a light spot in the image. "See this mass. This is what we thought was brain cancer. You said your psyche is 'scarred' from a traumatic event. I think that mass may be the 'scar.'"

Inside the bore of the MRI, Ben drifted into a slumber. After a few moments, his eyes flickered.

The MRI chirped and banged until the first image displayed on Riya's monitor. Both Tom and Riya studied it.

"What the hell happened to him?" Tom asked.

Ben's brain scan revealed three small masses and one massive one. If traumatic events caused these, Riya couldn't imagine what Ben had experienced. She examined the image further. Dark winding bands showed blood flow, and they avoided the areas, except for a trickle near the first mass.

The second image popped up. Dark bands now ran around the massive scar and moved towards the first and smallest scar.

Riya traced the blood flow with her finger. "Look at that."

"What is it?" Tom looked at Riya for answers.

"What are you doing in here?"

Tom and Riya whirled around to find the security guard in the doorway with his hand on his gun.

CHAPTER 62

INDIA, 323 B.C.

ABOVE RIYA'S VILLAGE, the soft blue sky with billowy clouds could not be more picturesque and peaceful. Even the sun seemed extra serene, offering just the right amount of heat rather than the stifling, miserable temperatures in recent days. In the largest hut, Nisha and Maya sat with the oldest villagers nibbling on fruit and meat. All looked happier and healthier after two days of full stomachs.

Alisa walked into the camp. Everyone sprang to their feet and ran out to give her a heroine's welcome, engulfing her in hugs and kisses. Even Nisha nodded in gratitude. The outpouring of appreciation left a lump in Alisa's throat. She choked back her emotions and tried to remain a pillar of stability in this otherwise turbulent time.

Maya gave Alisa the biggest hug of all, and Alisa squeezed her right back. She missed Maya like a daughter.

"Did you save the king?" she asked.

"Of course she did," Nisha replied in her typical biting manner. "Where do you think the food came from?"

Maya ignored Nisha and looked up at Alisa. "Maybe the king will marry you, and you will be a queen! You always said you were destined for something more."

Alisa dabbed Maya's chin and corrected her like a loving parent. "I said *we* are destined for more."

Maya hugged her again.

Alisa beamed. Happiness hadn't come often in her life, so when it did, she savored it. More than anything, Alisa appreciated being valued. She looked up at the beautiful sky and to the gods smiling down on her from the clouds. "Thank you," she whispered.

After an hour of catching up with friends, Alisa surveyed the village. A lot of work still needed to be done if they were to survive, and she was unsure if they had enough able-bodied people to do it. She couldn't stop herself from hoping that Alexander and his army would stay, or at least maybe he would. Her foot knocked over a couple of empty water pots, which brought her back to reality. She grabbed them and followed the trail to the riverbank. The last time she made this journey, it was a tedious task, but today, she relished every tranquil step. Upon reaching the riverbed, she dipped one pot and let the cool water run through her fingertips. She closed her eyes and enjoyed the peace.

"Alisa!" Maya raced along the path toward her. "Something is going on. The Greeks are gathering!"

Alisa dropped the pots and hurried off. She scampered up a hill with Maya struggling to keep up. As she reached the top, Alexander delivered a speech to his men.

"But it's time for a new work. Time to tend to our fields. Re-build our cities. And lead our people. It's time to go home. We leave tomorrow."

Alisa's face dropped, and her heart sank as a deafening cheer erupted from the soldiers. She turned and walked down the hill, bewildered. She saved him. How could he leave her again?

Maya attempted to console Alisa, but she waved her off and wandered the hills in a stupor. After her legs refused to go further, Alisa summoned the strength to go to Alexander's tent to gather her things. When she entered, she looked around. Even though she'd only been here for a week, the transformative events made it seem like it had been years. Alisa had put so much energy and emotion into saving Alexander. They had a connection, or so she thought. Angry that she had let her guard down, Alisa hurled her clothes in a pile on the floor.

"What are you doing?"

She recognized Alexander's voice but didn't turn around. She didn't want to see his face or those eyes that lied to her. "I needed to get my things. You're leaving tomorrow."

"We're not leaving tomorrow."

"You're not?" Alisa asked, now confused.

"No. I'm glad I caught you before you left," he said in a soft voice.

Alisa stopped packing as Alexander walked over to her. "Why?" She turned and faced him.

"Because I don't want you to leave."

As Alisa looked into Alexander's eyes, she could see he cared about her. The connection was real.

"It feels like we were almost at this same moment a few weeks ago," he said. "It's not often you get a second chance."

Alisa raised an eyebrow. "A second chance at what?"

"That first night, I wanted to kiss you."

"I didn't."

Alexander deflated.

Alisa stared into his eyes to make sure he understood. "But, I do now." She pressed against Alexander's chest and kissed him.

It was an intoxicating first kiss, one that neither would forget. The passion continued to build. Alexander slipped off Alisa's cloak and met her eyes. He didn't want to move too quickly. She tugged his regal robe off, which exposed his bare chest. She wanted this as much as he did. He lifted her onto his bed, and they made passionate love by the beautiful glow of the small fire. Enmeshed together, their faces were hidden by Alisa's long, black locks. Two flesh had become one. The moment was ethereal. Total bliss. When they pulled apart for just a moment, a tear fell from Alisa's cheek.

"What's wrong?" Alexander asked.

"Nothing is wrong," she said, stroking his cheek. "I'm happy. Thank you for believing in me."

"Thank you for saving me."

Alisa caressed his face. She'd felt nothing like this before. Maybe it was destiny, or maybe it was simply love. Either way, the gods answered her prayers. "I believe we were brought together for a reason," she said.

She leaned in and kissed him again.

THE SUN ROSE on the east. The camp remained quiet as most of the men slept off the night of heavy partying. Alisa awakened in Alexander's bed to find him pacing about. "What's wrong?"

"We found the traitors." He said with none of the emotion from a few hours earlier.

"That's good, right?"

Alexander stroked his chin. "It's not who I thought it would be. Philip, my doctor, told me some things that surprised me. He said you didn't heal me."

Alisa sat up in the bed to defend herself. "Alexander, that's—"

Alexander interrupted, "And he said you were taking supplies."

His cold eyes and the truth paused her. She had taken food, but he had to understand why she took them. "People were starving. They were going to die."

"So, it's true? I thought I could trust you." He shook his head and chuckled to himself. "We were brought together for a reason?"

This struck a nerve. Alisa threw her clothes on and rushed out on the verge of tears. She passed by hungover soldiers, staring at her. She needed out of this place. Anywhere was better than here. Hurrying away, she found herself by the river, leaning against the large tree. Her legs dropped from under her and she sobbed. She stopped long enough to glare at the cold blue sky—to the gods. "I don't know what you want. Do I matter to you? Do I matter at all?"

The tears dried up as fast as they came, and her face hardened. All of her emotions didn't matter. Her dreams also didn't matter to anyone except herself. Nisha was right. The gods don't care about her. If she wanted something, she needed to take it. She couldn't depend on Alexander or this strange army from a foreign land. She looked again at the sky. The clouds moved across the blue backdrop, the same as they'd done when she was so happy and content earlier in the day. The gods didn't care about the village. Then she realized. Nisha was only half right. The gods didn't care because they didn't exist.

CHAPTER 63

Nighttime had arrived. Darkness filled the dungeon except for a streak of light from the torches in the entry room. There, a guard sat at a table, feet resting on top, half-asleep. Curled up in the cell's corner, Smeme snored. After hours of searching for a way to escape, Alexander lay motionless on the opposite side, perhaps resigned to his fate. Morning was fast approaching. With it would come brutal torture. Rome and finding Hephaestion seemed impossible.

A faint rustling emanated from a hole in the wall. The noise grew until a ten-pound snaggle-toothed rat emerged and scurried into the dungeon in search of food. It crawled over to Smeme and sniffed. Smeme swatted it away, and the vermin wriggled over to Alexander, who laid motionless. His eyes were open and transfixed, as if in a trance. The rat sniffed closer, and his whiskers brushed against Alexander's cheek.

Alexander sprang to life and seized the giant rodent. It squirmed and squealed in terror. Alexander turned his back to Smeme and wrenched his arms until the squealing stopped.

Smeme furrowed his brow, curious by Alexander's actions.

A moment later, Alexander rolled over and revealed blood-soaked hands clutching large rat bones. With wild eyes, he scooted over to Smeme and whispered, "Do you know how to get to Rome?"

Smeme stared slack-jawed in disbelief and fear. "No. But the traders do. They leave in caravans most mornings. Look for their carts near the gates."

Alexander slithered to the dungeon door. He reached his hand through the barred window down to the lock. He maneuvered two rat bones inside. Click. It popped open.

Alexander nudged the door open and tiptoed into the adjacent room with the sleeping guard. The door leading outside was only a few yards to the right. Alexander snuck towards the door. Freedom was so close. His thoughts shifted to the next step and his escape from the city. He'd get to the caravans by the gates, stow away in a cart, and be back on the road to Rome by dawn. No problem.

Inside the dungeon, the cracked door tempted Smeme to follow. He mustered his courage and went for it. He pushed the door further, and it let out a loud creak.

The guard glanced up and almost fell out of his chair upon finding his prisoner out of the dungeon. "Hey!" He reached for his sword, but Alexander bolted outside. Smeme rushed out a moment later.

Alexander limped as fast as his injured leg would let him. Smeme ran in the opposite direction.

The guard dashed outside the prison, ringing a loud bell. "Prisoners are escaping!"

CHAPTER 64

Virginia, 2018

THE GUARD KEPT his distance from Tom and Riya while maintaining one hand on his holstered pistol. Riya remained frozen, unsure how she'd talk her way out of this situation, but she had no choice. If security arrested them, the Pantheon would find them.

"Where's Macy?" the guard asked.

Riya attempted to sound confident and composed. "I'm not sure, but I'm a doctor at this hospital and allowed to be here. We're in the middle of a critical MRI."

"Let me see your badge."

Riya fumbled through her purse, pretending to find the badge that Greg took. Ben's heart rate spiked, and the monitor beeped. With the memory of Tom's MRI still fresh, Riya glanced at the screen, concerned. Tom had flat-lined in seconds.

"I need to tend to the patient." Riya stood, but the guard held out his hand for her to stop.

"Where's your badge?" he demanded.

"I must've left it at home."

The guard snatched his radio off his belt. "I've got unauthorized people in the MRI suite. Request support."

The plan had unraveled. They were about to be arrested, and Ben was on the verge of cardiac arrest. "I'm a doctor. I need to tend to the patient." She pushed her chair back to leave.

The guard withdrew his pistol. "Stay put."

IN THE BORE of the MRI, Ben's eyes flittered, his breathing intensified, and his mind *flashed*.

He emerged on the mountaintop and spotted Alisa on the other hill, waving to him. This was it—no turning back. With the anesthesia, he no longer controlled his ability to wake up. He scrambled down the hill, and when he reached the bottom, he carefully walked forward, determined not to trip this time. He jumped over the rock that hobbled him twice before, but it didn't stop the wall from appearing, which now loomed in front. Ben stepped to the wall and pressed hard into the cold stone. The enormous barrier tilted and buckled. Ben dug in and pushed harder, causing the massive wall to topple over with a thunderous boom.

As the dust cleared, Ben saw her—Alisa. Her beautiful smile and captivating eyes were just a couple hundred feet away. She turned and raced up the hill. Ben gave chase, and like last time, Alexander emerged and blocked his path. "I told you before. You can't go there."

Ben shoved Alexander away. "You can't stop me."

Alexander squared off for the inevitable fight. "I beg to differ, friend."

Ben straddled his legs in a defensive posture and shadowed Alexander, who circled like a shark. Moving in a slow, rhythmic pace, Alexander tried to lull Ben to relax even for a second. When his moment arrived, Alexander attacked with a series of punches and kicks. Ben blocked the first wave, but a follow-up strike landed in his gut, sending him reeling backward. He shook it off, but Alexander charged again. Ben avoided the punches, then swept Alexander's legs, knocking him to the ground. Seizing the advantage, Ben launched a flying front kick to Alexander's head, flooring him. Ben spied Alisa disappearing over the hill. He raced off to catch her, but Alexander grabbed his leg, tripping him.

"I don't think so." Alexander sprang back to his feet and readied himself for another round.

Ben scrambled away, but before he could defend himself, Alexander kicked him in the stomach and then followed with a powerful strike to the face that sent him to the floor. Alexander jumped on top of him, pulled him up by the shirt, and punched him with all his strength. Blood poured out of Ben's nose, and his head lulled to the side. Alexander pounded again and again. The thrashing continued until, mercifully, Alexander stopped and dropped Ben to the ground. "What were you thinking?"

Through swollen eyes, Ben glared at Alexander. "I need to be with her."

"You can't be with her," Alexander said.

"Danger is coming. The Pantheon is after her. I need to protect her."

Alexander chuckled. "You. Protect her? That's a joke. What were you planning? You don't even know the people you're with. After all these years, you still have learned nothing." Alexander gave Ben one last shove to the ground and then climbed off. "Never come back here, or I will kill you."

Ben grimaced as he pulled himself to his feet. "Alexander."

Alexander stopped and turned around. "Did you hear what I said? Why don't you wake up and leave? I *will* kill you."

Ben held up his hands to fight and smiled. "I can't wake up."

Alexander walked towards Ben. When he was just a couple of feet away, he shook his head, irritated. Ben's eyes were all but swollen shut. "I don't want to do this," Alexander said.

"Then let me pass," Ben said.

"You know I can't do that."

This was it. Ben needed to defeat Alexander, or he'd die trying. He waited for his moment to strike and then mustered all his strength. His fist sailed through the air towards Alexander's jaw, but Alexander caught Ben's hand mid-strike. And it wasn't even difficult. Ben looked on in horror as Alexander delivered a vicious uppercut that sent Ben on his back. Alexander was mounted on top of Ben in seconds, delivering pulverizing punches.

In the MRI control room, Ben's heart monitor climbed to over 200 beats per minute, a rate associated with extreme physical activity. This wasn't safe. It reached 220 beats and then crashed. *Beeeeeeeeep.*

A medical alarm rang. Ben had flatlined.

CHAPTER 65

INDIA, 323 B.C.

OUTSIDE THE REMAINS of her mud hut, Alisa ground millet with a mortar and pestle. Her tears had been replaced with a sharp, dour disposition. The millet bore the brunt of her emotions, which became a fine paste.

"Hello."

She recognized Alexander's voice but ignored him and continued to grind away.

"Hephaestion was one of the few people I trusted." Alexander paused, then corrected himself. "He was the only person I trusted. When he died, I didn't know who to turn to. But there was something about you. Something I was drawn to. I can't explain it, really. I don't care about the supplies."

Alisa continued to work away. Alexander still didn't get it.

Craterus rode over with two other soldiers and Bucephalus. "We broke the traitors."

Alexander held up a finger. He needed a moment. "I don't care that Philip saved me."

Alisa dropped the pestle and turned around. "You know what hurts the most? I thought someone believed in me. Believed I was capable of more. That I mattered." Alisa pointed at him. "Philip didn't save you."

"But you said..."

"I took some food. Because people were starving." She waved her hands at the poverty of her village.

Craterus interjected, "The information led our scouts five miles west. They spotted an old man escaping on a donkey. We've found him."

Alexander leaned into Alisa and whispered, "How did you know how to save me?"

Alisa considered whether to share her secret dreams, afraid Alexander might find it stupid, but she was so angry she didn't care. "I had a vision. A dream."

Craterus's impatience grew. "If he gets to the Hydroatis, we may lose him forever. We must go now!"

Alexander eyed her as he walked backward to his horse. "I must go. I have one more battle to fight. But we will continue this talk when I return."

"Killing this man will not bring your friend back," Alisa said.

"I gave him my word." Alexander dashed towards Bucephalus, but stopped at the horse's side. "I'll return soon. And when my army leaves, you and your people will all come with us."

Alisa refused to let her guard down again. "I don't believe you."

"Now, you have my word." Alexander mounted Bucephalus and charged off.

Nausea settled in the pit of Alisa's stomach. Watching him leave stung. A part of her had hoped he'd stay. It was that same part that had opened up to him and started to fall for him.

Maya walked up beside her. "The gods will deliver us."

Alisa grabbed her pestle and resumed her work. "No. We're on our own."

OVER THE NEXT WEEK, the villagers attempted to restart their lives. They endeavored to move past the horror of the barbarians, and Alisa tried to forget Alexander. It was hard at first, especially with the Greek army camped beside them. She half expected Alexander to come back and talk to her at some point, but she never saw him again. Alisa assumed he'd found the man that killed his friend and had moved on. Then one day, the Greek army packed up and marched out, which only solidified her belief. Alisa didn't even bother to watch them leave. They no longer existed in her mind. Her attention turned to her remaining friends and family.

More time passed. One afternoon, Alisa scoured the flat plain for tubers and anything else edible. As she dug into the earth, she realized it had been where the Greek army camped. It might have even been where she saved Alexander's life. Now, not a trace remained. Alisa buried this last bit of nostalgia and sadness and continued to hunt for food.

The hard work of Alisa and the villagers paid off. They established something of a routine, and while they weren't thriving, they'd figured out how to survive, due in no small part to Alisa's leadership. Girls weaved reeds to support the huts' roofs, others prepared modest meals, and Alisa kept her job bringing water back to camp. She could've found someone else to do the simple task, but she still found solace by the riverbed.

Despite the improved conditions, they remained vulnerable. Never was that more apparent once the sun set, and one moonless, cloudy night, blackness surrounded the encampment. The only light came from one large fire in the middle of the village. Everyone huddled around it to keep warm and stay safe from the unknown dangers lurking in the dark.

Monkeys howled, and birds squawked from the trees—normal noises of nature during the day, but ominous and hair-raising at night. A rustling in the forest caused everyone to freeze. Alisa grabbed a stick by her side. Maya clutched her arm.

"The animals won't come near the fire," Alisa assured.

The sounds stopped, and that moment when everything becomes too quiet followed. A battle cry erupted from the trees. Marduk and the remnants of the heathens emerged from the shadows like ghosts. The villagers sprang to their feet and fled in every direction. Two girls, both young and fleet-footed, darted away, accidentally knocking burning logs from the fire. One rolled into a hut and ignited it.

The savages attempted to corral and capture the fleeing girls as the fire found fuel and grew. One heathen captured Maya and slung her over his shoulder. Alisa whacked him on his leg with the stick. He howled and dropped Maya.

Marduk emerged behind Alisa, picked her up, and flung to the ground. Knocked senseless, she struggled to regain her footing. Her vision blurred, and the sounds heightened. Shrieks of terror. Battle cries. Was this really life? Could it get any worse?

The heathen reclaimed Maya, but she bit him on the neck. He slammed Maya down, then raised his battle-axe. Alisa's world spun. She let out a furious scream full of rage, despair, and hopelessness as Maya's life ended with one strike. Horror surrounded her—fire, death, depravity.

A shadowy figure emerged through the smoke. The mysterious person fought the heathens with a sword and was winning! Savage after savage stepped up, only to be cut down. Marduk's turn. He let out a vicious battle cry and attacked. The heroic figure remained poised with smooth and deliberate movements.

As Alisa watched, it reminded her of Alexander. She drifted in and out of consciousness, and her heart hoped. It was Alexander; it had to be. He'd come back to save her, just as he'd promised.

Marduk charged. The figure sidestepped the attack, then struck. Marduk, the giant, fell down dead, cut down like he was nothing. Smoke thickened, and flames closed in. The man surveyed the area for anymore threats. Then, he checked the bodies for survivors. One-by-one, he searched, getting closer and closer to Alisa. He looked like a demon warrior through the smoke, but for Alisa, he was her savior. He reached out his hand to her. She took it.

It was Gabriel.

CHAPTER 66

Alexander fled from the jail. If he was recaptured, he knew the horrible fate that awaited. There would also be no chance of getting to Rome to fulfill his promise to Hephaestion. Escape was his only option, but the odds were stacked against him. Injured and outnumbered by at least a hundred to one, it was only a matter of time before the guards found him. He scurried through the streets, turning whenever he was able. In the distance, a guard shouted to reinforcements. "One went that way, the other went this way."

Alexander's mind raced as he kept to the shadows. He followed the streets, and when he turned one corner, the main gate came into view. Beside it, several carts sat parked just as Smeme said, but he didn't mention soldiers with swords guarding them. Behind Alexander, guards searched the streets and closed in. With seconds to react, he dove between the fence posts of a small corral. Squirming his way into the darkness amidst the hay, he came face-to-face with a giant pig. It snorted.

"Nice piggy. Please be quiet," Alexander begged.

The guards scoured the area outside the corral. Alexander eyed the pig, praying it wouldn't give him up. The guards continued their search down another path. Alexander exhaled. The giant hog licked his cheek, but he didn't care. Moments ago, his future included brutal torture, so a swine licking his face was just fine. He laid his head in the hay and allowed himself a brief rest. His eyes closed, and he slipped into a slumber.

THE FIRST RAYS of morning sunlight peaked across the mountain. Alexander stirred awake in the corral. Curled up beside him was the giant pig. Cute, but Alexander was still being hunted, and the city would soon be alive with activity.

As if on cue, the corral's owner opened the gate, entered, and began the dawn feeding. Hidden in the shadows and hay, Alexander lay still, careful not to make a peep. The owner started on the far side of the pen, but with each scoop of slop that he hurled to the hungry goats, pigs, and chickens, he stepped closer to Alexander.

With no time to waste, Alexander snuck out of his hiding spot and moved to the fenced edge of the corral. He looked at the main gate— soldiers still guarded it. Making matters worse, the traders were leaving with the carts and wagons.

The owner made another step in Alexander's direction. Did he dare make a run for it on an injured leg?

Clip clop. Clip clop. Clip clop. A colt pulled a wagon by the corral. The patron from the restaurant walked beside the horse and eyed Alexander. "Get in."

Alexander froze. Who was this stranger?

"You can stay, but I don't think it will end well for you," the patron said.

Alexander glanced at the soldiers near the gate, then looked behind him. The owner of the corral approached, leaving him with no choice. He scurried out and hopped into the wagon. He discovered a bunch of soft fabrics and clothing.

"Lie down," the patron ordered.

As soon as Alexander was on his back, the patron covered him with a purple cloak, then tapped the horse. The wagon continued down the street, past the soldiers, and through the open gate. For the next two hours, Alexander stared at the color purple as his mind raced. Would he escape the city? Where was he going? And who was this strange man? Curiosity got the best of him. He peeked his head out from under the cloak. With Sirmium now in the distance, Alexander sat up and eyed the stranger who saved him.

"Who are you? What do you want?"

"My name is Michael. I'm sure you have many questions. They will be answered soon enough." He tapped the horse to continue plodding forward.

"I need to get to Rome. I need to find my friend," Alexander said.

Michael smiled. "Fortunately for you, all roads lead to Rome."

CHAPTER 67

Virginia, 2018

Beeeeeeeeep.

The medical alarm blared. The guard either didn't know the alarm's meaning, didn't care, or didn't know what to do. Frozen, he kept his gunned aimed at Tom and Riya.

Beeeeeeeeep.

Every precious second that passed could mean the difference between life and death. Riya had to act. "I need to check on my patient. You can shoot me, and we both die, or I can treat him, and then I'll go wherever you want."

Not wanting to be responsible for someone's death, the guard nodded but motioned for Tom to stay put.

Riya rushed to Ben, slid him out of the MRI, and pulled out an adrenaline shot. She popped the cap and injected it into his thigh. His eyes twitched back and forth like crazy, but as soon as he was out of the tube, his heart rate stabilized, his eyes calmed down, and then cracked opened.

"Ben, you okay?" Riya asked.

He lulled his head in the affirmative.

With Ben safe, Riya shifted her attention to the security guard. She ripped off Ben's heart monitor, causing the medical alarm to blare. *Beeeeeeeep.* It appeared as if Ben had flat-lined again.

"He's crashing. I need help in here!" she screamed in her best-panicked voice.

The gun-toting guard escorted Tom into the room.

Riya waved at Tom, then to the other side of Ben. "I need him here now." She pointed at the guard, then to a spot near the MRI. "You can stand there and see what we're doing."

The guard kept his pistol aimed and moved into position. Before he could react, the enormous magnetic force snatched the gun from his hand and it crashed into the bore of the machine.

Tom cracked him with a left hook and knocked him out. The gun remained wedged against the inside of the MRI. Tom eyed it in disbelief.

"That's why you don't bring metal in here," Riya said, as she helped Ben out of the head coil and off the gurney.

She and Tom each put one of his arms around their shoulder and carried him semi-conscious through the MRI suite. They grabbed his clothes and continued down the hallway towards the exit.

At the opposite end of the hall, security guards emerged and broke out into a sprint. Tom and Riya did their best to hurry, but Ben's weight slowed them down to almost a crawl. The guards closed in fast. Tom and Riya burst through the back door. Carlos screeched the Escalade up, threw it into park, and jumped out to help Tom heave Ben in. They hopped in, and Carlos sped away just as the guards poured out the back door.

LATER THAT EVENING, Ben rested in the guest bedroom of Tom's estate. With the anesthesia out of his system, he felt like himself again. He glanced up and found Riya standing on one side of the bed. With arms crossed, Tom towered over him on the other side, glaring down.

"Well," Tom said. "What did you see?"

Ben didn't have an answer—at least not an answer Tom wanted. He shook his head.

"You gotta be kidding me. You saw nothing?" Tom asked, doubtful.

Ben didn't know how to explain that he'd kill himself before revealing whatever was locked inside his mind. He didn't even understand it himself. He looked down, ashamed.

"Don't lie to us. You had to have seen *something*," Tom said.

Ben snapped back, "I'm not lying. Nothing made any sense. She kept... running away."

Tom rubbed his head beyond frustrated. "Unbelievable."

Riya touched Ben's arm for support. "I believe you, Ben."

Tom threw up his hands. "Well, hoo-ray for that. We risked our lives for nothing, but she believes you."

Riya sat on the edge of the bed. "I don't think it was for nothing. I saw something on the MRI images."

"What did you see?" Ben asked.

"You remembered things about your life as Alexander when you went to Pella, right?" Riya asked.

Ben nodded.

"In the first image, there was almost no blood flow near the 'scars' in your brain—just a little by the first one."

"And?" Tom asked.

Riya turned to Ben. "Do you remember any more about your life as Alexander?"

Ben thought about it. Riya was right. He now remembered lots of details that he hadn't before—his father, his favorite foods, some of the ancient battles. It was still fuzzy, but there was more. He even recalled bits and pieces from what felt like another lifetime. "Yeah. I do."

"I'm not following. How did that happen?" Tom asked.

Riya explained, "In the second MRI image, more blood flow had moved to the first scar. The blood is helping him remember. If we can trigger those memories, the blood flow should increase—the more blood, the more he'll be able to remember."

Tom was intrigued. "How do we increase the blood flow?"

"We start backward and work our way up to the event that is stopping him from remembering." She turned to Ben. "If you remember pieces of your life as Alexander, where should we go next?"

Ben rubbed his chin for a long moment. "Rome."

Tom clapped his hands. Progress. "Okay, I'll make the reservations."

"Wait," Ben said. Something Alexander said worried him. He didn't know Riya, and he especially didn't know Tom. "The only way I'm going anywhere is if you tell us about the Pantheon… and you. And don't lie to *me*."

Tom gritted his teeth. Ben didn't waver. He wasn't moving unless Tom started talking, and a short, cryptic answer would not cut it this time. Tom slouched down in the chair beside the bed and scratched his forehead. "Fine. If you want to understand me, you need to understand the Pantheon, and to understand them, you need to know about the person who created it. To do that, you have to go all the way back to the beginning."

CHAPTER 68

Mongolia, 4132, B.C.

No one has this year marked in any history book, but it was then that the world's truth was revealed—at least according to one man. With truth comes wisdom, and with wisdom comes power. Too often, that truth smacks us in the face when we've reached the end of our life—when it can no longer be used. What, then, is the point? This man believed he'd answered that question.

———————————————

The sun rose over a vast plain covered with grass, shrubs, and the occasional tree. A tribe of families lived in huts made of earth, reeds, and sod. The day began like most for these primitive people. Women carried baskets, and men worked a small field digging up roots and tubers. All were tired and hungry.

A young man traveled the path leading to the village with a wooden spear in hand and a deer carcass slung over his shoulder. Everyone took notice because the food meant life. Like so many early peoples, they scraped by. They survived by utilizing defined roles and a hierarchy within the clan. One man ruled over everyone else, and the young hunter believed it was his destiny to be that man.

In another lifetime, this hunter would become a man named Sargon. His story became a myth. Those aware of his existence believed it to be true, but no one could be certain. His name in this life had been lost to time, but that didn't matter. What did matter was what happened to him.

Sargon approached the largest hut with the carcass. An elder motioned for him to stop while drooling at the dead animal. "They are praying to the Earth Mother."

Sargon peeked into the hut. Borgamon, the leader of the tribe, and his teenage son, Nob, bowed before a large rock adorned with flowers and carvings. They rose from their knees with arms outstretched, then bowed again.

Sargon's patience ran out. "I have food."

Borgamon turned and spied the carcass dangling off Sargon's shoulder. He approached, with Nob following behind. Sargon tossed the deer at Borgamon's feet.

Borgamon smiled at his son. "Earth Mother has found favor in our offering."

Sargon bristled. Their offering had nothing to do with his skill as a hunter. "I have provided much food. I have defeated enemies in battle. I built most of these dwellings." He clenched his jaw, holding himself back from saying something he'd regret.

"You have served well. What is it you want?" Borgamon asked.

"I want to rule," Sargon replied.

Borgamon recoiled from the shock of being threatened to his face.

Sargon lowered his head in deference. "When your time comes, of course."

Borgamon grunted. "My son, Nob, will rule." He motioned to Nob.

This was the expected order—like a law of nature. Sargon had been told this since he was a boy, but he refused to accept it. "If you want your legacy to continue, then we must be strong. I am the strongest—after you."

Borgamon grunted again. "It is true you have done many good things, but..." He turned to Nob. "What do you think?"

Nob tapped his chest. "I am the strongest."

Sargon bowed his head toward the shrine inside the tent. "Let's have Earth Mother decide."

"What do you mean?" Borgamon asked.

"Let us fight. Earth Mother will support who she wants to win."

Nob's eyes widened, no longer as confident.

Borgamon grunted a third time. "It shall be so."

Sargon smirked—this would be an easy victory. He didn't believe in the spirits or some random rock, but if the people thought it had powers, he'd use it to show he was "chosen."

Hours later, the tribe gathered for the big event. The men surrounded Sargon and created a fighting ring. Borgamon emerged from his hut with Nob following behind. When Borgamon stepped into the ring, everyone kneeled in homage. He waved Sargon and Nob to their feet so they could face one another.

He placed a hand on each of their shoulders. "When one asks for mercy or can no longer stand, the fight is over. No weapons. We are one tribe. One family."

The two took a knee, lowered their heads, and placed one hand on the other's shoulder.

Borgamon motioned everyone else to bow in prayer. He reached down and touched the heads of Sargon and Nob. Eyes closed, he prayed. "Earth Mother, you provide us with food, water, shelter, and you provide us with life. You keep us safe from evil; from the demons of night. We now ask for your wisdom in choosing our next leader. Show us the light, the future of our tribe."

Borgamon released Sargon and Nob, and the people rose to their feet. Sargon attempted to stand, but Nob continued to hold his shoulder and press him down. Nob coughed and clutched his throat with his other hand.

Sargon pulled away in fear as Nob fell to the floor in anguish. The tribe watched, confused, as Nob struggled to breathe.

"What is it, my son?" Borgamon pleaded.

Nob held his throat with one hand and pointed at Sargon with the other. "He's choking me."

Borgamon turned his ire to Sargon. "Earth Mother has spoken. He's a dark spirit!" He pointed to the men, then at Sargon. "Take him."

The mob descended on Sargon as Nob recovered his breath.

Sargon backed away in fear. "I didn't—"

"Silence!" Borgman said. "I knew there was something evil about you." He waved the men forward. "Burn him."

The men bound Sargon with rope and tied him to a tree. One brought two burning logs. Sargon panicked as the men placed the wood near his feet. Flames burned the grass around him and rose. As the searing sensation hit, Sargon bellowed in horrific agony. Worse than any nightmare, the fire grew bigger, and the pain—the jolting, blistering pain—magnified tenfold with each second. As the end drew near, Sargon made eye contact with Borgamon and Nob. A hint of a wry grin cracked across Borgamon's face. In that moment, as he burned, Sargon realized the truth.

He never had a chance to rule.

CHAPTER 69

OUTSKIRTS OF ROME, 268 B.C.

MICHAEL AND ALEXANDER had traveled together for over a month, but they spoke very little. Alexander slept for long stretches as his thigh healed. Every so often, they'd engage in idle talk, but when Alexander pressed for information, Michael always replied, "Your questions will be answered when we get to Rome."

In the middle of nowhere, with an injured leg, Alexander was at the mercy of Michael, something he hated. He couldn't trust Michael as he knew nothing about him, but why had Michael risked his life by smuggling him out of the city?

As a new day began, something weighed on Alexander's mind, something that had plagued him since the moment they met. Michael passed by right when Alexander reached the fence. "Did you know I was hiding in the corral?"

Michael nodded.

Alexander considered the implications. None of this was random. Michael waited and wanted him for a reason. "Why did you save me?"

Michael kicked a couple of rocks as he walked. "Word spread that you were a demon. In all my years, I have yet to find one. People fear what they don't understand. I don't intend any harm. I only wish to introduce you to someone. Fair enough?"

Alexander nodded, satisfied to be told something meaningful.

"So, why do you want to go to Rome?" Michael asked.

"To find a friend. His name is Hephaestion. Do you know him?"

Michael shook his head.

Alexander stretched his leg in the wagon. "He should be in Rome. If he's there, I'll find him."

Michael smiled. "You haven't been to Rome before, have you?"

"Why do you say that?"

The wagon crested a hill, and Rome came into view in all its splendor. Even by modern standards, it was a large, expansive metropolis. Tucked beside the Tiber river and surrounded by hills, it was stunning to see so many buildings crammed together. Home to hundreds of thousands, and many more came and went each day.

Alexander's jaw dropped.

When they reached the city's wall, Michael "parked" his cart. With so many traders, the noise from the wagons had become unbearable for the citizens, so wares had to be transported by hand. Guards kept watch over what was essentially an ancient parking lot. They eyed Michael and Alexander as the two entered the city.

Once inside the walls, Michael spotted an elderly man and waved him over. The man hobbled over. Michael leaned down and whispered. "We have a prospect. We'll be there soon."

Alexander marveled at the city's scope—the magnificent columned buildings, the statues to the gods, and the mass of humanity walking the streets.

Michael guided Alexander through the curving lanes amid the bustle of vendors. They passed a market square and then turned down a street that led to a quieter residential area containing estates of Rome's privileged. Rome's poor lived in the insulae—large apartment complexes. Some were several stories high, unstable, and unsafe. Each estate, known as a domus, was uniquely crafted. The variances coincided with the stature of the individual owning the domus—the larger and more elaborate, the more successful and influential the owner.

Michael led Alexander to a domus at the end of the street that appeared average relative to its neighbors. One distinguishing feature was the marbled sculpturing around the archway of the home. At the top, a pyramid with an eye in the center had been carved. Michael stepped to the doorway and withdrew a small brick near the foundation. He reached his hand inside the void and pulled out a hidden key, unlocked the door, and entered.

Alexander stepped into a modest entrance hall. Michael waved Alexander further inside. They passed through the atrium, which contained a small pool and manicured trees and flowers. Then, they moved into the culina—the kitchen with a hearth and oven for cooking. The room also included a large stone table for preparing food. Michael used all his strength to swivel it to the side about two feet, revealing a secret staircase underneath.

Michael led Alexander down the long, narrow staircase. The temperature dropped ten degrees as they descended. They entered a dark tunnel and Alexander grabbed his arms for warmth, while following Michael, confused. Where was he going, and why did such a tunnel system exist?

Before Alexander could ask, Michael offered, "This was originally a mining shaft—created by the Etruscans. We use it for a warehouse and other reasons."

Alexander ran his finger across the narrow passageways that had been chiseled into the tufa rock. As they pressed further, a glow from a fire illuminated an area up ahead. They entered a room with a low semi-circular ceiling. There was a second entrance on the opposite side.

A diminutive old man in a simple robe waited by a fire with a walking stick in hand. The man never took his eyes off Alexander, not even for a second. In a raspy voice, he said, "A pleasure to meet you... if we haven't already. We can dispense with further small talk and get right to it. You remember your past lives, correct?"

Alexander considered lying, but the man spoke with such certainty it didn't seem to make much sense.

"So do we. We've found there's one identity you associate with more than others, so for the sake of interactions with each other, we forgo the names in this life and refer to one another by the name of who we are. I am Solomon," he said, motioning to himself.

Solomon stared at Alexander, waiting for him to introduce himself.

"I'm... Alexander of Macedon."

Solomon nodded. "A warrior king."

"A failed king," Alexander corrected.

"Why do you say that?"

"I encountered a man named Gabriel. He could also remember his past lives. He murdered my friend, and then his men poisoned me."

Solomon dug in the ground with his staff, absorbing every word Alexander spoke. "That's not what history says about your death."

"The history is wrong."

Solomon took a deep breath. "The man you describe as Gabriel is likely someone else."

Alexander furrowed his brow.

"He's a master manipulator. A liar. He often assumes identities," Solomon explained.

"He was pretending to be Gabriel?" Alexander asked.

Solomon continued to dig into the ground. "From what you describe, yes. You never know who he or his followers are until it is too late."

"Who is he then?"

Solomon stopped digging and focused on Alexander. "We think we finally know who he is, but until we can confirm it, we can't share that information."

"Why not?"

Solomon stared at Alexander with cold, judgmental eyes. "Because he's that smart. And he's that good at manipulating. We must know who you are first."

"I already told you."

"I wish it were that simple. There can be no doubt that you remember past lives and that you are not with him." Solomon removed a bejeweled dagger from his robe and handed it to Alexander. "Knowing you have past lives means death should not be feared. Offer this life as a sacrifice. When you return, you will be entrusted with the secrets of the world."

Alexander stared at the dagger, then at Solomon. Was he serious? Solomon's silence offered the answer.

CHAPTER 70

Virginia, 2018

Police scoured the cordoned off MRI facility of the Virginia Hospital Center. Detectives dusted for fingerprints and inspected the control room for any evidence, and another interviewed the guard that Tom had knocked out. The guard described in melodramatic detail how it all happened. He pointed to where he was told to stand and motioned to his gun, still wedged inside the MRI machine. The detective in charge of the investigation was Varus, but these people knew him as Detective Harper Peterson. He knew this was the hospital where Riya had worked. He also knew she'd been fired, which explained why she had to "break in," but it did not explain why she would take such a risk or why she or Ben needed an MRI. He mulled over these questions as a detective presented him with an open laptop.

"What is this?" Varus asked.

"The security cameras got a video of the getaway vehicle."

The detective pressed play, and a video showed Vance's Escalade pulling out of the hospital parking lot.

"Run the plate," Varus said.

"Already did. Belongs to Congressman Tom Vance."

Varus smiled. All his questions would be answered soon enough.

"STAY STILL and look at the camera," Ron said, and then clicked the iPhone button to take the picture.

His subject, Ben, sat on a stool in front of a white backdrop, which was nothing more than a sheet strung up against the wall of Tom's study. Ron glanced at the image. Satisfied with his results, he waved Ben away and motioned Riya to the seat.

Ben snuck a glance at Tom and overheard him talking to Carlos in the back of the room. "Go with Ron and use the photos to get us passports, with new identities. They have to be top-notch."

"Where are we going?" Carlos asked.

"Trust me, okay?" Tom asked as if it was a question, but it wasn't.

As Ben listened and watched, he both marveled at and feared how Tom had convinced Ron and Carlos to do whatever he needed. The blind obedience was the manipulative behavior that the Pantheon had perfected. Plus, Tom had started his story about the Pantheon when Ron and Carlos conveniently interrupted it. Tom had only rehashed a myth about an early life of Sargon, the god-like leader of the Pantheon.

When Ron snapped the last picture of Riya, Carlos tapped him on the shoulder. The two left the study and exited the house. Ben waited until he heard the Escalade pulling out of the driveway and then turned to Tom. "Shall we continue?"

"What do you mean?" Tom asked.

"You never finished the story about the Pantheon. I'd like to get back to that."

"Of course," Tom said, as if he was more than happy to do that, but his cold eyes suggested otherwise.

"And I still need to know about you," Ben said.

"We're getting there," Tom said. "You need to hear the rest of Sargon's story first."

"Good, because so far, his tale sounds kind of sad, almost like we should feel sorry for him." Ben couldn't help but wonder if Tom was Sargon, especially after the warning from his past self.

"That's because you've only heard the beginning. You won't feel sorry for him for long." Tom settled down in his desk chair. "If you want to know how Sargon created the Pantheon, you have to go back to the life where he derived his name."

CHAPTER 71

Kɪsʜ, 2344 B.C.

Aɴ ɪᴍᴘᴏsɪɴɢ earthen wall surrounded Kish, a mid-sized city for the era. Built beside the life-giving Euphrates River, Kish boasted several multi-story buildings, with the most notable being the king's palace. Outside the walls, simple dwellings dotted the landscape.

An old man emerged from one of them, carrying water pots. His name was La'ibum. He walked to a nearby inlet overgrown with cattails. The wind blew, and the reeds rustled, creating an almost rhythmic beat. As La'ibum waded into the river, something caught his attention—a faint cry. He placed his pots on the shore and waded back into the river, towards the thickest patch of cattails. He pushed them aside and discovered a thatch covered basket. Another cry came from inside. He opened the lid, revealing a baby boy.

La'ibum was the gardener of King Ur-Zababa. A simple man, La'ibum had no children, so he took the infant and raised him as his own. He named the baby Sargon.

Sargon grew into a boy, then a teen. That's when the visions and night-mares began. The first vision occurred after Sargon concluded a successful trade with a neighbor—a pot of grain for a dead rabbit. Meat was a rare treat for Sargon and his father. Sargon had become an independent teen, capable of finding water, gardening, farming, trading, and even protecting himself from the thieves roaming the outskirts of town. He skinned the animal, disemboweled it, and placed it on a spit above the fire. It didn't take long for the tiny carcass to brown. Afraid the meal was burning, Sargon took it off with bare hands, which scorched his fingers. A minor injury, but the skin throbbed. The sensation triggered something in his mind —something psychological. He howled from the insignificant wound. His father rushed to help, but Sargon waved him away. He went into the corner to sulk, embarrassed he'd humiliated himself. That night, as Sargon slept, he dreamt of flames lapping at his feet, smoke rising into his eyes, and the excruciating pain of burning alive.

Over the next several months, the nightmares increased in frequency. Sargon did his best to conceal his feelings, but his father knew something was wrong. The sweet boy La'ibum had known for so many years had morphed into an angry young man.

One night, Sargon awakened from yet another nightmare. The sight of his father sleeping in the corner of their meager hut comforted him, but the slight warmth from the crackling fire filled him with rage and frustration. He reviled the modest fire. Every time he glanced at the flames, wretched screams echoed in his mind, or maybe they were insidious laughs mocking him. His face hardened. No one mocked him. Sargon flung a blanket over his shoulders and eyed the fire with contempt. He continued to scowl at the dancing flames, even though he feared they might come and get him. Then, a thought crossed his mind, and a calm washed over him. He tossed the blanket off and moved closer to the fire. Inches from the blaze, he marveled at the heat. He reached his arm out over the fire and gritted his teeth from the pain as his skin charred. He withdrew his hand and reveled in the sensa-tion that had once crippled him.

DURING THE TIME of Sargon's adolescence, King Ur-Zababa reigned. Relative prosperity marked the rule of the portly leader because of his keen political sense. There was always an enemy to fight or negotiate a treaty with, but the city still flourished. One morning, he stepped out onto his balcony and admired his domain. The sight of the Euphrates nourishing the growing metropolis delighted him. As he soaked up the view, Sargon, still in his teens, walked to the river's edge to fill water jugs. A trio of older boys spied on Sargon from bushes. They sprang out of hiding and stole Sargon's pots and anything else of value. Too far to send help, Ur-Zababa crossed his arms, frustrated he couldn't help the young boy. He'd worked hard to reduce crime, but Sargon was a commoner outside the walls, so no need to spend too much energy worrying about it.

Before returning inside, Ur-Zababa cocked his head in surprise as Sargon pummeled the three larger boys with an impressive array of jabs and spinning kicks. After they fled in tears, Sargon picked up his pots and resumed his work without giving the beat down a second thought. The king smiled. Justice prevailed. He sent two of his servants to summon Sargon to share a meal. Sargon found favor with the king, who invited him to become a member of the royal court as his personal cupbearer. Considered a prestigious duty by most, Sargon bristled at the menial task, but refusing the king's invitation never ended well. Hence, he accepted and soon became a trusted confidante, even if it meant having to "perform."

Ur-Zababa's entourage included a collection of strange individuals, all of whom possessed an extraordinary talent. One servant told dazzling stories, another juggled, and still, another burped and farted on command, which, though disgusting, was great if the mood ever needed to be lightened. Sargon's gift often served as entertainment during meals.

During one significant dinner party, Ur-Zababa met with the leaders of the surrounding tribes and the most powerful men of the city. They all sat on the floor around a long decorated rug covered with plates and bowls of gourmet food. Alcohol flowed, with many guests having had more than their fair share.

Ur-Zababa reclined at the head, adorned with jewels and a sparkling red robe, to signify his stature. His son, Ozil, dressed in similar attire, sat beside him. Sargon, now a young man, stood on the king's left with a jug of wine. Ur-Zababa motioned for a re-fill. Sargon obeyed.

A drunk guest, Moshi, pointed to Sargon. "You. Wine-boy. I hear you are quite the fighter."

Ur-Zababa smiled. "Be careful, Moshi. If you challenge him, you must fight, and Sargon does not lose."

"What's a dinner party without some fun?"

Moshi waved Sargon over to the area next to the feast. Everyone cheered. Sargon turned to Ur-Zababa, who flicked his wrist at Sargon. Time to perform. Annoyed, Sargon obeyed.

Hands held behind his back, Sargon breezed over to Moshi, who already had his arms raised, ready to fight. Moshi punched, and Sargon swiveled his chest and avoided the attack. Moshi swung again. Same result.

The crowd jeered Moshi, and his fun-loving bravado melted with his honor now at stake. He re-focused, feigned a punch, and kicked. Sargon caught Moshi's leg, twisted, knocked him to the ground, and delivered a blow to the face.

Moshi waved for mercy as he held his head. Sargon stepped back to his post as the crowd applauded and cheered.

The king's son, Ozil, bristled from the attention Sargon received. "Now my turn." He uncrossed his legs to stand.

Ur-Zababa subtly motioned for his son to remain sitting.

Sargon heard Ozil but refused to take the bait. "I could never defeat such a powerful warrior."

Ur-Zababa did not want his son's honor besmirched, especially at the hands of his servant. "We've already had enough entertainment."

Young and full of hubris, Ozil persisted. "No, Father. You said if you challenge, you must fight."

The guests watched the exchange, hoping for another fight.

Ur-Zababa waved at Ozil to stand down while grinning at his guests. "At the next feast, we will all enjoy your victory." He then held his hands out to his visitors. "Now, we tend to the reason I called you here. Lugal-zagesi."

The festivities of the dinner party stopped. The mere mention of this name instilled fear.

"He is eager for war. His army has threatened villages on the border. Many are defecting."

A boisterous guest held up his cup. "We will fight Lugal-zagesi!"

The guests cheered to support the idea.

Ur-Zababa appreciated the fighting spirit, but he was a rational man. "His numbers are too great."

The dinner guest, a "yes man" if there ever was one, raised his cup again. "We must sue for peace!"

The guests now clamored for a peace treaty.

Ur-Zababa nodded in agreement. "We must do what's best for the kingdom." He lifted his wine. The others followed suit in a toast. Ur-Zababa glanced at Ozil, who continued to glare at Sargon. "For our children."

A MODEST CARAVAN prepared to embark on a journey. Two slaves lifted a cart filled with gifts of cloth, gold, and silver. A white stallion with the mark of King Ur-Zababa stood in front, while a small contingent of soldiers surrounded the treasure.

Ur-Zababa exited the palace with Sargon. A servant followed behind them, carrying two clay tablets wrapped in a royal fabric and secured with the king's seal.

"Lugal-zagesi is a man of honor. You will be safe," Ur-Zababa said as he led Sargon to the caravan.

Hands clasped together, Sargon replied, "I trust you, my lord."

Ur-Zababa motioned to the tablets. "Deliver the peace terms and tribute. He should accept, but if he doesn't, he will honor my mark and give you safe passage."

"I trust you, my lord," Sargon said, knowing that if the king was wrong, he'd be killed.

Sargon mounted the stallion as the servant placed the tablets into the pack on the side. From atop the steed, Sargon looked down on Ur-Zababa and smiled. He was warming up to this trip.

Ozil exited the palace and walked beside his father.

Ur-Zababa waved to Sargon. "May the gods grant you a safe journey, my faithful servant."

Sargon eyed both father and son, and his smile disappeared. He bowed in deference. Then the cavalcade moved forward.

The caravan attempted to follow the river as much as possible, but eventually, they had to detour through miles of arid desert. They were a beacon of life and wealth in an otherwise barren landscape. The long and arduous journey took fourteen days, but they finally reached their destination—the glimmering city of Ur. Even from a distance, it appeared larger and more lavish than Kish. Sargon wondered what type of ruler could create such an incredible city.

Hours later, he stood outside the entrance to the king's palace with his horse and cart of tribute behind him. Lugal-zagesi's royal guards surrounded the slaves and escort troops. The king emerged in a flowing scarlet robe, golden jewelry, and encircled by an entourage of attendants.

Sargon bowed and presented the two tablets, now conspicuously unwrapped. An attendant accepted, then delivered them to a scribe standing beside Lugal-zagesi. The scribe read the tablets, eyed Sargon, and whispered to Lugal-zagesi.

"If you wish to kill me, here I am. Do as your enemy wishes," Sargon said.

Lugal-zagesi approached Sargon and looked him over from head to toe. "A servant who can read cuneiform?"

Sargon could kill Lugal-zagesi before the guards could reach him, but he had other plans. He kept his eyes and head down. "I know many languages."

Lugal-zagesi circled Sargon and studied every inch of him. "Then you know you are a peace offering. A sacrifice. And Ur-Zababa proposes an annual tribute." Lugal-zagesi motioned to the cart of treasure. "Why should I not accept this?"

Head still bowed, Sargon replied, "He knows he cannot defeat you, which is why he sues for peace. He is a coward who fears his own servant. If you do his bidding, are you then not his servant? And this tribute, is your protection not worth at least three times this? Let me defeat him, and you shall be honored with a proper tribute."

Lugal-zagesi considered Sargon's proposal while Ur-Zababa's guards eyed each other, unsure what this would mean for their lives.

On that day, the boy who was a cupbearer became a man that commanded an army. Sargon returned to Kish and exacted his revenge on the king, who was so willing to toss his life away. He also killed Ozil, but not before granting his wish. Sargon engaged in a hand-to-hand fight to the death. The one-sided contest unleashed a lifetime of pent up rage against the prior father and son duo.

Sargon had convinced Lugal-zagesi to let him lead a small contingent of troops to defeat Ur-Zababa. When Kish had been conquered, Sargon lavished the soldiers with gifts, women, liquor, and the promise of even grander treasure if they served him—and serve they did. After rallying all the nearby tribes, Sargon led a massive army against Lugal-zagesi. The battle was fierce and bloody, but in the end, Sargon emerged victorious.

The grand city of Ur became his. Sargon moved into Lugal-zagesi's palace and did what he had always dreamed of doing. He ruled. Now, people bowed to him. It was how it should be.

For decades, Sargon the Great reigned supreme. Ruling with an iron fist, his subjects learned that it was easier and safer to follow him without question.

One day, during his twilight years, servants presented him with the latest in fashion. He slipped on a majestic purple robe in his royal chambers. Extracted secretions of marine snails had stained the soft linen a brilliant color, unlike anything anyone had seen before. Sargon clapped for a servant to bring a giant polished obsidian stone that served as a primitive mirror. Eager to admire himself, Sargon inspected his dark reflection. His face had crow's feet and deep wrinkles across his forehead. His hair had greyed, and his shoulders slouched over.

At that moment, Sargon realized he had a problem.

CHAPTER 72

Rome, 268 B.C.

Alexander gripped the jeweled dagger in the cold, underground secret chamber and considered his options. Should he accept Solomon's offer and plunge it into his own chest? Should he strike Solomon instead? Maybe he should make a run for it? He considered everything, then dropped the knife.

"I don't fear death. But I also won't embrace it until I've fulfilled a vow to my friend. I'll find Gabriel or whatever his name is, and I will have my vengeance."

Solomon pondered over Alexander's response. "Those that follow this man choose death. We choose life. As did you... but it is to end the life of another." Solomon picked the dagger up off the floor and mused over the puzzling answer.

Alexander arched an eyebrow, confused. Was that a test? Did he pass? "What do you want with me?"

Solomon twirled the blade in his hand. "We have people throughout the world, searching for those who can remember. So does the enemy. We need more to join us if we're going to have any chance."

"Any chance at what?" Alexander asked.

Solomon stared at Alexander. "Stopping him. He believes he's a god who should rule. He and his followers call themselves the Pantheon. We are the Lux Mundi. We must lead instead of him."

"So people follow you? How are you any different from them?" Alexander asked, his suspicion growing.

Solomon huffed. "We couldn't be more different. He is the darkness. We lead people to the light. Do you know what we've accomplished here—in Rome? We've created a republic. There is not one monarch or king. A senate does the will of the people, but as the republic grows, we need more of 'us' to keep it a republic. Will you join us?"

Alexander's head spun. Two opposing sides, one claiming to be the light, the other the darkness, and a manipulative leader who pretends to be someone he's not. How could he trust anyone? "I'm grateful for your offer, but I must respectfully decline. My purpose is to find my friend in Rome."

Solomon bobbed his head, disappointed. "Finding people like us is rare, especially since you can't recognize one another physically."

"We have a special hand signal to recognize each another," Alexander said.

"Clever. But even with that, Rome is a massive city. The odds of you and your friend being here at the same time... are not good."

"I understand, but I gave him my word."

Solomon sheathed the dagger. "I appreciate your honesty, even if it is disheartening."

Alexander turned to leave.

"Alexander?"

He swung back around. Solomon tossed him a small but heavy pouch that jingled. "You'll need money if you're going to be in the city."

Alexander opened it, revealing silver coins. He bowed in gratitude.

"And Alexander, let's say you kill this man. What then?" Solomon asked.

"What do you mean?"

"You know he will return—in another life. What will you have accomplished?"

Alexander paused. He hadn't considered this.

"Did he ask you to join him?"

Alexander ran through his memories. "When I was dying, his men told me I'd get one more chance to choose."

Solomon crossed his arms and stroked his face, hoping Alexander would see the inevitable. "You must choose a side, Alexander. The light or the darkness. Whether in this life or another. And sometimes not choosing a side actually is."

Alexander furrowed his brow, unsure how that made sense. He bowed in gratitude for the coins. "I just need to find my friend."

Solomon offered one last piece of advice. "Don't allow yourself to be captured unless you intend to join the Pantheon. This man is dangerous. Far more than you realize. He won't be so kind as to kill you quickly. He will torture you and keep you alive as long as possible so that it takes longer for you to reemerge to challenge him again."

"Why does he torture? Why doesn't he just imprison you?"

Solomon shook his head. "He's the darkness."

CHAPTER 73

Virginia, 2018

In Tom's study, Riya and Ben sat on the edge of their chairs, listening to Tom tell the tale of Sargon from behind his desk. Riya's mind spun. The account was unlike any history lesson she'd ever heard growing up. Like so many things for Ben, the story felt familiar, but he didn't know why—it was like hearing a song he recognized, but he couldn't recall the title even though it was on the tip of his tongue.

"So, what was Sargon's problem?" Riya asked.

"As he grew older, he knew that ruling in one lifetime would never be enough, and his time as Sargon the Great was running out."

Ben leaned back in his chair, frustrated. "That still doesn't explain the creation of the Pantheon or how you know about it."

Before Tom could respond, his phone dinged, indicating a text message. His face dropped after reading it. He exited the study without a word, leaving Ben and Riya alone.

"What do you think that was about?" Ben asked.

"I don't know, but something's off," Riya said.

"Yeah, he keeps talking around the details of the Pantheon."

"And he doesn't want to expose them either," she added. "Do you think he's Pantheon?" Riya asked.

Ben rubbed his chin like he often did when he pondered. "I don't want to wait to find out."

Riya nodded in agreement, and they both crept to the door of the study. Ben peered out and found Tom in the living room, engrossed with something on the television. Riya pointed to the front door. This was their chance.

On the television, a solemn news anchor delivered a breaking news announcement. "We've received word that Congressman Tom Vance is wanted for drug possession and attempted theft of narcotics from the Virginia Hospital Center."

In the foyer, Ben turned the handle of the door. As he opened it, sirens erupted from two police cruisers pulling up to the gate.

An officer on a loudspeaker called out, "Congressman Vance, we need you to open the gate and come out of the house with your hands in the air."

Tom rushed over. "Close the door!" He shoved the door shut. All three stared out the window as more police cars pulled up. Tom pointed them towards the backdoor. When they reached it, they found officers on the other side of the fence line. A helicopter circled overhead, causing more concern. They were surrounded.

The news report on the television now showed a split-screen. On the left, the anchor, and the right featured a location reporter standing outside the Vance estate not too far from the police cruisers. "We're live at the home of Tom Vance, who is wanted along with Dr. Riya Patel and Ben Preston."

Riya's jaw dropped. "What? That's absurd."

"No, that's the Pantheon," Tom said.

As the reporter continued to provide details, officers periodically came into view behind her. One of them was Varus. He motioned the news van to back up and stay clear.

Ben pointed at the screen. "That's the guy that tried to kill us."

"Yeah. His name is…" Riya racked her brain trying to remember his name. "Harper Peterson."

"No. His name is Varus," Ben said.

Tom seized Ben by the arm. "Varus? Are you sure?"

"I'm sure. Do you know him?"

Tom took a deep breath. "Yeah. I know him."

CHAPTER 74

Ur, 2280 B.C.

Sargon wallowed in an almost catatonic state in his mammoth cedar bed while servants stood ready to assist. One tried to tempt him with figs. No reaction. Another offered wine. Not interested. A concubine stroked his cheek. Nothing. Deep in thought or depression, Sargon stared straight ahead.

A graying and much older Moshi, the man Sargon beat up at the dinner party years ago, entered and bowed. Sargon stirred, the first sign of life. "What have the oracles said? Can one live forever?"

Moshi looked at the ground. "Regretfully, all said man must return to the earth."

Sargon waved Moshi away. "Then why have you returned? Did I not make myself clear when you left? My body grows older and more decrepit by the day."

Moshi swallowed hard, unsure if he should speak further. "Because there is one oracle I have not met. He may have the answer."

"Why have you not met with him?" Sargon barked.

"Many believe he is a myth. He is rumored to be 700 years old and has discovered the fountain of youth."

Sargon leaned up in the bed, his attention piqued. "Find out if this is true." He pointed Moshi out the door to locate this man.

Moshi didn't move. "I don't know where he is. Only that he's rumored to be," he dropped his voice to a hush, "in the valley of death."

Even in a whisper, Sargon's servants overheard. The mere mention of the valley had a chilling effect. Filled with myth and legend, the valley of death was a place one did not travel to by choice.

Sargon considered his options. "Death comes for me, anyway. I shall spare it the journey."

He ordered two donkeys to be mounted with provisions, and his royal horse readied. Within hours, Sargon had cleaned himself up and prepared to leave. He marched out of the palace, climbed on his horse, and grabbed the reins. Servants and advisers stood by confused. Their king arranged for an expedition he would not return from.

One servant approached. "Will my lord reconsider embarking on this perilous trip?"

Sargon ignored him.

"Then will you at least bring some men with you? The deserts are filled with enemies."

Sargon had already considered all this. He motioned his horse forward. "If anyone tries to take my throne while I'm gone, you'd better hope I do not return."

The royal court watched, dumbfounded, as Sargon left.

After leaving the safety of the city, it didn't take long before Sargon found himself in an empty wasteland, but his journey had only begun. Day after day, he plodded forward in the scorching heat, determined to reach the infamous valley. The provisions carried on the backs of the donkeys dwindled, along with Sargon's vigor. Soon, two donkeys became one as Sargon sacrificed the first for food. The meat and blood didn't last long in the brutal sun. Still, Sargon pressed on until his horse neighed in a cry of anguish before falling to the ground, sending Sargon rolling into the dirt.

Abused and beaten, Sargon picked himself up and looked at his dead horse. The animal had been worked to death. Sargon grabbed a knife and carved up the carcass. He salvaged as much blood as possible, packed it on the donkey, hopped on its back, and continued.

He reached a canyon littered with the bones of dead animals. The walls contained pictographs that showed images of what appeared like people being sacrificed. Further ahead, the trail narrowed. Strange markings covered this wall. Who had been out in this wasteland? The marks unsettled Sargon.

He hopped off the donkey and tapped its side to go forward. When it passed the markings on the wall, it tripped on a hidden line of sinew. Darts shot out from the sides of the walls, tagging the animal. The donkey reared and galloped away in fear, almost knocking Sargon over. Fearing he was under attack, Sargon reached for his sword but paused before unsheathing. This trek hadn't been taken to fight. He dropped the blade to the ground, removed his tunic, and stood up stark naked. Arms outstretched, he walked forward. "I come in peace. I come for knowledge," he said.

A voice echoed against the walls. "Don't move."

Sargon stopped. A spry, middle-aged man in a tawny robe emerged from behind a rock. "If you take one more step, you'll fall into a pit."

Sargon studied the ground, then nodded in gratitude.

"Put your clothes on, but leave your weapons outside and follow me." The man disappeared behind the rock.

Sargon tossed his tunic on and walked around the hidden pit to the rock, where he discovered a tiny opening that led to a cave. He squeezed inside and followed a narrow tunnel illuminated by torches. As he maneuvered through the tight space, he emerged in an enormous cavern with a natural spring in the middle and a campfire beside it. He passed by something resembling a miniature catapult, then found another contraption with wooden gears and pulleys. As he surveyed the floor, he discovered all manner of wooden and metallic creations, along with a rock table containing crystals and bowls filled with colored powders.

The man emerged from a small room with a plate of bread. He placed it on the table and motioned Sargon over. Sargon approached and ate.

"Thank you."

Sargon and the man eyed one another with suspicion and curiosity.

His mouth stuffed with bread, Sargon garbled, "Who are you?"

"You can call me Ubarum. You?"

"Sargon."

"Ah, the ruler of Sumer," Ubarum said, unimpressed.

Sargon surveyed the cavern and then stared at the natural spring. "What is this place?"

"It's where I figure things out."

Sargon's eyes narrowed, confused.

"Toss a little of that black powder into the fire." Ubarum pointed to a small bowl on the table.

Sargon took a pinch, walked to the fire, and tossed it in. *Poof!* The powder ignited into a burst of flame. Sargon recoiled in fear and amazement.

"What was that?"

Ubarum stepped to the fire, trying to comprehend what he'd just witnessed, even though he'd performed this experiment many times. "You mean, why does it do that? Or even what is fire? Why does it consume some material and make other things strong?"

"What does it make strong?"

Ubarum unsheathed a steel sword, something supposedly not created for another 900 years. He handed it to Sargon, who admired the beauty of the blade.

Ubarum stroked the side of the blade and its shiny, smooth surface. "Forged in the hottest of fires. Stronger than any bronze weapon your army possesses."

After a moment of study and admiration, Sargon handed the weapon back.

"Is that not what you came for, Sargon the Great?" Ubarum asked with more than a hint of sarcasm. "New weapons for conquering?"

Sargon shook his head. "I come for the fountain of youth." He glanced at the natural spring.

Ubarum crossed his arms. "How did you hear of it?"

"People know you cannot die because of this water."

Ubarum walked to the spring, knelt down, and dipped his hand in the life-giving water. "You have traveled a great journey, Sargon. Few people attempt to cross that desert." He waved his hand over the water, welcoming Sargon to enjoy. "You have proved yourself worthy. You may drink."

Sargon walked to the water's edge. Timidly, he knelt down and peeked at his reflection. An old man stared back. He cupped his hands and drank several restorative handfuls. Eyes closed, he let the power of the water fill his soul.

"Look at your reflection. You look younger already!" Ubarum shouted.

Sargon's eyes snapped open. He scanned the water to find his reflection. The same old man stared back.

Ubarum howled with laughter, pleased with his practical joke.

Sargon sneered. "No one mocks me." He rose to his feet to fight.

Ubarum stood up. "Old man, you can see I am well prepared. Don't you think I have ten ways to kill you right now?" He tapped the handle of the steel sword hanging on his belt.

Sargon relented, fell to his knees, and looked down in despair. "It must be true. You have more than a lifetime of work here."

Ubarum walked back to the table. "I'll never understand people's need to explain the unexplainable with the supernatural. It's as if their little brains can't uncover the truth, so to protect their fragile pride, they conclude no one can, and therefore, it must be some mythical force." Ubarum chuckled, but then grew serious. "You're going to die, Sargon. Accept it."

Sargon clenched his teeth and stood up. "No."

"Why on earth would you want to live forever, anyway?"

"My mind already does."

Ubarum paused and looked Sargon up and down. "Is that so?" He searched through a collection of baskets behind the table and pulled out a strange scepter. Made of gold with long thin ends on each side, it encased a clear crystal in the middle. He held the scepter in his right hand, then handed it to Sargon. "Hold both ends of this."

Sargon grabbed both sides of the rod, and the crystal in the middle glowed like a soothing Tuscan sunset. Sargon marveled at what appeared to be magic. How could light be created out of nothing?

Ubarum took the scepter back with one hand. The crystal stopped glowing. Before Sargon could ask, Ubarum explained, "You're emitting energy. An aura that is only given off by people who are re-born, or at least who remember their past lives."

Ubarum grabbed both ends of the scepter, and the crystal glowed again.

CHAPTER 75

Rome, 268 B.C.

Alexander limped along Rome's stone streets, passing by stranger after stranger with his hands gripped in the secret hand signal taught to him by Hephaestion. People eyed him, confused. He realized how stupid he must look and the long odds of finding his friend. He paused and held his aching thigh.

"Any luck?"

Alexander startled as he turned to find Michael standing behind him. "Are you following me?"

"No," Michael said, but then admitted, "not really."

Alexander looked him up and down. What did he want?

"I get a minor reprieve from being in that dinky town where I found you. I get some time to enjoy the greatest city on earth. But it's kind of boring alone, you know," Michael said.

Alexander didn't know. This was a first for him, at least as far as he could remember. Alexander sat down and leaned his back against a building. He continued to rub his thigh, hoping to ease the pain.

"Maybe I can help you find your friend," Michael said.

"I don't see how."

Uninvited, Michael hunched down beside Alexander, uncomfortably close. "Who is he? I mean, really think about who your friend is. What did he do? What did he like? Things that he might not even realize. Did he always wear specific colors? Did he like certain foods? Those little quirks make us who we are."

Alexander stared at the small space separating them, hoping Michael would take the hint. He didn't. "I'll find my friend, but if you want to help, can you point me toward a doctor who can help with the pain in my leg?"

"Doctors here aren't that good," Michael said, but then pointed down the road. "But there's one about three streets down that's supposed to be decent."

Alexander struggled to his feet and limped off. He passed by the buildings with each one appearing more foreign. They all had odd signs hanging above the door. He recognized one because it was a Greek symbol—two snakes wound around a staff—the image associated with Asclepius, the Greek god of healing. With nothing better to go on, Alexander entered.

A doctor in a flowing blue toga sauntered in, but his face dropped at the sight of Alexander in his animal skin clothing. People who lived off the land rarely had money.

"Can you help with the pain in my leg?" Alexander held up the bag of coins.

The doctor's eyes lit up, and he beamed, happy to be wrong. "Yes, indeed." He whisked Alexander further inside. "Your humors are out of balance. Sit here and let me consult my literature."

Alexander rested on a mat on the floor and leaned his back against the wall. He closed his eyes, grateful to relax, even if only for a moment.

In the backroom, the doctor discussed the wound with an old woman. She argued with the doctor, then came out to inspect Alexander's leg. It was Alisa, only much, much older. When Alexander opened his eyes, she had already returned to the backroom. Alisa directed the doctor to the correct remedy.

The doctor shooed her away, snatched the medicine, and returned to Alexander's side. "I have just the thing. First, for your pain." The doctor offered a bowl with plant shavings.

Alexander scooped them up and ate them. The doctor undressed the wound and cleaned it with a cloth. Alexander winced as the doctor scrubbed the sensitive skin clean.

"Close your eyes and imagine something other than what I'll be doing."

Alexander nodded. He'd been through this routine before. He closed his eyes just as Alisa walked back out with a pot filled with medicine and a bowl full of water. "We're low on several medicines. I must go to the market."

The doctor grabbed the pot and snapped, "Hurry it up. I don't pay you to shop."

"Understood," Alisa said.

Something in Alisa's voice triggered Alexander's memory. He opened his eyes but only glimpsed Alisa's back as she left for the market. He closed his eyes again. Michael's advice rang in his head. Who was Hephaestion? What did he like? Alexander smirked as he remembered a party with a half-drunk Hephaestion bellowing for more Chios, a high-end wine. He refused the wine from Bactria. "I'd rather drink camel piss," was a phrase he repeated throughout the night.

Alexander's mind shifted to another memory—to a feast thrown in their honor by a small tribe that had been loyal to Persia. Rather than fight, they offered their support to the Greeks. To show their fealty, they presented a bountiful banquet for the officers of the Greek army. The main course consisted of roasted pork. Hephaestion devoured his meal, and it soon became a joke that he'd eaten an entire pig all on his own.

The smile only grew bigger as Alexander relived the good times with his friend. After defeating the Persians and taking over Persepolis, he remembered Hephaestion ogling the women. Their dark hair enthralled him, especially when they let it down. He turned into a teenage boy, enamored by the female form.

"There you go. All set," the doctor said.

Jarred out of his trip down memory lane, Alexander opened his eyes and realized he'd been out of it. He looked at his leg and found a very secure bandage. He stood and tested it out. "This is amazing. How did you do that?"

"I'm an incredible doctor. Tell your friends."

In the backroom, Alisa chafed as the doctor took all the credit.

Feeling infinitely better, Alexander now walked with only a slight limp. Traveling to the market, he found local vendors selling crafts, jewels, smoked meats, and fresh bread from carts. After surveying the scene, Alexander spotted what he wanted and approached a jeweler.

"You like?" the vendor asked.

The necklace had a stone similar to the one Hephaestion wore, except without the carvings. Alexander paid the jeweler, then moved onto another merchant and bought a hunting knife. He found a spot on the steps in front of the Temple of Jupiter and got to work carving the same symbols from Hephaestion's medallion into the stone. Once he finished, he admired his work. Not bad.

Alexander slipped the necklace on and wandered the streets of Rome, making sure the markings remained facing out. He passed by a wine shop and inquired with the owner about wine from Chios. Unfortunately, he didn't have any.

Later in the afternoon, Alexander visited a thermopolium, which was the equivalent of an ancient takeout restaurant. He purchased an enormous chunk of pork, sat down not too far away, and started eating. When other customers selected pork, Alexander drifted in front of the person holding his plate of pork and the medallion. This only resulted in confused stares.

The sun set and Alexander sheepishly asked a man where he could find "female companionship." After being directed to the nearest bathhouse, Alexander lost his nerve after witnessing young women chatting up men and offering their "services."

Back on the steps at the Temple of Jupiter, he stared at the medallion and rubbed the carvings. He missed his friend. "It was a good idea anyway," he said, trying to cheer himself up.

Alexander rose to his feet and walked through the market while the vendors packed up their carts for the day. He turned down a small alley. Out of nowhere, a man shoved him against the wall and stuck a knife against his throat.

"Who are you?" the man demanded.

"Alexander. From Macedon."

The man pressed the knife harder against Alexander's throat. "Do you know what that medallion says, Alexander from Macedon?"

The tip of the blade pierced Alexander's skin. "Fear controls the lesser man." Alexander performed the hand signal in front of his chest as he spoke.

The man let down his knife and his guard. He pulled Alexander close and embraced him. "I can't believe it. My friend."

Alexander couldn't believe it either. After all this time, he'd found Hephaestion!

CHAPTER 76

Riya never liked Tom and the more she learned about him, the less she liked. It troubled her that Tom didn't want to release the information on Anjali's Zip drive to the public, which might expose the Pantheon. Maybe it was possible that the Pantheon could bury the data, but Tom believed it was a certainty, which made no sense. And now, he admitted that he knew the person who had tried to kill her. Who was Tom? Until now, he revealed a calculated façade based on partial answers, and he loved to talk about trust, which was ironic given how much she distrusted him. Riya watched him as he stared pale-faced at the television.

"How do you know him?" she asked.

Tom didn't answer. He leered at Varus as if he were a ghost.

"Tom! How do you know him?"

Tom shook his head and snapped out of his daze. "I need to talk to Varus alone."

"No," Riya said.

Tom's bravado returned. He stepped toward Riya and stared her down. "Do you want to have any chance of getting out of this?"

Riya got right back in Tom's face. "How do you know the guy that tried to kill us?"

Ben stood behind Riya. He demanded answers, too. In this standoff of wills, the numbers didn't favor Tom. Something or someone had to give. "You want to know what caused my memory block?" Tom asked. "Torture. Brutal, extreme torture. Sargon ordered it done. That's how he maintains power. He tortures those that don't serve him. The pain stops you from remembering."

Another partial answer that deflected from Riya's original question. "How do you know Varus?"

Tom looked again at the television screen. "Varus was a friend—once. He doesn't want to follow Sargon. He just doesn't feel like he has a choice."

Ben shook his head. "He seemed more than willing when he tried to kidnap and kill Riya."

"He's doing what he's told." Tom raised his voice. "Listen, he won't help unless he feels he can trust me. I need to speak to him alone."

There was that word again—*trust*. Riya trusted that Tom still hid information. She also trusted that neither Tom nor Ben seemed that concerned about the murder of her sister, and Anjali's death had to mean something. It had to matter. If it didn't, then for Riya, at least, nothing did. "OK, but here's the thing, Tom. You need to trust *this*. If you're not being honest with me, the Zip drive goes public. Maybe the Pantheon can hide it. Maybe they can't. Either way, I'm releasing it. Understood?"

"Fair enough."

Tom took his phone out and dialed. "Carlos. It's Tom. Yeah, I saw the news. Where are you?" Tom paced the living room as he listened to the response. "Good. I need you to do another job. I need you to deliver a message."

OUTSIDE THE GATES of the estate, officers waited in position. Many looked bored and wondered why they had a congressman of all people holed up like a dangerous terrorist. Varus, the only one aware of the real reason, talked to another detective about re-positioning the men closer in preparation for the final assault.

An officer approached. "Sir."

Varus didn't answer.

"*Sir.*"

Varus stopped, annoyed by the interruption.

The officer handed Varus a piece of paper. "Someone has a message about the standoff. They said it was from an old friend—Mr. Craterus."

Varus glanced at the paper slip, then stepped aside and dialed his phone. He listened and with every second that passed, his jaw clenched tighter and tighter. His calculated plans were ruined. He hung up and gripped the phone like he wanted to crush it. Without a word, he stormed off towards the estate. The other officers tried to stop him, but he held up his hand.

"No one does anything until I return." Varus charged toward the front door of the estate.

Time for old friends to meet.

CHAPTER 77

VALLEY OF DEATH, 2280 B.C.

SARGON INSPECTED the golden scepter and the encased crystal. He held both ends, causing the crystal to illuminate, then let go. He repeated this process, unable to comprehend how he could emit energy that caused the stone to light up.

"I thought I was the only one with this gift," Sargon said.

Ubarum watched Sargon play with the scepter, amused. "There are others. Not many, but there are others."

"Your body dies?" Sargon asked.

Ubarum nodded.

Disappointed, Sargon sat down. This journey had been all for naught. Ubarum plopped down beside him.

"Why does it matter that your body dies if your mind doesn't?" Ubarum asked.

"Every lifetime you have to rebuild. If you're not born into the right family, you can't use these abilities without being viewed as a freak or being enslaved." Sargon shook his head at the frustration and agony he'd experienced.

"If you want anything of physical value in another life, use your brain." Ubarum tapped his forehead.

Sargon eyed Ubarum, jealous. He had life all figured out. "How do you do it?"

Ubarum held up a finger and then disappeared into a cave. While he waited, Sargon continued to toy with the scepter and the magic of the glowing crystal. How did Ubarum figure all this out? Was he that much smarter?

From inside the cave, Ubarum shouted. "What do you want more than anything? Is it to transfer your wealth to the next life?"

"Yes," Saron said, assuming that was the answer Ubarum wanted. As the words left Sargon's lips, the crystal stopped glowing for a split second, then resumed. Sargon cocked his head with curiosity.

Ubarum returned with a heavy sack covered with dirt. He opened it, revealing coins and jewels. "I often bury my gold and gems. I choose locations that are sure to remain in another life."

Sargon held up the scepter. "Do you know how this works?"

Ubarum shook his head. "Not entirely, but you're still asking the wrong question."

"What's the right one?"

"How is this even possible?" Ubarum motioned to his cave of inventions, then to Sargon and himself. "Why are we born with this gift?"

"I don't know."

Ubarum took a deep breath. "I don't know the answer either, but I've got nothing but time to figure it out."

An idea brewed in Sargon's head—one that grew bolder by the second —an idea that solved the riddle of growing old. He pointed to Ubarum's sword. "How do you turn weak metal into that?"

Ubarum smiled, eager to share his knowledge with someone who could genuinely appreciate it. "Let me show you." He walked to the fire.

Sargon snatched the bowl of black powder and slipped it under his cloak.

Ubarum took a knee next to the fire. Sargon knelt down on the opposite side.

"This fire is hot." Ubarum held his hands to the fire. "But it is nothing compared to the heat of a volcano. I once journeyed to one and could see the molten inferno changing everything—even the rock. Sometimes, the things that emerged from the fire were stronger than what went in."

Sargon stared at the flames. "You've learned a lot, Ubarum. I've learned some things too. Have you ever been burned?"

"A little once. That was all I needed to respect its power."

Sargon smirked at the dancing flames. "Indeed, it does have tremendous power. I've been burned. I probably died in less than a minute, but the pain was so unbearable that each second felt like a lifetime. It was so bad that in my next lifetimes, I didn't want to remember my past. The pain echoed into my present. I lost this gift for a long time. I can only imagine how long I would've lost it if that suffering had gone on for any longer than it did." Sargon raised his gaze to Ubarum. "But I want to find out."

Ubarum tilted his head, confused by the statement. Sargon tossed the black powder into the fire in front of Ubarum. It burst into a giant fireball that consumed Ubarum. He shrieked in horror and flailed, trying to put the flames out.

Sargon waited several seconds as Ubarum burned and then shouted, "Jump in the water."

Ubarum ran into the spring and submerged himself. The fire extinguished, and Ubarum floated to the surface. Sargon grabbed one of his legs and yanked Ubarum out.

Ubarum's charred robe smoked, and the skin on his legs was blistered and melted. He wallowed in extreme, hopeless suffering. He would die. It was just a question of when and how much agony he would endure.

Sargon took the scepter, the bag of treasure, and then removed the steel sword from Ubarum's side. "If you and I cross paths again, the pain you feel now will be nothing compared to what I will inflict."

Ubarum could only moan in response. Sargon grabbed a log from the fire and then set all the tables filled with Ubarum's work on fire. He left Ubarum to die a slow, miserable death alone in the dark.

Sargon trotted out of the cavern with a bounce in his step. He'd discovered his version of the fountain of youth.

CHAPTER 78

Rome, 268 B.C.

ALEXANDER AND HEPHAESTION embraced like long-lost brothers in the hidden alleyway. In a matter of seconds, joy and optimism replaced years of aching frustration. Overcome with emotion, a tear streamed down Alexander's cheek.

"I had almost given up hope," Alexander said.

"Me too," Hephaestion replied, but then pulled away in panic. "I don't have long. I must return. I'm a slave to a noble. An arrogant prick."

"A slave?"

Hephaestion nodded. "On my travels to Rome, a legion captured me. I became a spoil of 'war.' It's how this town prospers—on the backs of its slaves. Now I fetch food for my dung heap of a master."

"Why don't you run?" Alexander asked.

"They smashed my ankles when I was sold. Even walking is now painful." Hephaestion said with a twinge of pain in his voice from just speaking of it.

"What can I do?" Alexander asked.

Hephaestion leaned into Alexander's face and whispered. "We must bring down Rome. The people who infiltrated our army are running it."

"The Pantheon, right?"

Hephaestion pulled away, now suspicious of Alexander. "Who told you that?"

"I've met some people. They have the gift too. They're working behind the scenes to stop the Pantheon."

"Who?" Hephaestion asked.

"One is named Solomon. The other Michael. I don't know the others. They helped establish the republic. To give the power to the people so the Pantheon can't have it."

Hephaestion stepped back from Alexander. "So, they created the republic that turns millions like me into slaves. *That* is for the people?" His face hardened. "Do you remember when I told you to be wary of Gabriel?"

Alexander looked at the ground in shame. His naivete was the reason they were in this predicament.

Hephaestion paced in the alley, frustrated by Alexander. "Have you not learned anything?"

Alexander snapped back, "I didn't join them. I came to find you."

Hephaestion softened. "And I, you. I can't believe it. After all this time." He grabbed Alexander by both arms and looked him in the eye. "Rome is going to be the center of the world. We must help lead it. We can't be afraid to fail."

Alexander shook his head in agreement, but he was afraid to fail. That's precisely how he felt, and it's how he felt every day that he led the Greek empire.

"I'm going to find a way to escape. I'll meet you outside the south gate in two days. Be careful of anyone following you." Hephaestion limped off.

Alexander waited a moment to give Hephaestion a head start so no one would know they'd been speaking. He emerged from the alleyway and scanned the remaining people in the market square in fear. Was anyone out for him?

His paranoia grew as he moved through the streets. Each person he passed looked more suspicious than the next. He maneuvered his way through the city until he reached an inn. He entered and rented a room for the night.

A moment later, he found himself inside a simple room with a mat for sleeping. He slid the bar across the door to lock it, laid down on the mat, and exhaled. He was safe. His body needed sleep, but his mind had other ideas. Could he lead Rome? What if he failed? What if the Pantheon outsmarted him again? The faces of the men from his army flashed through his brain—men who died serving him. He let many people down, including Alisa. He'd promised to return and keep her safe, but he didn't. That failure bounced around his head. He wanted to forget it, but he couldn't. He hated imagining how she must've felt when he never returned, but he smiled, thinking about her eyes—those big, beautiful brown eyes. That thought comforted him and lulled him to sleep.

A BOOMING KNOCK snapped Alexander from his slumber. How long had he been asleep? Panic set it. Maybe the Pantheon figured out where he was staying.

"Who is it?" he asked.

The voice from the innkeeper put him at ease. "You paid for the night. Time for you to pay more or leave."

Alexander opened his money pouch and found it empty. Guess it was time to leave. Moments later, Alexander returned to the bustle of the big city. Roman citizens rushed to and fro. No one gave him much notice, which provided a break from his paranoia. He wandered through town until he reached the market square. Maybe it was the smell of warm bread that drew him back, but he had no money and could only stare at the steaming loaves, fresh fruit, and skewered meats. He stood beside the bread wagon, which teased him with intoxicating aromas that rumbled his stomach. The owner sold a bread basket to a paying customer, which provided a tempting opportunity. One little loaf rested on the edge of the cart. Who would miss that?

An arm patted Alexander on the shoulder. He whirled around and found Michael.

"Hungry?" Michael asked.

Alexander stepped away from the bread cart, embarrassed he had even considered stealing.

"Rome is an expensive city. If you spent the money we gave you, allow me to buy you a meal."

"No, I'm fine. Thanks."

"Did you find your friend?" Michael asked.

"No. Like you thought, too many people."

The two walked through the market square. "What are you going to do?"

"Probably going to head out," Alexander said.

"That's disappointing," Michael said. "Solomon and I were hoping you might change your mind. We think you could be a tremendous help to us. Solomon even liked your idea of a hand signal."

Alexander wondered why Michael kept appearing out of nowhere and why he was so interested in what he would do next. Had he been following him this whole time?

As they walked, Alexander glanced back. Michael did too. A trio of Roman soldiers tracked them in the background. "Alexander, don't be alarmed, but I think we are being followed."

Alexander whirled around to see what he'd missed. "What?"

The soldiers began pushing through the crowds to get to Alexander and Michael.

"Never mind. Time to be alarmed. Come!" Michael broke out into a sprint.

Alexander tried to keep up as Michael darted through the market square, then turned down a narrow street. He bolted across the stone path, then sprang through a small crevice between buildings. Aware of every nook, shortcut, and hidden route, Michael led them to a residential area in the poorer part of town. He motioned to a four-story insula. "We can stay here." Michael opened the door and stepped inside.

Fear gripped hold, and Alexander stopped. This had all happened too fast. Maybe this was a setup. Maybe Michael was Pantheon. Unsure of anything, Alexander backed away from the door.

"We must hurry," Michael said.

Alexander turned and ran down a street, away from Michael. As soon as he was able, he turned onto another road, but unlike Michael, he didn't know his way around the city. Ambling about, he turned a corner and found the soldiers on the other end of the street. They spied Alexander and dashed after him. Alexander backtracked, hung a left down a small alley, and then hit a dead end. The soldiers caught up with swords drawn. He had two choices—fight, and he'd likely be killed, or he could surrender and hope the beating wouldn't be too bad. He dropped to his knees and held up his hands. The soldier in charge stepped forward and kicked him in the gut. Alexander keeled over, and the rest of the soldiers joined in the thrashing.

Minutes later, the soldiers dragged Alexander, bloodied and half-conscious, through the market square. Roman citizens stared at him with disdain, assuming he was guilty. His eyes met those of an older woman, and his mind *flashed*. He recognized those eyes. It was Alisa. Even in her advanced age, something about her gaze drew him in. "Alisa!"

Alisa watched him get dragged by her. How did this strange man know her name?

THE SOLDIERS FLUNG Alexander into a small cell. Except for a ventilation window perched high on one wall, the cell was empty. Too small for anyone to crawl through, it also had bars just to make sure. He curled up in the corner, his face bruised and bloodied, but his thoughts remained with Alisa. He couldn't believe she was still alive.

"Alexander?" a voice called out.

Alexander stirred and sat up. "Yes."

"Are you alone?" the voice asked.

It was Michael.

"Yes," Alexander replied.

"Place your hands together and interlock your fingers," Michal said.

"What?"

"Just do it. Hurry."

Alexander clasped his fingers together.

"Extend both your thumbs, your pointer finger, and little one, but keep the other two interlocked."

Alexander followed the instructions and looked at the result. "I don't understand."

"Commit that hand signal to memory and take this."

A small pouch flung through the window. Alexander unraveled it to find ground up powder. "What is it?"

"It will kill you," Michael said.

"What?" Alexander dropped the bag as if the mysterious poison could somehow jump inside him just from holding it.

"They are going to torture you. Take it and meet us in the tunnel in your next life. Commit everything to memory. I must go."

The sound of Michael's footsteps drifted into the distance. He stared at the pouch. Was Michael helping him or trying to trick him into poisoning himself?

Down the jail's hallway, faint footsteps grew louder with each step. Keys clanked in the lock. Alexander shook the powder out on the floor, then spread it out with his hands and tossed the small piece of cloth on the other side of the cell as the door swung open. A portly young man in a regal toga entered. This man stood out, less by his royal attire and more from his potbelly and beak nose. To say he was unattractive would be an understatement, and his arrogant disposition matched his appearance.

"We know you have the gift. Who are you? Don't pretend and don't lie," the ugly man said.

"I'm Alexander of Macedon."

The ugly man smiled, revealing crooked, stained teeth. "Ahh. We meet yet again, as I said we would."

Alexander's face dropped. "Varus?"

Varus knelt down beside Alexander. He fingered Alexander's necklace and the medallion. He then grabbed it and yanked it off Alexander's neck.

"I know who used to wear something like this. Amazing," Varus said. "I suppose you've seen him recently. Quite a reunion, I'm sure."

Alexander seethed as Varus pocketed the keepsake inspired by his friend.

"Do you remember what I told you before you died?" Varus asked.

Alexander nodded.

Varus stood over Alexander in a display of dominance. "This is your last chance to join us. Say no, and it's a no forever. We track everyone with the gift and find those that decline. When we do, they suffer. So, what's it going to be?

Brutal torture or selling his soul. Those were Alexander's choices. He bowed his head and mumbled, "I'll join."

Varus smiled and flashed those disgusting teeth.

"On one condition," Alexander added. "I want to tell your god, the leader of the Pantheon."

Varus's smile disappeared, replaced with a snarl.

CHAPTER 79

TICK. Tick. Tick.

With each second that passed in the Vance Estate, the antique clock hanging on the study's wall made a faint tick, but the room was so quiet every sound echoed.

Tick. Tick. Tick.

Tom and Varus sat on opposite sides of the desk and engaged in a silent, mental chess match with life and death consequences. Each stared at the other. Tom folded his hands and rested them under his chin, then leaned back. "It's good to see you, Varus."

Varus tapped his knee. "I wish I could say the same because this..." He gestured to Tom, then to himself. "Whatever this is... will put me in an awkward position."

Tom dropped his hands and leaned forward. "I know, and I'm sorry about that, but I wanted to make sure you and I talked in private, as we both know how easy it is for phone calls and e-mails to be monitored."

Varus exhaled. "Go ahead. Say what you have to say."

"I have Sargon's power." Tom removed the wooden chest and presented it on the desk. He lifted the top with a flourish, revealing the golden scepter in all its glory. Checkmate.

Varus shrugged and waved it away. "That thing is quaint."

Tom held up the stunning scepter. He wasn't buying the act. "Quaint? It's how Sargon corralled us into submission."

"You've been out of the mix for quite a while."

Tom's confidence dwindled. He looked at the wand, wondering if it no longer held any value.

"Times have unfortunately changed, and Sargon's power is well beyond that." Varus sneered and flicked his wrist at the golden stick.

Tom shifted in his chair. He thought he had bargaining power, a lifeline. He didn't have a backup plan.

Varus leaned forward to make sure he had Tom's attention. "He knows how to kill people like us permanently. And not just stop us from remembering for a couple of lifetimes. I mean, you're dead."

Tom shook his head. No way. He eyed Varus and assessed whether to believe him.

Varus huffed, amused Tom didn't trust him. He picked up the scepter with both hands. The crystal glowed. "Sargon knows how to kill us permanently."

The crystal remained glowing. Checkmate. Game over.

Tom swallowed, praying there was some other move, an option he hadn't considered. "How?"

Varus tossed the wand back on the desk like it was a toy from a Happy Meal. "You know he'd never share a secret like that."

Tom slumped in his chair. For the first time, he faced genuine mortality.

"I can't help you, so you may as well take me out," Varus said.

"You know that's not possible. I can't kill an officer."

Varus was keenly aware of this fact. "Quite a pickle we're both in. I can't let you go, and you can't let me go."

The two fell silent, and the sound of the ticking clock became unbearable.

Tick. Tick. Tick.

Tom needed a new plan, and he needed it now.

Tick. Tick. Tick.

Then he realized something. He looked at Varus and offered a coy smile. "Yes, you can let me go, and you need to."

"Is that right?" Varus asked, even though he had zero intention of doing so.

"Yeah. That's right. You're going to tell Sargon that I have proof past lives are real. I got it from the sister of one of the scientists working on the project. I think you paid her a visit. Right now, the documents are with an outside source. If I die or I'm captured, they'll be released to the public."

Varus pursed his lips and shifted in his seat. "You'd be hurting yourself as much as the Pantheon."

Tom had to play up the crazy card if he had any chance of this working, and unfortunately, it wasn't crazy. It was the truth. "Not if I'm going to be killed. If I'm going down, I have no choice. I'll take everyone with me. You tell him this," Tom waved his hands around wildly toward the melee of police outside the window, "this mess around my house—the cars, the investigation, it goes away. You have one hour to figure out how to do it."

Varus seethed.

Tom had put Varus in the mother of all binds. Varus had to call Sargon with this update. "I'm not bluffing. I have nothing to lose by releasing that information. Sargon has everything to lose."

Varus tapped the sides of his chair, then stood and stretched his arms, a calculated display to show he had no intention of hurrying because Tom ordered him.

Tom rose to his feet and leaned forward with his hands on the desk. "One hour."

Varus clenched his teeth. He walked to the door of the study, but paused before leaving. He turned to Tom. "Get ready for war."

CHAPTER 80

Ur, 2286 B.C.

Sargon perched atop his golden throne as servants offered him food and drink, his journey to the valley of death now a distant memory. Reinvigorated by life, he savored the succulent provisions. Magistrates brought scrolls containing government matters which Sargon perused, then declared his ruling. As soon as he'd given his command, the magistrate would disappear to carry out the order. Then, more treats and spirits, followed by the next magistrate. This continued until Moshi entered. He bowed and approached Sargon.

"My lord, I found one that fits what you describe. He is strange and possesses many talents."

Sargon bit into an apple. "You've brought others before who ended up being nothing."

"This one is different," Moshi said.

"We shall see."

Moshi bowed again. "I have traveled the ends of the earth for my lord.

Many times. If this man is what you seek, then I humbly request that I may go home and live out the rest of my days in peace."

Sargon crunched another bite of the apple and pretended to consider Moshi's appeal. "No. You are too valuable. You must locate more special ones. For each one you find, I will reward you and your family with wealth you can only dream about. If you do not, I can no longer guarantee protection for your family."

Moshi bowed in obedience and left. A moment later, a strange man in flowing clothes and bizarre jewels entered.

Sargon studied him and then waved to his servants to leave. As soon as they were alone, Sargon asked, "What do they call you?"

"I don't care what *they* call me. My name is Polassar."

Polassar carried himself with a confidence that spilled into arrogance. The presence of high royalty left him unaffected.

"I search the lands for gifted people, Polassar. People like you. You know how to speak many languages, yes?"

Polassar nodded.

"You are a skilled warrior, yes?"

Polassar nodded again.

"And you are very good with numbers?"

Polassar nodded a third time.

"How on earth did you obtain all these skills?" Sargon asked in a false, dramatic tone.

Polassar hesitated, having faced repercussions for answering such a question before. "I guess I was just born with it."

Sargon smiled. He'd found someone with the gift. "I was born with it, too."

The words pierced Polassar's arrogance. He'd met his equal, or perhaps his superior.

Sargon stood up from his throne. "How would you like to rule the world with me?"

CHAPTER 81

Rome, 268 B.C.

With his hands bound, Alexander sat with his back against the wall of his cell. Hours had passed since Varus paid him a visit, giving him plenty of time to think about whether he would come face to face with the mysterious leader of the Pantheon—Gabriel or whatever he called himself. The idea of exacting his revenge didn't seem likely given his current condition, but still, Alexander had to see Gabriel. He had to look the devil in the eye and tell him he wouldn't win. Evil would never win.

Outside the cell, heavy footsteps clapped against the stone floor. They grew louder until keys jingled against the lock. The cedar door creaked open. Standing before Alexander was a Herculean man with cold, damning eyes.

"You have been offered the privilege of serving me. If you accept and are loyal, you'll enjoy a life of unimaginable wealth and power. If you refuse..." the man trailed off to let Alexander's imagination run wild with the alternative.

As the man towered above Alexander, something didn't seem right.

This giant didn't talk like Gabriel. Even if he was that good of an actor, something was off—he used a different cadence of speech, a unique thought process. "Do you remember when we first met, you asked me about my father, Philip of Macedon?"

"Yes," the man said.

Alexander chuckled. "I don't. I know you all like to pretend to be different people, but you're not in charge."

The man snorted, accepting the ruse didn't work. "You cannot see him."

"Then, I won't join you."

"If you decline, we *will* torture you."

"Anyone who would torture just to torture is not someone I wish to follow," Alexander said.

"There's something you should know before you make your final decision. The torture does something to the gift. Your brain won't want to relive the horror, especially when it is long and cruel. You won't remember your past. Your skills, knowledge, and friends will all be lost. So, I ask for the last time, will you join the Pantheon?"

Alexander's stomach dropped. Who was he if he didn't have his memories? He couldn't bear the thought of not remembering Hephaestion. Or Alisa. "I'll join," he said, almost in a whisper.

"Very good. But let's make sure you're telling the truth."

"I'm prepared to sacrifice this life to show you," Alexander said, thinking he'd be presented with a dagger, similar to Solomon's feigned proposition.

"Who did you meet in Rome? I need the names and the places you met."

Alexander swallowed hard. There *was* a secret war going on. He didn't want to be the reason the wrong side won. Solomon's wisdom echoed in his mind. *Sometimes not choosing actually is.* He didn't understand what that meant at the time, but he did now. He stumbled for an answer. "What do you mean? I didn't meet—"

The giant man interrupted, "We know you did. I ask again, who did you contact—names and places?"

Alexander looked up at the man, then down at the ground. He would not speak, even if it meant he'd lose everything.

"Very well." The man turned to exit.

"What now?" Alexander asked.

The man shrugged. "You'll be destroyed."

Alexander burned at the man's callousness. As the door shut, Alexander shouted one more question. "So, who are you? For real?"

The man hesitated. "Does it matter?"

"I guess it doesn't since, at best, you're second in command around here. No one remembers the second."

This man smirked, then bowed with a flourish. "General Craterus at your service."

CHAPTER 82

TICK. Tick. Tick.

The only sound in the study was that damn clock, and Tom's one-hour deadline grew closer. Lines had been drawn, and war declared. Tom sat alone, coming to terms with his new reality. The Pantheon knew who he was *and* where he was. If they captured him, Sargon would kill him—permanently. That couldn't happen. If they called his bluff, only one option remained. Tom opened a drawer and removed a .357 revolver. He placed it on the desk and stared at it.

Tick. Tick. Tick.

In the living room, Ben and Riya watched the live news feed taking place outside the gates, oblivious to Varus's threat of war. Tom had conveniently kept that detail to himself after Varus left, and he filled them in on the conversation. As far as they knew, Tom convinced Varus to have the police gone within an hour, but with three minutes remaining before the deadline, there was no sign of that. One token of comfort Tom had was that neither Ron nor Carlos were around. At least they'd survive the onslaught that was only seconds away.

Riya drifted out of the living room and walked to the study. She peeked her head in to give Tom an update. "Nothing new, and I haven't seen any police cars leaving."

Tom exhaled, almost resigned to the fact that his ruse had failed. "I need to use the bathroom." He grabbed the gun before standing.

Riya noticed the pistol. "When did you get a gun?"

Tom ignored the question and meandered to the bathroom. He locked the door behind him, placed the gun next to the sink, and turned the faucet on. Scared of what might happen any minute, Tom splashed water on his face, exhaled and eyed the weapon. Time was running out. He gripped the gun.

Ben glanced out the window. Police cruisers made U-turns and left. A jingle on the television showed a breaking news bulletin. Ben rushed over. The anchor touched his earpiece. "We've just received an update on the standoff at Congressman Vance's estate. It was a huge misunderstanding. Congressman Vance is dying. His visit to the hospital was for tests and medicine to help with his suffering. Dr. Patel is his doctor, and Ben Preston is a family friend. Wow, what a turn of events! Our thoughts and prayers go out to Congressman Vance."

Riya raced over and caught the tail end of the good news. They might survive this after all. She and Ben gave each other a half hug, then Riya hurried to let Tom know.

In the bathroom, Tom placed the barrel of the gun to his head and applied pressure to the trigger.

Riya reached the door.

Ben ran back to the foyer and looked out the window. "They're all leaving!" he shouted.

As Riya reached out her hand to knock, it swung open, revealing Tom, calm and composed.

"The police are leaving," Riya said with a smile.

Tom straightened his shirt and exited, brimming with confidence. "I told you I took care of it. You need to trust me."

CHAPTER 83

Ur, 2284 B.C.

OLD AND FEEBLE, Sargon sculpted an object with sharp, metallic instruments. His workshop was a regal temple with burning incense. His eyes remained focused, and his movements precise. With each delicate swipe of a blade, he removed a small shaving of gold that dropped to the ground. One last stroke, and he stepped back from his creation. He marveled, quite pleased with his efforts. This masterpiece had taken months to complete, but the idea had been years in the making.

That evening, Sargon stood on the edge of a steep cliff overlooking the Euphrates River. He absorbed the beauty from the god-like view and took a deep breath that he held before exhaling with relief.

A muscular young man with black hair and dark skin climbed up the trail and met Sargon at the top of the bluff. "You called for me, my Lord."

"Yes, Varus. Is there any word from Moshi?" Sargon asked without turning around.

"He's sent messengers. He continues to search, but he has found no one new with the gift."

Sargon held out his hand. The cool breeze tickled his fingertips. "Order him back. Tell him to stop."

"He will be pleased to go home," Varus said.

Sargon watched wistfully as a pair of sand grouse cruised just above the water. "Take his lands and his money. He's old and will be dead soon, so it doesn't matter."

Varus nodded.

"And bring our brothers together at once. I have an urgent issue we must address," Sargon said.

Varus returned down the trail to carry out his orders. Sargon closed his eyes and took one last peaceful breath. When he opened them, they were cold with reptilian focus.

SARGON GATHERED the handful of people he'd found with the "gift" into his inner sanctuary. Marble floors, rich tapestries, and cedar furniture adorned the room. This restricted area within the palace was where the gifted met. The only other individuals allowed in the room were servants, prostitutes, and concubines. Sargon's subjects, all men, were Varus, Polassar, Ashur, and Senna. Sargon perched himself on a golden throne while his followers sat on cushions in front of him.

"This body is going to die in a week," Sargon said.

The men glanced at one another with skepticism. A week? Though old, Sargon wasn't sick, and a week was so specific. Polassar, the first man Sargon found with the gift, and the most arrogant, prostrated himself. "If you are feeling ill, take rest, my lord."

Sargon clarified, "But I will return. I need to know that you are loyal to me and will maintain this house we have built. We are gods among men, and I am the god among you."

Ashur, early twenties, dark-skinned and slender, was confident, intelligent, and manipulative. "You have our pledge of loyalty."

Sargon nodded, appreciative of the lip service, but he by no means trusted it. "If there's one thing we've learned through our lives, it's that the temptation to sin is great. If you sin against me, there will be consequences." Sargon paused to make sure that sank in. This was a den of snakes, and he had to force their obedience. "There is punishment, and there is reward. I have given you all lives you have only dreamed about. I will continue to do that, and more, if you remain loyal."

Senna, the youngest and most insecure of the followers, admired Sargon, but he also feared him. "You are our one and only, Sargon."

"There will be a short time where I am not with you physically," Sargon said. "If any of you take advantage of that, you will not receive mercy. I can take your gift away. Remember that."

Polassar replied, "We will not betray you, mighty Sargon."

"Power tempts not only us but the lesser beings as well. History has shown that whenever there is a change of leadership, those people try to exploit it. I need to find the right person among you to make sure we maintain power." Sargon eyed each of them as if he was peering into their soul. "But which one?"

CHAPTER 84

Rome, 268 B.C.

CHAINED IN A QUARTERED POSITION, Alexander's head drooped against his chest. He couldn't even scratch an itch, much less attempt an escape from his tiny cell. He yelled out, "I need water. Hey! I need water!"

A minute later, the door opened, revealing Craterus and his Herculean frame. He assessed Alexander. "You're fine. You get just enough to keep you alive."

Alexander jiggled his arms and motioned to the chains. "Take these off so I can at least stretch."

Craterus laughed. "This is the easy part of the torture. Wait until you get to Capri."

"What's that?" Alexander asked, unsure if he wanted the answer.

"That's where the real pain starts. You leave tomorrow so," Craterus waved his hands around the cell, "enjoy this."

Outside the jail, Roman citizens went about their lives, oblivious to the high-stakes politics taking place in the buildings they passed by. The sun traveled across the sky and began setting in the west. Through it all,

Alexander remained chained and miserable. With an inability to do anything physical, voices from his mind taunted him.

Hephaestion called out, "We must lead. We can't be afraid to fail."

Alexander stared ahead in a catatonic state as Solomon's voice broke through. "You have to choose the light or the dark."

Tears welled up in his eyes. He'd neither led nor chosen. He'd lived in fear, and the Pantheon had played him like a piece in a giant game, and now it looked like he had no more moves left. The shame left him sobbing until a soft female voice emerged. "Hello?"

Confused, Alexander surveyed the room. Was that in his head?

"How do you know me?" the voice asked.

Alexander looked up at the barred window. The voice came from outside. "Alisa?"

"How do you know my name?" Alisa asked.

"I don't expect you to believe me when I say we knew each other once. It feels like a lifetime ago." Alexander chuckled at his choice of words. "Because it was."

"Who are you?" She asked.

Alexander took a deep breath before answering. "It's me. Alexander."

Silence.

"Alisa?"

"Why did you leave me?" she asked.

"Because... I was stupid. I wish I could see you right now... or even some other time, but they're going to take me away and torture me, so I can't remember anything." Alexander muttered under his breath, "You're one of the few things I don't want to forget."

"When do they take you away?" she asked.

"Tomorrow."

"Look for the women in white," Alisa said.

"Women in white? Why?" Alexander asked.

"They are the Vestal Virgins. Any condemned man who sees them must be freed. It is a Roman custom. They rarely leave their temple or come to this part of the city, but I will make sure they do. I must go."

Alexander couldn't believe his ears. Was this true? Did he have hope? "Alisa?" he asked.

Silence. She was gone, but she remained in Alexander's thoughts. He wanted to tell her so many things, and he had questions. The last time he saw her as Alexander of Macedon, she said she had visions and dreams. He couldn't help but wonder if those were past lives. That notion filled him with hope and determination to escape. He'd never heard of a Vestal Virgin before, but if they somehow held the key to reuniting him with Alisa and all he had to do was see them, that's what he'd do. As the night wore on, he imagined all the ways these Vestals might be hiding or challenging to find. He had to be prepared for anything. Finally, his mind gave in to fatigue, and he drifted off to sleep, even in his quartered position.

When morning arrived, light streaked through the tiny window in the cell. Alexander didn't notice and slept on. He rested, slouched forward, arms outstretched, and his head lulled against his chin.

The door creaked open, and two guards entered. They kicked Alexander awake, unlocked the chains, and pulled him to his feet. His legs buckled after having spent hours restricted to the ground, but after a few moments, he found his footing. Simple movements never felt so good. Unfortunately, a new set of shackles replaced the old. This mobile version included a connecting chain between his ankles and wrists to prevent him from running, but he didn't need to run. All he needed was to see these women in white—the Vestal Virgins—and he'd be free.

The guards led Alexander down a corridor, and as he shuffled forward, two more guards emerged to escort him. Next, the group passed a hallway, and two more guards joined the entourage. This continued for three more hallways until they reached the end, and Craterus stepped in front to lead the group. Now surrounded by twelve guards, plus Craterus, it was impossible for Alexander to see anything besides his captors. His heart pounded in fear.

He could not see the Vestal Virgins.

CHAPTER 85

Virginia, 2018

A bead of sweat ran down Ben's cheek as he tapped his finger on the kitchen table beside Riya. Tom peeked through the curtains. They'd escaped the police and Varus, but they were now following Tom's lead, something Ben had little faith in.

"Anything?" Riya asked.

"No," Tom said.

"Are you sure they're coming?" Ben asked.

"Yeah, Ron and Carlos always come through."

"But even when they come back, the Pantheon still knows where we are," Ben said, pointing out the obvious.

"Yes, and they're going to follow us as soon as we leave."

"I don't understand. You took care of it with Varus," Riya said.

"I did for the moment, but the Pantheon are figuring out how to take us without letting their secrets out. Once they do, they won't hesitate. Until then, they're going to follow us wherever we go."

"So, how are we going to get away?" Ben asked.

Tom's Escalade, driven by Ron, rolled down the street.

"They're here."

The Escalade passed through the gates. Carlos hopped out and ran inside the front door as Ron backed the car up.

Tom waved everyone to the dining room. Carlos passed Tom a bulging envelope. Tom opened it and pulled out passports, driver's licenses, and phones. He glanced at the pictures, then handed one to Ben and Riya.

Ben studied his passport and read the name. "John Johnston?"

Carlos shrugged. "What? It's as good a white boy's name as any."

Tom dispersed the remaining documents. "The name doesn't matter. It just matters that you learn the info on these cards."

Tom held out his hand. "Okay, I need your wallets, purses, and everything else with your real identities."

Ben considered the request. He'd never felt comfortable as "Ben Preston," but the more he learned about his past as Alexander, the less certain he felt about anything. He didn't know who he wanted to be, but it wasn't some made-up character named John Johnston.

Tom picked up on Ben's hesitation. "We can't run any risks of you accidentally giving someone the wrong ID or swiping a card somewhere. That's the easiest way for the Pantheon to track you. Right now, all our personal information is with them. They're waiting for us to slip up."

"What about money?" Riya shared Ben's reluctance to turn over her credit cards and other items.

"Don't worry. I have you covered." Tom opened up his backpack, revealing stacks of cash.

The money was impressive, but Ben didn't take comfort from the idea of relying on Tom for anything, but he had little choice. He handed over his wallet, and Riya did the same with her purse.

"Thank you." Tom grabbed their items and passed them both a burner phone. "These are pre-programmed with two numbers. Mine and yours. Don't call anyone else. The phone is the second easiest way to be tracked."

Tom glanced out the window, careful not to expose himself. "Ron's ready to go."

Ron opened the front door and used it as a shield, then opened the back door.

Tom, Ben, and Riya sprinted the short distance to the Escalade, and all three jumped into the back seats as Carlos hopped in the front. As soon as they were in, doors locked. Ron shifted into gear and sped away.

Everything was taking place too fast. All these choices and decisions were happening for Ben. He was now John Johnston going to Rome because of Riya's bizarre idea, and he was led by Tom, someone he didn't trust. He had that sickening feeling like he was once again a pawn in someone else's game, and his fate was out of his hands. That fear solidified when a sedan pulled in behind the Escalade.

Carlos took note through the side mirror. "We got a tail."

"Act like we don't see him," Tom said.

Ron drove the speed limit until they approached a traffic light that turned yellow.

"Punch it!" Tom said.

Ron gunned the engine and guided the Escalade through the intersection as it turned red. He glanced in the rearview. The sedan had to brake, unable to make it through safely. "We lost him."

Tom didn't celebrate. "That won't stop them for long. Keep going to Dulles. Get on the freeway."

"We're going to hit rush hour, Tom," Ron said.

"Yep."

Carlos checked the side mirror. A silver sedan several cars back traveled at the same speed, never getting closer or further. "We got another tail."

Ron peered in the rearview. A black sedan lurked. "No. We got two."

"Get on the freeway," Tom said again.

Carlos shook his head as the on-ramp approached. "We can't lose them there."

"Do it, Ron," Tom commanded.

Ron pulled onto the freeway. Almost immediately, they found themselves in stop and go traffic.

Carlos threw his hands up. "I told you. We got nowhere to go."

Ben glanced at the cars all around. They were trapped.

CHAPTER 86

A BUSTLING ANCIENT TOWN, but much smaller than Rome, was built around a tiny oasis in the heart of the Arabian Desert—the equivalent of an old western backwater on the outskirts of "real" civilization. In the middle of the city, an auction took place. Two dozen shackled men walked out one at a time to "center stage." About fifty free men studied the prisoners with intense judgment.

A muscular dark-skinned man in a white turban, Ganges, ran the event. He motioned to a shackled individual—a scrawny teen—to come over. Scared, the boy shuffled forward until Ganges snatched him by the neck. "You don't have to worry about this one revolting, now do you?" Ganges poked the youngster, and the crowd laughed in mockery. "Come up and get a good look at him."

Several free men walked past and offered disapproving, disgusted glances. The teen may as well have been a stray dog.

"Let's start the bidding with one gold piece." Ganges searched the

345

crowd. No takers. "Come on, people. He's small, but he's not useless. He's good for domestic duties."

A man from the crowd seized the opportunity for a bargain and raised his hand. "Half a gold."

A feeble fellow next to the bidder coughed. It was Moshi, Sargon's servant, now old and sick.

"Fine. Half a gold." Ganges shoved the teen out of the way. "Barely worth my effort."

The next slave rose to his feet, and the spectators gasped. He rivaled Ganges in size, except with bigger muscles.

Ganges even appeared a bit intimidated and kept his distance. "Here's a fit one. Good for decades of service. Imagine what he could do for your fields. Come on now, step up and get a good look."

Ganges waved people forward. A few potential bidders approached to inspect the product, but the slave's glare kept them from getting too close.

Moshi drifted forward and stepped right in front of the slave. He unrolled a scroll and held it up for him to read. "Can you read any of these ancient languages?"

The slave looked at the parchment. "I can read two of them. They say the same thing."

"Then what's your answer?" Moshi asked.

"Yes. I want to meet Sargon," the slave said.

Moshi turned to Ganges. "Fifty gold."

The other spectators groaned in shock and disappointment.

Ganges beamed. "Sold!"

POLASSAR STROLLED the streets of Ur with Senna. He spoke of nothing of substance; he bided his time until he reached an isolated stretch where no one could hear him. A golden opportunity had presented itself, and they had to act.

"So, Sargon is dying, and one of us gets to keep his seat warm. Quite an honor, don't you think?" Polassar said.

"Do you want to do it?" Senna asked.

"No." Polassar stopped walking, and his arrogance poured out. "He thinks we follow him? He's no better than us."

Senna scanned the area to make sure they were alone, then leaned forward and whispered, "You don't think he can take our power away?"

Polassar spoke without whispering, "No. He's trying to scare us into submission. He said he'll be dead in a week." He resumed his walk down the street.

Senna caught up to him and still kept his voice in a whisper. "That doesn't worry you. He looks fine."

"A week, a month, a year." Polassar shrugged. "Does time matter for people like us?"

Senna grasped Polassar's arm. "He wants to meet with me."

"Me too."

"What should we say?" Senna asked.

Polassar smiled. "We say what he wants us to say. He's the ruler among us, and we follow him obediently. We then wait for him to die, and it's our turn to lead."

CHAPTER 87

Rome, 268 B.C.

Craterus and the contingent of twelve soldiers led Alexander outside to a covered corridor. Alexander's eyes darted in every direction. Armor, shields, and the backs of guards blocked his field of view. Panic coursed through his veins. How could he see anything, much less spot the mysterious Vestal Virgins? Aside from the fact that they wore white, he didn't know what they looked like, and the best he could manage was an occasional glimpse of people in the nearby courtyard.

The escort arrived at an uncovered staircase. As the guards in front of Alexander stepped down, he had a view of the outside world. This was his opportunity, perhaps his only one. He shuffled down each step as slowly as possible, exaggerating the limited mobility of the chains around his ankles. Dozens of people littered the courtyard, but no women in white. He'd almost reached the bottom of the stairs, his chance for freedom extinguished when, miraculously, in the distance, he spied three enchanting ladies in white sitting beside a fountain.

"Vestal Virgins!" Alexander raised his chained arm and pointed as much as he was able.

The crowd turned to see. "Vestals," a few citizens shouted.

The people stopped, faced the Vestals, and bowed.

A voice from the mass of humanity, a voice Alexander recognized, shouted to the guards. "The condemned man must be freed."

Alexander searched the crowd for the voice's origin.

Another spectator shouted, "The gods have spoken. He's innocent."

Craterus assessed his precarious position. It took little to incite a crowd into an angry mob, and disrespecting a religious custom was a severe infraction. "The law to free a condemned man who sees a Vestal Virgin only applies to Roman citizens." Craterus waved his arm over the good people of Rome and then pointed to Alexander. "This man is a barbarian from a faraway land. He came here to destroy Rome. But we won't let him."

Alexander watched in shock as the Roman people nodded in agreement and resumed their lives. Hope was lost. Alexander would not be released. Mercifully, or perhaps cruelly, he caught sight of Alisa in the crowd. Their eyes met. Those beautiful brown eyes still captivated him. Those eyes that he'd soon forget after the Pantheon tortured him to death.

Something peculiar drew Alexander's attention, something behind Alisa. On the roof of a two-story building, a man pulled back a bow. Who was this person, and what were they doing? Just as the figure released the weapon, Alexander realized it was Michael. An arrow whizzed through the air and struck Alexander in the chest with a force that knocked him down.

Craterus whirled around and found Alexander on the ground, gasping for breath. The wound was a death blow. "No!" Craterus fumed as half the guards rushed away to apprehend the assailant.

As his life faded, Alexander smiled at this Pyrrhic victory. His memories were safe.

TIME STOOD STILL or became irrelevant. A pinprick of white light pierced the blackness. Just like when he was born into the life of Azes, Alexander raced towards the light and began a new life. Compared to his rugged, Scythian tribe, he emerged in a much more regal dwelling. Servants swarmed him at birth, swaddling him in a blanket made from the softest cotton. In this life, he carried the name of his father, Marcus Junius Brutus, and the year was 85 B.C.

The days passed, and Alexander grew. Just like in his lifetime as Azes, he showed tremendous potential in both academics and athletics. Often, he'd watch his father and namesake talking politics with other members of Roman high society. Something about the subject intrigued Alexander. His dad noted his son's interest and encouraged him, giving him all types of scrolls. As one of Rome's wealthy families, they were fortunate to have access to an almost limitless supply. Alexander absorbed whatever his parents put in front of him.

When puberty hit, so did the nightmares, filled with vivid images of horrific battles and death. In some of his dreams, Hephaestion and Solomon mentally tortured him with guilt, urging him to lead and choose the light. Every once in a while, he'd be blessed with a dream of Alisa. On those rare nights, he slept peacefully.

During one nightmare, Alexander found himself in a cold, dark tunnel. At the end of the shaft, a small flicker of light. Screams of terror and anguish echoed from behind. They hunted him and drove him to the beacon. He emerged in a secret chamber, and then he jolted awake.

For the rest of the day, the dream and the secret room tugged at his mind. He walked the streets of Rome without direction, but he passed a domus at the end of one road and stopped. He glanced up and stared at the archway. A pyramid with an eye in the center compelled him to approach the door and knock. No answer. He pushed the door, but it was locked. A brick near the foundation caught his eye. He pulled it out and reached his hand inside. His fingers grazed something metallic. He plucked out a key and marveled at it, then unlocked the door. Inside, the simple entryway led to the atrium. As he ventured further, the culina attracted him. He discovered a large stone table. His mind *flashed,* and he remembered Michael moving it.

Alexander pushed with all his strength and slid it to the side. Underneath, he uncovered the secret tunnel. He took a burning log from the hearth and walked down the steps. The cold air made his skin crawl. Alexander considered retreating when light and voices emanating from a room ahead urged him forward. He summoned his courage and pressed on, moving closer to their source.

He entered and found the secret chamber from his dreams, except a small pillar that depicted a man killing a bull, now stood in the center. A handful of men gathered around a red-headed boy not more than thirteen years old. The young teen led the gathering. As soon as Alexander went in, all eyes turned to him. He clasped his fingers together and extended his thumb, index finger, and pinkie.

"Who are you?" The red-headed boy asked.

Alexander responded with four simple words. "I choose the light."

CHAPTER 88

Virginia, 2018

From the back seat of the Escalade, Tom ignored the anxious stares of Ben and Riya and scanned the cars around him as the freeway traffic inched forward. Ron cut in and out of lanes in the slowest car chase ever to get as much distance as possible, but the two sedans mirrored his actions and kept pace. Tom remained focused, but not worried. "How close are they?"

Carlos checked the mirror. "About ten cars."

"Get in the right lane," Tom said.

Carlos shook his head. "That lane is going the slowest."

"Do it."

Tom's commands tested even Ron's obedience, but he did as instructed and pulled into the slow lane.

A sign showed an exit a quarter of a mile away. Tom shouted, "Pull onto the shoulder. Now. Gun it. Go. Go!"

Ron sped up and drove the shoulder, while several drivers blared their horns to share their feelings about his line cutting. A few waved "hi" with their middle fingers.

The two sedans followed, but a pissed off driver in a pickup truck cut in front and gave them the finger. They could wait just like everyone else. Ron looked in the rearview. The pickup blocked the sedans. "Gotta love road rage." He exited the freeway and turned onto a road.

"Pull over," Tom said.

Ron followed the instructions. Tom hopped out and motioned for Riya and Ben to get out. Tom stuck his head back in the car as Ron and Carlos watched, confused.

"If you lose them, meet us at Dulles. Here." Tom handed Ron his cell phone. "Take my phone. I pre-programmed it with the number on the burner phone."

"I got my phone," Ron said.

"Just take it, but do not call unless you lose them. Understood?"

Ron nodded, but as usual, didn't understand Tom's plans.

Carlos asked, "What's this all about, Tom? Who's following us?"

"They're not following you, so you're safe. I have some documents they want. Now go."

Tom tapped on the hood, and the Escalade pulled away. Ben, Riya, and Tom hurried into the trees, where they ducked down and hid. A few moments later, the two sedans sped down the road in Ron and Carlos's direction.

Once the sedans were out of sight, Tom stood. "They probably put a tracker on the car."

"You should let Ron and Carlos know," Ben said.

"They'll be okay."

"You don't know that," Riya said.

Tom knew Riya was right, but that's why he gave them his phone. He was putting his faith in Varus, someone he hadn't known for years, and the irony was not lost on him. He was handing over the two people he trusted most to someone he wasn't sure he could trust at all. A pang of guilt set in, but Tom shook it off. The Pantheon might capture them all if he didn't go through with his plan. "Varus doesn't want them," he said to convince himself as much as Riya.

"They might lead them to Dulles," Ben said.

"I know, which is why we're not going to Dulles." Tom pulled out his phone and dialed a taxi company. "Hi, I'd like to order a taxi to JFK."

Hours later, the trio passed through the security checks at JFK International Airport. They made their way to their gate to wait for their flight to board. With time to kill, Tom stared at his phone, wondering when Ron, Carlos, or Varus would call.

"You still think they're okay?" Ben asked.

Over the loudspeaker, a gate attendant announced, "Flight 4506 to Rome is now boarding first class and business class passengers."

"That's us. Let's go. Ron and Carlos are fine." Tom made his way to the short line that had gathered.

A BALDING MAN typed at a ridiculous rate on his keyboard inside a small corporate office building with several high-tech computer stations. On his monitor, e-mails, text messages, bank and credit card account information popped up and disappeared at an almost blinding pace. He scanned and discarded the material in seconds.

Varus entered and approached. "Have you found them, Senna?"

Senna didn't bother glancing up from his screen and continued to pour over data. "Does it look like it?"

"Have you uncovered anything?"

"Not yet."

"Then you haven't gone deep enough," Varus said.

"There are no e-mails, texts, or any other digital record that any of them sent documents about past lives experiments, which leads me to believe they have nothing. Maybe they have something on them, or they sent a physical copy, but it's not likely based on what we know of their timeline."

"What about Tom's two guards?" Varus asked.

"They're in the conference room."

"Anything on their phones?"

"One number is in the pre-set, and Craterus left you a video." Senna handed Varus the phone.

Varus eyed the menu on the phone. The notes section contained a saved video file. He pressed play, and Tom appeared. "Varus, if you're seeing this, I'm long gone. Ron and Carlos know nothing, and they're not a part of this. I'm asking for your decency. Leave them alone."

Varus couldn't believe his luck. Craterus cared for these people. "Do you have the tracking software set up?"

Senna shot Varus a glance. Of course, he had that set up.

Varus pressed the pre-set number, and it rang.

Tom's phone buzzed as he was just about to reach the attendant, scanning the boarding passes. He glanced at the number. "It's Ron. You two board. I'll be on in a moment."

Tom stepped out of line and drifted to a secluded corner as Ben and Riya scanned their tickets and walked down the gangway.

Tom answered. "Ron?"

"No. It isn't Ron," Varus said.

Tom's head dropped. "What are you going to do with them, Varus?"

"I don't know. I was thinking of cutting off their fingers, maybe burning their feet, or gouging their eyes out. How does that sound?" Varus looked at the tracking software on Senna's screen. It showed the location—JFK airport. He made eye contact with Senna to see if they had anyone nearby. Senna shook his head no.

Tom stiffened at the memory of his torture. He wouldn't wish that on his worst enemy, let alone Ron and Carlos. "What happened to you, Varus? Are you going to follow Sargon forever?"

"Here's what you never grasped. If I'm Sargon's number two, then I'm above everyone else, and I always will be."

"A toady is still a toady."

"With insults like that, maybe you don't care about Ron and Carlos."

"I'm sorry. Don't hurt them, Varus," Tom said.

"Since when do you care about the lesser people?"

Tom paused. Why was he fighting to keep them alive? Tom had known them for about three decades, which was nothing in the context of his life-times. Even so, they'd been through a lot together in those thirty years. Ron and Carlos were always there for him, and they might be the only people throughout Tom's lives he could trust. Maybe now that he was facing genuine mortality, Tom had to admit that Ron and Carlos should never have trusted him. From the minute they met, Tom used them for his own goals. "I guess since now."

"That's nice," Varus said, his voice dripping with sarcasm. "What do I get?"

Tom thought for a moment. Varus wouldn't accept anything insignifi-cant. "I'll deliver you Alexander."

"Really?"

"You know there's no love lost between us," Tom said.

"When?" Varus asked.

"One week."

Varus chuckled, "A week? You're asking for quite a head start."

"Come on. He doesn't even have his memories back. You know Sargon wants him."

"We both know who he really wants."

Tom repeated, "One week."

"This is the second time you're putting a clock on me. I don't appre-ciate that."

Tom paced about in his quiet corner. "It's a fair trade. I will not give him up before I get what I need from him."

"Then I guess you don't care that much about Ron and Carlos. This gives me a week to find you on my own. If I do, all bets are off."

Tom stopped pacing. "Were we ever friends, Varus?"

Varus considered the question. "Yes, I would say we were."

"Then, please, don't hurt them. I'm asking. Do I have your word?"

Varus took a deep breath and exhaled. "Fine."

Tom breathed a sigh of relief. "Thank you." He pressed the button and hung up.

Varus turned to Senna. "See if you can get into the security feeds at JFK."

"That's a needle in a haystack, Varus."

"I'll let you tell Sargon that you failed." Varus left the computer area and drifted into the kitchenette.

Coffee brewed next to a box of donuts and bagels. Even Pantheon members needed to eat. Varus took a quick bite of a bear claw, then held the phone back up to his ear as if he was still on a call. He opened a side door that led into a large conference room with no windows and no furniture, except for three chairs. Ron and Carlos were bound and gagged, sitting in two of them. They looked up with terror-filled eyes.

Varus didn't look at them. He pretended to focus on the conversation. "Once again, you just cast people aside when you're done with them. Some things don't change. Hello?" Varus looked confused as he held the phone, then turned to Ron and Carlos. "Tom hung up. Guess you're stuck with me now."

357

CHAPTER 89

The Arabian Desert, 2284 B.C.

The blazing sun battered Moshi as he rode a dromedary camel through the blistering sand. With each breath, he wheezed until he coughed and spit up something brown and nasty. The slave he purchased walked beside him with his hands bound. The duo trudged forward, but it was not aimless. Moshi had made this trek many times before. To the untrained eye, navigating through the desert seemed an impossible task. Each dune looked indistinguishable from the next. It would be like a sailor trying to find his way in the ocean by reading the waves. Instead, Moshi used the rising and setting sun, the stars, and a handful of large rocks. He could make this journey with his eyes closed, which was good since he spent half his time sleeping on his camel and the other half struggling to breathe.

The slave eyed Moshi. Even with the restraints, the slave could run or kick his feeble captor to death if he chose. It just didn't make sense in the middle of a desert. Plus, Sargon's message intrigued him. "How much further to Ur?"

Moshi pointed to a rock far off on the horizon. "See that? A day's ride past it."

"Do you know what Sargon wants with me?" The slave asked.

Moshi coughed again. "You have made a name for yourself. You are special. Sargon appreciates that." Moshi hocked another phlegm ball into the sand.

"So, am I to be his slave?"

"Not a slave, but—" Moshi clutched his chest in pain. He slumped to his side and fell to the ground.

The slave rushed to his side to help, but Moshi let out his last gasp of air, and the life faded from his body. He was dead. Now a free man, the slave had no obligation to anyone. He could go wherever he chose and do whatever he wanted, but the desert seemed endless, and wandering it looked pointless. The rock leading to Ur called to him. This life and maybe all his lives had reached a crossroads. He grabbed the scroll from Moshi's satchel and read it one more time. He put it down and weighed his choice—freedom or meet this mysterious Sargon?

IN THE CITY OF UR, Polassar entered the sacred temple dedicated to Sargon. Torches and incense burned, creating an eerie and mystical ambiance. Holding an eight-inch crystal dagger, Sargon stood on a small pedestal at the front, wearing a majestic purple robe and a jewel-encrusted crown. Beside him rested a golden statue about the size of a dog but in the shape of a bull. This was the magnificent artwork Sargon had been sculpting. The golden creation was lifelike in its form except for its size and one odd, abstract feature. The horns extended horizontally in an unnatural position.

"Kneel before me, Polassar. Demonstrate your fealty," Sargon said.

Polassar prostrated himself at Sargon's feet.

"I leave something for my followers." Sargon pointed to the statue with his dagger. "The bull has long been a symbol of power and strength. People worship it, and while I'm gone, so shall you. This bull shall carry my spirit.

It is a reminder for you that I am here, and I am watching. I say again, kneel before me."

Polassar eyed the sculpture skeptically, but also fearfully, and considered Sargon's confusing command. He shuffled over and sat in front of the bull. He stared at its sapphire, jeweled eyes. Did it have any power?

"Bow before me. Take the horns," Sargon said.

Polassar placed his hands on the horns and glanced up.

"Head down!" Sargon ordered. "You don't look a god in the eye."

Polassar averted his eyes and stared at the ground. The moment grew more uncomfortable when the tip of the crystal dagger touched Polassar's head.

"Do you swear to follow me even when I'm gone?" Sargon asked.

"Yes, my lord." Polassar's heart pounded against his chest, and he squinted his eyes, afraid that Sargon knew he was lying. He was sure that the dagger would be thrust into his skull any second.

CHAPTER 90

Rome, 44 B.C.

ROMAN CITIZENS SETTLED in for a cold winter night while horses pulled carts through the stone streets, their hooves clip-clopping along, making it difficult for anyone sober to sleep. Torches hung on poles and kept the roads lit.

The palatial home of Alexander bustled with hushed activity. Senators and other influential members of Roman high society huddled by a fire, whispering ideas of rebellion to each other while drinking Rome's finest wine. In this life, Alexander, now 41, was known as Brutus, a well-respected Senator whose opinion mattered, but on this night, he simply listened. Little did his guests know, he was biding his time and waiting for them to arrive at the conclusion he so desperately wanted. If he was patient, it would be their idea, and they'd be more certain to carry it out.

One graying senator, Lucius, lamented about the current state of affairs, "With each day, he demands we bestow him with new honors while taking away the power of the senate."

Another senator, Cassius, rallied the others. "If Caesar continues to rule, the Republic will be doomed forever."

The others all nodded in agreement. Senator Casca, eager for blood, shook his fist. "We must strike now. We must kill Caesar."

The room fell quiet. A hint of a smile crept across Alexander's face.

"How would we do it? How would we kill him?" Lucius whispered.

The senators looked to one another for answers. It was one thing to talk about revolution, quite another to murder a man in cold blood.

Alexander's time to speak had come. He leaned in and offered his insight. "We must monitor him—look for opportunities in his daily schedule when he's vulnerable and his guard is down."

Casca clenched his fist. "I can't wait to plunge a dagger deep into his heart."

"We will all exact our vengeance against him. For Rome." Alexander raised a glass.

The other guests lifted their glasses and then drank to the blood inspired toast.

The conspirators spent the next hour plotting how they'd monitor Caesar over the coming week. Once the planning finished, the chatter dwindled. With the bottles of wine empty and the emotional vigor drained for the night, the men filed out and traveled down the streets to go home. Alexander shut the door after the last guest left and headed for bed.

A knock brought him back. He suspected someone forgot something, but when Alexander opened the door, he was surprised to find a red-headed man, about the same age as himself. It was Solomon, the boy from the secret chamber. He held his hands clasped with his thumb, index, and pinkie fingers extended. This had become the hand signal of The Lux Mundi, an idea originated from Alexander and Hephaestion. The symbol had morphed into something that was beyond just a mechanism for identifying one another. It was also used to show unity and demonstrate that the individual placed the Lux Mundi above oneself.

Alexander returned the gesture, then motioned Solomon inside. "To what do I owe the pleasure, Solomon?"

Solomon stepped into the house. "You've not shown at the last two Lux Mundi gatherings. I see you've had other meetings." He stared at the mess left by the previous guests.

"My job as a senator requires lots of extracurricular events."

Solomon chuckled under his breath. "A position we helped you procure for the good of the Lux Mundi if I recall."

"Yes, and I intend to help the Lux Mundi in a major way."

Solomon's tone became cold and demanding. "It isn't the right time to take out Caesar."

"I wasn't trying to hide it from you. I assumed you'd be keeping tabs on my late-night gatherings. You saw who left. You know I have the support of many in the Senate. I can make this happen," Alexander said.

"You don't even know for certain who Caesar is."

Alexander threw up his hands. "We know he's Pantheon. And we know he's looking to declare himself dictator for life and be worshipped like a god. Even you know it's him."

Solomon nodded, unable to deny the facts. "How long has it taken for us to find ourselves in this position?"

Alexander didn't want to respond.

Solomon didn't allow it to go unanswered. "More than a lifetime." He pointed at Alexander. "It's taken more than a lifetime to get close. We are fortunate that he trusts you and does not know who you really are. Do you realize we can figure out everyone that is Pantheon if we wait and watch him?"

Alexander held his ground. "If we cut off the head of the serpent, the body will die."

"You make it sound like it will be easy. He's smart. Do not underestimate him."

"He's gotten sloppy and arrogant." Alexander paced the room in frustration. "Are we to wait until he's destroyed the republic in its entirety?"

Solomon chortled. "The republic? You're doing this for your own personal vendetta. When we first met, you didn't even want to be a part of the Lux Mundi. Now you want to dictate its actions and put it at risk. Might I remind you of the price for your very existence?"

The words stung because they were true. "I know we lost Michael because of me," Alexander said.

Solomon stepped nose to nose with Alexander to ensure he had his attention. "That's right. After he gave you mercy, they captured him before he could take his own life. If even half of the rumors are true of the torture he endured..." Solomon trailed off and choked up.

"His suffering is a reason to act. He would not have wanted his pain to have been for nothing."

Solomon held up his hand. "Don't use his torture to push your agenda. Continue to watch and keep tabs on Caesar. Nothing more."

"So, the Lux Mundi stands by and watches as the Pantheon takes over Rome?"

"We will act when the time is right. There's something else you should know. Joshua has found someone with the gift in China. This person claims to have important information about the Pantheon," Solomon said.

Alexander raised an eyebrow. It was always significant news when they discovered an individual with the gift. "Who?"

"We don't know. We're trying to figure out if they can be trusted."

Alexander rubbed his chin, conflicted.

"You gave your word to your friend, and your word is important. I'm now asking for your word that you'll wait—a couple months at most. Given what we've done for you, that's not asking much."

Backed into a corner, Alexander gritted his teeth. He clasped his hands together and performed the secret signal. "Two months. You have my word."

CHAPTER 91

Virginia, 2018

Ron and Carlos groaned and whimpered with bloodied faces in the conference room. Their gags were off but remained around their necks. Varus sat beside them with his legs crossed while dabbing a wet paper towel on a bloodstain on his shirt.

"I hate doing this. It may seem like I enjoy it, but I don't. But I also won't stop until I get what I need." Varus tossed the towel aside and put his arm around Carlos. "Where are they going, pal?"

Carlos looked up with his right eye, his left swollen shut from the beatings. "I don't know. I promise. He said to meet him at Dulles if we didn't get caught."

"Stop talking, Carlos. We gotta trust Tom," Ron said through gritted teeth. Blood poured down his mouth and onto his shirt from his smashed nose.

"Tom's not here, Ron," Carlos snapped.

Varus patted Carlos on his back and spoke in a soothing tone. "That's right. He's not, and he's not coming back. You heard the call. You served his purpose. He's long gone. Did he promise you money? I have lots of money. We don't have to do this the painful way. Did he promise that you'd be at the top with him?"

Carlos looked away.

"He promised me that, too," Varus said.

On the verge of breaking, Carlos glanced at Ron, who shook his head, urging him with his eyes not to talk. Varus re-gagged Ron, pulled out his pistol with a silencer, pointed it at him, and fired. *Pffft.* The bullet pierced Ron's shoulder. He slouched back in agony, but the gag muffled his screams. Tears streamed down Carlos's face.

"Decision time, boys. You can have a life you always dreamed of, or you can suffer. You both worked for him. He had you doing lots of things. What did you do?"

"Please. We don't know where he's going."

Varus pointed the pistol at Ron's head, but stared at Carlos.

"We ran errands for him. We got drugs, handled betting. We got fake IDs and passports."

Bingo. Just what Varus needed. "Do you know the names on those documents?"

Carlos's mind raced. "Umm, yes. I do remember one. John Johnston."

Varus lowered the gun, leaned down, and pulled Carlos's forehead against his. "You did good, Carlos. You did real good."

Varus stood and exited while Carlos dropped his head in shame. He'd been used by Tom and now Varus.

Varus hurried into the office space and over to Senna's workstation. "Check all the flight itineraries for a John Johnston."

Senna's fingers clicked into overdrive as he brought up various hacking software. Breaking into a system like this was child's play, and within minutes, he had infiltrated all the major airlines' reservations. Technology was both a blessing and a curse for the Pantheon. It forced them to adapt, but it also allowed their limited numbers to be leveraged in extraordinary ways.

"There it is." Senna moved his cursor over John Johnston's name and clicked it. "They're going to Rome."

"When do they land?"

"About an hour."

"Who do we have nearby?" Varus asked.

Senna looked at another screen that listed all the locations of Pantheon members around the world. There were over a hundred, and all were in or near major cities. "Ashur and Gregori. It will be close, but they might make it in time."

"Get them there now. And book me a private jet for Rome."

"Got it. What do you want to do about Ron and Carlos?"

Varus shook his head. He'd already forgotten about them. "Give me a second."

He walked through the kitchenette and into the conference room. He pulled out his pistol, aimed, and in two squeezes of the trigger, Ron and Carlos were shot dead like they were nothing.

THIRTY-FIVE THOUSAND FEET over the Atlantic Ocean, the crew of the Boeing 747 kept the lights of the cabin dim, as most passengers did their best to catch some sleep. Those fortunate enough to be in business class, like Tom, Ben, and Riya, found the task easier in their spacious seats that reclined. Tom sat behind Riya and was among the sleepers. Ben occupied the seat next to her but couldn't relax. His mind raced, trying to figure out what he should do next. He was on a plane to Rome with Tom, a guy with past lives who conveniently avoided sharing details with one exception— he had a vested interest in finding Alisa. Ben was the key to accomplishing that goal, and in the melee of escaping from the Pantheon, Tom had stripped Ben of his credit cards and left him with a fake ID.

Riya leaned over and whispered to Ben. "You okay?"

"No," Ben admitted.

"Me neither."

Ben looked at her eyes, and without a word, it became clear she had similar concerns. She nodded her head towards Tom. "Do you believe him that Ron and Carlos are okay?"

"That's what he said, but I don't know. It's hard to trust anything he says."

"Do you think you've ever met him—in your past?"

"Maybe, I just don't know."

"Is it getting *any* easier to remember?" she asked.

Ben shook his head.

"What does it feel like when you come up against this memory block?"

"There's a pain that's hard to describe," Ben said, and he wasn't going to try, but then his emotions got the better of him. "Imagine the worst thing you've ever experienced. There's that sickening feeling in the pit of your stomach. All you want is to go back in time and change it, but your mind replays that moment again, and again, and again until finally your brain sticks the memory in a hole and buries it so no one will find it, but that sickening feeling is always there... lurking." Ben shook his head. "I know that sounds stupid. I'm just tired and punchy," he said, hoping to cover up his vulnerability.

Riya appreciated his honesty. "Every time my sister pops into my mind, I remember that our last moment together was a fight. Her last memory of me was likely in anger, maybe even hate. And there's nothing I can do to change that, so no, that doesn't sound stupid. It makes perfect sense."

The two sat in silence, but for the first time, Ben felt like Riya understood him, and he understood her. It felt good to have that connection. It felt real. In his world of limited memories, doubts, and fears, he needed that more than he realized.

Riya shifted the topic. "Who is Alisa? Is she your wife or girlfriend?"

Ben drifted into his memories and considered Alisa—the mystery woman who left him with so many conflicting emotions. He was drawn to her, and yet she kept running away from him in his mind. "I don't think so."

"Do you know where to go in Rome?" Riya asked, hopeful.

Ben replayed the mishmash of memories in his mind—buildings, temples, and underground tunnels. They weren't just from his lifetime as Alexander anymore. They all pointed to Rome, but where exactly and why? He closed his eyes, trying to remember something else, some detail that might offer a hint or guidance. His mind *flashed*, but no memories. Just darkness. Frustrated, he opened his eyes and glimpsed his hands. They were folded with the thumb, pointer, and pinkie extended, and they were dripping with blood. He recoiled.

"You okay?" Riya asked.

Ben looked again at his hands, which were now clean. It was a memory —a clue.

"Ben? Do you know where to go?"

"Maybe, but I don't think I can remember with Tom around." Ben glanced back one more time at Tom, still asleep. "When we get to Rome, we need to get away from him."

"We don't have any money."

Ben considered the dilemma for a moment, then, saying nothing, he unbuckled his seat belt and bent down to the ground. Before Riya knew it, he was under her legs in a compromising position. She tossed a blanket over her lap to conceal his actions. A prying man from across the aisle looked over and shook his head in disgust. Riya smiled sheepishly.

Ben reached under Riya's seat to Tom's backpack. He tugged it closer to him and felt around for the zipper. He unzipped the main pouch and reached his hand inside. His fingers fell on one of the crisp stacks of cash. Tom shifted in his seat. Ben froze and waited for any other sign Tom was waking up. When the threat passed, Ben pulled his hand out and zipped the pack up. He slipped his head out from under the blanket and met the judgmental gaze of the passenger. He could try to explain his actions, but stealing wouldn't sound better than whatever he imagined, so Ben just gave him a wink and sat back in his seat.

He leaned over to Riya and furtively showed her the money. "Okay, when we get to Rome, we make our move."

CHAPTER 92

UR, 2284 B.C.

IN THE TEMPLE CHAMBER, Polassar quivered with his head bowed as he gripped the horns of the golden bull. Sargon held the tip of the crystal dagger against his hair. The tension was as thick as the incense burning. Did Sargon know he was lying? Would the blade thrust into his skull?

"If offered, would you rule as if you were me when I'm gone?" Sargon asked.

Polassar's mouth was dry from nerves, but he squeaked out, "Yes, my lord."

Silence.

"Do you promise to give me the authority and all the treasury back when I return?"

Polassar answered a second time, "Yes, my lord."

A longer moment of silence. Sargon removed the dagger from the top of Polassar's head.

"Rise," Sargon said.

Polassar released the horns, rose to his feet, but kept his eyes to the ground, terrified to meet Sargon's gaze, and petrified he knew the truth.

Sargon embraced Polassar. "Thank you, my son. You may go." Polassar shuffled out of the temple, perplexed by the entire ritual but relieved he'd pulled it off.

———

THAT EVENING, Sargon and his four followers enjoyed a lavish banquet in the inner sanctuary. Servants tended to their every whim and brought an assortment of liquors and delicacies. Seductive belly dancers performed nearby, much to the men's delight. Reminiscent of the feast when Sargon was a cupbearer, except now he held out his chalice to be filled. Polassar, Senna, Ashur, and Varus reveled in the pampering. This was the life that money and privilege provided. Even Sargon relished the moment until he clapped twice. "Privacy."

The servants, cupbearer, and dancers scurried into the back rooms out of sight.

Sargon addressed his four followers. "I have an announcement. The week is up. This body will be dead soon, so it is time to declare my successor."

"Don't give up, my lord. We need you." Polassar clasped his hands together and bowed towards Sargon.

"That's kind of you to say, Polassar, but this body is old. I'm ready for a new one, but fear not, I will be back. Thank you all for your pledge of loyalty."

Polassar eyed Senna and gave him the ever slightest smile.

Sargon continued with his speech, "However, someone was not truthful about their devotion."

A palpable uneasiness swallowed the room.

"As I told you, I am a god among you, so I know when you are lying. I can make you suffer, and I can take away your gift." Sargon stared at each of the men.

"Who is this traitor? We must do away with him!" cried Ashur.

"Well, let's not be hasty, Ashur. I believe in forgiveness, so I will give a second chance just this once. But remember this, next time, the penalty will be much worse."

One by one, Sargon stared at each man.

Senna squirmed in his seat until he couldn't take it anymore. "I'm sorry, Sargon. Please forgive me."

Sargon walked over and motioned for Senna to stand. Terror-stricken, Senna rose to his feet. With his head held low, he trembled.

"Look at me," Sargon said.

Senna raised his terrified gaze and made eye contact. Sargon reached out and gave him a firm yet loving hug. "Thank you for coming forward."

Senna exhaled, and Sargon returned to his seat.

"As punishment, you will take your own life." Sargon withdrew the crystal dagger, tossed it in front of Senna, and then took a sip of wine.

Senna looked at Sargon, confused.

"Now," Sargon said.

All eyes watched as Senna gripped the blade.

Sargon tilted his head and spoke in a soft but firm tone. "All will be forgiven after this. Do it."

Senna mustered his courage and thrust the dagger into his midsection. He dropped the blade, doubled over, and bled out near the food.

Sargon resumed his meal, eating a few choice bites of meat. "Polassar, finish him."

Polassar picked up the weapon, then sliced Senna's throat. Within seconds, Senna was dead.

"Fantastic. Now we can enjoy the rest of the meal." Sargon clapped twice. "More wine!"

Servants reappeared and filled everyone's glasses. Sargon motioned to his cupbearer for a refill. As the boy stepped to fill the king's cup, Sargon spoke paternally, "I was once in your place, young man." Once his chalice was full, he flicked his wrist. "Now, leave."

The servants and cupbearer once again departed.

Sargon turned to Varus. "Would you be so kind as to get my crown as it is time to anoint my successor?"

Varus bowed and then left. Polassar and Ashur eyed Senna's body with disgust as the blood pooled closer to them.

Sargon pointed at the corpse. "Senna will be welcomed back into the group. I do give second chances. Never a third. Is that understood?"

Polassar and Ashur nodded. Sargon raised his glass for a toast. "To second chances."

"To second chances." Polassar and Ashur lifted their glasses, then took healthy chugs.

Sargon sipped his fine blend. He savored the subtle flavors that danced on his tongue.

Ashur turned pale and doubled over in anguish.

"Are you okay?" Polassar asked. Then the sickness struck him, and he clutched his stomach. He writhed in agony as the almost empty cup of wine taunted him, inches from his face.

"Don't worry. You won't die from this poison," Sargon said.

Varus returned with the crown and found his friends lying in excruciating pain.

"Guards!" Sargon barked.

Soldiers entered and dragged Polassar and Ashur away, leaving Sargon and Varus alone. Varus handed the crown to Sargon.

"Varus, you and you alone were truthful. I will always remember that," Sargon said.

"What will you do with them?" Varus asked.

Sargon took another sip of his delicious untainted wine. "I'm a man of my word. They will get one more chance to follow me. For now, their eyes will be gouged out, and their tongues cut off, so they're mutes. I want them to think of nothing else in this life other than the error of their ways."

Sargon rose to his feet and kissed the top of Varus's forehead. "I will return soon. Be well, my dear, sweet Varus." He took a step to the door, then paused. "And don't drink the wine." He tossed his crown to Varus. "That's for you." Sargon exited the room.

Varus stood, bewildered. Was it true? Was he now the king? For the next hour, Varus wandered the palace halls in a stupor. He still held the crown. A servant approached and bowed before Varus.

"My lord, a man arrived. He says Moshi sent him to meet with the king. Shall I send him to you?"

My lord. Varus liked the sound of that. He looked at the crown, then placed it on his head. "Why wouldn't you?" Varus warmed to his new authority as he continued down the hallway, then entered the sacred temple.

The room was quiet. Maybe even peaceful. The only light came from the three torches mounted on the walls and a small fire pit near the center that burned incense. The dominating feature was the golden bull statue and its jeweled eyes that sparkled from the flames' reflected glow. Varus approached with deference. Was it Sargon? Better safe than sorry, he bowed down and grabbed the horns, but something felt different. He let go and inspected the sculpture closer. There was an indentation through the horns and back of the head—a void where it appeared something once fit. This gap was long and thin on both sides, with a circle in the middle. Varus rubbed his fingers across the space, clueless to its purpose.

The slave entered. "Are you Sargon?"

Varus turned. "I am the king. Who are you?"

The slave responded, "My name is Craterus."

Meanwhile, at the clifftop that overlooked the Euphrates River, Sargon dug a hole three feet deep. Satisfied with the depth, he removed the golden scepter from his robe and admired it. He placed it in the pit, buried it, then rolled a large rock over the spot. The effort left him exhausted. He stood and took one final breath. Without a second thought, he launched himself over the cliff and into the darkness.

Sargon was dead.

CHAPTER 93

Rome, 44 B.C.

On a cool, spring night, the same rebellious senators gathered again in Alexander's estate. They didn't whisper during this meeting. Instead, they argued. The group had been complaining about all the changes they wanted in Rome, but nothing could be done so long as Caesar remained on the throne. The senators bickered about when they should strike, how they should strike, and even if they should strike.

Cassius sliced the air with his hands to silence the squabbling. "Let's go over the possibilities again. When he goes on his evening walk, we could have someone waiting in the trees. When he crosses the bridge, someone could push him off. We could do it at a big event, and someone sneaks a weapon in."

Alexander shook his head. "These are too risky. Too much can go wrong."

Casca banged his fist against a table. "Why are we still talking? We need to act."

Alexander scratched at his chin in frustration. He wanted to act too, but he'd given his word to Solomon. "We only get one shot at this. We need to make sure we've thought through all the details."

Casca pointed at him. "No. You've gotten cold feet. Why? Are you afraid?"

"You're not?" Alexander said, throwing it back on Casca.

"It is only a matter of time before someone loyal to Caesar finds out about our plot. We must act now."

Lucius chimed in, "He's right. So much can happen before we get another chance."

Alexander turned to Lucius. "What do you mean before we'll get another chance?"

"Have you not heard? Caesar is going on another campaign. To conquer Parthia. He'll be gone for at least a year," Lucius said.

Casca stewed in his chair. "We thought you were a leader."

Alexander stroked his chin and considered the dilemma. He'd given his word, but that was before learning Caesar would be gone soon. The other senators were right, too. A lot could happen during that time. Their plot could be discovered, and that would be disastrous for everyone, including the Lux Mundi. Surely, Solomon would understand and agree they must act.

"Bring Caesar to the Theater of Pompey on the pretense of granting him more honors while also presenting issues that need his divine ruling," Alexander said. "It will be just like any other day, except we all carry our daggers. Whoever he turns his back to first must strike. We do this for Rome."

Casca nodded in agreement and rubbed his hands. Finally, some action. "When do we take back Rome?"

Alexander's eyes narrowed. "The day we settle debts. The Ides of March."

THE DAY OF RECKONING ARRIVED. The Tiber River snaked around the city like it always did, despite the murderous intention that lurked near the Theater of Pompey. Several conspirators milled about, just outside the pillared building. They tried and failed to appear inconspicuous. These senators were good at talking about assassinations and revolution, but they were not men of action. Alexander noted their weakness. Could they pull this off?

Lucius led Julius Caesar, decked out in a royal toga, towards them. He attempted to distract Caesar by asking for a political favor. Caesar waved him off, passed by the other senators, and entered the theater. The conspiring senators, including Alexander, glanced at one another. Their moment had arrived. They followed Caesar inside, where the rest of the senate gathered. Caesar failed to notice the predatory eyes that locked onto him as he moved further into the arena. He turned his back to Casca and greeted the other senators, looking to suck up to him. Alexander nodded to Casca to attack.

"Big talker" Casca withdrew his dagger with a trembling hand and delivered the weakest strike imaginable. He grazed Caesar's arm and inflicted a minuscule cut.

Caesar whirled around. "Casca, what are you doing?" He looked at the minor wound on his arm, not realizing the malice behind its intent.

Casca stood dumbfounded. "Now! Help!" Panicked, he looked at the other conspirators.

Lucius stepped forward with his dagger and thrust with only slightly more authority. Caesar whipped around and punched him. Fearing the moment would be lost, Alexander's heart raced. *Thump, thump. Thump, thump. Thump, thump.* He pushed his way through the melee.

When Caesar turned his back to anyone, a blade poked him. It was like death by a thousand papercuts. But, strong and skilled, Caesar fought like a warrior. He decked several conspirators, and it appeared he might survive this "onslaught."

Alexander stepped into the fray. *Thump, thump. Thump, thump. Thump, thump.* Carpe diem. He summoned his rage and struck with a ferocity and lethality that stunned the room. The dagger pierced deep into Caesar's chest —a death blow. Covered in blood from all the superficial cuts, Caesar staggered backward and fell to the floor.

Alexander exhaled, the weight of his anger and guilt now gone. He had slain the dragon. Brimming with confidence, he stepped forward and towered over Caesar. "I told you I'd end you."

"You—" Caesar coughed and sputtered.

Alexander leaned down and whispered, "That's for Hephaestion."

"You stupid boy." Caesar covered his face with his toga and waited for death to overtake him.

The other conspirators cheered and pumped their fists in the air. They did it—sort of. With blood dripping from his hands and the dagger, Alexander stood. He should feel elated, but something was off. Caesar's last words and the way he said them troubled Alexander.

The senators dashed through the streets, letting the citizens know the news. "The tyrant is dead! Rome is free!"

Alexander drifted outside and watched from the steps of the theater. Citizens covered their mouths, horrified. Alexander had made a grave mistake, but he had no idea just how big. He hurried to the residential section with the special domus. He rushed inside, passing through the entryway, atrium, and into the culina. The stone table had already been pushed aside. He raced down into the tunnel. Maybe the Lux Mundi could help mitigate whatever damage he'd caused. In his blood-stained toga, he entered the secret chamber and found Solomon and a half dozen other members of the Lux Mundi in an emergency meeting.

Solomon stood in the center next to a man Alexander didn't recognize. The stranger wore a long sleeve robe with ornamentation not of these parts. As Alexander stepped closer, Solomon caught sight of him.

Alexander bowed his head, clasped his hands, and extended his thumb, index finger, and pinkie. It was his way of trying to apologize.

A look of disgust filled Solomon's face. "Well, I guess we know what your word is worth."

Alexander dropped his head in shame. "He was going to leave soon. We wouldn't get another chance."

Solomon wasn't interested in an explanation or an excuse. He seethed with frustration and indignation. "Joshua has returned from China, as I said he would." Solomon motioned to the man Alexander didn't recognize.

"He found someone with the gift, but Alisa was sick and could not make the journey."

Alexander's heart skipped a beat. "What is her name?"

Joshua stepped forward. "Alisa. She is very sick, but she gave me the information we needed."

Alexander's world spun. "What information did she give?"

"She has the history of several key Pantheon, including their leader. She knows who they've been, and in some cases, who they are," Joshua said.

Alexander was almost afraid to ask, "Who is their leader?"

"His true name is Sargon," Solomon said. "He's a Roman named Octavian. Apparently, a long-lost nephew of the Caesar."

Alexander shook his head. "I've never heard of him. That can't be true."

"Of course, it isn't true. But the people of Rome don't know that, and Octavian is in Caesar's will as his heir," Solomon said.

"What?" Alexander asked, afraid to put the pieces together. He leaned against the wall for support.

Solomon responded, "You just made the leader of the Pantheon the new Caesar."

CHAPTER 94

Rome, 2018

Tom, Ben, and Riya departed the plane haggard and jet-lagged. They ambled down the jetway and into the international terminal of Fiumicino Airport. Tom read the signs and got his bearings for where to go next.

He pointed to the right. "We have to take the shuttle to get through customs."

"I need to use the restroom first," Ben said.

"Why didn't you take care of that on the plane?"

"I could go too," Riya admitted.

Tom threw up his hands. "Fine. We'll all go tinkle."

They walked through the gate, stretching their legs until they reached a bathroom. Riya disappeared into the ladies' room. Tom and Ben entered the men's. Once inside, Ben made a beeline for a stall. "I may be a while. Airline food is not sitting well. Sorry."

Tom drifted to the wall of urinals, unzipped and stretched his neck. Ben cracked his door, slipped out, and walked back into the terminal where Riya waited.

They broke into a sprint, dashed to the shuttle station, and hurried down the steps to the gangway. Out of breath, they looked around. No shuttle and the track was empty.

Tom finished relieving himself and washed his hands, unaware of anything amiss, until something caught his eye in the mirror. The door to Ben's stall was ajar. He walked over to inspect it. "Ben?"

No answer. Tom nudged the door open. Empty. He shot out of the restroom, almost bowling over two men entering.

Ben and Riya paced with nervous energy. Their ruse wouldn't give them much time, and there was nothing they could do to make the shuttle arrive faster. The rumble of the shuttle train in the distance offered a glimmer of hope. Seconds later, it rolled into the station. The doors slid open, and they hopped on. The shuttle remained stationary with the doors open for what seemed like an eternity. Tom stumbled down the stairs and onto the gangway. As he got back to his feet, the doors closed. Tom scanned the cabins of the shuttle until he spotted Ben and Riya. He shook his head as he pulled out his phone.

As the shuttle departed, Ben's phone rang. He answered, and it was, of course, Tom. "What are you doing, Ben?"

"I'm sorry, Tom. I need to do this on my own. I don't know who I can trust."

"Well, trust this. You can't go anywhere without me. I have the money."

Ben held up the stack of cash.

Tom clenched his teeth. "I'm trying to help. You stand no chance against the Pantheon alone. We will sort this out together, understood? Wait for me when you get off." Tom hung up.

Ben and Riya clung to the metal handlebars for support as the train rumbled on.

"He wants us to wait. He said he's trying to help," Ben said.

"Helping who?" Riya asked rhetorically.

The shuttle rumbled into the exit terminal, and Riya and Ben jumped off. They dashed up the stairs, scanning signs along the way. Tom would be on the next shuttle, so they had about a five-minute head start. They followed the signs for taxis and ran out of the airport until they found an open cab. They were going to escape! After hopping into the cab, the driver asked in a thick Italian accent, "Where to?"

It was the simplest of questions, but Ben and Riya were tongue-tied. Where were they going? The hesitation worried the driver. "Do you have money?"

Ben pulled out his stack of U.S. bills and showed the driver a hundred-dollar bill.

"You need euros or a credit card."

"We'll pay you double."

"The money changer is inside. You go now." The cabbie pointed his finger and waved for them to get out.

After all this, Ben and Riya were going to be done in by a cabbie with an attitude. They jumped out of the taxi and rushed back inside. Time was running out. Tom would arrive any minute. Fortunately, the kiosk for the money changer was just inside the baggage claim. While they waited for the next available teller, they didn't notice two men step out of a chauffeured SUV. Both wore expensive blue suits. One had long black hair tied up in a man bun. The other sported a tight buzz cut with a manicured beard. Man bun was Gregori, and buzz cut was Ashur. Both held their phones in front of them, and the screens displayed pictures of Ben, Riya, and Tom. They stepped into the baggage claim and scanned the passengers.

As Ben and Riya spoke to the moneychanger, they were oblivious that danger stood only a few feet away behind them.

Ashur continued to scan the area and began turning around. Before he faced Ben and Riya, Gregori tapped him on the shoulder and pointed. On the far end, Tom dashed into sight.

As soon as Tom saw Ben and Riya, he stopped running and walked towards them. He overlooked Ashur and Gregori at first, but their uncomfortable stare forced him to stop.

Ben collected his converted stack of euros, stepped away from the teller, then froze upon seeing Tom across the way. Ben's heart sank, thinking they'd been caught, but as Ashur and Gregori neared Tom, he saw fear in Tom's eyes. He and Riya needed to get away immediately. The Pantheon was already here.

CHAPTER 95

Ur, 2269 B.C.

The Euphrates River meandered behind the thriving city of Ur. Varus had done a commendable job of maintaining Sargon's legacy as the empire prospered under his reign. But, unfortunately, two decades of rule had taken its toll. Wrinkles and open sores covered Varus's pale skin. Death was closing in fast due in no small part to the stress of running a kingdom.

Varus wouldn't have lasted five years, let alone twenty were it not for Craterus, who decided to stay and join Varus's court. He became a critical member of the nobility and right hand to Varus.

The two began each day as they always did—with a walk to the sacred temple where they prayed to Sargon's statue. And on this day, Varus's failing health finally started to catch up with him. He coughed into his sleeve.

"Are you okay?" Craterus asked.

Varus answered by revealing his sleeve dotted with blood spittle. The two continued their stroll to the temple, and when they entered, the same torches illuminated the room with the same mystical glow. The same smoky incense burned, and the same ruby eyes bore down from the head of the golden bull.

Varus bowed before the statue and grasped the horns. "Great Sargon, we thank you for all that you have provided and continue to provide. Please return soon. Your humble servant, Varus." He finished his prayer and kept his head lowered as he backed away.

Craterus stepped to the bull next and performed the same ritual, except as he clasped the statue's horns, he dared to look up into the empty ruby eyes. "Do you ever wonder if this is real? Is he watching? Is he really a god?"

Any pretense of transcendent ambiance vanished. They sat in an old, dimly lit, smoke-filled room. Varus coughed more blood into his sleeve before considering the question for a long moment. "Probably not."

Craterus looked at Varus, surprised. He'd assumed Varus believed wholeheartedly. "Then why do we do this?"

Varus glared at the lifeless statue. "If he is watching, then that means he is a god. If he isn't, then is it so bad living this life? What were you before this?"

"I was sold into slavery."

"And when I die, which does not appear too far off, you will be king. If you don't serve him, then all of this," Varus waved his hand at the opulence that surrounded them, "will be taken away. I've seen it happen to others. Until I know for certain he's not a god, I'll bow down to this statue."

Craterus respected Varus's honesty and logic. He bowed and prayed. As he gripped the horns, his fingers fell into the gaps on the backside. "I've always wondered, why is there this space?"

"You can ask him when he returns."

"Do you think he will return soon?" Craterus asked.

"Yes," Varus said, without hesitation. "And I can tell you he has a peculiar sense of knowing if you're lying to him. So, my suggestion would be, don't lie to him—ever."

As Varus and Craterus prayed, the warm wind blew on the cliff where Sargon had launched himself into the abyss. The mighty Euphrates drifted along, indifferent to time and the politics of the cities built against its banks. The setting was calm and peaceful, with one glaring exception—the ominous hole where the scepter had been buried.

CHAPTER 96

Illyria, 44 B.C.

Roman infantry soldiers organized in legion formation marched in a training exercise on the outskirts of Illyria. Meanwhile, the elite guards and officers squared off against one another with wooden swords. Among them was a haughty young man, Octavian, with polished armor. He faced Marius, a much larger opponent. With auburn locks and piercing grey eyes, Octavian studied his adversary with his sword by his side. Muscular and intimidating, Marius attacked. Octavian moved as if he could read his opponent's mind. He easily blocked two strikes, then cracked Marius on the side.

"Dead," Octavian said.

Marius stepped back in a huff and grabbed his side in pain. He positioned himself in his starting position, ready for another round. This time, Marius attempted a different strategy. He held a more defensive posture. Unbowed, Octavian took the initiative. He thrust his weapon and allowed Marius to block the first attack, then decked him with his free hand, and followed with a sword swipe to Marius' side.

"Dead," Octavian said, without emotion. This was like an adult beating a child in a game. There's no joy because it isn't a challenge.

Marius fumed and groaned from the pain of the second strike in the same place, but hubris forced him to prepare for another punishing round.

Just outside the camp, a messenger on horseback raced up the trail. Guards held up their swords to stop him.

"I come from Rome. I have urgent news," the messenger said.

Octavian heard the exchange and, for the briefest of moments, turned and let his guard down. Marius seized the opportunity and struck. Without looking, Octavian blocked the attack and smacked Marius on the side of the head with the wooden sword.

"Dead." Octavian left a smarting Marius and walked towards the legions. "Fall in line."

Within a few minutes, several thousand soldiers settled into precise ranks. The messenger opened the sealed document with trembling hands. Octavian stood in front of the troops with three other high-ranking commanders, including Marius. Everyone, except Octavian, curiously waited for the urgent news to be read.

"Loyal subjects of Rome. A tragedy has befallen us," the messenger read aloud. "Our hope, our deity, our Caesar, has been brutally murdered."

The soldiers reacted with dismay and bristled with a fighting spirit.

The messenger continued reading, "A tyrannical group of senators struck down our glorious leader. In death, Gaius Julius Caesar has declared his successor. He leaves all his wealth, and he leaves Rome, to his very capable and divinely ordained nephew, Gaius Octavian."

The soldiers glanced at Octavian. *He's the new leader of Rome?*

Even Marius appeared stunned. He leaned over and whispered to Octavian, "I didn't know you were related to the Caesar."

"I'm a man of many secrets," Octavian said.

The messenger finished the scroll. "Caesar states, 'I trust you will serve him as you served me. Long live Rome.'"

In unison, the soldiers shouted, "Long live Rome."

Peculiar silence ensued. What now? In a grand public display, Marius turned and faced Octavian, then dropped to one knee and bowed. "Hail Caesar!"

The soldiers followed Marius's lead. "Hail Caesar!"

Octavian stepped forward to address the men in his first act as the new emperor of Rome. "We all loved Caesar... like a father. He did so much. He didn't deserve to be killed in this way. We now must take it upon us to avenge those that betrayed him."

The soldiers stewed, hungry for blood.

"We will return to Rome. We will find Caesar's murderers. And they will be punished. All of them."

IN THE SECRET UNDERGROUND CHAMBER, the Lux Mundi discussed the next steps now that Sargon, masquerading as Octavian, was the new Caesar. It was concluded that he must've known something about the assassination attempt; otherwise, why would he have arranged Julius Caesar's will so that he'd be named heir? If he knew that, then he knew of the Lux Mundi, which meant they were all in imminent danger, and it was all because of Alexander.

Solomon had Alexander pulled to the side for a private, heated conversation. "Your stupidity has destroyed an opportunity to stop the Pantheon, and you've put us all at risk. And above all, you gave me your word. Who are we if we don't live by our words?"

Sick to his stomach, Alexander promised, "I'll make it right. I'll stop Sargon."

Solomon stared at Alexander with contempt. "No. You are not the light."

"What does that mean?" Alexander asked.

"It means I made a mistake inviting you into the Lux Mundi. We will change our secret hand signal and our meeting place. You are no longer welcome," Solomon said.

Alexander despised himself because Solomon was right. For years,

Alexander had sought revenge. He hadn't used his gift to help people. Two other Lux Mundi members overheard the exchange and stared at him like a pariah. Alexander nodded in acceptance of his banishment and hurried out in shame. He raced through the tunnel, up the stairs, and exited the house into the early nighttime air. Alexander didn't stop until he turned a corner. Breathing heavily, he leaned against the wall, slid down, and buried his head between his knees. How could he have been so stupid? He wanted desperately to go back and plead for a chance at redemption, but how could he? Alexander delivered the power and wealth of the greatest empire in the world into the hands of his sworn enemy.

Shouting and footsteps echoed from the opposite street corner. Alexander peered around to see the source of the commotion. A dozen Roman soldiers marched to the domus with the secret chamber.

The soldier in charge pointed to half the men. "Seal the tunnel and stand guard." He then motioned to the remaining troops. "You five, come with me. There's only one other exit."

While the Lux Mundi had been studying the Pantheon, they'd been doing the same. They knew about the secret chamber. In minutes, the Lux Mundi would be trapped. Alexander needed to save them. Maybe this was his chance at redemption.

CHAPTER 97

Rome, 2018

As the two men in suits stepped closer to Tom, dread filled his face. Ben didn't need to see more. He seized Riya's hand, yanked her out of the baggage claim, and flagged down the next taxi. They hopped inside, and the driver waited for instructions. Ben's mind raced. *Where to?*

"The Theater of Pompey," Ben blurted out.

As the cab pulled into traffic, Ben and Riya craned their necks, trying to find any sign of Tom or the two men.

"Who were those guys?" Riya asked.

"They found us already," Ben said.

"That's not possible. How could they find us that fast?"

Ben shook his head. "I don't know, but they did."

They rode in silence for the next half hour. Ben picked at the cracked vinyl seat of the cab. Maybe Tom was right. Maybe they didn't have any chance without him, or maybe they just didn't have any chance at all. Ben questioned his suspicion of Tom. When he saw the men in suits, Tom was frightened.

As they neared the heart of Rome, Riya asked, "Is the Theater of Pompey where we need to go?"

"I'm not sure. My mind is a blur. It's a mess of feelings and images." Ben looked out the window, not wanting to talk about it anymore. They were on a journey guided by nothing more than Ben's jumbled and suppressed memories.

"I've been doing some thinking," Riya said. "I think the scars in your brain differ from Tom's. You have three smaller scars and a huge one. If someone tortured Tom as badly as he says, then it's hard to imagine that anyone could've been tortured that much worse. Something else happened to you. The other odd part is you'd think you'd remember your most recent lives first. You have flashes from lives way in your past. Why do you think that is?"

Ben thought about his struggle to push past the memory block. The beating Alexander inflicted remained fresh in his mind. "In the MRI, a part of me would rather die than remember."

"Right. But there's also a part of you that wants to remember; otherwise, we wouldn't be here. On the plane, you said it felt like you buried your memories so no one will find them. You didn't say, so you won't find them."

Ben refused to look at Riya or acknowledge the statement.

"Tom isn't here. You can't run from it anymore, Ben. This isn't just about you. They killed my sister. And if you care about Alisa, the Pantheon is going to find her. They found us."

As if on cue, the cab parked on a street—the Largo di Torre Argentina. Ben and Riya exited the vehicle and walked to a fence that ran around the perimeter of a sunken square containing the excavated remains of four Roman temples and pieces of the Theater of Pompey. A staircase led down to the ruins that included portions of weathered pillars rising from the ground like massive tree stumps.

From above, the site reeked of dichotomies. Mud and wild grass replaced the splendor of the once pristine grounds. Feral cats skittered through the hallowed paths where senators and the Caesar himself had walked. Where the once-grand theater towered, now honking cars drove on bustling streets.

Ben closed his eyes and took a deep breath. Modern Rome melted away, and the ancient buildings sprouted from the ground like saplings. He wandered the ancient roads, almost in a trance. Riya did her best to make sure Ben avoided the busy streets. He passed around a corner into an alleyway behind several businesses. The existing architecture revealed the curvature of the theater's interior, but in Ben's mind, the spectacular semi-circular seats blossomed like a flower. He now stood on the main stage of the theater.

Something stirred inside his stomach—a deep-seated nausea. His mind *flashed.*

As Brutus, he knelt down beside Caesar after stabbing him.

"You stupid boy," Caesar said as he died.

With closed eyes, Ben reached out and touched the spot where Caesar uttered those words. The memories of his actions that day, his feelings, his guilt, all flooded back.

"What is it?" Riya asked.

"I messed up." Ben opened his eyes. "But there's something more. This was just the beginning."

"Where do we go next?" Riya asked.

SHORTLY LATER, Riya and Ben walked in the back of a tour group inside the Basilica of San Clemente. The church contained three naves divided by arcades on marble pillars. Decorative geometric stones checkered the floor. Behind the primary nave, a grand sanctuary stood beneath a half-domed canopy raised by four columns over the shrine of Clement. A wooden frame and ethereal Christian mosaics adorned the ceiling.

Riya studied the impressive architecture with a confused look. The timing seemed off. Ben had only hinted at events that were before the birth of Christ, let alone a church built in the twelfth century.

A perky tour guide soon provided the answer. "This church sits atop a second, earlier church, and beneath that is the home of an ancient Roman nobleman, and beneath that there's a secret temple of Mithras."

The first chance they got, Ben and Riya slipped away from the tour to the steps leading to the structures below. They didn't stop until they descended to the lowest level, which contained excavated tunnels and rooms. The artificial lights provided a very different experience from Ben's hazy memories, so much so that he questioned if this was the right place. But then, he found himself outside a room protected by an iron gate. Inside was a space with a semicircular ceiling and a small pillar that depicted a man slaying a bull. It was the secret chamber.

Riya leaned over and whispered to Ben, "You were in here?"

Ben nodded.

Riya held her arms for warmth. "It's cold. What happened?"

Ben didn't hear the question. His gaze and mind were lost to this place when the Lux Mundi once met, but it now felt old, abandoned, and worthless.

Riya read the placards fastened to the wall just outside the gate. "This says that in the first century, A.D., you worshipped the god of Mithras. Is that right?"

Ben shook his head. "This place is older, and we didn't worship here."

"What happened here?" Riya asked.

"I failed them," Ben said.

CHAPTER 98

UR, 2270 B.C.

THE SOMBER CITIZENS of Ur gathered in the city's center, which featured a giant golden statue of a bull. It was an idol for the people. The cult of Sargon lived on. Servants carried the wrapped body of Varus atop a small burial platform through the weeping masses. When it reached the town square, servants placed it on an altar in front of the giant sculpture.

Craterus, now wearing the king's crown, stood beside the body and addressed the citizens, "People of Akkad, our wise king has passed on. He is with Sargon, and one day they shall both return to us. Until then, we continue to serve them as loyal subjects."

The mourners cried and shouted lamentations. Amongst the citizens was a shadowy figure in a dark brown cloak. His Asian features gave away his foreign origins. He watched with curiosity and awe as Craterus choked up while presenting a sacrifice to the golden bull.

That evening, Craterus paced the hallways of the compound. As he passed several servants, they bowed to pay respect to the new king. As with

Varus, he warmed to his new position. However, he also remembered Varus's advice, and so he continued the daily prayer ritual.

He entered the temple and knelt before the original golden bull statue that Sargon crafted. As he placed his hands on the sculpture's horns, a burst of flame and smoke erupted near the torches beside him.

Craterus stumbled backward, away from the danger. He glanced up, trembling.

The Asian man loomed over him and removed the hood from his cloak. "I am Sargon."

Craterus threw himself down at Sargon's feet. "Oh, mighty Sargon, I've prayed for this day to arrive."

Sargon marveled at Craterus's sincerity. "You have been loyal to me, yes?"

Head still bowed, Craterus clutched Sargon's feet. "Of course, my lord."

"Swear your allegiance to me again." Sargon motioned for Craterus to bow before the golden bull. Craterus grabbed the horns and lowered his head. Still in shock, he didn't notice that the void behind the horns had been filled. The golden scepter now rested in the space, a perfect fit. The crystal lit up.

"I promise to serve you, my lord," Craterus said.

The crystal remained lit. Sargon smiled. "Rise, my son."

Craterus stood. "Whatever you ask, I shall do. You are the true king." He took off his crown and offered it to Sargon.

Sargon held his hand out to stop him. "No. You have been loyal. You shall continue to sit on the throne as a reward. The people of Akkad might also find it odd to have someone that looks different from them as their king."

"As you wish, my lord." Craterus kept the crown but refused to wear it.

Sargon put his finger against Craterus's chest. "But you will serve me, and you will start by capturing two warlords north of Akkad. They are attempting to unify the local tribes and attack my kingdom. They do not fear me, but they will. Strike now and deliver these rebels to me."

"As you wish, my lord. What are their names?"

Sargon turned and left the temple. He was ready not only to restore his power but to expand it. "They go by different names to their people, but I know who they really are."

CHAPTER 99

Rome, 44 B.C.

Hidden in the shadows, Alexander sized up the two soldiers standing guard outside the domus. Unless he could take out the half-dozen men, both inside and outside, the Lux Mundi would be ambushed by the soldiers who went to seal off the other entrance. That left little time to come up with a plan. He snuck up behind the first guard and snapped his neck. Before the second had time to react, Alexander flung a dagger that tagged him in the throat.

Alexander burst through the door. Three legionaries rushed back from the culina, and without thinking, Alexander's instincts and lifetimes of fighting experience flooded out. The numbers didn't favor him, but he used the tight hallway to his advantage and only had to face one soldier at a time. After capturing the sword of the first man, the rest of the battle was easy. The three soldiers were killed or knocked unconscious in seconds.

Alexander raced down into the secret tunnel and pressed forward through the darkness towards the circle of light at the end. He called out in a loud whisper, "Solomon!"

No answer.

Alexander shuffled on until he reached the secret chamber, but he recoiled as soon as he entered. Corpses laid at his feet. Tiny leather satchels filled with powder rested beside several of the Lux Mundi. Alexander remembered the bag of poison Michael had offered him in the prior life. He was too late to save them.

Down the opposite tunnel, the footsteps of Roman soldiers echoed closer. Alexander retreated the way he came, and ran out of the house, back into the streets of Rome. He found an alley and hid in the shadows. Shouts of Roman officers and marching footsteps against the paved streets boomed throughout the city.

"Over here," a voice whispered.

Alexander spied Casca waving behind giant barrels and hurried over.

"They're hunting us," Casca cried.

"I know. We've got to get out of Rome."

The shouts from the Roman soldiers grew closer.

"This way." Alexander started down the street.

Casca remained frozen with fear. Alexander grabbed and shook him. "Casca. We must go."

Casca mustered every bit of courage he had in him, which wasn't much, and the two moved through the alley. As the soldiers' footsteps stomped closer, Alexander glanced over his shoulder. The light from their torches lit up the sides of the walls. They were going to get caught. Alexander furiously searched for a place to hide and spotted a toilet house just ahead. He yanked Casca inside.

"There's no way out," Casca said.

The two pushed further into the dark, foul-smelling building with their footsteps clapping against the stone floor, despite their best efforts to move in silence.

From outside the toilet house, a soldier yelled, "I think I saw someone go in there."

Alexander hunted for the access cover to the sewer. Seconds from being captured, fortune smiled. He found the heavy concrete lid, heaved it open, and waved Casca inside. Casca paused, but the choice was clear—filthy excrement-filled water or a painful execution.

Alexander and Casca entered a well-constructed tube about four feet in height, with about a third of it filled with wastewater. The putrid smell burned their eyes and caused them to dry heave. They buried their noses into their shoulders to mute the foul odor, but it was little help. Behind them, a soldier shouted, "They went into the sewer!"

Alexander and Casca pressed on, and the smaller tube spilled into the Cloaca Maxima, Rome's enormous main sewer line. They climbed down and entered chest-deep water that flowed in one direction.

"Where are we going?" Casca answered.

Alexander didn't have time to explain. He powered on, with Casca trailing like a scared puppy. Soldiers sloshed in the water behind, which urged both men to move faster. Finally, Alexander spotted what he was hoping for.

He pointed to an exit pipe. "Come on. This leads to the Tiber."

They followed the meandering water to the opening that spilled into the river. Under cover of darkness, they swam out. Almost immediately, the temperature dropped twenty degrees. Soldiers shouted from within the pipe and the streets above, trying to locate Alexander and Casca.

Their only chance was to remain in the river, but they couldn't survive for long in the frosty water. A tree branch floated by. Alexander swam over and grabbed the driftwood. "Casca, grab on."

Exhausted, Casca gripped the primitive life preserver, and the two let the current lead them away from the city. After several minutes, Alexander glimpsed back. The torches from the legions appeared as pin pricks of light. Rome was now safely in the distance, but the cold threatened, and each second in the frigid water felt like an hour.

"We need to get to shore." Alexander pointed to a small beach head. The two kicked towards it, despite their fatigue. Once ashore, they collapsed in the sand. Gasping for air and shivering, Alexander rolled over and found a Roman soldier with a sword at his throat. Five others stood behind him.

Yanked to their feet, Alexander and Casca were "escorted" by the soldiers to a camp a hundred meters inland. Concealed in the trees were three dozen legionaries and a handful of tents. Cassius emerged from inside one. Upon seeing Alexander and Casca, he rushed over and gave each a giant bear hug.

"It is good to see you, my brothers," Cassius said.

Casca shook from the cold and shock of escaping death.

Cassius patted Casca on the back. "Get a hold of yourself, Casca. This is all part of a revolution." He turned to Alexander. "And unfortunately, many of our supporters have been killed."

Cassius referred to the conspirators, but Alexander's thoughts were with Solomon and the Lux Mundi. He'd caused all of this. If only Alexander had listened to Solomon. "Yes, we lost a lot of good people," he said.

"But we have good news too," Cassius said. "Many of the legions are loyal to our cause."

Casca stopped his teeth from chattering long enough to ask, "What are we going to do?"

Alexander remained tortured by his guilt. His arrogance blinded him, and he'd handed Rome to the Pantheon.

Cassius nudged Alexander's shoulder. "What do you say? We still have hope. What do you want to do?"

A look of determination and anger overwhelmed Alexander. He had to fix this. Somehow, someway, he must atone for his sins. "Rally the legions that are loyal. We will fight. And we will win."

CHAPTER 100

Rome, 2018

Ben slouched on a bench in the Basilica of San Clemente atrium. Pedestrians passed by, but he didn't notice. Lost in a stupor, he tried to dig up memories he'd buried and sealed.

Riya sat beside him, unsure how she could help. "Ben, what do you want to do?"

Ben didn't respond. His mind still unpacked events and the emotional baggage they carried. Like uninvited guests, guilt, anger, fear, and shame all came to the party in his brain. He was a colossal failure of historical proportions, and yet there was something worse lurking in his mind.

"Ben?"

"This isn't it. Something else happened," he said.

"What happened?"

Ben shook his head, his face pale and unwell.

"Do you know where to go, at least?" Riya asked.

Ben closed his eyes and fought his mind to release an answer. "Philippi. We need to go to Philippi."

"Are you sure? That's a long way from Rome," Riya said.

Ben opened his eyes. "It started here, but it finished there."

VARUS STROLLED down the steps of the private jet. Ashur and Gregori waited beside a chauffeured SUV. No acknowledgment or introduction was necessary. These men had known each other for lifetimes, and they all knew Sargon's orders. Failure was never an option, which made Gregori's initial update less than ideal. "Craterus managed to get away."

"I hope you have something else to report," Varus said.

They climbed into the back of the SUV, and Gregori raised the privacy partition. Once secure, Ashur said, "Senna used airport security cameras and captured the license plate of the cab they got into this morning. We tracked down the driver. He dropped them off at the Largo di Torre Argentina."

An hour later, the SUV pulled up to the ruins of the temples. Ashur searched the area while Gregori scanned for security cameras. Varus showed pedestrians photos of Ben, Riya, and Tom. No one had seen them. Varus glanced down towards the vestiges of the grand theater, and a pang of remorse hit him. He knew what happened at this place over two thousand years ago, but he didn't know why it mattered today.

Varus's phone rang. He answered, and the ominous voice of Sargon asked, "Where are you?"

"We're searching the area where they were last reported."

Sargon chucked. "The Curia of Pompey."

Gregori walked over to Varus and whispered, "Senna just texted, and there's footage of them boarding a bus to Bari."

Varus relayed the new information. "They went to San Clemente church, and now we think they're on a bus to Bari."

Sargon fell silent.

"My lord. Are you there?"

Sargon snickered.

"What is it?" Varus asked.

"He doesn't have his memories back."

"How do you—"

Sargon interrupted. "They're not going to Bari. Check the passport numbers at the ferry crossing."

"Where are they going?" Varus asked.

"What happened after the assassination?" Sargon asked.

Varus hesitated, then replied, "Philippi."

CHAPTER 101

Ur, 2270 B.C.

The Akkadian army, led by Craterus, marched triumphantly through the city's gates with a long line of bound enemy captives. Citizens cheered and threw flowers at the feet of the victorious soldiers. The procession stopped when it reached the palace. Craterus dismounted and looked around. Where was Sargon?

He searched the estate, eager to present Sargon with the rebels he sought, but the community rooms, the dining hall, and even the grand indoor pool were all empty. Female giggles perked his ears. Craterus followed the laughter to a lavish bedroom, and inside, stunning women of all nationalities fawned over Sargon. He reveled as concubines fed him food and drink while tantalizing him with their seductive charm.

"My lord. I have the men you wanted," Craterus said, taken aback by the sight.

Sargon didn't offer a hint of gratitude. He didn't even look up as his gaze focused on the voluptuous woman in his lap. "Very well."

"What will you do with them?" Craterus asked.

"Leave them in the dungeon for a few weeks. Beyond that, they are not your concern." Sargon waved his hand at Craterus like he was shooing away a fly. Craterus bowed deferentially and left with gritted teeth.

WEEKS LATER, Sargon and Craterus hosted an enormous feast, but Sargon did most of the hosting. The two sat on opposite heads of the long dining carpet. Dancers paraded around a drunk Sargon while servants brought him delicacies and alcohol. With quiet disdain, Craterus sipped his wine. This had become a regular occurrence since Sargon's arrival.

"Those warlords are no longer in the dungeon. Did you execute them?" Craterus asked.

"They are not your concern." Sargon raised his glass. "Drink up, King of Akkadia. Enjoy the party." Sargon indulged in a long, healthy sip of wine, then let out a boisterous belch and laughed.

Craterus studied him. Sargon didn't act like a god.

The next morning, after Sargon sobered up, Craterus monitored him, curious to see what he did and where he went throughout the day. Most of his surveillance was uneventful. Sargon indulged himself with choice meats, bread, and treats. He spent hours reading scrolls on various topics—histories of people from neighboring territories, mathematics, and science. He took a swim in the pool with several concubines and then took a nap.

Late in the evening, Sargon walked one of the long palace hallways, and Craterus followed a safe distance behind. When Sargon turned a corner, Craterus snuck up and peered around, only to discover that Sargon had vanished.

Craterus searched the area with more vigor, but there was no trace of him. Maybe he was a god. Just as Craterus feared the repercussions of his actions, he noticed that the torch mounted on the wall was slightly askew. He grabbed the metal base, turned it, and a secret door cracked open. Craterus crept in and discovered a descending stone staircase. He tiptoed down each step, careful to avoid making even the slightest sound. When he reached the bottom, Craterus found a short hallway with a doorway off to the side. Sargon's voice echoed from within. Who was he talking to? Craterus debated whether he should continue, but his curiosity begged him forward. He had to know what Sargon was doing.

The room itself was nondescript, but the unusual devices that filled it raised an eyebrow. Small spikes lined one contraption designed for sitting. Another resembled a stockade, but Craterus had seen nothing quite like it. In the center, Sargon gripped a torch and breezed around one of the captured warlords. The man wore tattered clothes, and his hands were tied behind his back. A rope, strung through a metal ring in the ceiling, yanked his arms up, forcing him to arch his head towards the floor, but it wasn't long enough to allow him to lean against the ground for relief. His shoulders would rip out of their sockets if he went too far backward or forward. To avoid that outcome, the captive had to remain hunched over in a miserable position that grew more painful by the second. Since his hands were behind him, he didn't realize he gripped the scepter, and the crystal glowed.

The other warlord lay in the corner blindfolded, with his hands tied.

Sargon put the flame against the man's skin. He bellowed in anguish, but he couldn't move, or he'd experience greater pain from his shoulders.

"Please, Sargon. Give me one more chance to return to the Pantheon."

"You forget, Polassar. I was with your army," Sargon said.

Polassar. The name sounded familiar to Craterus. Varus had told him stories of former Pantheon members and their fate after lying to Sargon. But Varus also said they would be given a second chance. Maybe this was that opportunity.

"Every day you plotted to overthrow Akkad, the kingdom I built. When your men were afraid to attack the great kingdom of Sargon, you said he didn't exist. You said he was a spook story." Sargon teased the flame in front of Polassar's terrified eyes. Sargon pulled it back, then stuck his face in Polassar's. "Boo."

"Please, I'll do anything," Polassar begged.

Sargon stood and circled. "If I let you go, will you only serve me and do only as I ask?"

"I will. I swear," Polassar said, but the glowing crystal dimmed as the words left his mouth.

"Why do you not realize that I am a god? You've been lying for weeks. Do you not see the futility? Do you not understand the pain this will cause you?"

Sargon pulled the scepter out of Polassar's grip and slipped it under his cloak. He then untied the rope, and Polassar collapsed to the floor. Sargon threw a blindfold on and kicked him in the corner until he faced the wall. He seized the other man and put him in the same contraption. His arms wrenched up behind his back, which forced him into the subservient position. Sargon placed the scepter in the man's palms.

"Senna, my dear, sweet boy. Tell me again why you went with Polassar." Sargon removed the blindfold.

"I didn't know where you were," Senna said.

The light in the crystal glowed without dimming.

Sargon circled, intrigued. "Senna, do you remember the last dinner we had together?"

Senna nodded.

"You offered the truth. I appreciated that. I want the truth again, Senna." Sargon knelt down. "Look at me, Senna. This is your chance for redemption."

Senna trembled, horrified at what might follow once he looked up. Timidly, he lifted his gaze.

Sargon stroked the side of Senna's face. "All of this pain you feel right now will turn into the most incredible pleasure. Everything you want will be yours. Money, food, drink, women, or men, it doesn't matter to me. Whatever your heart desires can be yours. But I need to know that you are loyal to me. Will you serve me, Senna?"

Beads of sweat trickled down Senna's face. No more pain. He couldn't take any more pain. Quivering, he whispered, "Yes, my lord."

The crystal glowed.

"Tell me again. Will you serve me?" Sargon turned an ear to encourage Senna to speak up.

Senna brightened, praying the agony was over. He responded with more authority. "Yes, my lord."

The crystal remained lit. Sargon smiled. "Do you like Polassar? Is he your friend?"

Senna whimpered. He had to admit the truth, but he couldn't take any more suffering. "Yes."

Sargon patted Senna on the head, took the scepter out of his hands, and untied him, removing all restraints. Senna curled up on the floor and rubbed his wrists. Sargon beckoned with his finger, and Senna rose to his knees.

"Burn Polassar." Sargon thrust a torch into Senna's hand.

Senna looked over at his friend, huddled in the corner, then at Sargon.

"You said you will serve me." Sargon stared at Senna with cold eyes. This was not a request.

"No, please. Senna, we're friends," Polassar whimpered.

"A friend you killed at my command in the prior life, if I recall," Sargon said.

Senna's face hardened. He stuck the flame on the ripped clothing by Polassar's feet until it caught fire. Polassar shrieked in horror and agony.

Horrified, Craterus watched until he couldn't bear it anymore. He scurried back up the stairs as Polassar's screams chased him away. He ran out of the secret stairwell, closed the door, and raced down the hallway to his bedroom. For the rest of the night, Craterus sat alone, thinking and replaying the brutal images he witnessed. Varus's warning echoed in his mind. *"I can tell you he has a peculiar sense of knowing if you're lying to him. So, my suggestion would be, don't lie to him—ever."*

Every week since Sargon arrived, Craterus had to go to the temple and swear his allegiance before the sacred statue. How could he do that? Craterus could no longer worship him like a god now that he knew the truth, so how could he tell Sargon he'd serve him if he didn't believe it? He'd be tortured. He could escape and make a run for it, but Sargon could find him, just as he'd found Polassar and Senna. Craterus also didn't like the idea of seclusion. After living as a king, how could he live in isolation? Always hiding, never thriving. Varus's words of wisdom came back to mind. Craterus had been a slave, and now he was a king. Was this so bad?

The day came for Craterus to swear his allegiance. He walked down the hallway to the sacred temple. His heart raced a million miles an hour. As always, Sargon stood on the altar behind the golden bull. Craterus kept his head low and knelt before the statue. He grabbed the horns and then ever so slightly raised up off the ground while still keeping his head down. In this new position, Craterus could see a hint of the glow from the crystal behind the bull's head.

"I will serve you in this life," Craterus said.

The crystal remained glowing. He did it! He had passed the test, but he did it by telling the truth—at least enough of it. He would have to serve Sargon in this life.

In fact, Craterus ended up having to serve Sargon for over 1,500 years across multiple lifetimes, and he had to make the same promise every week, but it wasn't wasted time. Craterus learned everything he could about Sargon, and when he was General Craterus to Alexander of Macedon, the opportunity presented itself when he could at long last put his master plan into effect.

The moment he waited so patiently for occurred as he stood over Alexander after poisoning him with Varus. As Alexander's breaths became more shallow, Craterus's breathing intensified. Could he trust Varus? Through the years, Craterus had learned that he never knew who he could trust, but he knew who he couldn't. Still, opportunities like this didn't happen often, and this one was several hundred years in the making. He couldn't let it slip away without at least trying.

"If Sargon is a god, why was he afraid of Alexander?" Craterus asked and then froze, unsure how Varus would respond.

"I don't know," Varus said.

"We worship Sargon, but what if he's just like us?" Craterus said, floating out a stronger hint of rebellion.

"You know what happens if you challenge him," Varus said, unwilling to take the bait.

"We know Sargon's gone—at least for a little while." Craterus needed to convince Varus. He couldn't go through life pretending to worship Sargon.

"And we know he'll be back. What if you're wrong?"

"I'm not. He's just a man." Craterus sensed both Varus's curiosity and skepticism. "You want proof? Sargon has had us bow before the same statue for hundreds of years. In the next life, he will not do that."

"How do you—"

Craterus put his finger up for Varus to listen to the speech he'd been practicing for ages. "In the next life, we come back and reconnect with Sargon like we always do. When he no longer has us bow before the bull, you're going to ask me then how I know. When I'm proven right, you can decide if you still want to worship a man."

CHAPTER 102

PHILIPPI, 42 B.C.

SWORDS CLANGED against each other as men dueled for their lives. When a strike found its mark, a hair-raising scream reverberated across the battlefield. A disgusting ruddy brown slop covered the ground as the crimson blood mixed with the dusky soil. The gruesome battle pitted Roman against Roman in the hills a half-mile outside the walled city of Philippi. The war was between the Republic and the Empire—the conspirators versus Caesar's supporters.

Alexander rode with the cavalry and displayed his athleticism and skill as a warrior reminiscent of, but not identical to, his life as Alexander the Great. His sword strikes easily cut through the enemy, but he appeared less confident and even less convicted. These were fellow Romans, after all. He didn't have the comfort of believing the people he killed were evil barbarians.

The butchery weighed on his conscience and distracted him. An enemy seized the opportunity and attacked. Alexander blocked the sword swipe just in time, but the force sent him tumbling off his horse. He sprang to his feet and sliced through the man. As his blade pierced the man's stomach, a sickening scream echoed in his ear. Everything slowed down and the shriek seared in his mind. He held his head in agony.

More men charged. He regained his composure and vanquished the "enemy."

The opposing forces recognized the inevitability of defeat and began withdrawing from the area. Sensing victory, Alexander's men shouted, "They're retreating. The spoils of war are ours."

Alexander knelt down and reached his hand to the ground for support. The blood-soaked earth overwhelmed his senses. How many people had died to cover the battlefield like this? As his men rushed off to raid the enemy camp, he tried in vain to stop them. "No. You can't allow them to regroup."

His men either didn't listen or couldn't hear him as they raced off. He took several deep breaths to calm himself, then walked back to his camp. He passed by the dead and wounded from both armies. Among the injured, an enemy soldier, no older than sixteen, struggled to breathe. Panic filled his eyes upon seeing Alexander pacing towards him. Alexander knelt down and held the boy's hand. "It's okay. Just breathe."

Startled by the kindness, the young boy did his best to comply, but his lungs had been punctured and were filling with blood.

Alexander urged him on. Maybe he could save at least one. With each breath, the boy suffocated a little more. Alexander cradled the teen in his arms and did his best to comfort him as he struggled for air. Death overtook the boy, and his distant gaze fell on Alexander.

Alexander closed the boy's eyes out of respect and to avoid the guilt from the corpse's stare. Another life wasted, at least in part, because of Alexander. What would the boy have become if Alexander had not existed? He left the body and drifted back to his camp, passing by two high-ranking soldiers. "Find Cassius and the other officers. Have them meet in my tent for a post-battle assessment."

Safely in his tent, Alexander rubbed his hands in a small pot of water that had already turned a sickening red from all the blood that covered them. He'd fought so long that on several parts of his arms, blood had dried and caked onto his skin.

A table showed a crude mockup of the battlefield in the middle of the room. Marble figurines represented the armies—white was Alexander's and red Caesar's. There were about ten pieces per side. Two commanders and Casca stood at attention while waiting for Alexander to finish. A third commander entered.

"Where's Cassius?" Alexander asked as he dried his hands on a towel.

"He's dead," the commander answered.

Alexander's head dropped as he approached the table. "And the rest of the casualties?"

The second commander pulled three of the white pawns off the table. "We lost anywhere from seven to ten thousand men."

"What!" Alexander wanted to vomit.

The first commander removed five of the red figurines and smiled. "The good news is that Octavian and Antony's forces lost almost double that."

"Yes, that is good news," Alexander said sarcastically.

Casca smacked the back of one commander. "Then we won the battle! That's great news. We must hit them again."

Alexander held up his hand. "No. The strategic advantage is ours. We have the position on the hills, and we control the nearest seaport. We can be resupplied. They cannot. No one else needs to die right now."

"We must fight and destroy them!" Casca shook his fist.

Alexander hurled a white figurine at Casca's chest. "I said no. We will win by using our advantages. I won't put anyone else's life at risk just because it will be quicker."

A centurion rushed into the tent. "Sir. A messenger has sent word that Octavian wants to meet you. Alone."

Alexander paused. To the men in the room, this was Octavian, emperor of Rome, but to Alexander, it was Sargon, ruler of the Pantheon, liar, and murderer of his friend and the Lux Mundi.

"What does he want?" Casca asked.

"He wants to offer you something," the centurion said.

Casca turned to Alexander. "It could be peace terms for a new government."

"It could be a trap," one commander warned.

The group argued about the merits and risks of meeting with Octavian.

Alexander waved his hands. "Silence!"

No one said another word, and all eyes stared at Alexander. What would he do?

"I'll meet him."

CHAPTER 103

PHILIPPI, 2018

BEN AND RIYA attempted to sleep on a crowded bus to Philippi. This was the last leg of an epic twenty-two hour journey that included almost all forms of mass public transportation. It was all they could afford, given their limited funds. First, they had to take a train from Rome to Bari. From there, they boarded a ferry that took them across the Strait of Oronto to Struga. A taxi ride to Pogradec followed. They finished their travels with a series of bus rides, the first of which brought them to Thessaloniki, the second to Kavala, and finally, they found themselves on the bus to Philippi.

As Riya shifted in her seat, she glanced out the window. The ruins of the ancient city rose from the base of a modest mountain. She nudged Ben awake. He looked out and stared at the remnants. The answer was out there, but was Ben ready for it?

After pulling into the visitor parking lot of the historical site and paying the fee to enter, they walked through the ruins. Ben's face was pale and his eyes glassy. He touched his temple. "My head hurts."

"Maybe that means this is it."

They continued to wander the remnants of the city. Ben climbed a series of small steps built into the side of a knoll, which gave him a view of the landscape outside the city. The hills beckoned him. "Out there." He pointed to the valley, which he didn't realize consciously was the site of the ancient battlefield.

Ben and Riya left the ruins. As they hiked to the field, the sounds of war echoed in Ben's mind. Swords clashed. Men screamed in agony.

Ben's world spun, and a flood of bloody memories overwhelmed him. Two primitive tribes collided and bashed one another with wooden clubs and spears. Then, the barbarians he cut down as Alexander the Great lay in huge piles across an endless field. Finally, the gore and death from Philippi attacked his senses as he relived those horrendous moments. The closing image in his mind was the young boy's face and his dead eyes staring into nothing. Reliving the experiences overloaded Ben's psyche, causing him to collapse.

Riya rushed over. "Ben!"

His face was white, and his eyes distant. As he laid on the ground, collecting himself, a distinctive rock outcropping on the ridge of one hill above them caught his attention. Ben forced himself to his feet.

"You need to rest for a moment, Ben."

Ben ignored Riya and stumbled up the hill. The answer was there.

CHAPTER 104

Rome, 318 B.C.

THE METROPOLIS of ancient Rome glowed in the sunlight. An emaciated young man with a long beak nose in modest clothing rode to the city's edge on the back of a mangy horse. This was Varus in his remarkably unattractive physical form during the lifetime when Alexander was Azes. Born into a tribe in Gaul that struggled to find enough food, Varus found it a simple decision to set out on a two-month journey to Rome when he began having visions of the grand city. Distinct memories of Sargon promised him riches and power beyond anything he could imagine.

Varus followed his memories through the streets until he reached a spectacular columned temple. A guard stood at the entrance. Varus approached. "I come to pledge my loyalty."

"To whom do you wish to pledge?" the guard asked.

Varus lowered his voice, "My lord, Sargon."

The name of Sargon was something only those in the Pantheon knew. The guard pointed to a room inside. "Wait there while I get him."

Varus entered a receiving area with marble floors, soft daybeds, and a bubbling fountain along with a table filled with olives, figs, pears, fresh bread, and choice wines. He smiled as he gorged on the luxurious food. His long journey had been worth it.

After stuffing himself until he couldn't eat another bite, he lounged on a daybed, sipping wine when the guard returned. "He's ready for you."

Varus sat upright, and his nerves kicked into overdrive. His visions drew him here, but they also told him to fear Sargon. He followed the guard into the inner sanctuary to a torch-lit room similar to the one from Ur. Small fires burned incense, giving it the same musty aroma and magical glow. With Sargon presiding on a throne elevated on a platform, the familiarity of the setting reminded Varus of his duties. He needed to bow before the golden bull and swear his allegiance, but where was the statue? Varus searched the room. It was nowhere to be found.

"Who enters?" Sargon asked.

"A loyal subject of the one and only, Sargon."

"And who am I speaking with?" Sargon asked.

"It is I, Varus. Your servant since the days in Akkad."

"Kneel before me and vow your loyalty." Sargon motioned to the area just in front of him.

"Where is the statue?"

"That is no longer necessary. Kneel and kiss my feet." Sargon extended his ragged feet out from under him.

The change in the process triggered another memory. Craterus warned Varus that this would happen. He said Sargon wasn't a god. Was he right? Concealing his doubt, Varus prostrated himself and gingerly kissed the tips of Sargon's gnarled toes. "I will serve you, my lord."

"Rise," Sargon commanded.

Varus stood but kept his eyes to the ground, afraid Sargon would see the uncertainty swirling inside him.

Sargon embraced Varus like a father hugging his child. "Welcome home, my son."

Over the next several hours, Sargon re-indoctrinated Varus, and he was given something of a makeover. Concubines bathed him and tended to his needs. A servant cut his hair and styled it like a Roman noble, and a dresser replaced his filthy clothes with a soft linen toga. When he stood, Sargon crooked his neck. A significant improvement indeed, but Varus's odd physical appearance remained. Varus didn't care. He was thrilled to be in the lap of luxury, but he still had that seed of doubt in the back of his mind. Despite all the pampering, he couldn't help but wonder if this was all a ruse.

"I trust you're feeling more like yourself," Sargon said.

"Yes, thank you, my lord."

"Of course. This is what loyalty brings." Sargon walked over and put his arm around Varus. "But we have a problem."

"How may I serve?"

"We have a new enemy. Others share our gift, but they do not believe like we do."

"Who are they?" Varus asked.

"They call themselves the Lux Mundi, and they're trying to take what is ours."

"We shall stop them. Where are these people?"

"We only know of one with certainty. We must be patient and find out who they all are. Talk to Craterus. He will give you the details."

Varus perked up. Craterus was already here.

CRATERUS, as the large beast of a man who will one day interrogate Alexander in the jail cell, reviewed scrolls in a tiny, ancient library, in the temple's underbelly.

Varus entered. "Craterus?"

Craterus looked up from his reading but didn't react as he stared at the strange, ugly individual before him.

"It's me. Varus."

Craterus assessed Varus's less than ideal physical appearance and laughed. "You didn't luck out with this body, did you?"

"No, and why are you always a giant?" Varus shook his head as Craterus stood and gave him a hug.

Varus didn't return the hug. He eyed Craterus. "How did you know?"

Craterus grew serious. "Walk with me." He led Varus outside.

The two walked in silence through the streets of Rome, passing by everyday citizens. When they reached a stretch where no one was within earshot, Varus asked in a hushed tone, "How did you know he'd stop using the statue?"

Craterus pulled out the golden scepter, showed it to Varus, and then slipped it back under his toga.

"What is that?" Varus asked, wanting to have a better look.

Craterus kept it hidden under his toga. "This is how he knows if we're lying. This is what was in the golden bull."

"How did you get it?" Varus asked.

"I've been studying him. Watching his patterns. For lifetimes. I saw where he buried it in the prior life." Craterus smiled, quite pleased with his accomplishment.

"What does it do?" Varus asked.

"I'll show you later how it works, but do you believe me now?"

Varus nodded as they passed by a Roman popina, a pub of sorts whose primary ware was wine.

Craterus stopped. "Then let us drink to celebrate our freedom."

The duo sat at a secluded table in the back, which was concealed by a small wall. Two empty bottles of wine rested on the table, and a third bottle would soon meet the same fate. The alcohol had no effect on Craterus and his massive frame. Varus, on the other hand, looked tipsy as he played with the golden scepter. He marveled at the glowing crystal when he held both ends.

"I can't believe it. After all these years. How were you able to defeat this? How did you lie to him?" Varus asked.

"I didn't. Each time, I told him I'd serve him in this life. I was referring to his life, so I served him until he died. After that, I served myself." Craterus sneered as he took a big swig.

Varus put the scepter down and raised his drink. "To Craterus, my leader. You now rule the Pantheon."

Craterus lifted his cup. "In the next life, I'm going to lead Rome. But *we* share the power. Rome will be ours."

The two downed their glasses.

After another bottle, the drunk duo stumbled through the streets of Rome.

"What's your plan?" Varus asked.

"We use this life to figure out where he keeps all the money."

"His secret vaults?" Varus asked.

Craterus nodded. "We find them, and in the next life, we don't come back to him."

"He'll suspect we did it if we don't come back," Varus said.

Craterus smiled. "No, he's going to suspect this new group, the Lux Mundi. We plant the seed that they have the same powers Sargon possesses. They know how to stop us from remembering our past. He's going to think they stole this scepter, raided his vaults, and killed us."

Varus nodded. A solid plan, but a hint of doubt remained.

"What is it?" Craterus asked.

"Are you sure he's not a god?"

Craterus stopped and stared at Varus. "If he were a god, then we'd already be doomed."

CHAPTER 105

Alexander sat atop his horse with Casca and the three commanders by his side. He peered across the open valley, and a similar entourage gathered across the field. Sargon was among them. Alexander had been waiting almost 300 years for this moment, but fear crept into his mind. What if Sargon was as smart as Solomon said?

A commander turned to Alexander. "Are you sure about this?"

"Yes, I must go alone." Alexander kicked the sides of his horse, signaling it forward. On the other side, Sargon, as Octavian, rode his majestic steed wearing a red tunic and a loric plumata—a silver chain mail shirt with feather-like scales that glistened in the sun. He didn't bother with his crested helmet, a good sign he didn't intend to fight, or perhaps, he was so confident in his abilities, he had no use for the protection.

Alexander's heart sped up as the two stepped closer to one another. Once they were about fifty feet away, Sargon stopped, dismounted, and removed his sword belt. Alexander mirrored his actions.

Each man never took his eyes off the other until Sargon reached into the pouch of his horse and withdrew a modest chest. Alexander considered retrieving his sword, fearful the chest might contain a weapon, but Sargon held it out in front to alleviate any worry. It was too small to be dangerous.

Step by step, the two men approached one another. When they were within about ten feet, they stopped. Neither man spoke as each sized up the other.

Alexander broke the silence. "I know who you really are. You're Sargon, leader of the Pantheon."

Sargon shook his head. "I know who *you* are, Alexander, but you don't know me." He held out the small box. "I offer a gift."

"Is this a request for peace?" Alexander asked.

"Peace for you. I've come to relieve the burden you carry."

"What burden?" Alexander asked.

"You swore to avenge your friend, Hephaestion."

"And I intend to."

"You don't need to avenge him," Sargon said.

"You can't get inside my mind anymore, Sargon. You did it once when you pretended to be Gabriel. Hephaestion warned me about you. And I *will* avenge him."

Sargon ominously shook his head and took five steps forward.

Alexander held up his hand. "That's far enough."

Sargon stopped, nodded, then placed the chest down and returned to the side of his horse. "Open it."

Alexander approached the chest with apprehension. Something inside him was terrified. How could such a little box instill such fear? He leaned down, picked it up, and opened it. Inside, he found two medallion necklaces—the one Hephaestion wore and the replica Alexander made to find his friend. The events came crashing together.

Alexander stared at Sargon. "You… were Hephaestion?"

Sargon only barely held a giant smile from spreading across his face. "When I met you, I realized you were weak, but you were the son of a king, so I needed to rule through you."

Alexander searched his memory to grasp the deception. "You killed yourself? Why?"

"The bigger picture. I don't just think about one lifetime, Alexander. I'm two steps ahead, and I always will be. You were going to destroy the army from all that garbage Gabriel was spewing."

"Who was Gabriel?"

"Gabriel was... unexpected. He threatened our control of the Greek Empire, not just at that moment, but in the future."

"I've blamed him for centuries," Alexander said.

"Yes, and you've never ruled since," Sargon said, pleased with the effectiveness of his ruse. "I will always command the most powerful civilizations, Alexander. Just as I now control Rome. It is my destiny to rule. You don't have a destiny, remember?"

Alexander stumbled for a response.

Sargon continued with the verbal and mental assault. "You have no power. No wealth. You have no friends. And now, you don't even have the idea of revenge to comfort you. You've got nothing."

The words cut Alexander deeper than a sword because they were all true. Solomon was right. Sargon was too smart.

"Why would you want to live anymore? I actually pitied you when you said you wanted the gods to take away your gift," Sargon said in a soft tone, as if he cared. "I'm here now, and I can do that for you."

Alexander stumbled backward in a daze, still processing the reality that his best friend was actually his worst enemy. He mounted his horse and rode back.

Sargon called out, "Or you can go back to your pitiful excuse for an army and fight. I'll kill every one of them. It will all be your fault. Offer your surrender, and I'll take away your pain. You have until mid-day." Sargon chuckled. He reveled in his devilish victory that had been years in the works. He lived for these moments.

CHAPTER 106

Ben continued his ascent of the hill to the distinctive rock outcropping, stumbling the last steps before collapsing at its edge. This was it. The answer he did not want, but must have, was here. He grabbed a sharp stick and started digging.

Confused, Riya watched, then dropped to the ground and joined in. The two burrowed, moving large chunks of dirt and rock. A sizable hole emerged. When Riya reached down to scoop another handful of muck, her hand struck a firm object. "I think I've got something."

Ben paused and stumbled back, afraid to face what a part of him already knew was waiting. Riya pulled out a tiny object bound in a cloth. She unwrapped it, revealing the two medallions.

Ben's mind *flashed* to the wrestling match that started the relationship with Hephaestion. He thought he'd won in a thrilling comeback, but did he? Or did Hephaestion allow himself to be flipped and pinned?

After the bout, the two shared their feelings, except Hephaestion's were

426

manufactured. "It is a relief to know I'm not alone anymore. I hope we can be friends."

His memories ventured to the moment when Hephaestion boosted Alexander's morale after defeating the barbarians. "We didn't have a choice. We acted. We saved. And now, we celebrate that. Good triumphed."

But really, the Pantheon triumphed as Hephaestion used the Greek army to slaughter people, subjugate the survivors, and take all their wealth. All of it was on the false pretense that they were vanquishing evil and liberating the world.

He remembered Hephaestion warning him about Gabriel. "Something scares me about Gabriel. There's something he's not telling us. Knowing about this gift for centuries provides a huge advantage. What if he's playing us?"

The truth was Sargon had known about the gift for centuries and was playing Alexander.

Ben recalled the Battle of Philippi and riding away from Sargon after learning the truth. Sargon's chuckle—his mockery at Ben's stupidity—reverberated in his mind.

Tears streamed down Ben's face. "I thought he was my friend. He used me. From the moment he met me. I fought so many battles... killed so many... for him."

Riya put her hand on Ben's back. "Everyone makes mistakes, Ben."

"Not like this." Ben reburied the medallions.

"What are you doing?" Riya asked.

Ben kept piling dirt onto the tokens of his shame. "Burying them. I may need the reminder again. He's too smart. I just need to forget." Ben finished filling the hole, rose to his feet, and marched down the hill.

Riya watched, stunned. "Where are you going?"

"I've been searching for the answer to these strange visions, but I now know why I can't remember. I don't want to because I can't beat him. Are my thoughts even my thoughts, or is it all his grand plan?" Ben retreated down the slope.

"I followed you all this way for what? So, you can walk away and forget?" Riya shouted.

Ben kept walking.

Riya collapsed on the ground and wept. "My sister was killed. I'm not going to forget that, *ever*. Her death mattered. Don't act like it didn't matter. It had to have mattered."

Ben didn't dare turn around. Riya might not understand it, but if she stayed with him, she'd end up dead, just like so many of the people that had followed him in the past. No one else could die because of him.

A whirring sound echoed between the hills. Ben froze. The noise grew in intensity until the source revealed itself. A helicopter flew around the hill and faced them. Ashur piloted the bird, and Varus watched from the copilot seat. Gregori hung out the side with a rifle in hand. He took aim and shot at Riya, who dove behind a small rock just in time.

Ben dashed back towards Riya. Ashur maneuvered the helicopter around to give Gregori a clear shot. Ben jumped on top of Riya and waited for the end.

CHAPTER 107

ROME, 46 B.C.

A PROCESSION OF SOLDIERS, captives, and spoils of war entered Rome through the Porta Triumphalis. It was led by Craterus as Julius Caesar. Wearing a laurel crown and an all-purple, gold-embroidered toga picta, he stoically rode a four-horse chariot. His red painted face showed his near-divine status. The triumph continued through the streets of Rome, which were lined with shouting and cheering citizens. He had won the civil war against Pompey the Great and was now the undisputed ruler of the Roman Republic, a term he intended to change. The Roman Empire sounded so much better. The Senate could exist for a while, but he had ambitious plans for Rome. A bunch of simpletons and bureaucrats couldn't slow him down. He had outsmarted Sargon, after all. The masses roared with joy he reached the Temple of Jupiter. Craterus had done it.

He came. He saw. He conquered.

That evening, he began the next phase of his grand plan by reviewing the legal documents outlining Rome's governmental rules and laws with his assistants until a Roman elite, Quintus, entered. Craterus motioned to the assistants. "Leave us."

In seconds, it was just the two of them. A Duchenne smile erupted on Craterus's face. He pulled Quintus close and hugged him. "My dear friend, 'Quintus.'"

Quintus shook his head. "Stop with that. It's bad enough I have to suffer most people in this life calling me that name."

Craterus smacked him on the shoulder. "Could be worse. You could still have that beak nose and pot belly."

Quintus was Varus, and he offered a forced smile.

"Enjoy the moment. We did it just as I told you we would." Craterus motioned to the palatial estate around him.

Varus avoided eye contact.

"What's wrong?" Craterus asked.

"Nothing. This has all gone just as you've said."

"You're worried about Sargon, aren't you? Still paranoid, he's some omnipresent god."

Varus didn't need to respond to confirm Craterus's suspicion.

"We have his money. We have his power. And so, we rule. Not him. Sargon is gone." Craterus waved his hands all around to emphasize his point.

"What about when he comes back?" Varus asked.

———

ALMOST TWO YEARS LATER, it was the Ides of March. Craterus had more honors and powers than even he thought possible. The Senate feared him so much they were going to declare him emperor for life. And he was planning ahead, beyond this life. He'd already built his own secret vaults, just as Sargon had done.

In the palace, Craterus stood as his royal attendants dressed him in a regal toga. Varus sat in a chair off to the side, tapping his foot and biting his fingernails.

Craterus's wife, Calpurnia, entered a little wobbly from too much wine. "I had a terrible dream, my love," she slurred.

Craterus groaned. He found his spouse lovely, but a simpleton, to be sure. Confined to one life, she spent large portions of her limited time drinking her senses into oblivion. She also enjoyed looking to the stars, nature, and dreams for omens about the future. "What is it this time, Calpurnia?" Craterus asked.

"You were killed," she said.

Varus stopped tapping his foot.

Craterus turned to his attendants. "Do you see why you shouldn't drink too much?"

The room chuckled, but Calpurnia remained unbowed. "Please stay home. For me."

Craterus tipped her chin up like a child. "If I listened to all your warnings, my dear, I'd never have time to govern Rome." He let go and waved her away.

The attendants added the finishing touches of gold jewelry to the outfit. Craterus took one more admiring look at himself in the mirror. Satisfied, he pointed to Varus. "I'll see you at the Senate. Let's make it official. Emperor for life." Craterus sauntered out of the room.

Shortly after, Craterus breezed into the Theater of Pompey as senators gathered. The room's energy shifted the moment he stepped in, something he reveled in. He glad-handed a few of the politicians and could see the fealty in their eyes. He owned them. Venturing further through the sea of senators, a pinprick on his arm caused him to whirl around. Casca stared at him, terrified.

"Casca, what are you doing?" Craterus inspected the small cut.

"Now! Help!" Casca shouted.

Craterus scanned the room, confused. Lucius stepped forward with his dagger and thrust with slightly more authority, but only grazed the side of Craterus's ribs. Craterus whirled back and punched him. Other senators swiped with their blades. Enraged, Craterus decked several, but the attackers were coming from every direction. Alexander emerged through the swarm and struck with a speed and ferocity that Craterus did not expect and could not defend. The dagger pierced deep in Craterus's chest. Dumbfounded, he staggered backward and fell to the floor. *How did this happen? What did he miss?*

Alexander stepped forward and towered over Craterus. "I told you I'd end you."

Craterus looked up at Alexander. Was this Sargon? "You…" He coughed and sputtered.

Alexander leaned down and whispered, "That's for Hephaestion."

Craterus let out a weak, almost inaudible groan. Of all the people, it was the idiot who Sargon tricked. "You, stupid boy." He covered his face with his toga in shame and waited for death to come.

The senators cheered, then stormed out of the theater to declare the good news. One senator remained seated. It was Varus, and he had watched the entire sequence in silence. Once alone, Varus walked over to Craterus's body. He tugged open the blood-stained toga and found the golden scepter sheathed. As he unclasped the scepter and removed it, a slight moan startled him. Craterus was alive, but just barely. Varus removed the toga from his face.

The sight of Varus was like another dagger to Craterus. "You too, Varus?"

Varus looked to the ground in shame. "I'm sorry. Sargon knew what we were doing. He knew all along. He caused this to happen."

Craterus spat up blood. "How is that possible?"

"He's a god, Craterus."

Craterus attempted to process the defeat in his last moments. "No. He's just smarter than you."

"Maybe, but how much smarter do you need to be before you're a god?"

Craterus hung on that question as his breath failed him.

CHAPTER 108

PHILIPPI, 42 B.C.

ALEXANDER RODE BACK in a stupor after his encounter with Sargon. Casca and the other generals waited for an update, but Alexander drifted by without a word. When he reached the camp, he disappeared inside his tent to think. How did he get here? Alexander once commanded an army that defeated the world's worst tyrants. But maybe he was the tyrant. Or perhaps he was just a pawn, never controlling anything. Thousands of men had followed him in the past, and many had died for him. The shame and guilt overwhelmed Alexander, but he couldn't dwell on it because thousands of men were outside his tent now, counting on him to lead them to victory. Sargon had been playing the long game, thinking beyond the current lifetime, but these men didn't have that luxury. They needed to defeat Sargon *now*.

A commander popped his head into the tent. "The enemy prepares for battle."

The message didn't register as Alexander gave no response. His mind swirled. How could he defeat someone like Sargon? Was it even possible?

"What are your orders?" the commander asked.

Alexander had to say something. He could only muster three confusing words. "I must pray."

Baffled, the commander watched as Alexander drifted out of the tent. "Shall I prepare the men for battle?"

Alexander nodded and then hiked the hillside until he found a distinctive rock formation. He dug a hole and buried the medallions. When he finished, he looked out at the vista. Aside from the armies preparing to fight to the death, the view was beautiful and peaceful. As he admired the beauty, an intriguing thought dawned on him. Who was Gabriel? Did Sargon want to keep the two of them apart? How was Gabriel even a threat? He wandered the world as a historian, telling people the true histories. That couldn't be the answer. And what about Alisa? Sargon was right that Alexander no longer had revenge for Hephaestion to provide a purpose, but he was wrong that he had nothing. Every time he thought of her, he got butterflies in his stomach. Alisa had visions of healing, and someone named Alisa had given Joshua information about the Pantheon members in China. That seemed too much of a coincidence. It was possible that she also possessed the gift to remember her past lives. The odds of finding her again were minuscule, but it was something. It was at least hope.

But that hope would have to wait. Alexander turned his attention back to the armies, positioning themselves to destroy one another.

THE TIME for the battle of Philippi had arrived. Petrified soldiers squared off, separated by only a few hundred yards. Dressed and armed for combat, Alexander sat atop his horse. He looked strong, pristine, and capable, but his eyes were distant, still deep in thought.

Sargon rode his stallion on the other side of the field with callous indifference. These men were nothing but pawns in his quest for power. Riding beside Sargon was Varus, loyal subject and toady.

Alexander closed his eyes. The sounds of war that had plagued him for lifetimes reverberated in his mind. Swords clashed. Men screamed in terror and agony. Alexander's eyes snapped open, and the noises stopped, but the armies still faced each another. No one had died today, at least not yet. He couldn't ask these men to fight and die for a reason they didn't even know about. This was not their battle.

"Men, I pray for your forgiveness," Alexander said.

Confused, his men glanced back. The battle hadn't even begun.

Alexander withdrew his sword and thrust it into his belly. His attendants stepped in to stop him, but it was too late. As life faded from him, he called out, "Retreat and save yourselves!"

CHAPTER 109

GREGORI HUNG off the helicopter's side and took aim as Ben covered Riya with his body as a human shield.

Just as Gregori was about to pull the trigger, Varus shouted, "Stop! Sargon must kill him." Varus pressed the button for the loudspeaker. "Move down to the bottom of the hill with your hands up."

Ben couldn't believe his ears. He assumed they'd already be dead. He looked at Riya, huddled in a ball under him. This wasn't her fight, even if she wanted it to be. The Pantheon didn't care about her but would kill her without hesitating. They'd already done that with her sister. He pulled himself up, stared at the helicopter, and pointed to her. "Leave her out of this, and I'll do what you want!"

Varus couldn't hear Ben over the rotors' noise, but he saw enough from his gestures to understand. He pressed the loudspeaker button. "We'll leave her alone if you come down now."

Ben motioned for the helicopter to land in the valley.

Varus turned to Ashur. "Put it down. As soon as we've got him, we'll get rid of the woman."

Ben pulled Riya up off the ground. "Get out of here! Enough people have died because of me." He raised his hands and walked down towards the landing site.

Riya scampered through the loose rocks and dirt to the other side of the hill.

The chopper touched down, and Gregori hopped out with his rifle aimed at Ben as he approached. There was nothing left for Ben to do at this point. He could make a run for it and force them to shoot, but then they'd likely kill Riya, something he knew was already a possibility. The only thing he could do was meander down the hill to give her as much of a head start as possible.

When Alexander was twenty-five yards away, Gregori pointed to the ground. "Get down with your hands behind your head."

Alexander knelt down on the dirt. Gregori took two steps towards Alexander when a gunshot rang out. Gregori dropped dead. Ben scanned the area, confused.

An off-road truck zoomed towards Ben. A man fired a pistol from the driver's seat and tagged the helicopter. It was Tom.

Varus shouted to Ashur. "Go! Go! Go!"

The blades swirled, and the chopper took to the skies. Tom drove the truck beside Ben and slammed on the brakes. "Get in."

Ben hesitated, unsure if he should trust Tom.

Irritated, Tom pointed to the helicopter with his gun. "He's turning around. Get in."

"Only if you get Riya," Ben said.

Tom nodded. Ben hopped in, Tom spun the tires, and they sped up the hill towards Riya.

Varus climbed out of the copilot's chair and grabbed a second rifle in the back. "Bring it around."

Tom pulled up alongside Riya. She dove into the back seat in time to see the chopper approaching. Varus now hung off the side. Tom punched the accelerator, and the truck peeled away. The vehicle bounced, jolted, and banged its way down the backside of the hill.

"How are we going to lose a helicopter?" Riya asked.

"Don't know. This is a new experience for me, too." Tom handed Ben the pistol. "If you get a shot, take it."

Ben grabbed the gun and opened the window. He slid his head out to get a clear shot.

Varus motioned for the chopper to get closer. He took aim, but so did Ben. Who would get the shot off first?

Tom looked in the rearview, and as Varus was about to fire, he swerved.

Varus lost his shot, and Ben struggled to maintain his balance, Varus regrouped, aimed, and fired. The back right tire exploded.

The jolt knocked the pistol from Ben's hand. "I lost the gun."

Tom stomped on the accelerator even though the vehicle was now slowed considerably. As they reached the bottom of the hill, a forest came into view a quarter of a mile away. Tom steered the vehicle toward it. Within seconds, they barreled through a thicket of trees. Branches and leaves smacked against the windshield, making it impossible to see in front. Ben clicked himself into the seat belt.

As the car whipped through the foliage, Tom didn't notice the large tree stump until the truck smashed into it. Airbags burst open, and they came to an instant halt. A stillness followed, except for the hissing smoke coming from the engine and the whirring chopper overhead. The vehicle's left front was crushed inward, causing the steering wheel carriage and airbag to wedge Tom to his seat, unconscious. Ben's head drooped against the passenger airbag. His eyes flickered, and his mind *flashed.*

Ben found himself on the peaceful hilltop. He spotted Alisa waving at the bottom of the next hill. Ben focused his thoughts, and the ground zoomed under his feet toward her. The massive wall emerged, and he headed straight towards it. He closed his eyes and then passed through it like a ghost. Alisa dashed up the hill to a small hut, and Ben knew what was coming next. Alexander stepped out of the shadows.

"Back again?" Alexander asked. "When are you going to realize we're on the same side? I'm protecting you because I'm protecting myself."

"I'm not Alexander. My name is Ben Preston, and I'm going to the top of the hill."

Alexander shook his head. Time to deliver another beating. He circled Ben, who didn't move to defend himself. Instead, he waved his hand, and Alexander slammed back against the wall, unable to move by the invisible force of Ben's imagination. He jogged up the hill as Alexander shouted, "No! You don't want to know."

Ben continued on and crested the top. Alisa stood near the hut, and his heart skipped a beat. She offered a warm, brilliant smile that would light up any room, then slipped inside the hut. Ben's stomach filled with butterflies. He pulled back the cloth flap that served as a modest door. As he stepped inside, a man's voice caught him by surprise.

"It's been a long time."

Ben's face turned white. It was Gabriel. Alisa held his hand and put her head on his shoulder. A sickening feeling overwhelmed Ben's senses. Alisa, the woman he loved with all his heart, was someone he could never be with. *Ever.* He stumbled backward out of the shelter. His world spun, and he collapsed. Alexander was right. He didn't want to know. This pain could never be healed. Each and every lifetime, his heart would remain broken. As he sat on the ground, Gabriel exited and knelt beside him. Ben looked up. He wanted to hate Gabriel, but he couldn't anymore. Ben had chosen to leave Alisa. He had his chance.

"You were right," Gabriel said.

"Right about what?"

"We weren't given this gift to be historians. The temptation to indulge in the power it brings *is* great, but we have to be greater. We need you."

Strange voices behind Ben distracted him and jarred his senses.

Ben snapped awake in the truck. Dazed, Ben turned around and found Tom unconscious beside him and Riya knocked out in the back. Something caught his eye through the rear window. In the distance, the helicopter had landed. Varus and Ashur hopped out with guns drawn. Filled with dread, Ben hurried out of the truck and fled.

Leaves and branches lashed Ben as he escaped into the brush. He couldn't allow himself to be captured. If he was caught, he'd be killed. Then a curious thought turned his sprint into a jog. Why was he running? A moment ago, he had been willing to give himself up. Another revelation turned his jog into a walk. He'd faced his fear. It was worse than anything he could have imagined, so what was left to be afraid of? He stopped in his tracks as his thoughts, dreams, and memories melded together.

He remembered his first conversation with Hephaestion after the wrestling match.

"What do you see in your dreams?" Hephaestion asked.

"I see battles. War. Fighting. Sometimes there are other things, but mostly I see... suffering," Alexander said.

Ben looked back at the smoking car. With rifle in hand, Varus approached the vehicle from a distance. Ashur carried a pistol.

Ben's mind *flashed* one more time.

Alexander and Hephaestion commiserated about their visions.

"What if the people who are suffering are haunting us because we need to save them? What if these dreams are our destiny?" Hephaestion asked.

"You mean we're seeing our future?"

Hephaestion nodded. "What if we're supposed to save the world?"

The epiphany struck hard. Sargon lied to Ben, but he also told him the truth—the truth of his purpose—and if he loved Alisa, he couldn't abandon her or pretend she didn't exist.

Varus and Ashur marched closer to the truck, now about three hundred feet away.

Varus whispered, "Go around from that side."

Ashur took a wide berth and approached the vehicle from the opposite side.

Tom's eyes flickered, and he awoke. He attempted to move but realized he was trapped in the seat. Through the rearview mirror, Tom spied Varus approaching, so he ducked down and reached into his left pant pocket to fish something out. With his arms wedged, he struggled until he pulled out a small bag with a pill—another form of escape. Tom smiled, but then the bag slipped and fell between the side of the door and the seat.

With his gun raised, Ashur closed in on the crash, now only about 150 feet away. A whirring sound to his left distracted him. He turned. *Bam!* A rock tagged Ashur in the head.

Varus looked over. Ashur lay motionless on the ground. Varus crept over to Ashur, all the while keeping an eye out for any movement.

"I remember you, Varus," Ben called out, hidden within the trees.

Varus shifted his rifle to the right.

"Over here," Ben said.

Varus swiveled to the left. Where was he? He walked forward with his weapon ready. A dangerous ravine dropped on one side, a fallen tree with stripped branches loomed in front, and an unusual group of trees swayed in the breeze to his right. One tree nook stood out. Was that Ben's head trying to hide? Varus smirked as he leaned down and put the rifle scope to his eye. As he took aim, he deflated—just a brown leaf.

Then, that whirring sound. Varus turned just in time to see a rock crash into his scope, knocking the rifle stock into him. The impact stunned him and gave Ben an opportunity. Racing out from his hiding spot, he jump-kicked, but Varus ducked and avoided the attack. He swung the rifle around for a shot, but Ben seized hold, and they wrestled for control. Neither man could gain the upper hand until Varus kicked Ben in the stomach, causing him to let go.

Before he could aim, Ben punched Varus and followed with a foot to the gut. Varus fell back and almost over the edge of the ravine. To catch himself, he dropped the rifle, which slid down to the bottom.

Varus stepped away from the drop and squared off for a fight. "All right, Alexander. Let's do this."

Ben nodded, then attacked with a series of punches. Varus blocked them all and responded with his offensive assault. Both men executed perfect martial arts attacks and counters, but mistakes are inevitable, even for those who have practiced for lifetimes. Varus snuck a punch past Ben's defense and attempted to seize the advantage, but Ben regrouped and delivered a throttling uppercut. Now it was Ben who took the initiative. He let fly a powerful roundhouse punch, but Varus deflected it, grabbed Ben's neck, and locked on like a python.

Ben struggled to breathe as Varus maneuvered behind.

"Give it up, Alexander. You're nothing," Varus taunted.

Ben's eyes bulged as the oxygen wore out. His vision became fuzzy, and he was on the verge of passing out. His gaze locked onto the dead tree and its stripped branches in front of him—one last gasp. Ben stepped back, bent down with all his force, and flipped Varus over and onto a dead tree branch, impaling him upside down.

Varus was dead.

Ben collapsed onto the ground and regained his breath. He survived, but just barely. Out of nowhere, a phone rang. Was someone else in the forest? Panicked, Ben scanned the trees until he discovered the source of the ring—Varus's pocket. Ben patted the body down and found the phone. He answered and heard an ominous voice.

"Do you have him?"

"No. He doesn't have him," Ben said.

A long pause. "Alexander. Shall I assume you have your memories back?" Sargon asked.

"I have enough of them," Ben said.

"Do you remember what happened in your last life?"

Ben didn't answer.

"I'll take that as a 'no.' Then I won't spoil the surprise," Sargon said.

The statement paused Ben.

"You know, I've always regretted that you didn't choose to follow me. You would've been so much happier, and you would've been amazing for me. But of course, you were amazing for me, even when you were against me," Sargon said.

"My name is Ben, and times have changed. I know who I'm fighting against and what I'm fighting for."

Sargon chuckled. "You've never had any idea. So, shall we perform this play again, Alexander? One last time?"

"Yeah. This is the last time." Ben clicked the phone and hung up.

CHAPTER 110

December 15, 2018

This day changed the world. No one knows why, except for a select, perhaps chosen few. Most defining moments in history center on a death or deaths—assassinations, coups, wars, revolutions, executions—but not all of them. On this day, a peculiar video was put out in cyberspace. In the cacophony of news headlines and onslaught of information—stock market updates, political turmoil around the globe, sports scores, celebrity gossip, social media posts—the masses missed or overlooked it, but it wasn't meant for the masses. The video's link was posted to a host of message boards and websites about topics like past lives, dreams, and historical conspiracies. The video showed Riya standing on a small stage without an audience.

"On September 17, 2017, my sister was killed, along with seven of her colleagues. It was a day I'll never forget. The next year, I tried to figure out what they were studying. It turns out they made a miraculous discovery. They proved that we've been here before. We've had past lives. I know what some of you are thinking. That's crazy, and that's fine. If you feel that way, stop this video. It isn't for you. For those of you who are open to this possibility, let me ask you a few questions. Have you ever had a strange feeling in your gut that guided your decision? Have you ever experienced déjà vu? Do you have strange, unexplainable dreams? Maybe even recurring dreams of people you've never met? Do you have an unusual fascination with history? These things may be caused by pieces of your past lives, moving from your subconscious to your conscious. You might be asking, is there a way to remember your past lives consciously? Maybe some people already do."

As Riya spoke, she held her hands together and extended her thumb, index, and pinkie fingers. It appeared like a natural public speaking quirk, but something about it caught the eye of a twenty-year-old Spanish man watching. He listened to Riya speak, but his eyes focused on her hands. His mind *flashed* to a time and place long ago. Rome. The secret chamber. The Lux Mundi.

The man journeyed alone from Spain to Rome for some strange reason that came deep from within the recesses of his mind and gut. He didn't know why, but the mysterious force guided him to the Basilica of San Clemente. He purchased a ticket for a tour, and as he followed the guide and a small group of foreigners, he soon found himself in the building's lowest level. When he reached the gated "Temple of Mithras," a chill went down his spine. After the guide explained the chamber's history incorrectly, the tour moved on, but the young man remained. The room felt familiar, and something compelled him to hold his hands, just like Riya had done in the video. A hidden camera in the darkened corner of the gated doorway captured the moment.

And in a quaint restaurant in an unknown city, Ben read a history book about the fall of Rome. Beside him were stacks of historical books about various other subjects. His phone beeped with a notification. It was an email from Tom with a subject line that read, *We have one.* He swiped right, which opened a link containing a video. Ben pressed play and watched the young man performing the secret hand signal.

The Lux Mundi was reborn.

THANK YOU!

History of Lies has been a labor of love for us. It took years researching various historical events and weaving them all into a coherent story. We hope you enjoyed it. If you did, please consider leaving a review on the site where you acquired the book. Reviews are tremendously helpful, and we love receiving feedback from readers! If you have questions or if you're interested in other books and short stories, please visit https://www.maynardmcnally.com.

Thanks for reading, and thank you for your support!

Made in United States
Orlando, FL
28 January 2023

29174359R00248